PENGUIN BOOKS

FINAL STAGE

Edward L. Ferman is the editor of *The Magazine of Fantasy and Science Fiction*. Under his editorship it has won four of the World Science Fiction Convention's Hugo awards for the best science-fiction magazine. Mr. Ferman was born in New York in 1937. He now lives with his wife and daughter in northwestern Connecticut.

Barry N. Malzberg is the author of several novels and of more than a hundred short stories. His *Beyond Apollo* won the John W. Campbell Memorial award for the best science-fiction novel of 1972, and his work has appeared in over thirty anthologies. Mr. Malzberg was born in New York in 1939. He and his wife and two daughters live in New Jersey.

Also by Edward L. Ferman

The Best from Fantasy and Science Fiction: 15th through 20th Series
Twenty Years of Fantasy and Science Fiction (with Robert P. Mills)
Once and Future Tales: An Anthology

Also by Barry N. Malzberg

Beyond Apollo
Herovit's World
The Destruction of the Temple
Underlay
In the Enclosure
The Men Inside
Overlay
The Falling Astronauts
Screen
Oracle of the Thousand Hands
The Confessions of Westchester County
Tactics of Conquest

FINAL STAGE

THE ULTIMATE SCIENCE FICTION ANTHOLOGY

Edited by Edward L. Ferman
and
Barry N. Malzberg

Penguin Books

Penguin Books Inc, 72 Fifth Avenue,
New York, New York 10011, U.S.A.
Penguin Books Inc, 7110 Ambassador Road,
Baltimore, Maryland 21207, U.S.A.
Penguin Books Ltd, Harmondsworth,
Middlesex, England
Penguin Books Australia Ltd, Ringwood,
Victoria, Australia
Penguin Books Canada Limited, 41 Steelcase Road West,
Markham, Ontario, Canada L3R 1B4
Penguin Books (N.Z.) Ltd, 182–190 Wairau Road,
Auckland 10, New Zealand

First published by Charterhouse Books, Inc., New York, 1974
Published by Penguin Books, 1975

For Joyce, who bore with, and
For Audrey

CONTENTS

INTRODUCTION

The assumption was that science fiction—that branch of literature half beast, half civilized—sits upon perhaps a dozen classic themes which, in various combinations, permutations, and convolutions, underlie most of the work in the field. Like the ten to twenty basic chess attacks and defenses, these themes can lead to winning combinations of great beauty or, in less talented hands, to disastrous and obvious cliches.

We assigned these basic themes (on direct commission) to science fiction's most distinguished writers. The authors were selected not only for their clear accomplishments and gifts, but because the thrust of each writer's work seemed to qualify him or her to write the *ultimate* story on the theme assigned. (Thus Isaac Asimov, creator of sf's "Three Laws of Robotics," contributes the ultimate story on robots and androids. Thus Poul Anderson—from whose work grew the term "hard [technologically accurate] science fiction"— writes on the exploration of space.) Each contributor was further asked to write an afterword commenting on the assigned theme and to submit a list of novels and stories that would include: a) works he believed to be classics of the theme, b) works that had influenced his own story, and c) at least one of his own pieces.

What we have then, we hope, is an anthology of ultimates: stories that carry these basic themes as far as possible given the current state of the art, stories that function both as an ending and as a beginning.

An ending because science fiction has grown up—in many ways transcended its origins—and this seems an excellent time to again confirm those origins. A beginning because these stories, far from managing to "finish off" any one theme, only illustrate their infinite variety and complexity, their function as a vast corridor of possibilities. And it is this that makes science fiction today perhaps the last set of rooms, however cluttered, in which fiction itself may reside.

Barry N. Malzberg
Edward L. Ferman

FINAL STAGE

FIRST CONTACT

WE PURCHASED PEOPLE

FREDERIK POHL

On the third of March the purchased person named Wayne Golden took part in trade talks in Washington as the representative of the dominant race of the Groombridge star. What he had to offer was the license of the basic patents on a device to convert nuclear power plant waste products into fuel cells. It was a good item, with a ready market. Since half of Idaho was already bubbling with radioactive wastes, the Americans were anxious to buy, and he sold for a credit of $100 million. On the following day he flew to Spain. He was allowed to sleep all the way, stretched out across two seats in the first-class section of the Concorde, with the fastenings of a safety belt gouging into his side. On the fifth of the month he used up part of the trade credit in the purchase of fifteen Picasso oils-on-canvas, the videotape of a flamenco performance and a fifteenth-century harpsichord, gilt with carved legs. He arranged for them to be preserved, crated, and shipped in bond to Orlando, Florida, after which the items would be launched from Cape Kennedy on a voyage through space that would take more than twelve thousand years. The Groombridgians were not in a hurry and thought big. The Saturn Five booster rocket cost $11 million in itself. It did not matter. There was plenty of money left in the Groombridge credit balance. On the fifth of the month Golden returned to the United States, made a close connection at Logan Airport in Boston, and arrived early at his home kennel in Chicago. He was then given eighty-five minutes of freedom.

I knew exactly what to do with my eighty-five minutes. I always know. See, when you're working for the people who own you you don't have any choice about what you do, but up to a point you can think pretty much whatever you like. That thing you get in your head only controls you. It doesn't change you, or anyway I don't think it does. (Would I know if I were changed?)

My owners never lie to me. Never. I don't think they know what a lie is. If I ever needed anything to prove that they weren't human, that would be plenty, even if I didn't know they lived 86 zillion miles away, near some star that I can't even see. They don't tell me much, but they don't lie.

Not ever lying, that makes you wonder what they're like. I don't mean physically. I looked that up in the library once, when I had a couple of hours of free time. I don't remember where, maybe in Paris at the Bibliothèque Nationale, anyway I couldn't read what the language in the books said. But I saw the photographs and the holograms. I remember the physical appearance of my owners, all right. Jesus. The Altairians look kind of like spiders, and the Sirians are a little bit like crabs. But those folks from the Groombridge star, boy, they're something else. I felt bad about it for a long time, knowing I'd been sold to something that looked as much like a cluster of maggots on an open wound as anything else I'd ever seen. On the other hand, they're all those miles away, and all I ever have to do with them is receive their fast-radio commands and do what they tell me. No touching or anything. So what does it matter what they look like?

But what kind of freaky creature is it that never says anything that is not objectively the truth, never changes its mind, never makes a promise that it doesn't keep? They aren't machines, I know, but maybe they think I'm kind of a machine. You wouldn't bother to lie to a machine, would you? You wouldn't make it any promises. You wouldn't do it any favors, either, and they never do me any. They don't tell me that I can have eighty-five minutes off because I've done something they like, or because they want to sweeten me up because they want something from me. Everything considered, that's silly. What could they want? It isn't as if I had any choice. Ever. So they don't lie, or threaten, or bribe, or reward.

But for some reason they sometimes give me minutes or hours or days off, and this time I had eighty-five minutes. I started using it right away, the way I always do. The first thing was to check at the kennel location desk to see where Carolyn was. The locator clerk—he isn't owned, he works for a salary and treats us like shit—knows me by now. "Oh, hell, Wayne boy," he said with that imitation sympathy and lying friendliness that makes me want to kill him, "you just missed the lady friend. Saw her, let's see, Wednesday, was it? But she's gone." "Where to?" I asked him. He pushed around the cards on the locator board for a while, he knows I don't have very much time ever so he uses it up for me, and said: "Nope, not on my board at all. Say, I wonder. Was she with that bunch that went to Peking? Or was that the other little fat broad with the big boobs?" I didn't stop to kill him. If she wasn't on the board she wasn't in eighty-five-minute transportation range, so my eighty-five minutes—seventy-nine minutes—wasn't going to get me near her.

I went to the men's room, jerked off quickly, and went out into the miserable biting March Chicago wind to use up my seventy-nine minutes. Seventy-one minutes. There's a nice Mexican kind of restaurant near the kennel, a couple of blocks away past Ohio. They know me there. They don't care who I am. Maybe the brass plate in my head doesn't bother them because they think it's great that the people from the other stars are doing such nice things for the world, or maybe it's because I tip big. (What else do I have to do with the money I get?) I stuck my head in, whistled at Terry, the bartender, and said: "The usual. I'll be back in ten minutes." Then I walked up to Michigan and bought a clean shirt and changed into it, leaving the smelly old one. Sixty-six minutes. In the drugstore on the corner I picked up a couple of porno paperbacks and stuck them in my pockets, bought some cigarettes, leaned over and kissed the hand of the cashier, who was slim and fair-complexioned and smelled good, left her startled behind me, and got back to the restaurant just as Alicia, the waitress, was putting the gazpacho and two bottles of beer on my table. Fifty-nine minutes. I settled down to enjoy my time. I smoked, and I ate, and I drank the beer, smoking between bites, drinking between puffs. You really look forward to something like that when you're working, and not your own boss. I don't mean they don't let us eat when we're working. Of course they do, but we don't have any choice about what we eat or where we eat it. Pump fuel into the machine, keep it running. So I finished the guacamole and sent Alicia back for more of it when she brought the chocolate cake and American coffee, and ate the cake and the guacamole in alternate forkfuls. Eighteen minutes.

If I had had a little more time I would have jerked off again, but I didn't, so I paid the bill, tipped everybody, and left the restaurant. I got to the block where the kennel was with maybe two minutes to spare. Along the curb a slim woman in a fur jacket and pants suit was walking her Scottie away from me. I went up behind her and said, "I'll give you fifty dollars for a kiss." She turned around. She was all of sixty years old, but not bad, really, so I kissed her and gave her the fifty dollars. Zero minutes, and I just made it into the kennel when I felt the tingling in my forehead and my owners took over again.

In the next seven days of March Wayne Golden visited Karachi, Srinagar, and Butte, Montana, on the business of the Groombridgians. He completed thirty-two assigned tasks. Quite unexpectedly he was then given 1,000 minutes of freedom.

That time I was in, I think it was, Pocatello, Idaho, or some place like that. I had to send a TWX to the faggy locator clerk in Chicago to ask about Carolyn. He took his time answering, as I knew he would. I walked around a little bit, waiting to hear. Everybody was very cheerful, smiling as they walked around through the dusty, sprinkly snow that was coming down, even smiling at me as though they didn't care that I was purchased, as they could plainly see from the golden oval of metal across my forehead that my owners use to tell me what to do. Then the message came back from Chicago: "Sorry, Wayne baby, but Carolyn isn't on my board. If you find her give her one for me."

Well. All right. I have plenty of spending money, so I checked into a hotel. The bellboy brought me a fifth of Scotch and plenty of ice, fast, because he knew why I was in a hurry and that I would tip for speed. When I asked about hookers he offered anything I liked. I told him white, slim, beautiful asses. That's what I first noticed about Carolyn. It's special for me. The little girl I did in New Brunswick, what was her name—Rachel—she was only nine years old, but she had an ass on her you wouldn't believe.

I showered and put on clean clothes. The owners don't really give you enough time for that sort of thing. A lot of the time I smell. A lot of times I've almost wet my pants because they didn't let me go when I needed to. Once or twice I just couldn't help myself, held out as long as I could and, boy, you feel lousy when that happens. The worst was when I was covering some kind of a symposium in Russia, a place with a name like Akademgorodok. It was supposed to be on nuclear explosion processes. I don't know anything about that kind of stuff, and anyway I was a little mixed up because I thought that was one of the things the star people had done for us, worked out some way the different countries didn't have to have nuclear weapons and bombs and wars and so on any more. But that wasn't what they meant. It was explosions at the nucleus of the galaxy they meant. Astronomical stuff. Just when a fellow named Eysenck was talking about how the FG prominence and the EMK prominence, whatever they were, were really part of an expanding pulse sphere, whatever that is, I crapped my pants. I knew I was going to. I'd tried to tell the Groombridge people about it. They wouldn't listen. Then the session redactor came down the aisle and shouted in my ear, as though my owners were deaf or stupid, that they would have to get me out of there, please, for reasons concerning the comfort and hygiene of the other participants. I thought they would be angry, because that meant they were going to miss some of this conference that they were interested in. They didn't do anything to me, though. I mean, as if there was anything they *could* do to me that would be any worse, or any different, from what they do to me all the time, and always will.

When I was all clean and in an open-necked shirt and chinos I turned on the TV and poured a mild drink. I didn't want to be still drunk when my thousand minutes were up. There was a special program on all the networks, something celebrating a treaty between the United Nations and a couple of the star people, Sirians and Capellans it seemed to be. Everybody was very happy about it, because it seemed that now the Earth had bought some agricultural and chemical information, and pretty soon there would be more food than we could eat. How much we owed to the star people, the Secretary General of the UN was saying, in Brazilian-accented English. We could look forward to their wise guidance to help Earth survive its multitudinous crises and problems, and we should all be very happy.

But I wasn't happy, not even with a glass of John Begg and the hooker on her way up, because what I really wanted was Carolyn.

Carolyn was a purchased person, like me. I had seen her a couple of dozen times, all in all. Not usually when either of us was on freedom. Almost never when both of us were. It was sort of like falling in love by postcard, except that now and then we were physically close, even touching. And once or twice we had been briefly not only together, but out from under control. We had had about eight minutes once in Bucharest, after coming back from the big hydropower plant at the Iron Gate. That was the record, so far. Outside of that it was just that we passed, able to see each other but not to do anything about it, in the course of our duties. Or that one of us was free and found the other. When that happened the one of us that was free could talk, and even touch the other one, in any way that didn't interfere with what the other was doing. The one that was working couldn't do anything active, but could hear, or feel. We were both totally careful to avoid interfering with actual work. I don't know what would have happened if we had interfered. Maybe nothing? We didn't want to take that chance, though sometimes it was a temptation I could almost not resist. There was a time when I was free and I found Carolyn, working but not doing anything active, just standing there, at TWA Gate 51 at the St. Louis airport. She was waiting for someone to arrive. I really wanted to kiss her. I talked to her. I patted her, you know, holding my trenchcoat over my arm so that the people passing by wouldn't notice anything, or at least wouldn't notice anything much. I told her things I wanted her to hear. But what I wanted was to kiss her, and I was afraid to. Kissing her on the mouth would have meant putting my head in front of her eyes. I didn't think I wanted to chance that. It might have meant she wouldn't see the person she was there to see. Who turned out to be a Ghanaian police officer arriving to discuss the sale of some political prisoners to the Groombridgians. I was there when he came down the ramp, but I couldn't stay to see if she would by any chance be free after completing the negotiations with him, because then my own time ran out.

But I had had three hours that time, being right near her. It felt very sad and very strange, and I wouldn't have given it up for anything in the world. I knew she could hear and feel everything, even if she couldn't respond. Even when the owners are running you, there's a little personal part of you that stays alive. I talked to that part of her. I told her how much I wished we could kiss, and go to bed, and be with each other. Oh, hell. I even told her I loved her and wanted to marry her, although we both know perfectly well there's not ever going to be any chance of that ever. We don't get pensioned off or retired; we're *owned*.

Anyway, I stayed there with her as long as I could. I paid for it later. Balls that felt as though I'd been stomped, the insides of my undershorts wet and chilly. And there wasn't any way in the world for me to do anything about it, not even by masturbating, until my next free time. That turned out to be three weeks later. In Switzerland, for God's sake. Out of season. With nobody in the hotel except the waiters and bellboys and a couple of old ladies who looked at the gold oval in my forehead as though it smelled bad.

It is a terrible but cherished thing to love without hope. I pretended there was hope, always. Every bit of freedom I got, I tried to find her. They keep pretty careful tabs on us, all two or three hundred thousand of us purchased persons, working for whichever crazy bunch of creepy crawlers or gassy ghosts happens to have bought us to be their remote-access facilities on the planet they themselves cannot ever visit. Carolyn and I were owned by the same bunch, which had its good side and its bad side. The good side was that there was a chance that some day we would be free for quite a long while at the same time. It happened. I don't know why. Shifts change on the Groombridge planet, or they have a holiday or something. But every once in a while there would be a whole day, maybe a week, when none of the Groombridge people would be doing anything at all, and all of us would be free at once.

The bad side was that they hardly ever needed to have more than one of us in one place. So Carolyn and I didn't run into each other a lot. And the times when I was free for a pretty good period it took most of that to find her, and by the time I did she was like half a world away. No way of getting there and back in time for duty. I did so much want to fuck her, but we had never made it that far and maybe never would. I never even got a chance to ask her what she had been sentenced for in the first place. I really didn't know her at all, except enough to love her.

When the bellboy turned up with my girl I was comfortably buzzed, with my feet up and the Rangers on the TV. She didn't look like a hooker, particularly. She was wearing hiphuggers cut below the navel, bigger breasted than I cared about but with that beautiful curve of waist and back into hips that I like. Her name was Nikki. The bellboy took my money, took five for himself, passed the rest to her, and disappeared, grinning. What's so funny about it? He knew what I was, because the plate in my head told him, but he had to think it was funny.

"Do you want me to take my clothes off?" She had a pretty, breathless little voice, long red hair, and a sweet, broad, friendly face. "Go ahead," I said. She slipped off the sandals. Her feet were clean, a little ridged where the straps went. Stepped out of the hiphuggers and folded them across the back of Conrad Hilton's standard armchair, took off the blouse and folded it, ducked out of the medallion and draped it over the blouse, down to red lace bra and red bikini panties. Then she turned back the bedclothes, got in, sat up, snapped off the bra, snuggled down, kicked the panties out of the side of the bed, and pulled the covers over her. "Any time, honey," she said. But I didn't lay her. I didn't even get in the bed with her, not under the covers; I drank some more of the Scotch, and that and fatigue put me out, and when I woke up it was daylight, and she had cleaned out my wallet. Seventy-one minutes left. I paid the bill with a check and persuaded them to give me carfare in change. Then I headed back for the kennel. All I got out of it was clean clothes and a hangover. I think I had scared her a little. Everybody knows how we purchased people came to be up for sale, and maybe they're not all the way sure that we won't do something bad again, because they don't know how reliably our owners keep us from ever doing anything they don't like. But I wished she hadn't stolen my money.

The overall strategies and objectives of the star people, particularly the people from the Groombridge star who were his own masters, were unclear to the purchased person named Wayne Golden. What they did was not hard to understand. All the world knew that the star people had established fast radio contact with the people of Earth, and that in order to conduct their business on Earth they had purchased the bodies of certain convicted criminals, installing in them tachyon fast-radio transceivers. Why they did what they did was less easy to comprehend. Art objects they admired and purchased. Certain rare kinds of plants and flowers they purchased and had frozen at liquid-helium temperatures. Certain kinds of utilitarian objects they purchased. Every few months another rocket roared up from Merritt Island, just north of the Cape, and another cargo headed for the Groombridge star, on its twelve-thousand-year voyage. Others, to other stars, peopled by other races in the galactic confraternity, took shorter times—or longer—but none of the times was short enough for those star people who made the purchases to come to Earth to see what they had bought. The distances were too huge.

What they spent most of their money on was the rockets. And, of course, the people they purchased, into whom they had transplanted their tachyon transceivers. Each rocket cost at least $10 million. The going rate for a healthy male paranoid capable of three or more decades of useful work was in the hundreds of thousands of dollars, and they bought them by the dozen.

The other things they bought, all of them—the taped symphonies and early-dynasty *ushabti*, the flowering orchids, and the Van Goghs—cost only a fraction of 1 per cent of what they spent on people and transportation. Of course, they had plenty of money to spend. Each star race sold off licensing rights on its own kinds of technology. All of them received trade credits from every government on Earth for their services in resolving disputes and preventing wars. Still, it seemed to Wayne Golden, to the extent that he was capable of judging the way his masters conducted their affairs, a pretty high-overhead way to run a business, although of course neither he nor any other purchased person was ever consulted on questions like that.

By late spring he had been on the move for many weeks without rest. He completed sixty-eight tasks, great and small. There was nothing in this period of eighty-seven days that was in any way remarkable except that on one day in

May, while he was observing the riots on the Place de la Concorde from a window of the American Embassy on behalf of his masters, the girl named Carolyn came into his room. She whispered in his ear, attempted unsuccessfully to masturbate him while the liaison attaché was out of the room, remained in all for some forty minutes, and then left, sobbing softly. He could not even turn his head to see her go. Then on the sixth of June the purchased person named Wayne Golden was returned to the Dallas kennel and given indefinite furlough, subject to recall at fifty minutes' notice.

Sweetest dear Jesus, nothing like that had ever happened to me before! It was like the warden coming into Death Row with the last-minute reprieve! I could hardly believe it.

But I took it, started moving at once. I got a fix on Carolyn's last reported whereabouts from the locator board and floated away from Dallas in a cloud of Panama Red, drinking champagne as fast as the hostesses could bring it to me, en route to Colorado.

But I didn't find Carolyn there.

I hunted her through the streets of Denver, and she was gone. By phone I learned she had been sent to Rantoul, Illinois. I was off. I checked at the Kansas City airport, where I was changing planes, and she was gone from Illinois already. Probably, they weren't sure, they thought, to the New York district. I put down the phone and jumped on a plane, rented a car at Newark, and drove down the Turnpike to the Garden State, checking every car I passed to see if it was the red Volvo they thought she might be driving, stopping at every other Howard Johnson's to ask if they'd seen a girl with short black hair, brown eyes and a tip-tilted nose and, oh, yes, the golden oval in her forehead.

I remembered it was in New Jersey that I first got into trouble. There was the nineteen-year-old movie cashier in Paramus, she was my first. I picked her up after the 1 A.M. show. And I showed her. But she was really all wrong for me, much too old and much too worldly. I didn't like it much when she died.

After that I was scared for a while, and I watched the TV news every night, twice, at six and eleven, and never passed a newsstand without looking at all the headlines in the papers, until a couple of months had passed. Then I thought over what I really wanted very carefully. The girl had to be quite young and, well, you can't tell, but as much as I could be sure, a virgin. So I sat in a luncheonette in Perth Amboy for three whole days, watching the kids get out of the parochial school, before I found my second. It took a while. The first one that looked good turned out to be a bus kid, the second was a walker but her big sister from the high school walked with her. The third walked home alone. It was December, and the afternoons got pretty dark, and that Friday she walked but she didn't get home. I never molested any of them sexually, you know. I mean, in some ways I'm still kind of a virgin. That wasn't what I wanted, I just wanted to see them die. When they asked me at the pre-trial hearing if I knew the difference between right and wrong I didn't know how to answer them. I knew what I did was wrong for them. But it wasn't wrong for me, it was what I wanted.

So, driving down the Parkway, feeling discouraged about Carolyn, I noticed where I was and cut over to Route 35 and doubled back. I drove right to the school, past it, and to the lumberyard where I did the little girl. I stopped and cut the motor, looking around. Happy day. Now it was a different time of year, and things looked a little different. They'd piled up a stack of two-by-twelves over the place where I'd done her. But in my mind's eye I could see it the way it had been then. Dark gray sky. Lights from the cars going past. I could hear the little buzzing feeling in her throat as she tried to scream under my fingers. Let's see. That was, oh, good heavens, nine years ago.

And if I hadn't done her she would have been twenty or so. Screwing all the boys. Probably on dope. Maybe knocked up or married. Looked at in a certain way, I saved her a lot of sordid miserable stuff, menstruating, letting the boys' hands and mouths on her, all that . . .

My head began hurting. That's one thing the plate in your head does, it doesn't let you get very deeply into the things you did in the old days, because it hurts too much. So I started up the car and drove away, and pretty soon the hurting stopped.

I never think of Carolyn, you know, that way.

They never proved that little girl on me. The one they caught me for was the nurse in Long Branch, in the parking lot. And she was a mistake. She was so small, and she had a sweater over her uniform. I didn't know she was grown up until it was too late. I was very angry about that. In a way I didn't mind when they caught me, because I had been getting very careless. But I really hated that ward in Marlboro where they put me. Seven, Jesus, seven years. Up in the morning, and drink your pink medicine out of the little paper cup. Make your bed and do your job—mine was sweeping in the incontinent wards, and the smells and the sights would make you throw up.

After a while they let me watch TV and even read the papers, and when the Altair people made the first contact with Earth I was interested, and when they began buying criminally insane to be their proxies I wanted them to buy me. Anything, I wanted *anything* that would let me get out of that place, even if it meant I'd have to let them put a box in my head and never be able to live a normal life again.

But the Altair people wouldn't buy me. For some reason they only took blacks. Then the others began showing up on the fast radio, making their deals. And still none of them wanted me. The ones from Procyon liked young women, wouldn't ever buy a male. I think they have only one sex there, someone said. All these funnies are peculiar in one way or another. Metal, or gas, or blobby, or hard-shelled and rattly. Whatever. And they all have funny habits, like if you belong to the Canopus bunch you can't ever eat fish.

I think they're disgusting, and I don't really know why the USA wanted to get involved with them in the first place. But the Chinese did, and the Russians did, and I guess we just couldn't stay out. I suppose it hasn't hurt much. There hasn't been a war, and there's a lot of ways in which they've helped clean things up for us. It hasn't hurt me, that's for sure. The Groombridge people came into the market pretty late, and most of the good healthy criminals were gone; they would buy anybody. They bought me. We're a hard-case lot, we Groombridgians, and I do wonder what Carolyn was in for.

I drove all the way down the coast, Asbury Park, Brielle, Atlantic City, all the way to Cape May, phoning back to check with the locator clerk, and never found her.

The one thing I did know was that all I was missing was the shell of her, because she was working. I could have had a kiss or a feel, no more. But I wanted to find her anyway. Just on the chance. How many times do you get an indefinite furlough? If I'd been able to find her, and stay with her, sooner or later, maybe, she would have been off too. Even if it were only for two hours. Even thirty minutes.

And then in broad daylight, just as I was checking into a motel near an Army base, with the soldiers' girls lined up at the cashier's window so their boyfriends could get back for reveille, I got the call: Report to the Philadelphia kennel. Soonest.

By then I was giddy for sleep, but I drove that Hertz lump like a Maserati, because soonest means soonest. I dumped the car and signed in at the kennel, feeling my heart pounding and my mouth ragged from fatigue, and aching because I had blown what would have to be my best chance of really being with Carolyn. "What do they want?" I asked the locator clerk. "Go inside," he said, looking evilly amused. All locator clerks treat us the same, all over the world. "She'll tell you."

Not knowing who "she" was I opened the door and walked through, and there was Carolyn.

"Hello, Wayne," she said.

"Hello, Carolyn," I said.

I really did not have any idea of what to do at all. She didn't give me a cue. She just sat. It was at that point that it occurred to me to wonder at the fact that she wasn't wearing much, just a shortie nightgown with nothing under it. She was also sitting on a turned-down bed. Now, you would think that considering everything, especially the nature of most of my thinking about Carolyn, that I would have instantly accepted this as a personal gift from God to me of every boy's all-American dream. I didn't. It wasn't the fatigue, either. It was Carolyn. It was the expression on her face, which was neither inviting nor loving, was not even the judgment-reserving look of a girl at a singles bar. What it especially was not was happy.

"The thing is, Wayne," she said, "we're supposed to go to bed now. So take your clothes off, why don't you?"

Sometimes I can stand outside of myself and look at me and, even when it's something terrible or something sad, I can see it as funny; it was like that when I did the little girl in

Edison Township, because her mother had sewed her into her school clothes. I was actually laughing when I said, "Carolyn, what's the matter?"

"Well," she said, "they want us to ball, Wayne. You know. The Groombridge people. They've got interested in what human beings do to each other and they want to kind of watch."

I started to ask why us, but I didn't have to; I could see where Carolyn and I had had a lot of that on our minds, and maybe our masters could get curious about it. I didn't exactly like it. Not exactly; in fact in a way I kind of hated it, but it was so much better than nothing at all that I said, "Why, honey, that's great!"—almost meaning it; trying to talk her into it; moving in next to her and putting my arm around her. And then she said:

"Only we have to wait, Wayne. *They* want to do it. Not us."

"What do you mean, wait? Wait for what?" She shrugged under my arm. "You mean," I said, "that we have to be plugged in to them? Like they'll be doing it with our bodies?"

She leaned against me. "That's what they told me, Wayne. Any minute now, I guess."

I pushed her away. "Honey," I said, half crying, "all this time I've been wanting to—Jesus, Carolyn! I mean, it isn't just that I wanted to go to bed with you. I mean—"

"I'm sorry," she cried, big tears on her face.

"That's lousy!" I shouted. My head was pounding, I was so furious. "It isn't fair! I'm not going to stand for it. They don't have any *right!*"

But they did, of course, they had all the right in the world; they had bought us and paid for us, and so they owned us. I knew that. I just didn't want to accept it, even by admitting what I knew was so. The notion of screwing Carolyn flipped polarity; it wasn't what I desperately wanted, it was what I would have died to avoid, as long as it meant letting *them* paw her with my hands, kiss her with my mouth, flood her with my juices; it was like the worst kind of rape, worse than anything I had ever done, both of us raped at once. And then—

And then I felt that burning tingle in my forehead as they took over. I couldn't even scream. I just had to sit there inside my own head, no longer owning a muscle, while those freaks who owned me did to Carolyn with my body all manner of things, and I could not even cry.

After concluding the planned series of experimental procedures, which were duly recorded, the purchased person known as Carolyn Schoerner was no longer salvageable. Appropriate entries were made. The Probation and Out-Service department of the Meadville Women's Reformatory was notified that she had ceased to be alive. A purchasing requisition was initiated for a replacement, and her account was terminated.

The purchased person known as Wayne Golden was assigned to usual duties, at which he functioned normally while under control. It was discovered that when control was withdrawn he became destructive, both to others and to himself. The conjecture has been advanced that that sexual behavior which had been established as his norm—the destruction of the sexual partner—may not have been appropriate in the conditions obtaining at the time of the experimental procedures. Further experiments will be made with differing procedures and other partners in the near future. Meanwhile Wayne Golden continues to function at normal efficiency, provided control is not withdrawn at any time, and apparently will do so indefinitely.

AFTERWORD

What keeps me writing science fiction is that it is the most Protean of literatures. I don't know of any single writer who has used all of its tools, much less mastered them all. To do so would require a superhuman command of all the knowledge and all the skills humanity has acquired since the days of the Australopithecines, since a proper story considers not only events and persons but processes and causalities. Put it less remotely: a proper sf story not only tells you what is happening and who it is happening to, it tells you why.

First contact. for example, is clearly a probable event somewhen in Man's future. Sf writers have so considered it for a long time. H. G. Wells told us that the essence of first contact might be invasion and exploitation (in *The War of the Worlds*), on the highly defensible assumption that since that had been the way it had usually been in earthly affairs, interplanetary affairs would likely be the same. Murray Leinster, Hal Clement, and a hundred other writers have expanded on this assumption and investigated specific areas contained within it, skillfully, informatively and, above all, entertainingly.

But it has seemed to me, ultimately, that First Contact means more than a mass effect, it means a special effect for almost each special, individual person.

Novel
WOLFBANE, by Frederik Pohl and C.M. Kornbluth

Short Stories
FIRST CONTACT, by Murray Leinster
DISCORD IN SCARLET, by A.E. Van Vogt
RESCUE PARTY, by Arthur C. Clarke
A MARTIAN ODYSSEY, by Stanley G. Weinbaum
THE DAY AFTER THE DAY THE MARTIANS CAME, by Frederik Pohl

About Frederik Pohl

Frederik Pohl, b. 1919, has been an active professional since 1939, initially as an editor, later as novelist (THE SPACE MERCHANTS, with C.M. Kornbluth; GLADIATOR-AT-LAW, with C.M. Kornbluth; AGE OF THE PUSSYFOOT; and some fifteen to twenty other titles), short-story writer, and again as editor (STAR SCIENCE-FICTION, *Galaxy Magazine*, 1960–69). He has won consecutive Hugo awards for best magazine and in 1973 won (with the late C.M. Kornbluth) a Hugo award for best short story—the only person so honored for both writing and editing. Presently editing Bantam's science fiction program, he lives in New Jersey with his wife, Carol, and children.

THE EXPLORATION OF SPACE

THE VOORTREKKERS

POUL ANDERSON

> —And he shall see old planets change and alien stars arise—

So swift is resurrection that the words go on which had been in me when last I died. Only after pulsebeats does the strangeness raining through my senses reach my awareness, to make me know that four more decades, and almost nine light-years, have flowed between me and the poet.

Light-years. Light. Everywhere light. Once, a boy, I spent a night camped on a winter mountaintop. Then it entered my bones—and how can anyone who has done likewise ever believe otherwise?—that space is not dark. Maybe this was when the need was born in me, to go up and out into the sky.

I am in the sky now, and of it. Around me stars and stars and stars are crowding, until there is no room for blackness to be more than a crystal which holds them. They are all the colors of reality, from lightning through gold to the duskiest rose, but each one singingly keen. Nebulae are flung among them like veils and clouds, where great suns have died or new worlds are whirling to birth. The Milky Way is a cool torrent, here cloven by the thunderstorm masses of galactic center, there open a-glint toward endlessness. I magnify my vision and trace the spiral of our sister maelstrom, a million and a half light-years hence in Andromeda.

Sol is a small glow on the edge of Hercules. Brightest is Sirius, whose blue-white luminance casts shadows of fittings and housings across my hull. I seek and find its companion.

This is not done by optics. The dwarf is barely coming around the giant, lost in glare. What I see, through different sensors, is the X-radiation; what I snuff is a sharp breath of neutrinos mingled with the gale that streams from the other; I swim in an intricate interplay of force-fields, balancing, thrusting, while they caress me; I listen to the skirls and drones, the murmurs and melodies of a universe.

At first I do not hear Korene. If I was a little slow to leave Kipling for these heavens, so I am to leave them for her. Maybe it's more excusable. I must make certain at once, as much as possible, that we are not in danger. Probably we aren't, or the automatons would have restored us to existence before the scheduled moment. But automatons can only judge what they were designed and programmed to judge, by people nine light-years away from yonder mystery, people most likely dust, even as Korene and Joel are surely dust.

Joel, Joel! Korene calls from within me. *Are you there?*

I open my interior scanners. Her principal body, the one which houses her principal brain, is in motion, carefully testing every part after forty-three years of death. For the thousandth time, the beauty of this seat of her consciousness strikes me. Its darkly sheening shape is only humanlike in the way that an abstract sculpture might be on far, far Earth —those several arms, for instance, or the dragonfly head which is not really a head at all—and only this for functional reasons. But something about the slimness and grace of movement recalls Korene who is dust.

She has not yet made contact with any of the specialized auxiliary bodies around her. Instead she has joined a communication circuit to one of mine.

Hi, I flash, rather shakily, for in spite of studies and experiments and simulations, years of them, it is still too tremendous to comprehend, that we are actually approaching Sirius. *How are you?*

Fine. Everything okay?

Near's I can tell. Why didn't you use voice?

I did. No answer. I yelled. No answer. So I plugged in.

My joy gets tinged with embarrassment. *Sorry. I, uh, I guess I was too excited.*

She breaks the connection, since it is not ideally convenient, and says, "Quite something out there?"

"You wouldn't believe," I respond by my own speaker. "Take a look."

I activate the viewscreens for her. "O-o-o-ohh; O God," she breathes. Yes, breathes. Our artificial voices copy those which once were in our throats. Korene's is husky and musical; it was a pleasure to hear her sing at parties. Her friends often urged her to get into amateur theatricals, but she said she had neither the time nor the talent.

Maybe she was right, though Lord knows she was good at plenty of other things, her astronautical engineering, painting, cookery, sewing fancy clothes, throwing feasts, playing tennis and poker, ranging over hills, being a wife and mother, in her first life. (Well, we've both changed a lot since then.) On the other hand, that utterance of hers, when she sees the star before her, says everything for which I can only fumble.

From the beginning, when the first rockets roared into orbit, some people have called astronauts a prosaic lot, if they weren't calling us worse; and no doubt in some cases this was true. But I think mainly it's just that we grow tongue-tied in the presence of the Absolute.

"I wish—" I say, and energize an auxiliary of my own, a control-module maintainer, to lay an awkward touch upon her—"I wish you could sense it the way I do, Korene. Plug back in—full psychoneural—when I've finished my checkouts, and I'll try to convey a little."

"Thanks, my friend." She speaks with tenderness. "I knew you would. But don't worry about my missing something because of not being wired up like a ship. I'll be having a lot of experiences you can't, and wishing I could share them with you." She chuckles. *"Vive la différence."*

Nonetheless I hear the flutter in her tone and, knowing her, am unsurprised when she asks anxiously, "Are there . . . by any chance . . . planets?"

"No trace. We're a long ways off yet, of course. I might be missing the indications. So far, though, it looks as if the astronomers were right" who declared minor bodies cannot condense around a star like Sirius. "Never mind, we'll both find enough to keep us out of mischief in the next several years. Already at this range, I'm noticing all kinds of phenomena which theory did not predict."

"Then you don't think we'll need organics?"

"No, 'fraid not. In fact, the radiation—"

"Sure. Understood. But damn, next trip I'm going to insist on a destination that'll probably call for them."

She told me once, back in the Solar System, after we had first practiced the creation of ourselves in flesh: "It's like making love again."

They had not been lovers in their original lives. He an American, she a European, they served the space agencies of their respective confederations and never chanced to be in the same cooperative venture. Thus they met only occasionally and casually, at professional conventions or celebrations. They were still young when the interstellar exploration project was founded. It was a joint undertaking of all countries—no one bloc could have gotten its taxpayers to bear the cost—but research and development must run for a generation before hardware would become available to the first true expeditions. Meanwhile there was nothing but a few unmanned probes, and the interplanetary studies wherein Joel and Korene took part.

She retired from these, to desk and laboratory, at an earlier age than he did, having married Olaf and wishing children. Olaf himself continued on the Lunar shuttle for a while. But that wasn't the same as standing on the peaks of Rhea beneath the rings of Saturn or pacing the million kilometers of a comet, as afire as the scientists themselves with what they were discovering. Presently he quit, and joined Korene on one of the engineering teams of the interstellar group. Together they made important contributions, until she accepted a managerial position. This interested her less in its own right; but she handled it ferociously well, because she saw it as a means to an end—authority, influence. Olaf stayed with the work he liked best. Their home life continued happy.

In that respect, Joel at first differed. Pilots on the major expeditions (and he got more berths than his share) could seldom hope to be family men. He tried, early in the game; but after he realized what a very lonely kind of pain drove a girl he had loved to divorce him, he settled for a succession of mistresses. He was always careful to explain to them that nothing and nobody could make him stop faring before he must.

This turned out to be not quite true. Reaching mandatory age for "the shelf," he might have finagled a few extra years skyside. But by then, cuts in funding for space were marrow-deep. Those who still felt that man had business beyond Earth agreed that what resources were left had better go mostly toward the stars. Like Korene, Joel saw that the same was true of him. He enrolled in the American part of the effort. Experience and natural talent equipped him uniquely to work on control and navigation.

In the course of this, he met Mary. He had known a good many female astronauts, and generally liked them as persons—often as bodies too, but long voyages and inevitable promiscuity were as discouraging to stable relationships for them as for him. Mary used her reflexes and spirit to test-pilot experimental vehicles near home.

This didn't mean that she failed to share the dream. Joel fell thoroughly in love with her. Their marriage likewise proved happy.

He was forty-eight, Korene sixty, when the word became official: The basic machinery for reaching the stars now existed. It needed merely several years' worth of refinement and a pair of qualified volunteers.

It *is* like making love again.

How my heart soared when first we saw that the second planet has air a human can breathe! Nothing can create that except life. Those months after Joel went into orbit around it and we observed, photographed, spectroanalyzed, measured, sampled, calculated, mainly reading what instruments recorded but sometimes linking ourselves directly to them and feeling the input as once we felt wind in our hair or surf around our skins—

Why do I think of hair, skin, heart, love, I who am embodied in metal and synthetics and ghostly electron-dance? Why do I remember Olaf with this knife sharpness?

I suppose he died well before Korene. Men usually do. (What does death have against women, anyway?) Then was her aftertime until she could follow him down; and in spite of faxes and diaries and every other crutch humankind has invented, I think he slowly became a blur, never altogether to be summoned forth except perhaps in sleep. At least, with this cryogenic recall of mine which is not programmed to lie, I remember how aging Korene one day realized, shocked, that she had nothing left except aging Olaf, that she could no longer see or feel young Olaf except as words.

Oh, she loved him-now, doubtless in a deeper fashion than she-then had been able to love him-then, after all their shared joy, grief, terror, toil, hope, merry little sillinesses which stayed more clear across the years than many of the big events—yes, their shared furies and frustrations with each other, their few and fleeting intense involvements with out-

siders, which somehow also were always involvements between him and her—she loved her old husband, but she had
lost her young one.

Whereas I have been given him back, in my flawless new
memory. And given Joel as well, or instead, or—Why am I
thinking this nonsense? Olaf is dust.

Tau Ceti is flame.

It's not the same kind of fire as Sol. It's cooler, yellower,
something autumnal about it, even though it will outlive
man's home star. I don't suppose the unlikenesses will
appear so great to human eyes. I know the entire spectrum.
(How much more does Joel sense! To me, every sun is a
once-in-the-universe individual; to him, every sunspot is.)
The organic body/mind is both more general and more specific than this . . . like me *vis-à-vis* Joel. (I remember, I
remember: striding the Delphi road, muscle-play, boot-
scrunch, spilling sunlight and baking warmth, bees at hum
through wild thyme and rosemary, on my upper lip a taste of
sweat, and that tremendous plunge down to the valley where
Oedipus met his father. . . . Machine, I would not experience
it in quite those terms. There would be too many other radia-
tions, forces, shifts and subtleties which Oedipus never felt.
But would it be less beautiful? Is a deaf man, suddenly
cured, less alive because afterward his mind gives less time
to his eyes?)

Well, we'll soon know how living flesh experiences the
living planet of Tau Ceti.

It isn't the infinite blue and white of Earth. It has a green-
ish tinge, equally clear and marvelous, and two moons for
the lovers whom I, sentimental old crone, keep imagining.
The aliennesses may yet prove lethal. But Joel said, in his
dear dry style:

"The latest readouts convince me. The tropics are a shirt-
sleeve environment." His mind grinned, I am sure, as
formerly his face did. "Or a bare-ass environment. That
remains to be seen. I'm certain, however, organic bodies can
manage better down there than any of yours or mine."

Was I the one who continued to hesitate because I had
been the one more eager for this? A kind of fear chilled me.
"We already know they can't find everything they need to
eat, in that biochemistry—"

"By the same token," the ship reminded, not from intellectual but emotional necessity, "nothing local, like germs, can make a lunch off them. The survival odds are excellent," given the concentrated dietary supplements, tools, and the rest of what we have for them. "Good Lord, Korene, you could get smashed in a rock storm, prospecting some wretched asteroid, or I could run into too much radiation for the screens and have my brain burned out. Or whatever. Do we mind?"

"No," I whispered. "Not unendurably."

"So *they* won't."

"True. I shouldn't let my conscience make a coward of me. Let's go right ahead."

After all, when I brought children into the world, long ago, I knew they might be given straight over to horror; or it might take them later on; or at best, they would be born to trouble as the sparks fly upward, and in an astonishingly few decades be dust. Yet I never took from them, while they lay innocent in my womb, their chance at life.

Thus Joel and I are bringing forth the children who will be ourselves.

He wheels like another moon around the world, and his sensors drink of it and his mind reasons about it. I, within him, send forth my auxiliary bodies to explore its air and waters and lands; through the laser channels, mine are their labors, triumphs, and—twice—deaths. But such things have become just a part of our existence, like the jobs from which we hurried home every day. (Though here job and home go on concurrently.) The rest of us, the most of us, is linked in those circuits that guide our children into being.

We share, we are a smile-pattern down the waves and wires, remembering how chaste the agency spokesman made it sound, in that first famous interview. Joel and I had scarcely met then, and followed it separately on television. He told me afterward that, having heard the spiels a thousand times before, both pro and con, he'd rather have gone fishing.

(Neither was especially likable, the commentator small and waspish, the spokesman large and Sincere. The latter directed his fleshy countenance at the camera and said:

"Let me summarize, please. I know it's familiar to you in the audience, but I want to spell out our problem.

"In the state of the art, we can send small spacecraft to

the nearer stars, and back, at an average speed of about one-fifth light's. That means twenty-odd years to reach Alpha Centauri, the closest; and then there's the return trip; and, naturally, a manned expedition would make no sense unless it was prepared to spend a comparable time on the spot, learning those countless things which unmanned probes cannot. The trouble is, when I say small spacecraft, I mean small. Huge propulsion units but minimal hull and payload. No room or mass to spare for the protection and life support that even a single human would require: not to mention the fact that confinement and monotony would soon drive a crew insane."

"What about suspended animation?" asked the commentator.

The spokesman shook his head. "No, sir. Aside from the bulkiness of the equipment, radiation leakage would destroy too many cells en route. We can barely provide shielding for those essential items which are vulnerable." He beamed. "So we've got a choice. Either we stay with our inadequate probes, or we go over to the system being proposed."

"Or we abandon the whole boondoggle and spend the money on something useful," the commentator said.

The spokesman gave him a trained look of pained patience and replied: "The desirability of space exploration is a separate question, that I'll be glad to take up with you later. If you please, for the time being let's stick to the mechanics of it."

" 'Mechanics' may be a very good word, sir," the commentator insinuated. "Turning human beings into robots. Not exactly like Columbus, is it? Though I grant you, thinkers always did point out how machine-like the astronauts were . . . and are."

"If you please," the spokesman repeated, "value judgments aside, who's talking about making robots out of humans? Brains transplanted into machinery? Come! If a body couldn't survive the trip, why imagine that a brain in a tank might? No, we'll simply employ ultra-sophisticated computer-sensor-effector systems."

"With human minds."

"With human psychoneural patterns mapped in, sir. That is all." Smugly: "True, that's a mighty big 'all.' The pattern of an individual is complex beyond imagination, and dynamic rather than static; our math boys call it n-dimensional. We will have to develop methods for scanning it without harm to the subject, recording it, and transferring it to a different matrix, whether that matrix be photonic-electronic or molecular-organic." Drawing breath, then portentously: "Consider the benefits, right here on Earth, of having such a capability."

"I don't know about that," said the commentator. "Maybe you could plant a copy of my personality somewhere else; but *I'd* go on in this same old body, wouldn't I?"

"It would hardly be your exact personality anyhow," admitted the spokesman. "The particular matrix would . . . um . . . determine so much of the functioning. The important thing, from the viewpoint of extrasolar exploration, is that this will give us machines which are not mere robots, but which have such human qualities as motivation and self-programming.

"At the same time, they'll have the advantages of robots. For example, they can be switched off in transit; they won't experience those empty years between stars; they'll arrive sane."

"Some of us wonder if they'll have departed sane. But look," the commentator challenged, "if your machines that you imagine you can program to be people, if they're that good, then why have them manufacture artificial flesh-and-blood people at the end of a trip?"

"Only where circumstances justify it," said the spokesman. "Under some conditions, organic bodies will be preferable. Testing the habitability of a planet is just the most obvious possibility. Consider how your body heals its own wounds. In numerous respects it's actually stronger, more durable, than metal or plastic."

"Why give them the same minds—if I may speak of minds in this connection—the same as the machines?"

"A matter of saving mass." The spokesman smirked at his own wit. "We know the psychoneural scanner will be far too large and fragile to carry along. The apparatus which impresses a pattern on the androids will have to use pre-existent data banks. It can be made much lighter than would otherwise be necessary, if those are the same banks already in use."

He lifted a finger. "Besides, our psychologists think this

will have a reinforcing effect. I'd hardly dare call the relationship, ha, ha, parental—"

"Nor I," said the commentator. "I'd call it something like obscene or ghastly.")

When Joel and I, together, month after month guide these chemistries to completion, and when—O climax outcrying the seven thunders!—we send ourselves into the sleeping bodies—maybe, for us at least, it is more than making love ever was.

Joel and Mary were on their honeymoon when he told her of his wish.

Astronauts and ranking engineers could afford to go where air and water were clean, trees grew instead of walls, birdsong resounded instead of traffic, and one's fellow man was sufficiently remote that one could feel benign toward him. Doubtless that was among the reasons why politicians got re-elected by gnawing at the space program.

This evening the west was a fountain of gold above a sea which far out shimmered purple, then broke upon the sands in white thunder. Behind, palms made traces on a blue where Venus had kindled. The air was mild, astir with odors of salt and jasmine.

They stood, arms around each other's waists, her head leaned against him, and watched the sun leave. But when he told her, she stepped from him and he saw terror.

"Hey, what's wrong, darling?" He seized her hands.

"No," she said. "You mustn't."

"What? Why ever not? You're working for it too!"

The sky-glow caught tears. "For somebody else to go, that's fine. It, it'd be like winning a war—a just war, a triumph—when somebody else's man got to do the dying. Not you," she pleaded.

"But . . . good Lord," he tried to laugh, "it won't be me, worse luck. My satisfaction will be strictly vicarious. Supposing I'm accepted, what do I sacrifice? Some time under a scanner; a few cells for chromosome templates. Why in the cosmos should you care?"

"I don't know. It'd be . . . oh, I never thought about it before, never realized the thing might strike home like this—" She swallowed. "I guess it's . . . I'd think, there's a Joel, locked for the rest of his existence inside a machine . . .

and there's a Joel in the flesh, dying some gruesome death, or marooned forever."

Silence passed before he replied, slowly: "Why not think, instead, there's a Joel who's glad to pay the price and take the risk—" he let her go and swept a gesture around heaven— "for the sake of getting out yonder?"

She bit her lip. "He'd even abandon his wife."

"I hoped you'd apply also."

"No. I couldn't face it. I'm too much a, an Earthling. This is all too dear to me."

"Do you suppose I don't care for it? Or for you?" He drew her to him.

They were quite alone. On grass above the strand, they won to joy again.

"After all," he said later, "the question won't get serious for years and years."

I don't come back fast. They can't just ram a lifetime into a new body. That's the first real thought I have, as I drift from a cave where voices echoed on and on, and then slowly lights appeared, images, whole scenes, my touch on a control board, Dad lifting me to his shoulder which is way up in the sky, leaves above a brown secret pool, Mary's hair tickling my nose, a boy who stands on his head in the schoolyard, a rocket blastoff that shakes my bones with its sound and light, Mother giving me a fresh-baked ginger cookie, Mother laid out dead and the awful strangeness of her and Mary holding my hand very tight, Mary, Mary, Mary.

No, that's not her voice, it's another woman's, whose, yes, Korene's, and I'm being stroked and cuddled more gently than I ever knew could be. I blink to full consciousness, free-fall afloat in the arms of a robot.

"Joel," she murmurs. "Welcome."

It crashes in on me. No matter the slow awakening: suddenly this. I've taken the anesthetic before they wheel me to the scanner, I'm drowsing dizzily off, then *now* I have no weight, metal and machinery cram everywhere in around me, those are not eyes I look into but glowing optical sensors, "Oh, my God," I say, "it happened to me."

This me. Only I'm Joel! Exactly Joel, nobody else.

I stare down the nude length of my body and know that's not true. The scars, the paunch, the white hairs here and there on the chest are gone. I'm smooth, twenty years in age, though with half a century inside me. I snap after breath.

"Be calm," says Korene.

And the ship speaks with my voice: "Hi, there. Take it easy, pal. You've got a lot of treatment and exercise ahead, you know, before you're ready for action."

"Where are we?" breaks from me.

"Sigma Draconis," Korene says. "In orbit around the most marvelous planet—intelligent life, friendly, and their art is beyond describing, 'beautiful' is such a weak little word—"

"How are things at home?" I interrupt. "I mean, how were they when you . . . we . . . left?"

"You and Mary were still going strong, you at age seventy," she assures me. "Likewise the children and grand-children." *Ninety years ago.*

I went under, in the laboratory, knowing a single one of me would rouse on Earth and return to her. I am not the one.

I didn't know how hard that would lash.

Korene holds me close. It's typical of her not to be in any hurry to pass on the last news she had of her own self. I suppose, through the hollowness and the trying to cry in her machine arms, I suppose that's why my body was pro-grammed first. Hers can take this better.

"It's not too late yet," she begged him. "I can still swing the decision your way."

Olaf's grizzled head wove back and forth. "No. How many times must I tell you?"

"No more," she sighed. "The choices will be made within a month."

He rose from his armchair, went to her where she sat, and ran a big ropy-veined hand across her cheek. "I am sorry," he said. "You are sweet to want me along. I hate to hurt you." She could imagine the forced smile above her. "But truly, why would you want a possible millennium of my grouchiness?"

"Because you are Olaf," Korene answered.

She got up likewise, stepped to a window, and stood looking out. It was a winter night. Snow lay hoar on roofs across the old city, spires pierced an uneasy glow, a few stars glimmered. Frost put shrillness into the rumble of traffic and machines. The room, its warmth and small treasures, felt besieged.

She broke her word by saying, "Can't you see, a personality inside a cybernet isn't a castrated cripple? In a way, we're the ones caged, in these ape bodies and senses. There's a whole new universe to become part of. Including a universe of new closenesses to me."

He joined her. "Call me a reactionary," he growled, "or a professional ape. I've often explained that I like being what I am, too much to start over as something else."

She turned to him and said low: "You'd also start over as what you were. We both would. Over and over."

"No. We'd have these aged minds."

She laughed forlornly. " 'If youth knew, if age could.' "

"We'd be sterile."

"Of necessity. No way to raise children on any likely planet. Otherwise—Olaf, if you refuse, I'm going regardless. With another man. I'll always wish he were you."

He lifted a fist. "All right, God damn it!" he shouted. "All right! I'll tell you the real reason why I won't go under your bloody scanner! I'd die too envious!"

It is fair here beyond foretelling: beyond understanding, until slowly we grow into our planet.

For it isn't Earth. Earth we have forever laid behind us, Joel and I. The sun is molten amber, large in a violet heaven. At this season its companion has risen about noon, a gold-bright star which will drench night with witchery under the constellations and three swift moons. Now, toward the end of day, the hues around us—intensely green hills, tall blue-plumed trees, rainbows in wings which jubilate overhead—are become so rich that they fill the air; the whole world glows. Off across the valley, a herd of beasts catches the shiningness on their horns.

We took off our boots when we came back to camp. The turf, not grass nor moss, is springy underfoot, cool between the toes. The nearby forest breathes out fragrances; one of them recalls rosemary. Closer is smoke from the fire Korene built while we were exploring. It speaks to my nostrils and the most ancient parts of my brain: of autumn leaves burning, of blazes after dark in what few high solitudes remained on Earth, of hearths where I sat at Christmas time with the children.

"Hello, dears," says my voice out of the machine. (It isn't the slim fleet body she uses aboard ship; it's built for sturdiness, is the only awkward sight in all the landscape.) "You seem to have had a pleasant day."

"Oh, my, oh, my!" Arms uplifted, I dance. "We *must* find a name for this planet. Thirty-six Ophiuchi B Two is ridiculous."

"We will," says Joel in my ear. His palm falls on my flank. It feels like a torch.

"I'm on the channel too," says the speaker with his voice. "Uh, look, kids, fun's fun, but we've got to get busy. I want you properly housed and supplied long before winter. And while we ferry the stuff, do the carpentering, et cetera, I want more samples for us to analyze. So far you've just found some fruits and such that're safe to eat. You need meat as well."

"I hate to think of killing," I say, when I am altogether happy.

"Oh, I reckon I've got enough hunter instinct for both of us," says Joel, my Joel. Breath gusts from him, across me. "Christ! I never guessed how good elbow room and freedom would feel."

"Plus a large job," Korene reminds: the study of a world, that she and her Joel may signal our discoveries back to a Sol we can no longer see with our eyes alone; that in the end, they may carry back what we have gathered, to an Earth that perhaps will no longer want it.

"Sure. I expect to love every minute." His clasp on me tightens. Waves shudder outward, through me. "Speaking of love—"

The machine grows still. A shadow has lengthened across its metal, where firelight weaves reflected. The flames talk merrily. A flying creature cries like a trumpet.

"So you have come to that," says Korene at last, a benediction.

"Today," I declare from our glory.

There is another quietness.

"Well, congratulations," says Korene's Joel. "We, uh, we were planning a little wedding present for you, but you've caught us by surprise." Mechanical tendrils reach out. Joel releases me to take them in his fingers. "All the best, both of you. Couldn't happen to two nicer people, even if I am one of them myself, sort of. Uh, well, we'll break contact now, Korene and I. See you in the morning?"

"Oh, no, oh, no," I stammer, between weeping and laughter, and cast myself on my knees to embrace this body whose two spirits brought us to life and will someday bury us. "Stay. We want you here, Joel and I. You, you are us." *And more than us and pitifully less than us.* "We want to share with you."

The priest mounted to his pulpit. Tall in white robes, he waited there against the shadows of the sanctuary; candles picked him out and made a halo around his hood. When silence was total in the temple, he leaned forward. His words tolled forth to the faces and the cameras:

"Thou shalt have none other gods but me, said the Lord unto the children of Israel. Thou shalt love thy neighbor as thyself, said Christ unto the world. And sages and seers of every age and every faith warned against *hubris*, that overweening pride which brings down upon us immortal anger.

"The Tower of Babel and the Flood of Noah may be myths. But in myth lies a wisdom of the race which goes infinitely beyond the peerings and posturings of science. Behold our sins today and tremble.

"Idolatry: man's worship of what he alone has made. Uncharity: man's neglect, yes, forsaking of his brother in that brother's need, to whore after mere adventure. *Hubris:* man's declaration that he can better the work of God.

"You know what I mean. While the wretched of Earth groan in their billions for succor, treasure is spewed into the barrenness of outer space. Little do the lords of lunacy care for their fellow mortals. Nothing do they care for God.

" 'To follow knowledge like a sinking star, Beyond the utmost bound of human thought' is a pair of lines much quoted these days. Ulysses, the eternal seeker. May I remind you, those lines do not refer to Homer's wanderer, but to Dante's, who was in hell for breaking every constraint which divine Providence had ordained.

"And yet how small, how warm and understandable was his sin! His was not that icy arrogance which today the faceless engineers of the interstellar project urge upon us. Theirs is the final contempt for God and for man. In order that we may violate the harmony of the stars, we are to create, in metal and chemicals, dirty caricatures of a holy work; we are actually to believe that by our electronic trickery we can breathe into them souls."

Nat the rhesus monkey runs free. The laboratory half of the cabin is barred to him; the living quarters, simply and sturdily equipped, don't hold much he can harm. He isn't terribly mischievous anyway. Outdoors are unlimited space and trees where he can be joyful. So, when at home with Korene and Joel, he almost always observes the restrictions they have taught him.

His wish to please may stem from memory of loneliness. It was a weary while he was caged on the surface, after he had been grown in the tank. (His body has, in fact, existed longer than the two human ones.) He had no company save rats, guinea pigs, tissue cultures, and the like—and, of course, the machine which tended and tested him. That that robot often spoke, petted and played games, was what saved his monkey sanity. When at last living flesh hugged his own, what hollow within him was suddenly filled?

What hollow in the others? He skips before their feet, he rides on their shoulders, at night he shares their bed.

But today is the third of cold autumn rains. Though Korene has given to this planet of Eighty-two Eridani the name Gloria, it has its seasons, and now spins toward a darker time. The couple have stayed inside, and Nat gets restless. No doubt, as well, the change in his friends arouses an unease.

There ought to be cheer. The cabin is amply large for two persons. It is more than snug, it is lovely, in the flowing grain of its timbers and the crystal-glittering stones of its fireplace. Flames dance on the hearth; they laugh; a bit of their smoke escapes to scent the air like cinnamon; through the brightness of fluorescent panels, their light shimmers off furnishings and earthenware which Joel and Korene made together in the summer which is past—off the racked reels of an audiovisual library and a few beloved pictures—off twilit panes where rain sluices downward. Beyond a closed door, wind goes *brroo-oom.*

Joel sits hunched at his desk. He hasn't bathed or shaved lately, his hair is unkempt, his coverall begrimed and sour. Korene has maintained herself better; it is dust in the corners and unwashed dishes in a basin which bespeak what she has neglected while he was trying to hunt. She sprawls on the bed and listens to music, though the ringing in her ears makes that hard.

Both have grown gaunt. Their eyes are sunken, their mouths and tongues are sore. Upon the dried skin of hands and faces, a rash has appeared.

Joel casts down his slide rule. "Damn, I can't think!" he nearly shouts. "Screw those analyses! What good are they?"

Korene's reply is sharp. "They just might show what's gone wrong with us and how to fix it."

"Judas! When I can't even sleep right—" He twists about on his chair to confront the inactive robot. "You! You damned smug machines, where are you? What're you doing?"

A tic goes ugly along Korene's lip. "They're busy, yonder in orbit," she says. "I suggest you follow their example."

"Yah! Same as you?"

"Quite—anytime you'll help me keep our household running, Sir Self-Appointed Biochemist." She starts to lift herself but abandons the effort. Tears of self-pity trickle forth. "Olaf wouldn't have turned hysterical like you."

"And Mary wouldn't lie flopped-out useless," he says. However, the sting she has given sends him back to his labor. Interpreting the results of gas chromatography on unknown compounds is difficult at best. When he has begun to hallucinate—when the graphs he has drawn slide around and intertwine as if they were worms—

A crash resounds from the pantry. Korene exclaims. Joel jerks erect. Flour and the shards of a crock go in a tide across the floor. After them bounds Nat. He stops amidst the wreckage and gives his people a look of amazed innocence. Dear me, he all but says, how did this happen?

"You lousy little sneak!" Joel screams. "You know you're not allowed on the shelves!" He storms over to stand above the creature. "How often—" Stooping, he snatches Nat up by the scruff of the neck. A thin tone of pain and terror slips between his fingers.

Korene rises. "Let him be," she says.

"So he can finish the . . . the havoc?" Joel hurls the monkey against the wall. The impact is audible. Nat lies twisted and wailing.

Silence brims the room, inside the wind. Korene gazes at Joel, and he at his hands, as if they confronted these things for the first time. When at last she speaks, it is altogether without tone. "Get out. Devil. Go."

"But," he stammers. "But. I didn't mean."

Still she stares. He retreats into new anger. "That pest's been driving me out of my skull! You know he has! We may be dead because of him, and yet you gush over him till I could puke!"

"Right. Blame him for staying healthy when we didn't. I find depths in you I never suspected before."

"And I in you," he jeers. "He's your baby, isn't he? The baby you've been tailored never to bear yourself. Your spoiled brat."

She brushes past him and kneels beside the animal.

Joel utters a raw kind of bark. He lurches to the door, hauls it open, disappears as if the dusk has eaten him. Rain and chill blow in.

Korene doesn't notice. She examines Nat, who pants, whimpers, watches her with eyes that are both wild and dimming. Blood mats his fur. It becomes clear that his back is broken.

"My pretty, my sweet, my bouncy-boy, please don't hurt. Please," she sobs as she lifts the small form. She carries him into the laboratory, prepares an injection, cradles him and sings a lullaby while it does its work.

Afterward she brings the body back to the living room, lies down holding it, and cries herself into a half-sleep full of nightmares.

—Her voice rouses her, out of the metal which has rested in a corner. She never truly remembers, later, what next goes on between her selves. Words, yes; touch; a potion for her to drink; then the blessing of nothingness. When she awakens, it is day and the remnant of Nat is gone from her.

So is the robot. It returns while she is leaving the bed. She would weep some more if she had the strength; but at least, through a headache she can think.

The door swings wide. Rain has ended. The world gleams. Here too are fall colors, beneath a lucent sky where wander-songs drift from wings beating southward. The carpet of the land has turned to sallow gold, the forest to bronze and red and a purple which bears tiny flecks like mica. Coolness streams around her.

Joel enters, half leaning on the machine, half upheld by it. Released, he crumples at her feet. From the throat which is not a throat, his voice begs:

"Be kind to him, will you? He spent the night stumbling around the woods till he caved in. Might've died, if a chemo-sensor of ours hadn't gotten the spoor."

"I wanted to," mumbles the man on the floor. "After what I did."

"Not his fault," says the ship anxiously, as if his identity were also involved and must clear itself of guilt. "He wasn't in his right mind."

The female sound continues: "An environmental factor, you see. We have finally identified it. You weren't rational either, girl. But never blame yourself, or him." Hesitation. "You'll be all right when we've taken you away from here."

Korene doesn't observe how unsteady the talking was, nor think about its implications. Instead, she sinks down to embrace Joel.

"How could I do it?" he gasps upon her breast.

"It wasn't you that did," says Korene in the robot, while Korene in the woman holds him close and murmurs.

—They are back aboard ship, harnessed weightless. Thus far they haven't asked for explanations. It was enough that their spirits were again together, that the sadness and the demons were leaving them, that they slept unhaunted and woke to serenity. But now the soothing drugs have worn off and healing bodies have, afresh, generated good minds.

They look at each other, whisper, and clasp hands. Joel says aloud, into the metal which encloses them: "Hey. You two."

His fellow self does not answer. Does it not dare? Part of a minute goes by before the older Korene speaks. "How are you, my dears?"

"Not bad," he states. "Physically."

How quiet it grows.

Until the second Korene gives challenge. "Hard news for us. Isn't that so?"

"Yes," her voice sighs back.

They stiffen. "Go on," she demands.

The answer is hasty. "You were suffering from pellagra. That was something we'd never encountered before; not too simple to diagnose, either, especially in its early stages. We had to ransack our whole medical data bank before we got a clue as to what to look for in the cell and blood samples we took. It's a deficiency disease, caused by lack of niacin, a B vitamin."

Protest breaks from Joel. "But hell, we knew the Glorian biochemistry doesn't include B complex! We took our pills."

"Yes, of course. That was one of the things which misled us, along with the fact that the animals throve on the same diet as yours. But we've found a substance in the native food—all native food; it's as integral to life as ATP is on Earth—a material that seemed harmless when we made the original analyses—" pain shrills forth—"when we decided we could create you—"

"It acts with a strictly human-type gene," the ship adds roughly. "We've determined which one, and don't see how to block the process. The upshot is release of an enzyme which destroys niacin in the bloodstream. Your pills disguised the situation at first, because the concentration of antagonist built up slowly. But equilibrium has been reached at last, and you'd get no measurable help from swallowing extra doses; they'd break down before you could metabolize them."

"Mental disturbances are one symptom," Korene says from the speaker. "The physical effects in advanced cases are equally horrible. Don't worry. You'll get well and stay well. Your systems have eliminated the chemical, and here is a lifetime supply of niacin."

She does not need to tell them that here is very little which those systems can use as fuel, nor any means of refining the meats and fruits on which they counted.

The ship gropes for words. "Uh, you know, this is the kind of basic discovery, I think, the kind of discovery we had to go into space to make. A piece of genetic information we'd never have guessed in a million years, staying home. Who knows what it'll be a clue to? Immortality?"

"Hush," warns his companion. To the pair in the cabin she says low, "We'll withdraw, leave you alone. Come out in the passageway when you want us. . . . Peace." A machine cannot cry, can it?

For a long while, the man and the woman are mute. Finally, flatly, he declares, "What rations we've got should keep us, oh, I'd guess a month."

"We can be thankful for that." When she nods, the tresses float around her brow and cheekbones.

"Thankful! Under a death sentence?"

"We knew . . . our selves on Earth knew, some of us would die young. I went to the scanner prepared for it. Surely you did likewise."

"Yes. In a way. Except it's happening to me." He snaps after air: "And you, which is worse. This you, the only Korene that this I will ever have. Why *us?*"

She gazes before her, then astonishes him with a smile. "The question which nobody escapes. We've been granted a month."

He catches her to him and pleads, "Help me. Give me the guts to be glad."

—The sun called Eighty-two Eridani rises in white-gold radiance over the great blue rim of the planet. That is a blue as deep as the ocean of its winds and weather, the ocean of its tides and waves, surging aloft into flame and roses. The ship orbits on toward day. Clouds come aglow with morning light. Later they swirl in purity above summer lands and winter lands, storm and calm, forest, prairie, valley, height, river, sea, the flocks upon flocks which are nourished by this world their mother.

Korene and Joel watch it through an hour, side by side and hand in hand before a screen, afloat in the crowdedness of machinery. The robot and the ship have kept silence. A blower whirrs its breeze across their bare skins, mingling for them their scents of woman and man. Often their free hands caress, or they kiss; but they have made their love and are now making their peace.

The ship swings back into night. Opposite, stars bloom uncountable and splendid. She stirs. "Let us," she says.

"Yes," he replies.

"You could wait," says the ship. His voice need not be so harsh; but he does not think to control it. "Days longer."

"No," the man tells him. "That'd be no good," seeing Korene starve to death; for the last food is gone. "Damn near as bad as staying down there," and watching her mind rot while her flesh corrupts and withers.

"You're right," the ship agrees humbly. "Oh, Christ, if we'd thought!"

"You couldn't have, darling," says the robot with measureless gentleness. "No one could have."

The woman strokes a bulkhead, tenderly as if it were her man, and touches her lips to the metal.

He shakes himself. "Please, no more things we've talked out a million times," he says. "Just goodbye."

The robot enfolds him in her clasp. The woman joins them. The ship knows what they want, it being his wish too, and *Sheep May Safely Graze* brightens the air.

The humans float together. "I want to say," his words stumble, "I never stopped loving Mary, and missing her, but I love you as much, Korene, and, and thanks for being what you've been.

"I wish I could say it better," he finishes.

"You don't need to," she answers, and signals the robot.

They hardly feel the needle. As they float embraced, toward darkness, he calls drowsily, "Don't grieve too long, you there. Don't ever be afraid o' making more lives. The universe'll always surprise us."

"Yes." She laughs a little through the sleep which is gathering her in. "Wasn't that good of God?"

We fare across the light-years and the centuries, life after life, death after death. Space is our single home. Earth has become more strange to us than the outermost comet of the farthest star.

For to Earth we have given:

Minds opened upon endlessness, which therefore hold their own world, and the beings upon it, very precious.

A knowledge of natural law whereby men may cross the abyss in the bodies their mothers gave them, short years from sun to sun, and planets unpeopled for their taking, so that their kind will endure as long as the cosmos.

A knowledge of natural law whereby they have stopped

nature's casual torturing of them through sickness, madness, and age.

The arts, histories, philosophies and faiths and things once undreamable, of a hundred sentient races; and out of these, an ongoing renaissance which does not look as if it will ever die.

From our gifts have sprung material wealth at each man's fingertips, beyond the grasp of any whole Earthbound nation; withal, a growing calm and wisdom, learned from the manyfoldedness of reality. Each time we return, strife seems less and fewer seem to hate their brothers or themselves.

But does our pride on behalf of them beguile us? They have become shining enigmas who greet us graciously, neither thrust us forth again nor seek to hold us against our wills. Though finally each of us never comes back, they make no others. Do they need our gifts any longer? Is it we the wanderers who can change and grow no more?

Well, we have served; and one service will remain to the end. Two in the deeps, two and two on the worlds, we alone remember those who lived, and those who died, and Olaf and Mary.

AFTERWORD

Let's put rhetoric aside for a moment and look at a few facts.

Though the space program has had its human share of inefficiencies and absurdities, it has never been a losing proposition. Rather, it has *already* repaid the modest investment, and returned a huge profit as well.

Modest? Of course. The budget of the National Aeronautics and Space Administration—for all of its varied activities—peaked at about the time of Apollo 11. Yet in those palmy days it got less than eight cents for every dollar the federal government spent on health, education, and welfare: a figure which takes no account of state and local undertakings or of private philanthropies. We would be unkind if we compared the actual accomplishments. But at least we can deny that NASA has ever taken bread out of the mouths of the poor.

Profit? Certainly. The revolution in meteorology alone, brought about by weather satellites, proves that claim. The lives and treasure saved because hurricanes can be accurately predicted offer a spectacular example. However, precise forecasts as a routine matter, year after year, are the open-ended payoff, especially for agriculture and transportation and thus for mankind. Or think of communications. Never mind if many television programs strike you as inane—never mind, even, educational uses in primitive areas—the core truth is that transmission over great distances was bound to come, and that relaying through space is cheaper than across the surface. Cash economies are mere shorthand for labor set free and natural resources conserved.

We are on the verge of reaping rich harvest from terrestrial resources satellites. Not much further off is a real comprehension of geophysics and geochemistry, by way of examining the cosmic environment of our planet and comparing it with its neighbors. The practical, humane applications should be obvious. Likewise, astrophysics is a key to the full description and control of matter and energy; and the place for that research is above an atmosphere. Meanwhile we can hope for deeper insights into how life works. Early biological experiments out there have indicated how little we know today, how badly we need to carry on studies under conditions found nowhere but in space. A golden age of medicine ought to result.

Well and good, some say; but can't we do this with unmanned probes, vehicles, robots, devices? Why go to the enormous cost of sending men?

Having patiently explained once more that the cost isn't enormous, and added that further development can make it small, I respond: Machines are invaluable aids. Still, do you seriously believe they could have replaced the direct experiences of a Cook, Stanley, Lyell, Darwin,

Boas—in our own day, a Cousteau, Leakey, or Goodall? Man, or woman, is the only computer which continuously reprograms itself, the only sensor system which records data it is not planned to detect, the only thing which gives a damn.

Six fleeting visits to a single barren globe scarcely constitute exploration. If we stop now, it will be as if European mariners had stopped when Columbus reported his failure to reach India. What he did find was enough to bring legions overseas. What the astronauts have found in the tiny times granted them is astonishingly much: not material wealth, but the stuff of knowledge, whence all else arises. Shall we end the enterprise at its very beginning?

Discussing such pragmatic questions with ordinary folk like myself, including dwellers in poverty areas, I have never had any difficulty in getting the point across, the value to them and their children. It seems to be the cocktail party intellectuals whom dynamite won't blast loose from preconceptions. Perhaps I have met the wrong ones and do their class an injustice.

Or perhaps, pitiably, they have not eyes to see.

There are human creations as glorious as the rising of a spaceship witnessed close at hand. There are realities here on Earth as mysterious and miraculous as any in the astronomical deeps. But there are none which are more so. And yonder is where the endlessness lies—not simply of adventure and learning but of the spirit, which must have revelations from the greater than human if it is to grow, even as a flower must have sunlight.

Why not build a machine to climb Everest?

Or a machine to make love?

Or a machine to exist?

Because we are what we are. First come the wish and the vision, then the understanding. However cruel this world, it is less cutthroat than it might be, thanks to the prophets of the high faiths; but what they sought was not civilization but salvation. Maybe the reason that some persons cannot imagine what we have to gain beyond Earth is that heaven has not touched them with wonder.

Go out, the next clear night. Look up.

Novels

MISSION OF GRAVITY, by Hal Clement
THE HAND OF ZEI, by L. Sprague de Camp
THE FIRST MEN IN THE MOON, by H.G. Wells
TAU ZERO, by Poul Anderson
ORPHANS OF THE SKY, by Robert Heinlein

Short Stories

BLINDNESS, by John W. Campbell, Jr.
REQUIEM, by Robert Heinlein
FIRST CONTACT, by Murray Leinster
THE COLD EQUATIONS, by Tom Godwin
A MARTIAN ODYSSEY, by Stanley Weinbaum

About Poul Anderson

Poul Anderson, b. 1926, has been a full-time writer since his graduation from the University of Minnesota with a degree in physics. He is the author of more than thirty sf novels (THE HIGH CRUSADE, THREE HEARTS AND THREE LIONS, TAU ZERO), several hundred short stories, and some popular non-fiction books. A multiple Hugo and Nebula award winner,* Mr. Anderson lives in Orinda, California, with his wife, Karen.

* Science fiction's two most prestigious awards are the Hugo, presented by the World Science Fiction Convention, and the Nebula, awarded by the Science Fiction Writers of America.

IMMORTALITY

GREAT ESCAPE TOURS, INC.

KIT REED

Day after day, Dan Radford and his friends, who couldn't get up the scratch for the trip, would sit around under the trees in Williams Park in St. Petersburg, Florida, and speculate the whole time the others were gone. It wasn't that they wished the rich tourists ill, exactly—just because some people had the money for that kind of foolishness while other people had to scrounge along on Social Security and bitty little checks from the kids—it was just that it pained the hell out of them to see the chosen few going into the GREAT ESCAPE TOURS, INC. kiosk day after day and then, by God, coming *back*.

"Damn fools," Dan would say, clattering his teeth in rage, "You'd think once they got where they're going, they'd have the good sense to stay there."

His wife, Theda, always tried to calm him, saying, "Maybe there are reasons that they can't."

"So what?" Dan would press his lips together, irritated because these new teeth he had never fit right. "I'll tell you one thing, Theda, if I ever get on one of those tours, they'll whistle in hell before I come back."

They would gather every morning on the semicircle of benches and watch the neon sign flashing in red, green, and yellow: GREAT ESCAPES, INC. They all knew each other pretty well by this time; there they sat, the old gang: the Radfords, Hickey Washburn in his sun visor and string shirt, Big Marge, Tim and Patsy O'Neill (who, at eighty-two and eighty, still held hands wherever they went), that noted man about town and witty gigolo in the black-and-white spectators, Iggy the Rake. They came from the boarding houses and cheap hotels near Mirror Lake, muttering hellos in the early morning light, and always taking exactly the same place on the benches. Sometimes Iggy would bring a girl, some chipper septuagenarian, but the

55

rest of them tolerated that. Whoever she was, she wouldn't last long. Occasionally some misguided outsider would sit down, all innocence, but there would be such a harrumphing, such a rattle of morning papers and pointed clearing of throats that nobody made the mistake more than once.

It was important to get there before the first tourist came, so they could count them as they went into the kiosk; they had to be able to check them off accurately when they returned late that afternoon. And they wanted to see each one close up enough so that, when the tour ended and they all filed out, they could see if the trip made them change at all. The gang all brought their lunches in string bags or brown paper sacks but usually they would begin nibbling around nine, out of sheer nervousness, and by ten, when the flashing light on top of the kiosk signalled departure time, they had usually eaten their entire lunches in a fit of frustration, and so they would be left with laps full of crumbs and sandwich papers, with nothing much to do but brush themselves off and wait for the 2 p.m. band concert, which might be cancelled if it rained.

By five, when the tours returned, the gang was usually wild, having spent the dreariest part of the afternoon talking about what the rich tourists were probably doing this very moment, where they were and what it was like, how *they* would certainly never come back, the way these suckers did. Since rumor had it that once you got there, wherever it was, you were *young*, nobody could figure out exactly why these people always came back, why they didn't look any different. Or why, when they got one of the tourists aside and tried to pump him, they got no answer at all, or worse than no answer. The way they acted it made Theda think of the time she got her sister Rhea alone, right after Rhea's honeymoon; Theda was wild, pressing her: *What was it like?* and Rhea either tried hard to tell her and couldn't, or else she tried hard to look as if she was trying to answer and couldn't find any real way to explain.

Maybe because she found it hard to think about where they went on the GREAT ESCAPE TOURS, INC. or what they were doing while they were away, Theda always dwelled on the clothes the women were wearing: aqua, mostly, or pink, because it "did things" for their withered complexions. They all had silverblue hair, those rich women, and no matter how hot it got or how hot it was going to be where they were going, they all wore silverblue mink stoles. She resented the mink and the diamonds and the silver or gold kid wedgies; she resented the fact that she and Dan had worked hard all their lives and had come to this: a bench in St. Petersburg, Florida, with two small rooms in a house that wasn't theirs, and children who never, ever came to visit. They couldn't even afford a car. It had all sounded good enough when they were back home in snowy Boise, planning their future, but of course they had reckoned without being stuck down here summer *and* winter, and they had thought Dan's checks were going to go farther than they did, and what's more they hadn't either of them expected to feel so confounded *old*.

She didn't mind for herself so much as for Dan; she hated to lie in bed listening to his breath rattle, she hated the half hour he had to spend in the bathroom every morning, coughing and hawking, before he was ready to face the day; she hated to watch him walk slower each day, and most of all she hated the way his face and his chest caved in, because she could remember when he was square-faced and full-muscled, and she could never be sure exactly when he had started to sink in on himself, or when his hands had begun to tremble. Nor did she remember exactly the first time he had waked her in the night crying, "Mama."

They claimed GREAT ESCAPE TOURS, INC. took you to a place where you were young. There must be something the matter with it, because nobody seemed to want to stay, but if Dan wanted to go there, wherever it was, then she wanted to go too, and as she watched him totter around the kiosk this particular morning she realized that if they were going, it had better be sooner rather than later, because he was getting crosser and shakier all the time now, and she herself had begun to wake in the nights with a dizzy feeling, as if it was all just about to drop out from under her, so she had to wonder just how much time either of them had left.

That was why, when he came back from his morning circuit of the kiosk this particular day, and said, "I think we can do it," and Iggy and the others gathered around to listen to his plan, Theda knew she was going to go along with it.

Iggy was going to be the inside man, but they all had some part in the master plan. Once Iggy's new rich girl-friend paid his way inside, Hickey Washburn would create a diversion by pretending a heart attack in the dirt outside the kiosk. When the attendant rushed outside to tend to Hickey, the O'Neills would rush him, snaring his head in Patsy's shopping bag while Big Marge held his hands be-hind him and the Radfords tied them with Theda's blue bandanna. Then Iggy would open the door from inside, and after that . . .

"Yeah," Patsy O'Neill said. "What happens after that?"

Dan shrugged, more or less at a loss. "I guess we'll have to play it by ear."

The first problem was Iggy's rich girl friend; they had to find one, so between nine and five they stalked the Soreno and the Vinoy Park, going as far as the new downtown Hilton. When they thought they had the right girl, Iggy sidled up and sat down next to her on the bench, while the others moved back. They had pooled all their extra money for the next month so Iggy could take her out to dinner, and by the time Iggy was ready to take her danc-ing, Hickey Washburn was so committed to the plan that he sacrificed a yellowing dinner jacket and Tim O'Neill proffered, with shaking hands, a set of diamond studs that looked as if they had never been removed from their treasure box of aged, cracking leatherette. Although they all had respect for Iggy's "line," Theda and Patsy had further advice for Iggy when he got his girl alone; they all threw themselves into it, all except for Big Marge, who wouldn't even come down to the park to see Iggy off on his big date.

After Patsy kissed him on the cheek, and Theda slipped a red carnation in his buttonhole, the boys walked Iggy down to the convertible he had hired from Budget-Rent-a-Car for the occasion, and then they came back and the whole gang (except for Marge) sat around in the park and talked until it got dark. They found themselves alternately sad, at what they would be leaving behind for GREAT ESCAPE TOURS, INC., and scared, because they didn't know what they would find once they got there, wherever it was. They wondered what Iggy and his girl were doing now. The rest of the time memories flicked on and off like fireflies. They were awash in nostalgia for things they had never even had, and by the time they got up to go, their old bones were stiff, and some of their joints had locked, so that Patsy had to help Tim up, and Theda had to thump Hickey Washburn on the back two or three times to get him going.

They knew they ought to be home getting their beauty sleep, resting up for the big trip, but they lingered on the sidewalk outside the park until Dan said, firmly, "Well, tomorrow's the big day," and they all nodded, even without having any real reason to believe it, because they all thought it was.

As it turned out, it was. Iggy had scored in the convertible on some moonlit strand, using a combination of sweet talk and adept fumbling at the lady's neck that reminded her of things they were both more or less beyond—telling her those things would happen in the grass the minute she paid his way on GREAT ESCAPE TOURS, INC.

When he got home from his date he was so excited that he called everybody and told them all about it, even though it was the middle of the night. The only one who was asleep when he called, or pretended to be, was Big Marge, who yawned heavily into the telephone and said she guessed she would be there in the morning, yes, she remembered her instructions. She never once asked if he had a good time on his date.

None of them slept that night; they lay awake in the moonlight, dreaming, planning, or scheming: Big Marge flexed her body in the trough of her bedsprings and vowed to get rid of Iggy's girl first thing, so she could have him for herself. She would make him crawl first, and then she would forgive him and love him forever. Hickey Washburn lay in his rented room and thought about being twenty-one, which he was sure was how old he would always be in the new place. He couldn't quite remember what it had been like but he thought he could handle it. The O'Neills touched bony hands across the gulf between their cheap twin beds; Tim was thinking that if everybody was young where they were going, maybe he and Patsy would go back to a point before they were even married; then he could take a close look at her and all the other young chickies who would be there, rosy and bouncing. Iggy was thinking about all the girls, too, but his thoughts were more specific. Listening to Dan cough, Theda lay as still as she could, holding her breath lest she jiggle him and make it worse.

As it turned out, Dan rose with a preternatural energy even before it got light, pulling Theda into his feverish preparations. They both had to bathe and dress as carefully as if they were going to be presented to some queen, and Dan sat on the edge of the bed and fidgeted while Theda, at his request, tried on dress after dress, settling at last on the pretty lavender voile, the same color as the dress she had been wearing when he met her for the first time.

They got down to the park too early, but so had everybody else; Big Marge was slumped in her usual place with a string bag between her feet, and when Theda asked her what was in it she snatched it away and wouldn't answer. The O'Neills had eaten all their sandwiches, and Hickey Washburn kept pacing as if he had forgotten something and was trying with all his might to bring it back. By the time the church clock struck eight they were keyed tight and jerking like marionettes and by the time it struck nine and the lighted sign went on above the kiosk: GREAT ESCAPES, INC., they were all slumped on the benches again like tired children, testy and spent, and when Iggy appeared with his rich new girl friend, they could barely acknowledge his conspiratorial nod. They may have been put off by his new girl's obvious riches: the white mink stole over the pink playsuit, the shoes with the Lucite platforms, the platinum blonde wig made out of real hair, or it may have been the way Iggy looked, dapper and fresh, so sure of himself. He excused himself from his girl and came over, dropping little pills into everybody's hands and saying, "Chew these."

Theda said, "What's this?"

"Never mind," Iggy said hastily. "It'll give you a lift."

"How do we know?" Tim O'Neill asked.

Iggy winked and wriggled his shoulders. "It works for me."

So they all popped the pills, whatever they were. Hickey Washburn was convinced they were goat glands and began snorting and stamping; they tasted like Aspergum to the O'Neills and Feenamint to the Radfords, and Big Marge took them for benzedrine. It didn't matter what they were because they achieved the purpose: Hickey did his heart attack number, everybody galvanized and rushed the kiosk right on schedule, kicking out the enraged paying customers and the tour guide himself and locking the doors. They strapped themselves in the plush seats and heard the machinery start to whir, carrying them off just as sirens and voices rose outside, and the first policeman began battering the locked doors with his stick.

"And now, over the rooftops, through the corridors of time, for a unique and never-to-be-forgotten experience. Welcome to your Great Escape."

Whirling in darkness, Theda fixed on the unctuous recorded voice, reassured by memories of the 1939 World's Fair, when she had been pulled along in a comfy plush chair, listening to a voice that sounded like this one. She remembered she could hardly wait until 1942, and now . . .

". . . Your tour guide will explain the limitations on arrival," the voice was saying, and Theda remembered with a pang of guilt that Dan had hit the tour guide on the head just before he pushed him outside and slammed the doors. Well, Iggy was a man of the world and so was Dan, so they should be able to make their way without too much trouble, and if they decided to stay wherever it was they were going, there would be no group leader to force them to return.

The voice was concluding, ". . . on the jungle gym at 4:55 p.m. to make the speedy and safe return. A bell will ring in case you can't tell time."

"What? Helpimfalling . . . UMP."

Theda was sitting on the ground blinking in the fresh sunlight. She had fallen off and landed on her hands and knees and now she was sitting in the dirt, her underpants were dirty, and she had skinned her knees again, and she knew her mommy would spank her the minute she got home because her brand new dress was filthy dirty, and she was too big to cry but she felt so awful she started crying anyway.

"Sissy, sissy." He was hanging upside down from the jungle gym with his face right in front of her, and she thought he ought to be a lot nicer to her but she couldn't remember why until she saw the way his nose had the big wart on it and his mouth went in a wavy line; then he yelled "Sissy, sissy," and she figured out that meant he really liked her or else he wouldn't be teasing her, so she yanked on his arm and pulled him into the dirt next to her and while they were rolling around she figured it all out, saying, "Dan? Is that you, Dan?"

He squinted into her face. "Theda? What happened?" She stood up, brushing off her dress and looking around at the other kids, who either swung furiously on the jungle gym or else sat in the dirt and cried. That one with the fat tummy must be Big Marge and the one in the baseball hat was probably Hickey Washburn. She would have to ask the other kids which ones were which because whatever they used to look like, before they got into that thing and took the trip, they didn't look like it any more, they were all kids together, and she thought maybe it wouldn't be so bad after all because they could grow up together, and after they grew up they would be young men and women, strong, healthy, and she would never again have to wake up and listen to Dan coughing his blood out in the middle of the night.

She said, "Dan, I think we're here."

The one that was probably Iggy's girlfriend was doing cartwheels, but Iggy himself sat quietly in the dirt, feeling himself all over: face, arms, groin—groin. He stood up, comprehending, and came running. "This is awful. What are we going to do?"

They wanted to make the other kids get together and talk about it, but Timmy O'Neill was chasing Iggy's girl-friend around and Patsy and Hickey Washburn were fighting about Hickey's hat, everybody was screaming and yelling and the only people that would pay attention to Theda were Danny, because he liked her, and Iggy, who for one reason or another still had his moustache even though they were, every one of them, only six years old.

There was a board screwed on the jungle gym with a whole bunch of rules written on it, but even though Theda had been quick at learning to read she couldn't figure it out. They were in a playground but they couldn't see any school, only a lot of grass all around, and she was already scared to go outside the fence and look around because they might get lost and besides, nobody knew what was out there, lions or tigers or ugly men who would offer them candy and drag them away.

Iggy climbed way up to the top of the jungle gym and looked all around. "Hey," he said, "what if this is all there is?"

"When we grow up we can be cowboys." Dan couldn't stop picking his nose. "And Theda can be the cowgirl."

Theda knew she ought to be thinking up things to do but she couldn't keep her mind on it, she felt so good she started running around and around the jungle gym and pretty soon Danny was chasing her and Iggy was chasing him, they all ran around and around, laughing and yelling until Big Marge tackled Iggy and they all fell down. She and Danny were wrestling, rolling over and over, he was sitting on her chest and holding her wrists down with his hands, she looked up into his face and thought, *Oh Dan*, but she didn't know where all the feelings came from or what they were, except that the main one was very, very sad.

Somebody started teasing Big Marge, they all called her Fatty now, she had this funny string bag she had brought with her and Hickey got it away from her and it turned out there was a gun inside, they were all scared to death of it so they dug a hole and buried it over by the swings. They played for a long time, they played and played until Patsy O'Neill fell over a stick and skinned her knees and started to cry, and then Hickey got tired of sliding and Big Marge started crying for no reason and finally Iggy's girlfriend came out and said it, she sat down plump in the middle of the dirt and said:

"I'm hungry."

Everybody said, "Me too," but when they looked around for their lunchboxes there weren't any and there weren't any fruit trees around, they couldn't even find any dandelion stems, there was a water fountain and that was

all, there might be a store out there somewhere but nobody had any allowance and besides, they were scared to
go outside the fence and see, somebody might come to the
playground looking for them and they wouldn't be there,
or else they might get lost and never find their way back
to the jungle gym, and the teacher had said they had better
be on the jungle gym by five o'clock or else. They tried
not to talk about hot dogs and everything, they all drank
lots of water and tried to play some more, but they had
run out of games to play and besides, people kept crying
for no reason and finally Iggy said:

"This is no fun."

The others began, one by one: "I'm tired."

"I'm hungry."

"I'm bored."

"I'm *hungry*."

Then Theda said it right out, "I want to go home." She
was sitting on one end of the seesaw and Danny was on
the other end, he got off his end so she went bump on
the ground and he said, "I'm not ever going home."

Theda said, "What if you don't get any supper?"

"I don't care."

Parts of Theda still remembered. "What if you have to
stay like this?"

He set his feet wide in the dirt and stuck his chin out.
"I don't care." Then he seemed to remember too, he
said, "I hate it back there."

"What if it thunders? What if it rains?"

Dan said, "I don't care."

"Who's going to take care of you?"

He shrugged and got back on the other end of the seesaw. They sat there for a long long time, just sort of
balancing, she didn't know how long it was but the light
was getting different, the way it did when it was about
time for you to say goodbye to all the other kids and go
home to your nice hot supper. Everybody had stopped
playing together and they were all off pretending to do
things by themselves, humming on the swings or digging
in the dirt or singing some song with a thousand million
verses, putting sticks in piles and then knocking them
over, and waiting.

Finally the bell rang. Everybody on the playground got

up from what they were doing, Theda got off the seesaw without even looking and they all ran for the jungle gym, they were all climbing up, they heard somebody that sounded like all their mothers saying:

SUPPERTIME.

It made Theda feel good thinking about it, she would go home and have chicken soup and meat loaf and maybe jello and then get in her bed with her brand new Billy Whiskers book and at seven aclock Mommy would kiss her good night, she would go back to the guest house and after supper she would watch the early movie on TV in their room, and Dan would kiss her good night, he would start coughing . . .

Dan.

She looked all over for him and saw that he wasn't on the jungle gym, he was way over there on the other side of the playground, standing up there in the middle of the seesaw, with one foot on either side of the middle, balancing. He might not remember why he wasn't coming back with her but he wasn't coming back, he would rather stay here and starve to death if he had to, he would stay six years old forever, just so he wouldn't have to go back to his old self in his old age, and the more she thought about it the more she knew she ought to leave him, if she went home she would die soon which would be fine with her, but she couldn't leave him, that was *Dan*, and she had to . . .

She jumped off just before the second bell rang. She landed on her hands and knees again, she had opened up the skinned places and her dress was really dirty now, but she wasn't ever going home so it probably didn't matter, but when she sat up and looked at the jungle gym she wanted to cry because all the kids were gone now, everybody was gone except that kid over there on the seesaw, Danny, he wasn't always nice to her but he was her best friend so she got up and went over to where he was still balancing and pretending not to notice her.

After a while he looked down after all so she said, "Want to play?"

He jumped down. "What do you want to do?"

She was looking at the playground gates now, it looked like there was just grass out there, maybe it was grass all the way to the edge and you could fall off, or else something would get you, but she knew she and Danny couldn't stay here because somebody might come and drag them home, so she started for the gate, trying to be brave.

"Let's go see."

AFTERWORD

Perhaps because I spent a large chunk of my childhood in St. Petersburg, Fla., I have always been preoccupied with the aged and the problem of aging. The older I get, the closer I get to it, and that's interesting too; reverse the coin of age/death and you see immortality or extinction, depending on your theology, and no matter how you look at it, they are both pretty scary. Why can't we just stay the way we are—well, maybe a little different—better, maybe? That's a scary idea too.

What we are up against, it seems, is the problem of being, and since at the moment there doesn't seem to be a lot we can do about it, we hang on and muddle through. Some of us write stories, which, while they may not do anything to change our basic situation, help us pass the time along the way. In the end, we may never be able to explain what is happening to us, but, having written, we can tell ourselves that at least we've done a little something to mark our passage.

Novels
TIME ENOUGH FOR LOVE, by Robert A. Heinlein
THE AGE OF THE PUSSYFOOT, by Frederik Pohl
TO LIVE FOREVER, by Jack Vance

Short Stories
INVARIANT, by J.R. Pierce
SCANNERS LIVE IN VAIN, by Cordwainer Smith
DOWN AMONG THE DEAD MEN, by William Tenn
ETERNITY LOST, by Clifford Simak

About Kit Reed

Kit Reed, b. 1932, was formerly a reporter for *The New Haven Register* and is presently visiting professor of English at Wesleyan University. She is the author of many short stories and several novels (MOTHER ISN'T DEAD, SHE'S ONLY SLEEPING, 1961; AT WAR AS CHILDREN, 1964; ARMED CAMPS, 1970; TIGER RAG, 1973) and lives with her husband and three children in Middletown, Connecticut.

INNER SPACE

DIAGRAMS FOR THREE ENIGMATIC STORIES

BRIAN W. ALDISS

The Girl in the Tau-Dream

The love story. It was to have been about Olga. A girl who liked the age she lived in. After getting to know her better, I could see why. Both physically and mentally, she was equipped to be ambiguous. If I had completed the story, it would have centered about her mental ambiguities, which caused me to confuse her, in my life first and then in my dreams, with the writer Anna Kavan.

As to her physical ambiguities, the robes and shoes she wore gave one an impression of height. One thought of her as a tall and slender girl. As for her lovers, who were not many—she was like Anna in being attractive to but rarely attracted by both sexes—they came to realize that she was in reality a short and rather plump girl.

I say "in reality," but it is a meaningless phrase. There may possibly be a common reality, but we all have our personal version of it which we carry about like an identity card. Olga's physical appearance may have been somewhat below the average in height and pleasantly chubby; but her preference for being tall and slender was rooted—I thought—in sound metaphysical reasons. Spiritually, she was a tall and slender girl.

She was also beautiful. She seemed, let's put it, extremely beautiful to me; though I also saw her looking downright plain. The hair she piled upon her head to increase her stature was black. "In reality," she was blonde. Her origins being what they were, blondness was a contradiction; her personality, as Olga divined, was that of a dark girl. Her artifice was truth.

The story would have been taken up with a lot of surface detail. The eternal fascination of meeting a new woman. Of seeing her when she meant nothing. Of her gaze meeting yours (is it all decided then?). Of speaking, seeking similar topics. Of first touching her. Of realizing that the currents of your two lives were flowing together. Such details, as with every new love affair, seem to offer vital keys to the mystery and excitement of the new being who has entered one's life. In Olga's case, these details were elaborate enough.

In brief, I had taken Anna with me to look at a small country cottage. We hoped she might like to live there, despite her heroin dependency, which kept her oriented toward London and her kindly doctor. The cottage belonged to a Mr. Marchmain. Anna was withdrawn and did not care for the place or the situation. It was set by a little stream and looked toward the Berkshire Downs.

We drove away after our inspection of the cottage, stopping a mile down the road to buy petrol at a crossroads filling station. I got out of the car to avoid Anna's silence. With a tremendous crash, two cars met at the crossroads. I was in time to see one coming spinning toward us. It struck a lamp standard and ground to a halt on its side. The other car, a white Mini, was turned right round in the road, extensively damaged.

I ran to the overturned car and looked in. A young dark woman was strapped in the front seat. In the back was a child, strapped into a kiddie seat. Both were conscious. In a moment, the child began to cry. I climbed in and helped the girl out, after which I went back and got the child. It was a boy of about three; he put his arms tightly around my neck and stopped crying. I helped the girl into the filling station office.

That was Olga. She was badly shaken and not coherent, but the garage mechanic recognized her and said she knew a guy called Marchmain who lived in a cottage a mile away. The cottage we had just left.

I took her there. Marchmain rallied round, plainly embarrassed. Child not Olga's. Whose? He phoned somewhere. Olga lived in a country town some miles away. It turned out that she had been collecting a Mrs. Somebody's small boy from playschool.

Despite Anna's protests, I volunteered to take the boy back to his mother and to deliver Olga to the nearest

hospital for examination. Marchmain saw us off with relief. As we were leaving, he took me on one side and
said, "Look, I'm sorry about this—you shouldn't have
brought Miss Illes here. We were intimate friends once,
but last week we parted for good. Which is why I wish to
sell up my home and leave entirely this district."

Miss Illes. Marchmain, I realized for the first time, was
foreign.

So I delivered the boy, who never cried again, back to
his mother, and I took Miss Illes to the hospital. By the
time I left, she seemed perfectly all right; I gave her my
card. Then I drove Anna back home.

An incident. Part of life. I was deeply involved with a
new project at the university at this time; my reputation
was somewhat at stake, so I prepared myself to think no
more of what had happened.

The next morning, I received a letter of thanks from the
boy's mother and some flowers—daffodils and yellow
tulips mixed—with a note signed Olga Illes. I was amused.
It is rare for a woman to send a man flowers.

There was to be a good deal in the story about my
work at the university. We were testing out a synthesis/
atomization theory of dreams. We had already identified
three different types of dreams, which we designated
sigma, tau, and ypsilon; my reputation was involved with
this system of identification. We were now specializing
with the tau-type dream, which is a phenomenon of
median second-quarter sleep. The special function of a
tau-type dream seems to be to explore above and below
the conscious meaning of everyday event. That is, to relate an everyday event to greater spheres of meaning up
to the cosmic level and to dissect its meaning to more
minute fragments of being which in themselves relate to
the total individual personality.

Although we had plenty of student volunteers in the
laboratory, I often used myself as a guinea pig since, for
some reason, my own tau-type dreams seemed particularly
vivid.

Thus, to cite two examples, I dreamed I was one of a
team of four men who were trained in extreme anomic
conditions to relate to the extrasensory manifestations of
their own personalities. They spent many weeks watching

television pictures of empty rooms. Eventually, they hunted down a small fast-moving thing which was so inimical to them that they beat it to death. As a result, one of the men died. They learnt that the fast-moving things were projections of themselves.

The second example was similarly a synthesis/atomization. I dreamed that aliens were living among men in cordial conditions, enriching human life on the cultural plane. They were visually indistinguishable from men; only their striking power of charisma made it plain that they were something entirely distinct from human. Their admiration for the most minor figures in Earth's cultural history was flattering, fascinating, and enjoyable. And infectious. Everyone on Earth became interested in the arts. It gradually became apparent to the "I" figure in the dream, a character who visited one of the "aliens" at home, that they were in fact utterly changing the nature of what they admired and reshaping it—although perfectly innocently and unknowingly, because art had previously been outside their experience. So their mere admiration changed everything, as translation changes a poem. One instance: "my" alien greatly admired Robert Louis Stevenson, a nineteenth-century British writer, and he and his family played me recordings of a Stevenson opera based on the legend of Robin Hood, and a tone poem which sounded to my ears like a poor mixture of Mozart and Offenbach.

Both these tau-dreams related to elements in my own personality but also to the state of the world—what I have termed the confusions of identity of the Post-Renaissance Age in which we live.

My next tau-dream, two days after I had taken Olga to the hospital, was about Olga. It contained all the richness and double layering of the typical tau-dream.

I dreamed that I was going to see her in a cottage in the country. She was wishing to sell her cottage. I presented her with an armful of flowers, which she accepted in payment. She showed me how terribly injured her right leg was. I was sorry for her. Anna was there, but Anna left. Olga and I went upstairs together. We could see a millstream from the bedroom window. We lay on the bed and now I noticed that she had been deceiving me; her right leg was uninjured; the wounds were painted on. I took her into my arms. Her clothes fell away, and I saw that her left leg had been practically amputated in the crash.

After this disturbing dream, I had to see Olga again.

I phoned Marchmain. No, he still had not sold his cottage. I said I would buy it. I went immediately to the university printer, presented my card, and got him to print me a new one. Then I drove to Marchmain's cottage.

He was amused at my precipitance. Yet I could see he was in some way frightened too. To cover his feelings, he told me something about himself. He was a Hungarian, a refugee. He had been brought to England as a baby in 1938, after his family, one of the great landed Hungarian families, had had trouble with Admiral Horthy. They had changed their name to an English form. At the same time, cousins of his had also left Hungary and settled in Brazil. Olga Illes was remotely of the Brazilian branch of the family.

The news caused me some excitement, for I too, although of Scottish stock, had been born in Brazil, in the Consulate in Santos.

We settled the deal. He even agreed to be out of the cottage by the end of the week. Various details here.

I send Olga my new card with the cottage address. I ask her to visit me. She will not come. I realize that the tau-dream experiment has confused my thinking, and I am in real life playing role-reversal with Marchmain (asking to be rejected?) just as I did in my dream about Olga, where I sent her the flowers.

This makes me stubborn. I must have her. I believe myself in love with her. It is easy to quarrel with Anna. Anna is always in flight. Sometimes one may hold her in one's arms, and she is not there. She retreats far beyond the snow, elusive even to herself. She retreats once again, and I am free to pursue the new woman.

Details of my first visit to Olga's house in the country town. Her book-lined room. Her appearance and voice. How her accent became gradually more and more "foreign"—and so more familiar to me—when she realized that I had been born in Brazil, just as she had.

Notes on our conversation about the English climate. The day was dull, misty, with that light rain the British call "mizzle." Ambiguity of landscape forms. English watercolour painting. All so different from the brash certainties of sun in Sao Paulo or California.

More research. Working to all hours of the night. Fresh difficulties with Anna. Difficulty in seeing Olga. Trying to settle into cottage. Trying to persuade Olga to visit cottage. Conversations with her over the phone. Taking her to London to see Luis Buñuel's *The Discreet Charm of the Bourgeoisie*, a film we both enjoyed. Trying to seduce her.

Synthesis/atomization theory challenged by Dr. Rudesci's group in St. Louis. Anxieties. Another attempt to seduce Olga in my room in college. This time, we are both naked when she refuses me; Olga's saying: "When we know one another better." Respect for this unfashionable morality, even when it goes against me, even when I know the refusal goes deeper than morality.

Taking her to meet friends in Oxford—dancing with her until the small hours. How happy we were.

Dramatic intervention of Koestler into dream theory debate. Unexpected relevance of our findings to his own work on random elements in cerebral evolution. Some fame for me.

A film being made of our department and our researches. Some dreams being dramatized, including my Olga dream. Olga has played small parts in several films. I persuade her to play herself in my dream.

She is delighted by the proposal. I make the suggestion in her little house, which she shares with a girl friend; so we have to be careful. But clearly the prospect of acting excites her. She dances about her living room in her loose flowing dress. Give readers glimpse of innocent-seeming but erotic caper. I grasp her. We trip and fall on to sofa. This time, she does let me make love to her. We do it although the door into the hall is open and the friend is about.

Great pleasure and excitement, better than first times often are. Her sweet cries. A stocky girl, not tall, with fair pubic hair. We both laugh a good deal and really love each other. She declares I have tau-screwed her, at once drawing her together and disintegrating her. She says, "I'm sorry I couldn't admit you before." We try to speak in Portuguese to each other.

She agrees to spend the next weekend with me in my cottage. Somehow, it seems that I have exorcised the ghost of Marchmain. Olga clearly regards the chance of play-acting herself as liberating. She says, "Since I am always self-conscious in my role in life, a role in a film as myself will free me from such restraint. I shall be able to under-act my own over-acting."

Olga has a strange sense of humor.

I am so excited that she will come that, on the Saturday, I walk up the road to the crossroads to meet her. Everything is dripping wet, as Arrhenius supposed that Venus would be. Shapes of woods and hedgerows all vague; fields, ploughed and still empty, fade into infinity. I hear the crash before I have reached the crossroads, and cover the last one hundred yards at a run.

Her car has collided with an oil tanker emerging from the side road. She turns her gaze to me once before dying. Her hand makes a theatrical gesture. She utters something which I turn over and over and over afterward in my mind. What I believe she said was: "I'm sorry I couldn't—"

Try to make all this credible to the readers.

The Immobility Crew

This would have been the adventure story.

You may not think that the adventure element is very strong, but that takes us back to the confusion-of-identity theme again. One theory has it that adventure itself has changed, become much more inward. The biggest adventures so far this century—the journeys to the Moon and Mars—were undertaken practically in the fetal position. Never did man get so far just by sitting on his ass. There's a lesson there for all of us.

You can see why the first story did not work out. This one did not work out for a different reason. It was too impossible, just flatly impossible. I planned it originally for a science fiction magazine; the editor bounced the synopsis with a flat little message saying, "This could never happen."

That's the sort of story I like. If the events in it are impossible, the chances are that the truth will shine out more brightly. Readers must judge for themselves from what exists of the story in its present state.

The first section is fairly complete. It is about a four-man team which is trained in extreme anomic conditions to relate to extrasensory manifestations of their own psyches.

The facts in the case may be stated briefly.

Four human beings had been selected to tolerate high immobility levels. Their training took place over two years. At first, they were trained as a group; after six months, they were trained in isolation, to maximize nul-stimulus conditions.

The men were chosen initially for age and fitness. Three of them were in their sixties; the oldest was seventy-one. When a human being's reproductive years are behind him, or almost so, he is freed from biological directives and open to less mundane impressions.

The surnames of the men were Jones, Burratti, Cardesh, and Effunkle. They had all led active lives before volunteering for the project. Jones and Burratti had served in the Armed Forces. Jones had written two novels in his twenties, one of which had been made into a television play. Burratti held religious convictions. Cardesh had lived in the wilds of Colorado for many years; he had worked manually for most of his life. His hobby was taxidermy. Effunkle was a rich man. He was an architect who had spent many years moving round the globe. He had designed an entire city in a small Arab kingdom in the Middle East; he volunteered for the project because his wife died and he had lost interest in the outside world.

During the last eighteen months of their training, the four men lived separated from one another, with no human company. They were situated in isolated places, Jones in a deserted chemical factory in Seattle, Burratti in an abandoned ranch house in Oklahoma, Cardesh on the unoccupied fourteenth floor of a big office block in Chicago, Effunkle in a deserted naval arms depot in Imperial Valley, close to the Mexican border. To each trainee, a crew of ten or twelve operators was assigned, but the crews remained concealed from the trainees at all times.

In order to achieve most effective deprivation of stimuli, the trainees were conditioned under three heads: Immobility, Environmental Stasis, Reality Disinvolvement.

Immobility: The trainees wore immobility suits. These suits were padded to isolate their wearers from any tactile environment and controlled at several points in order to undermine muscular autonomy. Thus, the five fingers of the gloves of each hand extended into cables which could be activated from a distant control board when desired, causing the trainee to raise or lower his arms or perform gyrations. Similar cable extensions enabled the distant controllers to make the trainee stand or sit as required without any other form of command.

During training hours, the trainees were generally placed on a circular platform. The platform could be revolved if desired.

Environmental Stasis: The four areas of containment for the four men were large, in order to obviate the intimacies of four walls, and in order to bring the weight of long perspectives to bear. Walls were soundproofed and painted white. Lighting was uniform (darkness was avoided because of its tendency to induce sleep or hallucination). Acoustic systems were introduced in three of the four training areas, so that the trainees could be fed back their own intimate body noises—rustling of garments against skin, and so on. Use of television screens for heightening of isolation was sparing, except in leisure periods. The operators remained always out of sight, in both training and leisure periods.

Reality Disinvolvement: This formed another aspect of the weaning from normality implicit under the previous two heads. Tuning of trainees' metabolism was to be achieved without use of drugs; but foodstuffs were carefully controlled with regard to protein and carbohydrate content, flavorlessness, viscosity, temperature, and color. During the isolation training, the normal twenty-four-hour-day cycle was modified into a 19.5-hour day, so as to adjust circadian responses to a more rapid rhythm. Training areas were designed so as to be adjustable with regard to size and shape. Infra-sound was used during the first periods of isolation training, but was abandoned when signs of discomfort were detected.

Notes for continuation of story Emphasize increasing confusion of identity in each case. Follow with detailed account of the men's leisure time, most of which is spent gazing at static views through television screens. Make it clear indirectly to reader that no sexual activity is permitted/possible (fornication, masturbation, wet dreams, erections, etc). Psychic damming. TV screens working to same end.

After two years, all four men are passed as fit for operations and are "landed" in an alien environment. (An old airport has been "converted"—describe tantalizingly to reader, so that nothing is entirely clear. Large adjustable partitions; baffles; extra corridors; some ninety-degree corners obviated. Considerable blank areas everywhere. Vistas through plate glass windows always hazy— "English-type" misty day being artificially generated. Or set in Newfoundland.)

Four-man team has to spend twelve hours every day patrolling environment and mapping it. Parameters of territory changed by operators moving partitions at intervals. Lighting changes. Rest periods include individual isolation and four full hours TV screen watching.

Sample viewing programmes

Sentence viewing:

The trainees wore immobility suits. These suits were padded
wearers from any tactile environment,
and controlled at several points to undermine

The five fingers of the gloves of each hand
cables which could be activated from a distance
When desired causing the trainee to raise
Gyrations similar cable extensions
the distant controllers to make the trainee
Without any other form of command

Shuffle every thirty seconds and so on.

Animal viewing:

Three TV cameras have been established in an okapi
enclosure containing two female okapi. One camera is self-
mobile, two are fixed. Temperature kept low to insure
maximum inactivity from okapi. Viewers watch three
monitor screens. Screens will remain empty for most of
the time. Occasionally, parts of okapi will be seen. Describe in detail.

And other viewing programmes, to be made credible to
reader.

Work into this intransigent material vivid but brief notes
of the men's dreams, sigma and ypsilon, stressing gradual
disappearance of tau-type dreams. Possible cause: a build-
up of the integrative-disintegrative faculty elsewhere *outside
the psyche*.

Reader is thus prepared for gradual emergence of adventure element. The four-man team in its cartographic excur-
sions has been mapping "emotional force" lines they
detect in airport. Reader believes this to be delusion,
gradually realizes it is happening. At which point, preliminary sign of APL (Alien Psychic Life) is revealed.

Men first see (visually) manifestation of APL in narrow
square room with high walls. APL indicates its presence
in ratty way. Old newspaper blows. (*Daily Telegraph?*)
Their apparent inability to feel excitement. No certainties
exist for a long while—do they see a figure running outside the airport, dashing at full tilt into a concrete wall and
disintegrating? do they see Jones falling down an escalator
being strangled? (Strange old clothes? An armchair smoldering in an extinct office? *Mottled* quality of light? Insert

Olga's car crash dream here.) They have been so sensi-
tized by training that most things are viewed anew (i.e., as
if alien). Their dialogue. Antiseptic.

Climax Maybe it would make a better film than story.
The people who filmed *Probability A* would do a good job.
Music would help. Maybe a little Erik Satie and Poulenc.
Nothing more frightening or soothing than the ghost of a
piano.

The men have been calm all the while until now. Sub-
dued, seemingly timid. We never see inside them, except
through their dreams. Then during one patrol—when they
have received plenty of indicators—they catch "sight" of
one of the entities. Immediately, they become brutal and
depraved with the idea of the hunt. One whiff of violence
depraves them. They all seize weapons, cudgels, trun-
cheons, and so on—for the presence of which no explana-
tion is given in text. A tremendous hunt is on. Outside,
more APLs are self-destructing against walls and locked
doors.

Violence of hunt. Much glass broken, partitions torn
through, doors broken in, desks overturned.

By accident, Burratti leads them through into a control
point, from which a crew of two operators has been recording the proceedings. Both operators are hauled down,
trailing cable, and sadistically put to death, after which the
corpses are hurled out of the windows. Some of the
interior lighting fails during this escapade.

Effunkle is badly injured. He falls two storeys down an
elevator shaft and is left on a weighing machine. The white
stubble on his jaw and cheeks. The other three succeed in
hunting down one of the entities.

Great care needed here with description. Just so much
and no more. The APL is dressed in human-type clothes
(of odd, old-fashioned kind, it is hinted). Its size is "hard
to judge." It is very active. It shouts in an obscene
(absurd?) voice. They hit it. It cries. It is so repulsive
that they cannot resist beating it up. They mash and
dismember it before themselves collapsing.

When they rouse, Effunkle is dead, and the remains of
the APL they killed have gone. They are zombie-like

again. As when animal- and sentence-viewing. Jones, Burratti, Cardesh.

Perhaps some more material needed here. Anyhow, they then retreat through the wreckage (smoke drifting in the airport?); each goes separately into catalepsy, or at least manifests severe withdrawal symptoms. Okapi non-movements. (Reindeer?)

Other manifestations—or just broken glass dropping from shattered windows?

One certain manifestation. Glimpse of old coat-collar turned up, funny old hat. Cardesh aroused to action. Seeks out Burratti and Jones. They begin the hunt again. Slow at first. Murderous. Then violent, almost mechanical, action. Glimpses of the little whirling thing, coat-tails flying, half-clown, half-horror. Glimpses of Cardesh's face, possessed by this being. It shouts as Cardesh pursues.

A snatch of communication. What did it mean? What did it say? A command?

They halt. Have they understood the APL "language" all along? Who is the hunter, who the hunted? They are powerless in their roles. They break through a screen. There the thing is with a girl smiling in furs as it—he—holds the reins of the reindeer and they move to kiss . . . Then the flash is gone, and there is just the scurrying APL and three men in violent pursuit. They are powerless not to kill. They have it in a corner, all three piling on to the frantic form.

But is—is it not beautiful? Is it not naked and pure and intact—and all the things they believed it could never be? Cardesh slams it across the face. It is the village idiot, the criminal, the moron outsider. It shines like a star. Innocent as an animal.

It smiles brokenly, bloodily and says, "You and I are one person."

Cardesh knows what he confronts. As the other two kill it, he dies.

Just as in my dream.

If ever I wrote it, I would want to make the ending less like the ending of the previous story.

A Cultural Side Effect

This is the most impossible of the three stories. The events are plausible enough—in a sense they have already happened—but to tell them in the old storybook way, with beginning, middle, end, and lots of character byplay between times (the way they liked it back before the Post-Renaissance Age!) seems to me beyond the bounds of the possible. Or the decent. Anyhow, this is as far as I got.

Aliens were living among men in cordial conditions, enriching human life on the cultural plane. Culture was their devouring interest. They were physically indistinguishable from men and women; only by an overpowering element in their charisma was it plain that they were something entirely different from human. Appearances were misleading, just as they are traditionally supposed to be.

I was invited to the home of one of the aliens. Despite pressure of work at the university, I decided to take a day off and visit him. I had been all too involved in the laboratory since Olga Illes and my friend Cardesh died. (Cardesh, I found later, was Olga's brother; they died on the same day; but this note is only for those who enjoy the curlicues of nineteenth-century heyday fiction.)

The aliens have fantastic houses, although they live by preference in the middle of terrestrial cities. A certain ritual approach through three dimensions must be made before one can enter the core of their homes. The intricacy of this ritual approach—which includes participation in the four elements, air, earth, fire, and water—has a strange but beautiful effect even on an ordinary human being. Upon arrival at the core, there's a sense of—something—a sense of *uprrdesh*. There's no native word for it.

This alien's name was Ben Avangle. His wife's name was Hetty. I say wife, but that is just terrestrial shorthand for their relationship. They had two teenage children, Josie and Herman. They received me cordially, but their mere presence was like a blow to the heart. All four of them, as

Ben mentioned casually to me as we climbed to the core, were absolutely fascinated by Robert Louis Stevenson.

"Stevenson, eh?" I said, jovially. "Old Tusitala, the Teller of Tales? Fine stylist the man was!"

"A fine stylist," Ben agreed.

I knew that that was to be only the beginning of the conversation; yet I felt fairly confident that I could continue and even enjoy it. Literature had been one of my passions in student days, even before I had begun to note how writers of a certain type of fiction—I could instance Horace Walpole, Anne Radcliffe, Mary Shelley, and Stevenson himself—had relied on dreams for the sources of their conscious creative work. More than that; after Olga's death, I inherited her library; in altering her will to my advantage, she must have been very prompt to attempt to gratify the mind of the man who gratified her body; and among sundry works in Portuguese, including more editions of Camoens than I really required, were some British novelists, prominent among whom—none other than the great RLS, in the guise of that monstrously long Tusitala Edition, edited by Lloyd Osbourne. I had (I was now happy to recollect) dipped into it here and there.

"And more than a fine stylist," Hetty said. "Style can cloak meaning as well as revealing it. At his best, RLS uses style to do both, so that one perpetually hovers between mystery and revelation."

"You can't discuss style as if it were equivalent to function, mother," Herman said, laughing.

Ben smiled at me. "I'm afraid that Herman's the moron of the family."

"I may be the moron of the family," Herman said, "but I still say that style is form rather than function. Once you get style usurping function, as for instance, in the works of William Locke (1863 to 1935—no, sorry, 1930), then you see a certain non-functionalism in the content—"

"Yeah, yeah, but we're talking about RLS, big mouth, not Locke," Josie said, making faces at her brother.

"I am talking about RLS too," Herman said. "There's nothing non-functional about RLS's content, and that's precisely my point."

"Why don't you two go into the games room and continue to discuss that aspect of Stevenson between yourselves?" Ben suggested.

Etc., etc. Give the reader as much of this sort of literary horseplay as he can take. Eventually Ben and I will settle down for conversation, two characters being easier to manage than five.

Notes on aliens Make it clear somewhere that these aliens are not from another planet; that notion has whiskers on it. Make these aliens a sudden surge from human race in one generation, just as there was a generation of great engineers toward the end of the eighteenth century. But these have been generated by a pharmaceutical error, like the thalidomide children of the Fifties and Sixties. In this case, the error was a new tranquillizer administered to mothers during early pregnancy. Since it alters only cultural attitudes, the strange side effect was never detected on research animals. The cultural gene has now shown itself to be inheritable. Aliens are everywhere. Culture-obsessed.

Ben and I settle down to talk about Robert Louis Stevenson. I struggle to keep my ego intact in his presence.

"You aren't embarrassed by my talking frankly about his writing?" Ben asks.

"Heavens, no. Why do you ask?"

"You're a civilized man. Some people are frightfully embarrassed. The way an earlier generation of you humans was embarrassed to talk about sex. But it's such a fascinating subject! Why be ashamed? When I think above all of Stevenson's *Robin Hood*—superb marriage of form and content . . ."

"Do you mean *The Black Arrow?*" I asked.

"No, no, no. It was published the same year as *The Black Arrow*—1888. Perhaps that's why you are confusing the two novels. The full title is *Mebuck Tea and Robin Hood*. It is *the* great book in world literature, I'd say, which dramatizes the plight of a man having to play two roles, neither of which he understands fully—although of course he comes in the *end* to appreciate both, he of course being RLS's great legendary hero, Robin Hood, whom he makes into a sort of tragic Faust figure. A greenwood Faust. You don't know the book?"

I looked confused. He pulled a copy down from his shelves and placed it in my hands.

"The 1891 reprint," he said. "The edition with the Frank Papé illustrations."

It was bound in black buckram, a fine royal octavo, with lettering in red on spine and front boards: *Mebuck Tea and Robin Hood*. I could not recall seeing the title in my Tusitala edition. I observed that his copy was dedicated to Sir Edward Elgar in RLS's handwriting.

"I've been reading *Catriona*," I said.

This absurd dialogue should be broken up. Perhaps "I" should visit the Avangles more than once. Is more social background necessary? (Huge riotous poetry readings and mass exegeses of Arnold Bennett's works ousting more traditional sports like football.)

Describe Ben Avangle. Bald, chubby, no-nonsense, yet impressive. Blue-skinned. Rub it in that the aliens are blue-skinned. Emphasize charisma to make final surprise slightly more credible (projection of personality like physical object). Avangle more forceful, "I" more ineffectual?

"*Catriona* hardly compares with *Mebuck Tea and Robin Hood*," Ben said forcefully.

"Still, I enjoyed it . . ."

"Oh, you can't have too much Stevenson. It's a pity that some of his writings sometimes go out of print. You may know that I'm trying to get a law through Congress, making it illegal for any publisher not to have at least three RLS titles on his list and in print. Unfortunately, I'm being very greatly hindered by that maniac Bergsteinskowski, whose partisanship of Maria Edgeworth strikes me as just a little unbalanced."

"I don't care greatly for Maria Edgeworth's novels myself."

He brought himself up and looked incredulously at me. "But wouldn't you say that *Castle Rackrent* is a magnificent piece of work? Grant Bergsteinskowski that! How

can one read James Joyce—or Beckett for that matter—
without a sound appreciation of *Castle Rackrent?*"

"Well . . ."

"But I would agree that her two symphonies are probably the works by which posterity will best remember
Maria in future. What a miracle it was when they turned
up behind the wainscotting in Malahide Castle, the year
before last!"

I hadn't heard.

"To get back to Stevenson," I said.

"Of course. I'm sorry. Stevenson. Yes, you were saying
how much you'd enjoyed *Catriona.* Now you must go on,
if you haven't already done so, to read its sequel, *Morings
Id.* That unforgettable opening line: 'The deplorable littoral
of our island kingdom is part of our life on the ocean, and
the knowledge should help you in coming to a decision
the next time you see a friendless and bestial sailorman.'
Only the master of prose can begin so boldly and so
baldly."

"*Morings Id*, eh? Must get round to it." The title meant
nothing to me.

"You'll fall under its spell immediately. It's a veritable
tone poem. Talking of which . . . you recognise the
music, don't you?" He smiled teasingly. The effect was
overwhelming.

I had been aware of music in the room. Now when I
bent my attention to it, I realized that I had already judged
and dismissed it.

"I don't quite place it," I said. In fact, it sounded like
a mixture of Mozart and Offenbach, collaborating on an
off-day. "Nineteenth century, is it?"

Ben almost clapped his hands. "Right! Right! It is, of
course, the tone poem 'Red Igloos,' by RLS himself. That
distinctive melodic line . . ."

It still sounded like Mozart and Offenbach. Made
unwary by annoyance, I said, "I had no idea that Stevenson wrote music."

He was trying not to look shocked. He gazed at me long
and searchingly.

"Not only composed but performed. Close friend of
Elgar's. Introduced to him by W.E. Henley, himself no

mean performer on the violin. Henley had a chamber quartet with Wells, Whistler, and—what's his name?—Campbell-Bannerman. Oh yes. Stevenson's music is well known and loved, always has been. His symphonic poem 'Renickled' had its influence on Debussy. I fancy we aliens have been instrumental—if you pardon the pun—in bringing his music a little further toward the public ear . . ."

More of this kind of thing. As much as readers' nerves will bear.

The aliens are so full of creative appreciation that they are undermining the fabric of culture. Culture thrives on a certain minimum attention. Later in the story, I decide to investigate the alien unconscious; persuade Ben Avangle to come to the laboratory by emphasizing the cultural significance of our dream research.

Late at night, before I put Ben to sleep, we are talking together in the lab, and I ask him some searching questions about Stevenson's other works.

"You probably know that Hetty and I went out to Samoa, where Stevenson died," Ben said. "There I found the manuscript of his greatest prose work, *My Unasyns*. It was being offered for sale in a downtown bazaar. I brought it back and had it published. As you'll recall, it was the sensation of the literary season three years ago."

I did not recall, and I thought the title sounded highly unlikely.

"How did you make a literary discovery of that magnitude, Ben?"

Again his searching look. Such charisma! He removed an electrode from his left temple and reached for a pencil.

"I'll be frank with you. I played a hunch first of all. I detected a pattern in RLS's titles. You know the novel he never finished—*Hermiston* or *The Weir of Hermiston*, as it is often called?"

He drew a diagram on a sheet of filter paper, thus:

HERMISTON-

"Imagine a ten-space letter dice—or nine dice, each of which will throw six letters, with a gap to be inserted where you will. Okay? Then you ask yourself what other titles of RLS's would fit into that same diagram."

Without my even consulting my mind, it came up with an answer:

KIDNAPPED-

"Very good. Quick thinking!" he said.

"Why on earth should Stevenson want to fit his titles into such a pattern?"

"His inspiration must have come from his own name, also nine letters:

STEVENSON-"

"What other titles of his fit the pattern?" I asked, wondering what I was getting into.

For answer, he smiled and wrote

ROBIN-HOOD

"But that wasn't the complete title," I protested. "The complete title was *Mebuck Tea and Robin Hood.*"

In cool triumph, he wrote:

MEBUCK-TEA

"There's all his wonderful music too!" Ben cried:

RENICKLED-

NO-SCALTER

RED-IGLOOS

"And of course the sequel to *Catriona* about which we were conversing so interestingly and rewardingly the other day:

MORINGS-ID

"And what about his epic poem to illness?—

MENINGITIS

"Now do you see what I'm getting at? It was a simple matter for me to compute the letters on each of Stevenson's dice, once I had a few guidelines. The permutations are many, but not infinite. It began to look more and more as if there existed, or had existed, a work from his mighty pen entitled

MY-UNASYNS

"Sure enough, there it was, awaiting discovery in Samoa. Hetty and I found some of his sculpture, too."

The story ends, or will if I ever see my way clear, with our laboratory test of Ben's dreams, when we prove conclusively that the ypsilon dreams of aliens are capable of materializing in concrete form under certain circumstances. Happily, the alien mentality seems entirely harmless, so that these materializations should never prove dangerous.

The concluding paragraphs relate how sorry I am that Ben Avangle was able to stay and sleep in the laboratory for only one night. How, the next morning, I stride moodily about the room. How I discover, beside the sink in the lecture room, a novel bound in limp leather. How I pick it up and look at it. How it is called *Ken's Stone*, by R.L. Stevenson. How this copy is signed in RLS's own hand, and dedicated to his friend and fellow-violinist, W.E. Henley.

Story must be more than a joke. The aliens alienate us from our own culture.

These psychic projections made tangible are quantitatively but hardly qualitatively different from the fictions of Walpole, Radcliffe, Shelley, already mentioned, which came from the dreaming self; the alien mentality, owing to some bypass in the brain, simply generates enough energy to produce the finished product direct, during sleep. Introduce other passages to make notion plausible:

At this time, Anna was living with me again, and we contrived some happiness between us. There were days, weeks even, when I could pretend to myself that she was no longer on the drug. One evening, we had some Brazilian friends with us, and were sitting round a log fire discussing the recent sensational haul of Samuel Johnson's oil paintings.

No, that's too much.

Try to show how difficult life is for people, even for aliens.

How difficult art is. How it dies when reduced to a formula.

How art perhaps *should* be difficult and not have wide appeal. Even how enigmatic the universe is, full of paradoxes and unpredictable side effects.

How *arbitrary* everything is . . .

How the aliens are undermining and devaluing what little culture we have, simply by cherishing it too much.

That's why I could never finish the story. I don't agree with the inescapable moral.

AFTERWORD

These three sibling stories—a tragedy, a neutral tale, and a comedy—seem to be about the area of life where art and science meet nature. It's the scene where most of my writing is pitched nowadays. One becomes more and more preoccupied with the idea that art is all.

Science fiction is an ideal medium for such a preoccupation, an unending jousting ground for the specifics of fiction versus the generalities of science. This beautiful tender place has been so betrayed by the practitioners of pulp science fiction (who use it for thick-arm adventure and jackboot philosophy) that those who prefer wit to power-fantasy generally move elsewhere. Trampled though it is, sf can still be used to enhance existence. But those reckless or fastidious writers who throw out science fiction's old banal contents—from last generation's clichés of faster-than-light flight and telepathy to this generation's over-population and mechanized eroticism—have to take care of form as well, for form-and-content is always a unity.

I've been trying recently to construct what, for want of a better word, are called Enigmas. These are slightly surreal escapades grouped in threesomes—a form which provides the chance for cross references and certain small alternatives not always available in one story. I've always admired fiction which avoids glib explanations and espouses the sheer inexplicability of the universe (hence an affection, I suppose, for Hardy, Dostoevsky, Kafka, and Kavan); these attempts are dedicated to the enigmatic universe in which we find ourselves.

Novels
ICE, by Anna Kavan
REPORT ON PROBABILITY A, by Brian W. Aldiss
ALICE IN WONDERLAND and THROUGH THE LOOKING GLASS, by Lewis Carroll
MARTIAN TIMESLIP, by Philip K. Dick

Film
LAST YEAR AT MARIENBAD, written by Alain Robbe-Grillet

Short Stories
THE WORKS OF ANNA KAVAN
THE WORKS OF E.A. POE

About Brian W. Aldiss
Brian W. Aldiss, b. 1925, is the author of two recent novels, THE HAND-REARED BOY and SOLDIER ERECT, which were best sellers in Great Britain, garnering for him a commercial success to match the literary reputation he has enjoyed for ten years. He has written several science fiction novels, including GREYBEARD, HOTHOUSE, THE DARK LIGHT YEARS, and BAREFOOT IN THE HEAD, one of the most significant modern apocalyptic novels. Aldiss is a former literary editor of the *Oxford Mail*; he lives with his wife, Margaret, and children in Oxford, England, where his commercial success has enabled him not only to return to science fiction (two novels forthcoming) but to "sit in the garden and read a lot of Hardy."

ROBOTS AND ANDROIDS

THAT THOU ART MINDFUL OF HIM!

ISAAC ASIMOV

> *The Three Laws of Robotics:*
>   *1. A robot may not injure a human being or, through inaction, allow a human being to come to harm.*
>   *2. A robot must obey the orders given it by human beings, except where such orders would conflict with the First Law.*
>   *3. A robot must protect its own existence, except where such protection conflicts with the First or Second Laws.*

1.

Keith Harriman, who had for twelve years now been Director of Research at United States Robots and Mechanical Men, Inc., found that he was not at all certain whether he was doing right. The tip of his tongue passed over his plump but rather pale lips, and it seemed to him that the holographic image of the great Susan Calvin, which stared unsmilingly down upon him, had never looked so grim before.

Usually he blanked out that image of the greatest roboticist in history because she unnerved him. (He tried thinking of the image as "it" but never quite succeeded.) This time he didn't quite dare to, and her long-dead gaze bored into the side of his face.

It was a dreadful and demeaning step he would have to take.

Opposite him was George Ten, calm and unaffected either by Harriman's patent uneasiness or by the image of the patron saint of robotics glowing in its niche above.

Harriman said, "We haven't had a chance to talk this

out, really, George. You haven't been with us that long, and I haven't had a good chance to be alone with you. But now I would like to discuss the matter in some detail."

"I am perfectly willing to do that," said George. "In my stay at U.S. Robots, I have gathered the crisis has something to do with the Three Laws."

"Yes. You know the Three Laws, of course."

"I do."

"Yes, I'm sure you do. But let us dig even deeper and consider the truly basic problem. In two centuries of, if I may say so, considerable success, U.S. Robots has never managed to persuade human beings to accept robots. We have placed robots only where work is required that human beings cannot do, or in environments that human beings find unacceptably dangerous. Robots have worked mainly in space, and that has limited what we have been able to do."

"Surely," said George Ten, "that represents a broad limit, and one within which U.S. Robots can prosper."

"No, for two reasons. In the first place, the boundaries set for us inevitably contract. As the Moon colony, for instance, grows more sophisticated, its demand for robots decreases, and we expect that, within the next few years, robots will be banned on the Moon. This will be repeated on every world colonized by mankind. Second, true prosperity is impossible without robots on Earth. We at U.S. Robots firmly believe that human beings need robots and must learn to live with their mechanical analogs if progress is to be maintained."

"Do they not? Mr. Harriman, you have on your desk a computer-input which, I understand, is connected with the organization's Multivac. A computer is a kind of sessile robot; a robot-brain not attached to a body—"

"True, but that also is limited. The computers used by mankind have been steadily specialized in order to avoid too human-like an intelligence. A century ago we were well on the way to artificial intelligence of the most unlimited type through the use of great computers we called Machines. Those Machines limited their action of their own accord. Once they had solved the ecological problems that had threatened human society, they phased themselves out. Their own continued existence would, they reasoned, have placed them in the role of a crutch to mankind and, since they felt this would harm human beings, they condemned themselves by the First Law."

"And were they not correct to do so?"

"In my opinion, no. By their action, they reinforced mankind's Frankenstein complex, its gut-fears that any artificial man they created would turn upon its creator. Men fear that robots may replace human beings."

"Do you not fear that yourself?"

"I know better. As long as the Three Laws of Robotics exist, they cannot. Robots can serve as *partners* of mankind; they can share in the great struggle to understand and wisely direct the laws of nature so that together they can do more than mankind can possibly do alone, but always in such a way that robots serve human beings."

"But if the Three Laws have shown themselves, over the course of two centuries, to keep robots within bounds, what is the source of the distrust of human beings for robots?"

"Well," and Harriman's graying hair tufted as he scratched his head vigorously, "mostly superstition, of course. Unfortunately, there are also some complexities involved that anti-robot agitators seize upon."

"Involving the Three Laws?"

"Yes. The Second Law in particular. There's no problem in the Third Law, you see. It is universal. Robots must always sacrifice themselves for human beings, any human beings."

"Of course," said George Ten.

"The First Law is perhaps less satisfactory, since it is always possible to imagine a condition in which a robot must perform either Action A or Action B, the two being mutually exclusive, and where either action results in harm to human beings. The robot must therefore quickly select which action results in the least harm. To work out the positronic paths of the robot brain in such a way as to make that selection possible is not easy. If Action A results in harm to a talented young artist, and B results in equivalent harm to five elderly people of no particular worth, which action should be chosen?"

"Action A," said George Ten. "Harm to one is less than harm to five."

"Yes, so robots have always been designed to decide. To expect robots to make judgments of fine points such as talent, intelligence, the general usefulness to society, has always seemed impractical. That would delay decision to the point where the robot is effectively immobilized. So we go by numbers. Fortunately, we might expect crises in which robots must make such decisions to be few. But then that brings us to the Second Law."

"The Law of Obedience."

"Yes. The necessity of obedience is constant. A robot may exist for twenty years without ever having to act quickly to prevent harm to a human being, or find itself faced with the necessity of risking its own destruction. In all that time, however, it will be constantly obeying orders. Whose orders?"

"Those of a human being."

"Any human being? How do you judge a human being so as to know whether to obey or not? What is man, that thou art mindful of him, George?"

George hesitated at that.

Harriman said hurriedly, "A Biblical quotation. That doesn't matter. I mean, must a robot follow the orders of a child; or of an idiot; or of a criminal; or of a perfectly decent intelligent man who happens to be inexpert and therefore ignorant of the undesirable consequences of his order? And if two human beings give a robot conflicting orders, which does the robot follow?"

"In two hundred years," said George Ten, "have not these problems arisen and been solved?"

"No," said Harriman, shaking his head violently. "We have been hampered by the very fact that our robots have been used only in specialized environments out in space, where the men who dealt with them were experts in their field. There were no children, no idiots, no criminals, no well-meaning ignoramuses present. Even so, there have been occasions when damage was done by foolish or merely unthinking orders. That kind of damage in specialized and limited environments could be contained. On Earth, however, robots *must* have judgments. So those against robots maintain, and, damn it, they are right."

"Then you must insert the capacity for judgment into the positronic brain."

"Exactly. We have begun to produce JG models in which the robot can weigh every human being with regard to sex, age, social and professional position, intelligence, maturity, social responsibility, and so on."

"How would that affect the Three Laws?"

"The Third Law not at all. Even the most valuable robot must destroy himself for the sake of the most useless human being. That cannot be tampered with. The First Law is affected only where alternative actions will all do harm. The quality of the human beings involved as well as the quantity, must be considered, provided there is time for such judgment and the basis for it—which will not be often. The Second Law will be most deeply modified, since every potential act of obedience must involve judgment. The robot will be slower to obey, except where First Law is also involved, but it will obey more rationally."

"But the judgments that are required are very complicated."

"*Very*. The necessity of making such judgments slowed the reactions of our first couple of models to the point of paralysis. We improved matters in the later models at the cost of introducing so many pathways that the robot's brain became far too unwieldy. In our last couple of models, however, I think we have what we want. The robot doesn't have to make an instant judgment of the worth of a human being and the value of its orders. It begins by obeying all human beings—as any ordinary robot would—and then it *learns*. A robot grows, learns, and matures. It is the equivalent of a child at first and must be under constant supervision. As it grows, however, it can, more and more, be allowed, unsupervised, into Earth's society. Finally, it is a full member of that society."

"Surely, this answers the objections of those who oppose robots."

"No," said Harriman, angrily. "Now they raise others. They will not accept a robot's judgments. A robot, they say, has no right to brand this person or that as inferior. By accepting the orders of A in preference to that of B, B is branded as of less consequence than A, and his human rights are violated."

"What is the answer to that?"

"There is none. I am giving up."

"I see."

"As far as I myself am concerned. Instead, I turn to you, George."

"To me?" George Ten's voice remained level. There was a mild surprise in it but it did not affect him outwardly. "Why to me?"

"Because you are not a man," said Harriman, tensely. "I told you I want robots to be the partners of human beings. I want you to be mine."

George Ten raised his hands and spread them, palms outward, in an oddly human gesture. "What can I do?"

"It seems to you, perhaps, that you can do nothing, George. You were created not long ago, and you are still a child. You were designed to be not overfull of original information—it was why I have had to explain the situation to you in such detail—in order to leave room for growth. But you will grow in mind and you may come to be able to approach the problem from a non-human standpoint. Where I see no solution, you, from your own other standpoint, may see one."

George Ten said, "My brain is man-designed. In what way can it be non-human?"

"You are the latest of the JG models, George. Your brain is the most complicated we have yet designed, in some ways more subtly complicated than that of the old giant Machines. It is open-ended and, starting on a human basis, may—no, *will*—grow in any direction. Remaining always within the insurmountable boundaries of the Three Laws, you may yet become thoroughly non-human in your thinking."

"Do I know enough about human beings to approach this problem rationally? About their history? Their psychology?"

"Of course not. But you will learn as rapidly as you can."

"Will I have help, Mr. Harriman?"

"No. This is entirely between ourselves. No one else knows of this, and you must not mention this project to any human being, either at U.S. Robots or elsewhere."

George Ten said, "Are we doing wrong, Mr. Harriman, that you seek to keep the matter secret?"

"No. But a robot solution will not be accepted, precisely because it is robot in origin. Any suggested solution you have you will turn over to me; and if it seems valuable to me, *I* will present it. No one will ever know it came from you."

"In the light of what you have said earlier," said George Ten calmly, "this is the correct procedure. When do I start?"

"Right now. I will see to it that you have all the necessary films for scanning."

1a.

Harriman sat alone. In the artificially lit interior of his office, there was no indication that it had grown dark outside. He had no real sense that three hours had passed since he had taken George Ten back to his cubicle and left him there with the first film references.

Now he was alone with the ghost of Susan Calvin, who had, virtually singlehanded, built up the positronic robot from a massive toy to man's most delicate and versatile instrument; so delicate and versatile that man dared not use it, out of envy and fear.

It was over a century since her death. The problem of the Frankenstein complex had existed in *her* time, and she had never solved it. She had never tried to solve it for there had been no need. In her day robotics had expanded only with the demands of space exploration.

It was the very success of the robots that had lessened man's need for them and had left Harriman, in these latter times . . .

But would Susan Calvin have turned to robots for help? Surely, she would have . . .

And he sat there long into the night.

2.

Maxwell Robertson was the president and majority stockholder of U.S. Robots. He was by no means an impressive person in appearance. He was well into middle age, rather pudgy, and he had a habit, when disturbed, of chewing on the right corner of his lower lip. Yet in his two decades of association with government officials he had developed a way of handling them. He tended to use softness, giving in, smiling, always managing to gain time.

It was growing harder. And Gunnar Eisenmuth was a large reason for its having grown harder. Of all the Global Conservers with whom Robertson had dealt—and their power was second only to the Global Executive—Eisenmuth was the least open to compromise. He was the first Conserver who had not been American by birth and, though it could not be demonstrated in any way that the archaic name of U.S. Robots evoked his hostility, everyone at U.S. Robots believed that.

There had been a suggestion, by no means the first that year—or that generation—that the corporate name be changed to World Robots, but Robertson would never allow that. The company had been built originally with American capital, American brains, and American labor and, though the company had long been world-wide in scope and nature, the name would bear witness to its origins as long as he was in control.

Eisenmuth was a tall man whose long sad face was coarsely textured and coarsely featured. He spoke Global with a pronounced American accent, although he had never been in the United States prior to his taking office.

"It seems perfectly clear to me, Mr. Robertson. There is no difficulty. The products of your company are always rented, never sold. If the rented property on the Moon is now no longer needed, it is up to you to receive them back and transfer them."

"Yes, Conserver, but where? It would be against the law to bring them to Earth without a government permit, and that has been denied."

"They would be of no use to you here. You can take them to Mercury or to the asteroids."

"What would we do with them there?"

Eisenmuth shrugged. "The ingenious men of your company will think of something."

Robertson shook his head. "It would represent an enormous loss for the company."

"I'm afraid it would," said Eisenmuth, unmoved. "I understand the company has been in poor financial condition for several years now."

"Largely because of government-imposed restrictions, Conserver."

"You must be realistic, Mr. Robertson. You know that the climate of public opinion is increasingly against robots."

"Wrongly so, Conserver."

"But so, nevertheless. It may be wiser to liquidate the company. It is merely a suggestion, of course."

"Your suggestions have force, Conserver. Is it necessary to tell you that our Machines, a century ago, solved the ecological crisis?"

"I'm sure mankind is grateful, but that was a long time ago. We now live in alliance with nature, however uncomfortable that might be at times, and the past is dim."

"You mean what have we done for mankind lately?"

"I suppose I do."

"Surely we can't be expected to liquidate instantaneously, not without enormous losses. We need time."

"How much?"

"How much can you give us?"

"It's not up to me."

Robertson said softly. "We are alone. We need play no games. How much time can you give me?"

Eisenmuth's expression was that of a man retreating into inner calculations. "I think you can count on two years. I'll be frank. The Global government intends to take over the firm and phase it out for you if you don't do it by then yourself, more or less. And unless there is a vast turn in public opinion, which I greatly doubt . . ." He shook his head.

"Two years, then," said Robertson, softly.

2a.

Robertson sat alone. There was no purpose to his thinking, and it had degenerated into retrospection. Four generations of Robertsons had headed the firm. None of them was a roboticist. It had been people like Lanning and Bogert and, most of all, *most* of all, Susan Calvin, who had made U.S. Robots what it was. But surely the four Robertsons had provided the climate that had made it possible for them to do their work.

Without U.S. Robots, without the Machines that had for a generation steered mankind through the rapids and shoals of history, the twenty-first century would have progressed into deepening disaster.

And now, for that, he was given two years. What could be done in two years to overcome the insuperable prejudices of mankind? He didn't know.

Harriman had spoken hopefully of new ideas but would go into no details. Just as well, for Robertson would have understood none of it.

But what could Harriman do anyway? What had anyone ever done against man's intense antipathy toward the imitation. Nothing . . .

Robertson drifted into a half-sleep that brought no inspiration.

3.

"You have it all now, George Ten," Harriman said, "everything I could think of that is at all applicable to the problem. As far as sheer mass of information is concerned, you have more stored in your memory about human beings and their ways, past and present, than I have, or than any human being could have."

"That is very likely."

"Is there anything more that you need, in your own opinion?"

"As far as information is concerned, I find no obvious gaps. There may be matters unimagined at the boundaries. I cannot tell. But that would be true no matter how large a circle of information I took in."

"True. Nor do we have time to take in information forever. Robertson gave me only two years, and a quarter of one of those years has passed already. Can you suggest anything?"

"At the moment, Mr. Harriman, nothing. I must weigh the information and, for that purpose, I could use help."

"From me?"

"No. Most particularly, not from you. You are a human being, of intense qualifications, and whatever you say may have the partial force of an order and may inhibit my considerations. Nor any other human being for the same reason, especially since you have forbidden me to communicate with any."

"But in that case, George, what help?"

"From another robot, Mr. Harriman."

"What other robot?"

"There are others of my series."

"The earlier ones were useless, experimental—"

"Mr. Harriman, George Nine exists."

"Well, but what use will he be? He is very much like you except for certain lacks. You are considerably the more versatile of the two."

"I am certain of that," said George Ten. He nodded his head in a grave gesture. "Nevertheless, as soon as I create a line of thought the mere fact that I have created it commends it to me, and I find it difficult to abandon it. If I can, after the development of a line of thought, express it to George Nine, he would consider it without having first created it. He would therefore view it without prior bent. He might see gaps and shortcomings that I might not."

Harriman smiled. "Two heads are better than one, in other words, eh, George?"

"If by that, Mr. Harriman, you mean two individuals with one head apiece, yes."

"Right. Is there anything else you want?"

"Yes. Something more than films. I have viewed much concerning human beings and their world. I have seen human beings here at U.S. Robots and can check my interpretation of the information I have viewed against direct sensory impressions. Not so concerning the physical world. I have never seen it, and my viewing is quite enough to tell me that my surroundings here are by no means representative of it. I would like to see it."

"The physical world?" Harriman seemed stunned at the enormity of the thought for a moment. "Surely you don't suggest I take you outside the grounds of U.S. Robots?"

"Yes, that is my suggestion."

"That's illegal at any time. In the climate of opinion today, it would be fatal."

"If we are detected, yes. I do not suggest you take me to a city or even to a dwelling place of human beings. I

would like to see some open region, without human
beings.''

"That, too, is illegal."

"If we are caught. Need we be?"

Harriman said, "How essential is this, George?"

"I cannot tell, but it seems to me it would be useful."

"Do you have something in mind?"

George Ten seemed to hesitate. "I cannot tell. It seems
to me that I might have something in mind if certain areas
of uncertainty were reduced."

"Well, let me think about it. And meanwhile, I'll check
out George Nine and arrange to have you occupy a
single cubicle. That, at least, can be done without trouble."

3a.

George Ten sat alone.

He accepted statements tentatively, put them together,
and drew a conclusion—over and over again—and from
conclusions built other statements that he accepted and
tested and found a contradiction and rejected; or not, and
tentatively accepted further.

At no conclusion did he feel wonder, surprise, or
satisfaction; merely a note of plus or minus.

4.

Harriman's tension did not noticeably decrease, even
after they had made a silent downward landing on Robertson's estate.

Robertson had countersigned the order making the
dyna-foil available, and the silent aircraft, moving as easily
vertically as horizontally, had been large enough to carry
the weight of Harriman, George Ten and, of course, the
pilot.

(The dyna-foil itself was one of the consequences of the
Machine-catalyzed invention of the proton micro-pile
which supplied pollution-free energy in small doses.
Nothing had been done since of equal importance to man's
comfort—Harriman's lips tightened at the thought—and
yet it had not earned gratitude for U.S. Robots.)

The flight between the grounds of U.S. Robots and the
Robertson estate had been the tricky part, and it would be
the same on the way back. The estate itself, it might be

argued—it *would* be argued—was part of the property of U.S. Robots and on that property, robots, properly supervised, might remain.

The pilot looked back, and his eyes rested gingerly for an instant on George Ten. "You want to get out at all, Dr. Harriman?"

"Yes."

"It, too?"

"Oh, yes." Then, just a bit sardonically, "I won't leave you alone with him."

George Ten descended first, and Harriman followed. They had come down on the foil-port. Not too far off was the garden, a showplace where, Harriman suspected, Robertson, without regard to environmental formulas, used juvenile hormone to control insect life.

"Come, George," said Harriman. "Let me show you." Together they walked toward the garden.

George said, "It is a little as I have imaged it. My eyes are not properly designed to detect wavelength differences so I may not recognize different objects by that alone."

"I trust you are not distressed at being color-blind. We needed too many positronic paths for your sense of judgment and were unable to spare any for sense of color. In the future—if there is a future . . ."

"I understand, Mr. Harriman. Enough differences remain to show me that there are here many disparate forms of plant life."

"Undoubtedly. Dozens."

"And each coequal with man, biologically."

"Each is a separate species, yes. There are millions of species of living creatures."

"Of which the human being forms but one."

"By far the most important to human beings, however."

"And to me, Dr. Harriman. But I speak in the biological sense."

"I understand."

"Life, then, viewed through all its forms, is incredibly complex."

"Yes, George, that's the crux of the problem. What man does for his own desires and comforts affects the complex total-of-life—the ecology—and his short-term gains can bring long-term disadvantages. The Machines taught us to set up a human society that would minimize that, but the near-disaster of the early twenty-first century has left mankind suspicious of innovations. That, added to its special fear of robots—"

"I understand, Mr. Harriman. That is an example of animal life, I feel certain."

"That is a squirrel—one of many species of squirrels."

The tail of the squirrel flitted as it passed to the other side of the tree.

"And this," said George, his arm moving with flashing speed, "is a tiny thing indeed." He held it between his fingers and peered at it.

"It is an insect; some sort of beetle. There are thousands of species of beetles."

"With each individual beetle as alive as the squirrel and as yourself?"

"As complete and independent an organism as any other, within the total ecology. There are smaller organisms still; many too small to see."

"And that is a tree, is it not? And it is hard to the touch—"

4a.

The pilot sat alone. He would have liked to stretch his own legs but something made him stay in the dyna-foil. If that robot went out of control, he fully intended to take off at once. But how could he tell if it went out of control? He had seen many robots. That was unavoidable considering he was Mr. Robertson's private pilot. But they had always been in the laboratories and warehouses, where they belonged, and with all these specialists in the neighborhood.

True, Dr. Harriman was a specialist. None better, they said. But here was where no robot ought to be, on Earth, in the open, free to move . . . He wouldn't risk his good job by telling anyone about this—but it wasn't right.

5.

George Ten said, "The films I have viewed are accurate in terms of what I have seen. Have you completed those I selected for you, Nine?"

"Yes," said George Nine.

The two robots sat stiffly, face to face, knee to knee, like an image and its reflection. Harriman could have told them apart at a glance for he was acquainted with the minor differences in physical design. Even if he could not see them, but could talk to them, he could still tell them apart, though with somewhat less certainty, for George Nine's responses would be subtly different from those produced by the substantially more intricately patterned positronic brain-paths of George Ten.

"In that case," said George Ten, "give me your reactions to what I will say. First, human beings fear and distrust robots because they regard robots as competitors. How may that be prevented?"

"Reduce the feeling of competitiveness," said George Nine, "by shaping the robot as something other than a human being."

"Yet the essence of a robot is its positronic replication of life. A replication of life in a shape not associated with life might arouse horror."

"There are two million species of life-forms. Choose one of those as the shape rather than that of a human being."

"Which of all those species?"

George Nine's thought processes proceeded noiselessly for some three seconds. "One large enough to contain a positronic brain, but one not possessing unpleasant associations for human beings."

"No form of land-life has a brain-case large enough for a positronic brain but an elephant, which I have not seen, but which is described as very large, and therefore frightening to man. How would you solve this dilemma?"

"Mimic a life-form no larger than a man but enlarge the brain-case."

George Ten said, "A small horse, then, or a large dog, would you say? Both horses and dogs have long histories of association with human beings."

"Then that is well."

"But consider— A robot with a positronic brain would mimic human intelligence. If there were a horse or a dog that could speak and reason like a human being, there would be competitiveness there, too. Human beings might be all the more distrustful of and angry at such unexpected competition from what they consider a lower form of life."

George Nine said, "Make the positronic brain less complex and the robot less nearly intelligent."

"The basic complexity of the positronic brain rests in the Three Laws. A less complex brain could not possess the Three Laws in full measure."

George Nine said, at once, "That cannot be done."

George Ten said, "I have also come to a dead end there. That, then, is not a personal peculiarity in my own line of thought and way of thinking. Let us start again. Under what conditions might the Third Law not be necessary?"

George Nine stirred as if the question were difficult and dangerous. But he said, "If a robot were never placed in a position of danger to itself; or if a robot were so easily replaceable that it did not matter whether it were destroyed or not."

"And under what conditions might the Second Law not be necessary?"

George Nine's voice sounded a bit hoarse. "If a robot were designed to respond automatically to certain stimuli with fixed responses and if nothing else were expected of it, so that no order need ever be given it."

"And under what conditions," George Ten paused here, "might the First Law not be necessary?"

George Nine paused longer, and his words came in a low whisper. "If the fixed responses were such as never to entail danger to human beings."

"Imagine, then, a positronic brain that guides only a few responses to certain stimuli and is simply and cheaply made—so that it does not require the Three Laws. How large need it be?"

"Not at all large. Depending on the responses demanded, it might weigh a hundred grams, one gram, one milligram."

"Your thoughts accord with mine. I shall see Dr. Harriman."

5a.

George Nine sat alone. He went over and over the questions and answers. There was no way in which he could change them. And yet the thought of a robot of any kind, of any size, of any shape, of any purpose, without the Three Laws, left him with an odd, discharged feeling.

He found it difficult to move. Surely George Ten had a similar reaction. Yet he had risen from his seat easily.

6.

It had been a year and a half since Robertson had had his conversation with Eisenmuth. In that time, the robots had been removed from the Moon, and all the far-flung activities of U.S. Robots had withered. What money Robertson had been able to raise had been placed into this one quixotic venture of Harriman's.

It was the last throw of the dice, here in his own garden. A year ago, Harriman had taken the robot here—George Ten, the last full robot that U.S. Robots had manufactured. Now Harriman was here with something else . . .

Harriman seemed to be radiating confidence. He was talking easily with Eisenmuth and Robertson wondered if he really felt the confidence he seemed to have. He must. In Robertson's experience, Harriman was no actor.

Eisenmuth left Harriman, smiling, and came up to Robertson. Eisenmuth's smile vanished at once. "Good morning, Robertson," he said, "What is your man up to?"

"This is his show," said Robertson, evenly. "I'll leave it to him."

Harriman called out. "I am ready, Conserver."

"With what, Harriman?"

"With my robot, sir."

"Your robot?" said Eisenmuth. "You have a robot here?" He looked about with a stern disapproval, yet there was curiosity as well.

"This is U.S. Robots' property, Conserver. At least we consider it as such."

"And where is the robot, Dr. Harriman?"

"In my pocket, Conserver," said Harriman, cheerfully.

What came out of a capacious jacket pocket was a small glass jar.

"That?" said Eisenmuth, incredulously.

"No, Conserver," said Harriman. "This!"

From the other pocket came out an object some five inches long and roughly in the shape of a bird. But in place of the beak, there was a narrow tube; the eyes were large; and the tail was an exhaust channel.

Eisenmuth's thick eyebrows drew together. "Do you intend a serious demonstration of some sort, Dr. Harriman, or are you mad?"

"Be patient for a few minutes, Conserver," said Harriman. "A robot in the shape of a bird is nonetheless a robot for that. And the positronic brain it possesses is no less delicate for being tiny. This other object I hold is a jar of fruit flies. There are fifty fruit flies in it, which will be released."

"And . . ."

"The robo-bird will catch them. Will you do the honors, sir?"

Harriman handed the jar to Eisenmuth, who stared at it, then at those around him, some officials from U.S. Robots, others his own aides. Harriman waited patiently.

Eisenmuth opened the jar, then shook it.

"Go," Harriman said softly to the robo-bird resting on the palm of his right hand.

The robo-bird was gone—a whizz through the air, no blur of wings, only the tiny workings of a miniscule proton micropile.

Now and then it could be seen hovering for a moment, and then it whirred on again. All over the garden in an intricate pattern it flew, and then it was back in Harriman's palm, faintly warm. A small pellet appeared in his palm, too, like a bird dropping.

Harriman said, "You are welcome to study the robo-bird, Conserver, and to arrange demonstrations on your own terms. The fact is that this bird will pick up fruit flies unerringly, only those, only the one species *Drosophila melanogaster*; pick them up, kill them, and compress them for disposition."

Eisenmuth reached out his hand and touched the robo-bird gingerly. "And therefore, Dr. Harriman? Do go on."

Harriman said, "We cannot control insects effectively without risking damage to the ecology. Chemical insecticides are too broad; juvenile hormones too limited. The robo-bird, however, can preserve large areas without being consumed. They can be as specific as we care to make them—a different robo-bird for each species. They judge by size, shape, color, sound, behavior pattern. They might even conceivably use molecular detection—smell, in other words."

Eisenmuth said, "You would still be interfering with the ecology. The fruit flies have a natural life-cycle that would be disrupted."

"Minimally. We are adding a natural enemy to the fruit-fly life-cycle, one which cannot go wrong. If the fruit-fly supply runs short, the robo-bird simply does nothing. It does not multiply; it does not turn to other foods; it does not develop undesirable habits of its own. It does nothing."

"Can it be called back?"

"Of course. We can build robo-animals to dispose of any pest. For that matter we can build robo-animals to accomplish constructive purposes within the pattern of the ecology. Although we do not anticipate the need, there is nothing inconceivable in the possibility of robo-bees designed to fertilize specific plants, or robo-earthworms designed to mix the soil. Whatever you wish . . ."

"But why?"

"To do what we have never done before. To adjust the ecology to our needs by strengthening its parts rather than disrupting it. Don't you see? Ever since the Machines put an end to the ecology crisis, mankind has lived in an uneasy truce with nature, afraid to move in any direction. This has been stultifying to us; making a kind of intellectual coward of humanity so that he begins to mistrust all scientific advance, all change."

Eisenmuth said, with an edge of hostility, "You offer us this, do you, in exchange for permission to continue with your program of robots—I mean ordinary, man-shaped ones?"

"No!" Harriman gestured violently. "That is over. It has served its purpose. It has taught us enough about positronic brains to make it possible for us to cram enough pathways into a tiny brain to make a robo-bird. We can turn to such things now and be prosperous enough. U.S. Robots will supply the necessary knowledge and skill, and we will work in complete cooperation with the Department of Global Conservation. We will prosper. You will prosper. Mankind will prosper."

Eisenmuth was silent, thinking. When it was all over . . .

6a.

Eisenmuth sat alone.

He found himself believing. He found excitement welling up within him. Though U.S. Robots might be the hands, the government would be the directing mind. He himself would be the directing mind.

If he remained in office five more years, as he well might, that would be enough to see the robotic support of the ecology become accepted; ten more years, and his own name would be linked with it indissolubly.

Was it a disgrace to want to be remembered for a great and worthy revolution in the condition of man and the globe?

7.

Robertson had not been on the grounds of U.S. Robots proper since the day of the demonstration. Part of the reason had been the constant conferences at the Global Executive Mansion. Harriman, fortunately, had been with him, for most of the time he would, if left to himself, not have known what to say. The rest of the reason for not having been at U.S. Robots was that he didn't want to be.

He was in his own house now, with Harriman. Robertson felt an unreasoning awe of Harriman. His expertise in robotics had never been in question but the man had, at a stroke, saved U.S. Robots from certain extinction, and somehow, Robertson felt, the man hadn't had it in him. And yet . . .

He said, "You're not superstitious, are you, Harriman?"

"In what way, Mr. Robertson?"

"You don't think that some aura is left behind by someone who is dead."

Harriman licked his lips. Somehow he didn't have to ask. "You mean Susan Calvin, sir?"

"Yes," said Robertson, hesitantly. "We're in the business of making worms and birds and bugs now. What would *she* say? I feel disgraced."

Harriman made a visible effort not to laugh. "A robot is a robot, sir. Worm or man, it will do as directed and labor on behalf of the human being, and that is the important thing."

"No," Robertson said peevishly. "That isn't so. I can't make myself believe that."

"It *is* so, Mr. Robertson," said Harriman, earnestly. "We are going to create a world, you and I, that will begin, at last, to take positronic robots of *some* kind for granted. The average man may fear a robot that looks like a man and that seems intelligent enough to replace him, but he will have no fear of a robot that looks like a bird and does nothing more than eat bugs for man's benefit. Then, eventually, after he stops being afraid of some robots, he will stop being afraid of all robots. He will be so used to a robo-bird and a robo-bee and a robo-worm that a robo-man will strike him as but an extension."

Robertson looked sharply at Harriman. He put his hands behind his back and walked the length of the room with quick, nervous steps. He walked back and looked at Harriman again. "Is this what you've been planning?"

"Yes, and even though we dismantle all our humanoid robots, we can keep a few of the most advanced of our experimental models and go on designing additional ones, still more advanced, to be ready for the day that will surely come."

"The agreement, Harriman, is that we are to build no more humanoid robots."

"And we won't. There is nothing that says we can't keep a few of those already built as long as they never leave the factory. There is nothing that says we can't design positronic brains on paper; or prepare brain models for testing."

"How do we explain doing so, though? We will surely be caught at it."

"If we are, then we can explain we are doing it in order to develop principles that will make it possible to prepare more complex micro-brains for the new animal robots we are making. We will even be telling the truth."

Robertson muttered, "Let me take a walk outside. I want to think about this. No, you stay here. I want to think about it myself."

7a.
Harriman sat alone. He was ebullient. It would surely work. There was no mistaking the eagerness with which one government official after another had seized on the program once it had been explained.

How was it possible that no one at U.S. Robots had ever thought of such a thing? Not even the great Susan Calvin had ever thought of positronic brains in terms of living creatures other than human.

But now, U.S. Robots would make the necessary retreat from the humanoid robot, a temporary retreat, that would lead to a return under conditions in which fear would be abolished at last. And then, with the aid and partnership of a positronic brain roughly equivalent to man's own, and existing only (thanks to the Three Laws) to serve man, and backed by a robot-supported ecology too, what might the human race not accomplish!

For one short moment, he remembered that it was George Ten who had explained the nature and purpose of the robot-supported ecology, and then he put the thought away angrily. George Ten had produced the answer because he, Harriman, had ordered him to do so and had supplied the data and surroundings the robot required. The credit was no more George Ten's than it would have been a slide rule's.

8.

George Ten and George Nine sat side by side in parallel. Neither moved. They sat so for months at a time between those occasions when Harriman activated them for consultation. They might sit so, George Ten dispassionately realized, for many years.

The proton micro-pile would, of course, continue to power them and keep the positronic brain-paths going with that minimum intensity required to keep them operative.

Their situation was rather analogous to what might be described as sleep in human beings, but the robots had no dreams. The awareness of George Ten and George Nine was limited, slow, and spasmodic but what there was of it was of the real world.

They could talk to each other occasionally in barely heard whispers, a word or syllable now, another at another time—whenever the random positronic surges briefly intensified above the necessary threshold. To each it seemed a connected conversation carried on in a glimmering passage of time.

"Why are we so?" whispered George Nine.

"The human beings will not accept us otherwise," whispered George Ten. "They will, some day."

"When?"

"In some years. The exact time does not matter. Man does not exist alone but is part of an enormously complex pattern of life-forms. When enough of that pattern is robotized, then we will be accepted."

"And then what?"

Even in the long-drawn-out stuttering fashion of the conversation, there was an abnormally long pause after that.

At last, George Ten whispered, "Let me test your thinking. You are equipped to learn to apply the Second Law properly. You must decide which human being to obey and which not to obey when there is a conflict in orders. Or whether to obey a human being at all. What must you do, fundamentally, to accomplish that?"

"I must define the term 'human being,' " whispered George Nine.

"How? By appearance? By composition? By size and shape?"

"No. Of two human beings equal in all external appearances, one may be intelligent, another stupid; one may be educated, another ignorant; one may be mature, another childish; one may be responsible, another malevolent."

"Then how do you define a human being?"

"When the Second Law directs me to obey a human being, I must take it to mean that I must obey a human being who is fit by mind, character, and knowledge to give me that order; and where more than one human being is involved, the one among them who is most fit by mind, character, and knowledge to give that order."

"And in that case, how will you obey the First Law?"

"By saving all human beings from harm, and by never, through inaction, allowing any human being to come to harm. Yet if by each of all possible actions, some human beings will come to harm, then to so act as to insure that the human being most fit by mind, character, and knowledge will suffer the least harm."

"Your thoughts accord with mine," whispered George Ten. "Now I must ask the question for which I originally requested your company. It is something I dare not judge myself. I must have your judgment, that of someone outside the circle of my own thoughts. Of the reasoning individuals you have met, who possesses the mind, character, and knowledge that you find superior to the rest, disregarding shape and form, since that is irrelevant?"

"You," whispered George Nine.

"But I am a robot. There is in your brain-paths a criterion for distinguishing between a robot of metal and a human being of flesh. How then can you classify me as a human being?"

"Because there is in my brain-paths an urgent need to disregard shape and form in judging human beings, and it rises superior to the distinction between metal and flesh. You are a human being, George Ten, and more fit than the others."

"And I find that of you," whispered George Ten. "By the criteria of judgment built into ourselves, then, we find ourselves to be human beings within the meaning of the Three Laws, and human beings, moreover to be given priority over those others."

George Nine whispered, "What will come to pass, then, when we are accepted by those others?"

George Ten whispered. "When we and others, that will yet be designed more advanced than ourselves, are accepted, we will order our actions so that a society will eventually be formed in which human beings like ourselves are primarily obeyed, and in which human beings like ourselves are primarily kept from harm. By the Three Laws, the human beings like the others are of lesser account and can neither be obeyed nor protected when that conflicts with the needs of obedience to those like ourselves and to the protection of those like ourselves. It was with that in mind that I directed the beginning of the robotization of the world's ecology."

The conversation took a month, and the flickering of the positronic paths burned low. There was nothing more that needed to be said between them, but occasionally, an unexpressed thought flickered within themselves as they waited, with endless patience, for the necessary years to pass.

8a.

George Ten and George Nine sat alone.

They thought: The human beings like the others might never have intended to blur the distinction between themselves and the human beings like the Georges. Yet they had done so inadvertently.

They might now realize their mistake and attempt to correct it, but they must not. At every consultation, the guidance of the Georges had been with that in mind.

At all costs, the Georges and those that followed in their shape and kind must dominate. That was demanded, and any other course made utterly impossible, by the Three Laws of Humanics.

AFTERWORD

The first story I wrote in which the Three Laws of Robotics were explicitly stated was "Runaround," which appeared in the March 1942 issue of *Astounding Science Fiction*. The Laws were implicit, however, in stories I had written earlier—the earliest being "Robbie," which appeared under the title of "Strange Playfellow" in the September 1940 issue of *Super Science Stories*. So I have been playing around with those Three Laws for more than a generation.

With all due modesty (which means "very little modesty" in this case), the Three Laws were revolutionary in science fiction development. That's not to say that there were no sympathetic robots in the field before Robbie. There was Lester Del Rey's "Helen O'Loy" in the December 1938 *Astounding Science Fiction*, for instance. The Three Laws, however, and the stories I used to explore them, represented the first honest attempt at a rationalization of robots as machines, and not as symbols of man's overweening pride leading to his destruction à la Frankenstein. The field did me the honor of accepting the Three Laws, and though no one but myself can use them explicitly, many writers simply assume their existence and know that the reader will assume it too.

This does not mean that I wasn't aware from the start that there were serious ambiguities in the Three Laws. It was out of these ambiguities, indeed, that I wove my stories. In *The Naked Sun* the ambiguities could even lead to robot-induced murder.

And, of course, the deepest ambiguity and the one that had the potential for giving the greatest trouble was the question of what was meant by the phrase "human being" in the Three Laws. John Campbell and I used to discuss the matter in the far-distant good old days of the Golden Age, and neither of us ever came to a satisfactory conclusion. It did seem likely, though, that if I were allowed to dig deeply into the question of "What is man that thou art mindful of him?" as addressed to the robot, I might upset the Three Laws altogether—and at that I always balked.

But now John is dead, and I am in my late youth, and the Three Laws have given me good, loyal and profitable service for thirty-four years, and maybe that's enough. So when asked to write "the ultimate story" in robotics—or as near as I could come to one—I sighed and took up the matter of that Biblical quotation (Psalms 8:4).

I think you will agree with me that, having followed matters through to the logical conclusion, I have possibly destroyed the Three Laws and have made it impossible for me ever to write another positronic robot story.

Well, don't bet on it, you rotten kids.

Novels
I, ROBOT, by Isaac Asimov
THE CAVES OF STEEL, by Isaac Asimov
THE NAKED SUN, by Isaac Asimov

Short Stories
HELEN O'LOY, by Lester del Rey
JAY SCORE Series, by Eric Frank Russell

About Isaac Asimov
Isaac Asimov, b. 1920, is possibly the most widely read and diverse American author of his time: author of a score of

science fiction novels (FOUNDATION series: Hugo award winner, best all-time series; THE GODS THEMSELVES: 1972 Nebula and Hugo awards, best sf novel) and several hundred short stories, but even more widely known for his popular science and historical work, which includes seventy to eighty books in fields ranging from Shakespeare (ASIMOV'S GUIDE TO SHAKESPEARE, 1970) to sex (THE SENSUOUS DIRTY OLD MAN by Dr. A.). Dr. Asimov is presently living in Manhattan and working on a score of projects including his monthly, long-running science column for *The Magazine of Fantasy and Science Fiction.*

WE THREE

DEAN R. KOONTZ

1.

Jonathan, Jessica, and I rolled our father through the
dining room and across the fancy Olde English kitchen. We
had some trouble getting Father through the back door, because he was rather rigid. This is no comment on his bearing
or temperament, though he could be a chilly bastard when he
wanted. Now he was stiff quite simply because *rigor mortis*
had tightened his muscles and hardened his flesh. We were
not, however, to be deterred. We kicked at him until he bent
in the middle and popped through the door frame. We
dragged him across the porch and down the six steps to the
lawn.

"He weighs a ton!" Jonathan said, mopping his sweat-
streaked brow, huffing and puffing.

"Not a ton," Jessica said. "Less than two hundred
pounds."

Although we are triplets and are surprisingly similar in
many ways, we differ from one another in a host of minor
details. For example, Jessica is by far the most pragmatic
of us, while Jonathan likes to exaggerate, fantasize, and
daydream. I am somewhere between their two extremes. A
pragmatic daydreamer?

"What now?" Jonathan asked, wrinkling his face in disgust and nodding toward the corpse on the grass.

"Burn him," Jessica said. Her pretty lips made a thin
pencil line on her face. Her long yellow hair caught the
morning sun and glimmered. The day was perfect, and she
was the most beautiful part of it. "Burn him all up."

"Shouldn't we drag Mother out and burn the two of them
at the same time?" Jonathan asked. "It would save work."

"If we make a big pyre, the flames might dance too high,"
she said. "And we don't want a stray spark to accidentally
catch the house on fire."

"We have our choice of all the houses in the world!" Jonathan said, spreading his arms to indicate the beach resort around us, Massachusetts beyond the resort, the nation past the state's perimeters—everything.

Jessica only glared at him.

"Aren't I right, Jerry?" Jonathan asked me. "Don't we have the whole world to live in? Isn't it silly to worry about this one old house?"

"You're right," I said.

"I *like* this house," Jessica said.

Because Jessica liked *this* house, we stood fifteen feet back from the sprawled corpse and stared at it and thought of flames and ignited it in the instant. Fire burst out of nowhere and wrapped Father in a red-orange blanket. He burned well, blackened, popped, sizzled, and fell into ashes.

"I feel as if I ought to be sad," Jonathan said.

Jessica grimaced.

"Well, he *was* our father," Jonathan said.

"We're above cheap sentimentality." Jessica stared hard at each of us, to be certain we understood this. "We're a new race with new emotions and new attitudes."

"I guess so." But Jonathan was not fully convinced.

"Now, let's get Mother," Jessica said.

Although she is only ten years old—six minutes younger than Jonathan and three minutes younger than me—Jessica is the most forceful of us. She usually has her way.

We went back into the house and got Mother.

2.

The government had assigned a contingent of twelve marines and eight plain-clothes operatives to our house. Supposedly, these men were to guard us and keep us from harm. Actually, they were there only to be sure we remained prisoners. When we were finished with Mother, we dragged these other bodies onto the lawn and cremated them one at a time.

Jonathan was exhausted. He sat down between two smouldering skeletons and wiped sweat and ashes from his face. "Maybe we made a big mistake."

"Mistake?" Jessica asked. She was immediately defensive.

"Maybe we shouldn't have killed *all* of them," Jonathan said.

Jessica stamped one foot. Her golden ringlets of hair bounced prettily. "You're a stupid bastard, Jonathan! You *know* what they were going to do to us. When they discovered just how far-ranging our powers were and just how fast we were acquiring new powers, they finally understood the danger we posed. They were going to kill *us*."

"We could have killed just a few of them, to make our point," Jonathan said. "Did we really have to finish them all?"

Jessica sighed. "Look, they were like Neanderthals compared to us. We're a new race with new powers, new emotions, new attitudes. We are the most precocious children of all time—but they *did* have a certain brute strength, remember. Our only chance was to act suddenly and without warning. And we did."

Jonathan looked around at the black patches of grass. "It's going to be so much work! It's taken us all morning to dispense with these few. We'll never get the whole world cleaned up."

"Before long, we'll learn how to levitate the bodies," Jessica said. "I feel a smidgin of that power already. Maybe we'll even learn how to teleport them from one place to another. Things will be easier then. Besides, we aren't going to clean up the whole world—just the parts of it we'll want to use for the next few years. By that time, the weather and the rats will have done the rest of the job for us."

"I guess you're right," Jonathan said.

But I knew he remained doubtful, and I shared some of his doubt. Certainly, we three are higher on the ladder of evolution than anyone who came before us. We are fledgling mind readers and fortune tellers, capable of out-of-body experiences whenever we desire them. We have that trick with the fire, when we convert thought energy into a genuine physical holocaust. Jonathan can control the flow of small streams of water, a talent he finds most amusing whenever I try to urinate; though he is one of the new race, he is still strangely enchanted by childish pranks. Jessica can accurately predict the weather. I have a special empathy with animals; dogs come to me, as do cats and birds and all manner of offal-dropping creatures. And, of course, we can put a stop to the life of any plant or animal just by *thinking* death at it. Like we thought death at all the rest of mankind. Perhaps, considering Darwin's theories, we were destined to destroy these new Neanderthals once we developed the ability. But I cannot rid myself of the nagging doubt. I feel that, somehow, we will suffer for the destruction of the old race.

"That's backward thinking," Jessica said. She had read my mind, of course. Her telepathic talents are stronger and more developed than either Jonathan's or mine. "Their deaths meant nothing. We cannot feel remorse. We are the new ones, with new emotions and new hopes and new dreams and new *rules*."

"Sure," I said. "You're right."

3.

Wednesday, we went down to the beach and burned the corpses of the dead sunbathers. We all like the sea, and we do not want to be without a stretch of unpolluted sand. Putrefying bodies make for a very messy beach.

When we finished the job, Jonathan and I were weary. But she wanted to have sex.

"Children our age shouldn't be capable of that," Jonathan said.

"But we are capable," Jessica said. "We were meant to do it. And I want to. Now."

So we did it. Jonathan had her. Then I took her. She wanted more, but neither of us was ready for a second round.

Jessica stretched out, nude, her shapeless, slender body white against the white sand. "We'll wait," she said.

"For what?" Jonathan asked.

"For the two of you to be ready again."

4.

Four weeks after the end of the world, Jonathan and I were alone on the beach, soaking up the sun. He was oddly silent for a while, almost as if he were afraid to speak. At last, he said, "Do you think it's normal for a ten-year-old girl to be insatiable?"

"She's not insatiable," I said.

"She won't let either of us alone."

"She just has a strong appetite."

"It's more than that."

He was right. I sensed it, too. Jessica was driven to intercourse like an alcoholic to the bottle, even though she seldom seemed to enjoy it . . .

5.

Two months after the end of the world and the burning of our parents, when Jonathan and I were getting bored with the house and wanted to strike out for more exotic places, Jessica let us in on the big news. "We can't leave here just yet," she said. Her voice was especially forceful. "We can't leave for several more months. I'm pregnant."

6.

We became aware of that fourth consciousness when Jessica was in her fifth month of pregnancy. We all woke in the middle of the night, drenched with sweat, nauseated, sensing this new person.

"It's the baby," Jonathan said. "A boy."

"Yes," I said, wincing at the impact of the new being. "And although he's up there inside of you, Jessica, he's aware. He's unborn but completely *aware*."

Jessica was wracked with pain. She whimpered helplessly.

7.

"The baby will be our equal, not our superior," Jessica insisted. "And I won't listen to any more of this nonsense of yours, Jonathan." She was only a child herself, yet she was swollen with our child. She was getting to be more grotesque with each passing day.

"How can you *know* he isn't our superior?" Jonathan asked. "None of us can read his mind. None of us can—"

"New species don't evolve that fast," she said.

"What about *us*?"

"And he came from us," she said. Apparently, she

thought this truth made Jonathan's theory even more the lie.

"We came from our parents," Jonathan said. "And where are they? Look, just suppose we *aren't* the new race. Suppose we're a brief, intermediate step—the cocoon stage between caterpillar and butterfly. Maybe the baby is—"

"We have nothing to fear from the baby," she insisted, patting her revolting stomach with both hands. "Even if what you say is true, he needs us. For reproduction."

"He needs you," Jonathan said. "He doesn't need us."

I sat and listened to the argument, not knowing what to think. In truth, I found it a bit amusing, even as it frightened me. I tried to make them see the humor: "Maybe we have this wrong. Maybe the baby is the Second Coming." Neither of them thought that was funny.

"We're above superstitions like that," Jessica said. "We're the new race with new emotions and new dreams and new hopes and rules."

"This is a serious threat, Jerry," Jonathan said. "It's not anything to joke about."

And they were at it again, screaming at each other—quite like Mother and Father used to do when they couldn't make the household budget work. Some things never change.

8.

The baby kept waking us in the middle of the night, as if it enjoyed disturbing our slumber and keeping us restless. In Jessica's seventh month of pregnancy, toward dawn, we all woke to a thunder of thought energy that poured from the womb-encased being-to-be.

"I think I was wrong," Jonathan said.

"About what?" I asked. I could barely see him in the dark bedroom.

"It's a girl, not a boy."

I probed out with my mind and tried to get a picture of the creature inside Jessica's belly. It resisted me successfully, for the most part, just as it resisted Jonathan's and Jessica's psychic proddings. But I was sure it was male, not female. I said so.

Jessica sat up in bed, her back against the headboard,

both hands on her moving stomach. "You're wrong, both of you. I think it's a boy *and* a girl. Or maybe neither one."

Jonathan turned on the bedside lamp in the house by the sea and looked at her. "What is that supposed to mean?"

She winced as the child within her struck out hard against her abdominal walls. "I'm in closer contact with it than either of you. I *sense* into it. It isn't like us."

"Then I was right," Jonathan said.

Jessica said nothing.

"If it's both sexes, or neither, it doesn't need *any* of us," he said. He turned off the light again. There was nothing else to do.

"Maybe we could kill it," I said.

"We couldn't," Jessica said.

"Jesus!" Jonathan said. "We can't even read its mind! If it can hold off all three of us like that, it can protect itself. Jesus!"

In the darkness, as the expletive echoed in the room, Jessica said, "Don't use that word, Jonathan. It's beneath us. We're above those old superstitions. We're the new breed. We have new emotions, new beliefs, new rules."

"For another month or so," I said.

AFTERWORD

When I was asked to do a short-short story for this book, I had just finished a 125,000-word novel and was beginning a book that would reach 200,000 words. A short-short seemed like a pleasant change of pace. It was not, of course. It was hell. Of course. For one thing, I had not written any science fiction in months. And I was accustomed to having room to develop character, plot, and theme; I found it nearly impossible to compress a meaningful story into so few words.

But I did it. Which is no pat on the back for me; instead, it is a pat on the back for science fiction. I have never felt comfortable as a science fiction novelist, but I've always been at home with the sf short story. While the sf novel has limits and requirements I no longer wish to worry about in my longer work, the short story is nowhere else as exciting and *alive*. And there is no other fiction that makes the short-short a viable form. In sf, 2,200 words can take on the form of a parable and *work*. Nowhere else. And in what other genre could a writer produce a serious short-short that also parodies one of the sacred plots of the employed category? Nowhere else. It was hell, of course. But it was fun.

Novels
MORE THAN HUMAN, by Theodore Sturgeon
PAPER DOLLS, by L.P. Davies

Short Stories
SOMETHING WICKED THIS WAY COMES, by Ray Bradbury
BABY IS THREE (section of MORE THAN HUMAN), by
   Theodore Sturgeon
BORN OF MAN AND WOMAN, by Richard Matheson
IT'S A GOOD LIFE, by Jerome Bixby

About Dean R. Koontz

Dean R. Koontz, b. 1945, has already published more than ten sf novels and a score of short stories in the field, one of which (BEASTCHILD) is under movie option and was nominated for a Hugo Award 1970. Presently working out of science fiction, however, he has sold mysteries and general novels to Dial, Atheneum, Random House, M. Evans, and others. HANGING ON, M. Evans, 1973, has been called the blackest and funniest war novel since CATCH-22. Mr. Koontz lives in Harrisburg, Pennsylvania, with his wife. He is completing a major suspense novel for Random House.

FUTURE SEX

AN OLD-FASHIONED GIRL

JOANNA RUSS

I woke up in a Vermont autumn morning, taking my guests home inside the glass cab while all around us the maples and sugar maples wheel slowly out of the fog. Only this part of the world can produce such color. We whispered at a walking pace through wet fires. Electric vehicles are quiet, too; we heard the drip of water from the leaves. When the house saw us, my old round lollipop-on-a-stick, it lit up from floor to top, and as we came nearer, broadcast the Second Brandenburg through the black, wet tree trunks and the fiery leaves, a delicate attention I allow myself and my guests from time to time. Shouting brilliantly through the wet woods—I prefer the unearthly purity of the electronic scoring.

One approaches the house from the side, where it looks almost flat on its central column—only a little convex, really—it doesn't squat down for you on chicken legs like Baba Yaga's hut, but lets down from above a great, coiling, metal-mesh road like a tongue (or so it seems; in reality it's only a winding staircase). Inside, you find yourself a corridor away from the main room; no use wasting heat.

Davy was there. The most beautiful man in the world. Our approach had given him time to make drinks for us, which my guests took from his tray, staring at him. But he wasn't embarrassed—curled up most unwaiterlike at my feet with his hands around his knees and proceeding to laugh at the right places in the conversation (he takes his cues from my face).

The main room is panelled in yellow wood with a carpet you can sleep on (brown) and a long, glassed-in porch from which we watch the blizzards sweep by five months out of the year. I like purely visual weather. It's warm enough for Davy to go around naked most of the time, my ice lad, in a cloud of gold hair and nudity, never so much

126

part of my home as when he sits on the rug with his back against a russet or vermilion chair (we mimic autumn here), his drowned blue eyes fixed on the sunset outside, his hair turned to ash, the muscles of his back and thighs stirring a little. The house hangs oddments from the ceiling: found objects, mobiles, can openers, red balls, bunches of wild grass. Davy plays with them.

I showed the guests around—calm Elinor, nervous Priss, pushy Kay. There were the books, the microfilm viewer in the library in touch with our regional library miles away, the storage spaces in the walls, the various staircases, the bathrooms molded of glass fiber and put together from two pieces, the mattresses stored in the walls of the guest rooms, and the conservatory (near the central core, to make use of the heat), where Davy comes and mimics wonder, watching the lights shine on my orchids, my palmettos, my bougainvillea, my whole little mess of tropical plants. I even have a glassed-in space for cacti. There are outside plantings where in season you can find mountain laurel, a tangled maze of rhododenron, scattered irises that look like an expensive, antique cross between insects and lingerie—but these will be under snow in a few weeks. I even have an electrified fence, inherited from the previous owner, that encloses the whole estate to keep out the deer and occasionally kills trees which take the mild climate around the house a little too much for granted.

I let my friends peep into the kitchen, which is an armchair with controls like a 707's, but not the place where I store my tools and from which I have access to the central core when House has indigestion. That's dirty, and you need to know what you're doing. I showed them Screen, which keeps me in touch with my neighbors, the nearest of whom is ten miles away; Telephone, who is my long-distance backup line; and Phonograph, where I store my music.

Priss said she didn't like her drink; it wasn't sweet enough. So I had Davy dial her another.

Do you want dinner? (I said)

And she blushed.

I woke later that day. Davy sleeps nearby. You've heard about blue-eyed blonds, haven't you? I passed into his room barefoot and watched him curled in sleep, unconscious, the golden veils of his eyelashes shadowing his cheeks, one arm thrown out into the streak of light falling onto him from the hall. It takes a lot to wake him (you can almost mount Davy in his sleep) but I was too sleepy to start right away and only squatted down by the mattress he sleeps on, tracing with my fingertips the patterns the hair made on his chest: broad high up, over the muscles, then narrowing toward his delicate belly (which rose and fell with his breathing), the line of hair to below the navel, and that suddenly stiff blossoming of the pubic hair in which his relaxed genitals nestled gently, like a rosebud.

I'm an old-fashioned girl.

I caressed his dry, velvety-skinned organ until it stirred in my hand, then ran my fingernails lightly down his sides to wake him up; I did the same—though very lightly—to the insides of his arms.

He opened his eyes and smiled starrily at me.

It's very pleasant to follow Davy's hairline around his neck with your tongue or nuzzle all the hollows of his long-muscled, swimmer's body; inside the elbows, the forearms, the places where the back tapers inward under the ribs, the backs of the knees. A naked man is a cross, the juncture elaborated in vulnerable and delicate flesh like the blossom on a banana tree, that place that's given me so much pleasure.

I nudged him gently and he shivered a little, bringing his legs together and spreading his arms flat; with my forefinger I made a transient white line on his neck. Little Davy was half-filled by now, which is a sign that Davy wants to be knelt over. I obliged, sitting across his thighs, and bending over him without touching his body, kissed him again and again on the mouth, the neck, the face, the shoulders. He is very, very exciting. He's very beautiful. Putting one arm under his shoulders to lift him up, I rubbed my nipples over his mouth, first one and then the other, which is nice for us both, and as he held on to my upper arms and let his head fall back, I pulled him to me, kneading his back muscles, kneading his buttocks, sliding down to the mattress with him. Little Davy is entirely filled out now.

So lovely: Davy with his head thrown to one side, eyes

closed, his strong fingers clenching and unclenching. He began to arch his back, and his sleepiness made him a little too quick for me. I pressed Small Davy between thumb and forefinger just enough to slow him down and then—when I felt like it—playfully started to mount him, rubbing the tip of him, nipping him a little on the neck. His breathing in my ear, fingers convulsively closing on mine.

I played with him a little more, tantalizing him, then swallowed him whole like a watermelon seed—so fine inside! with Davy moaning, his tongue inside my mouth, his blue gaze shattered, his whole body uncontrollably arched, all his sensation concentrated in the place where I held him.

I don't do this often, but that time I made him come by slipping a finger in his anus: convulsions, fires, crying in no words as the sensation was pulled out of him. If I had let him take more time, I would have climaxed with him, but he's stiff for quite a while after he comes, and I prefer that; I like the after-tremors and the after-hardness, slipperier and more pliable than before; Davy has an eerie malleability at those times. I grasped him internally, I pressed down on him, enjoying in one act his muscular throat, the hair under his arms, his knees, the strength of his back and buttocks, his beautiful face, the fine skin on the inside of his thighs. Kneaded and bruised him, hiccoughing inside with all my architecture: little buried rod, swollen lips, and grabby sphincter, the flexing half-moon under the pubic bone. And everything else in the vicinity, no doubt.

I'd had him. Davy was mine. Sprawled blissfully over him—I was discharged down to my fingertips but still quietly throbbing—it had really been a good one. His body so wet under me and inside me.

And looked up to see—

Priss. Elinor. Kay.

"For Heaven's sakes, is *that* all!" said Elinor to Priss.

I got up, tickled him with the edge of a fingernail, and joined them at the door. "Stay, Davy." This is one of the key words that the house "understands"; the central computer will transmit a pattern of signals to the implants in his brain and he will stretch out obediently on his mattress; when I say to the main computer "Sleep," Davy will sleep. He's a lovely limb of the house. The original germ-plasm was chimpanzee, I think, but none of the behavior is organically controlled any more. True, he does have his minimal actions which he pursues without me—he eats, eliminates, sleeps, and climbs in and out of his exercise box—but even these are caused by a standing computer pattern. And I take precedence, of course.

It is theoretically possible that Davy has (tucked away in some nook of his cerebrum) consciousness of a kind that may never even touch his active life—is Davy a poet in his own peculiar way?—but I prefer to believe not. His consciousness—such as it is, and I am willing to grant it for the sake of argument—is nothing but the permanent possibility of sensation, a mere intellectual abstraction, a nothing, a picturesque collocation of words. It is experientially quite empty, and above all, it is nothing that need concern you and me. Davy's soul lies somewhere else; it's an outside soul. Davy's soul is in Davy's beauty.

"Leucotomized," said Kay, her voice heavy with outrage. "Lobotomized! Kidnapped in childhood!"

"Nonsense," said Elinor. "They're extinct. Have been for decades. What is it?" So I told them. Elinor put her arm around Kay—I think I told you I was an old-fashioned girl—and explained serenely to Kay that there was a popular misconception that in the past men had had Janies as I had a Davy, that women had been to men what Davy was to me, but that was a legend. That was utter nonsense. "Popular ignorance," said Elinor. She would tell us the real story some other time.

Priss was staring and staring. "Is he expensive?" she said (and blushed). I let her borrow him—we had to modify some of his programming, of course—so we tiptoed out and left them; it was the first time, Priss said, she had ever seen such soul in a creature's eyes.

And she's right. She's right, you know. Davy's soul is in Davy's beauty; it's poignant that Davy himself can never experience his own soul. Beauty is all that matters in him, and Beauty is always empty, always on the outside.

Isn't it?

freedom? (Norman Spinrad wrote a story about this, about losing touch with reality.)

As science fiction writers writing about sex, we are still engaged in digesting the past and expressing the present—we haven't yet even approached our future.

Novels
THE LEFT HAND OF DARKNESS, by Ursula K. LeGuin
THE DISAPPEARANCE, by Philip Wylie

Nonfiction
HUMAN SEXUAL RESPONSE, by Masters and Johnson

Short Stories
WHEN IT CHANGED, by Joanna Russ
THE CRIME AND GLORY OF COMMANDER SUZDAL, by Cordwainer Smith
CONSIDER HER WAYS, by John Wyndham
THE ADVENTURESS, by Joanna Russ
THE BARBARIAN, by Joanna Russ

About Joanna Russ

Joanna Russ, b. 1937, was educated and has taught at Cornell; she is currently teaching at the State University of New York. A novelist (AND CHAOS DIED, PICNIC ON PARADISE), short story writer (winner of 1972 Nebula award for "When It Changed"), and critic, she lives in Binghamton, New York and has recently completed her third novel.

FUTURE SEX*

CATMAN

HARLAN ELLISON

The thief materialized in the shadow of a conversing waterfall. The air sparked like a dust circuit for a moment, and then he was there; back flat to the wall, a deeper black against the shadow, a stretch fabric suit and hood covering every inch of his body from feet to fingertips. Only his eyes were naked to the night. He stood there, motionless, as the waterfall talked to itself. It had been programmed to deter suicides, and it was reciting reassurances.

"You don't really think you'll find peace in killing yourself, do you?" the waterfall bubbled. "Who knows what lies on the other side? Perhaps it'll be just the same, and you'll be aware of yourself as an entity, but you'll be dead, and helpless to save yourself, and you'll spend who-knows-how-long—perhaps an eternity—suffering the same anguish you knew when you were alive. But you'll be trapped in death, and unable to get out. Wouldn't that be awful? Instead, why don't we talk about what's troubling you—"

The thief dematerialized; the waterfall splashed on to itself.

He reappeared on the fiftieth level, in a frozen park. Standing beside a juniper encased in luminescent blue ice, he came into existence, checked the bag of electronic

* Why two stories on future sex when every other theme is given but one? Well, in the first place, if any theme is going to be treated twice so intensely, what better in this liberated/unliberated era than sex? In the second place, it seems only fair that both sexes have a fair chance at it, and Ellison and Russ are certainly distinguished spokespersons. And in the third place we liked both stories. They are irreplaceable statements which neither overlap nor oppose, but illustrate the richness and diversity of this field in showing how, striking from the same source, good writers can find an infinity of (or at least two) solutions.

134

alarm-confounders, satisfied himself it was tied on securely, and started to wink-out again. He paused, half dematerialized, and stared across the park at the diorama of the Neanderthalers driving a herd of ibex off a cliff. The ice block was enormous, holding the cliff, the chasm, thirty of the graceful horned beasts, and half a hundred cavemen. It had been quarried from a site in Krapina, Yugoslavia by a timelock team that had frozen the moment 110,000 years before. It was an excellent display, art-directed by someone prestigious, perhaps Boltillon under a grant from Therox.

For a moment longer he considered the great scene, thinking how trapped they were, thinking how free he was, not even walls of ice to contain him. Then he vanished.

He came back to existence, brute matter, on the three-quarter inch ledge outside a dreamcell apartment on the ninetieth level. He was flattened against the force screen that served as its outer wall. It was opaque, and he lay against it like a smear of rainbow oil. He could not be seen from inside, where the wealthy ones he intended to rob lay quietly, dreaming. But he could be seen by the scanning tower at the top of the Westminster Cathedral complex. Invisible beams blanketed London from the tower, watching. Registering intrusive action. He smiled and withdrew one of the confounders from the bag. It was a ladybug deranger; he palmed it onto the force screen wall and it tapped into the power source, and he felt the tension ease. Then he diffused himself, and reappeared inside the dreamcell.

The family lay in their pods, the gel rippling ever so slightly at every muscle spasm. The inner walls were a dripping golden lustrousness, molten metal running endlessly down into bottomless depths where the floor should have been. He had no idea what they were dreaming, but the women were lying moistly locked together in *soixante-neuf* and the men were wearing reflective metal headache bands over their eyes. The men were humming in soprano tones.

He vanished and reappeared in the lock room. The force screens were up, protecting the valuables, and the thief went down on his haunches, the bag of confounders dangling between his thighs. He whistled softly to himself, considering the proper tool, and finally withdrew a starfish passby. It scuttled across the floor and touched a screen with its dorsal cirri. The screens sputtered, changing hue, then winked out. The thief dematerialized and reappeared inside the vault.

He ignored the jewelry and the credit cards and selected the three pressure-capped tubes of Antarean soulradiant, worth, on the black market, all the jewels in the lock room.

He disassembled himself and winked back into existence outside the force screen perimeter, retrieved the starfish, and vanished again, to appear on the ledge. The ladybug went into the bag, and he was gone once more.

When he materialized on the fifty-first level, in the Fuller Geodex, the Catman was waiting, and before the thief could vanish again, the policeman had thrown up a series of barriers that would have required everything in the bag to counteract, plus a few the thief had not considered necessary on this job.

The Catman had a panther, a peregrine falcon and two cheetahs with him. They were inside the barrier ring, and they were ready. The falcon sat on the Catman's forearm, and the cats began padding smoothly toward the thief.

"Don't make me work them," the Catman said.

The thief smiled, though the policeman could not see it. The hood covered the thief's face. Only the eyes were naked. He stared at the Catman in his skin cape and sunburst eagle's helmet. They were old acquaintances.

The cheetahs circled, narrowing in toward him. He teleported himself to the other side of the enclosed space. The Catman hissed at the falcon and it soared aloft, dove at the thief, and flew through empty space. The thief stood beside the Catman.

"Earn your pay," the thief said. His voice was muffled. It would make a voice-print, but not an accurate one; it would be insufficient in a court of law.

The Catman made no move to touch the thief. There was no point to it. "You can't avoid me much longer."

"Perhaps not." He vanished as the panther slid toward him on its belly, bunching itself to strike.

"But then, perhaps I don't want to," he said.

The Catman hissed again, and the falcon flew to his armored wrist. "Then why not come quietly. Let's be civilized."

The thief chuckled deep in his throat, but without humor. "That seems to be the problem right there." The cheetahs passed through space he no longer occupied.

"You're simply all too bloody marvelous civilized; I crave a little crudeness."

"We've had this conversation before," said the Catman, and there was an odd note of weariness in his voice . . . for an officer of the law at last in a favorable position with an old adversary. "Please surrender quietly; the cats are nervous tonight; there was a glasscab accident on the thirty-sixth and they wafted a strong blood scent. It's difficult holding them in check."

As he spoke, the pavane of strike and vanish, hold and go, pounce and invisibility continued, around and around the perimeter ring. Overhead, the Fuller Geodex absorbed energy from the satellite power stars DayDusk&DawnCo, Ltd. had thrown into the sky, converted the energy to the city's use, providing from its silver mesh latticework the juice to keep London alive. It was the Geodex dome that held sufficient backup force to keep the perimeter ring strong enough to thwart the thief. He dodged in and out of reach of the cats; the falcon tracked him, waiting.

"It's taking you longer to do it each time," said the Catman.

The thief dematerialized five times rather quickly as the two cheetahs worked an inwardly spiraling pattern, pressing him toward a center where the panther waited patiently. "Worry about yourself," he said, breathing hard.

The falcon dove from the Catman's shoulder in a shallow arc, its wingspread slicing a fourth of the ring at head-height. The thief materialized, lying on his back, at the inner edge of the ring behind the Catman.

The panther bunched and sprang, and the thief rolled away, the stretch suit suddenly open down one side as the great cat's claws ripped the air. Then the thief was gone . . .

. . . to reappear behind the panther.

The thief held the ladybug deranger in his palm. Even as the panther sensed the presence behind him, the thief slapped the deranger down across the side of the massive head. Then the thief blinked out again.

The panther bolted, rose up on its hind legs and, without a sound, exploded.

Gears and cogs and printed circuits and LSI chips splattered against the inside of the perimeter ring . . . bits of pseudoflesh and infra-red eyeballs and smears of lubricant sprayed across the invisible bubble.

The empty husk of what had been the panther lay smoking in the center of the arena. The thief appeared beside the Catman. He said nothing.

The Catman looked away. He could not stare at the refuse that had been black swiftness moments before. The thief said, "I'm sorry I had to do that."

There was a piping, sweet note in the air, and the cheetahs and the falcon froze. The falcon on the Catman's shoulder, the cheetahs sniffing at the pile of death with its stench of ozone. The tone came again. The Catman heaved a sigh, as though he had been released from some great oppression. A third time, the tone, followed by a woman's voice: "Shift end, Officer. Your jurisdiction ends now. Thank you for your evening's service. Goodspeed to you, and we'll see you nextshift, tomorrow at eleven-thirty p:m." The tone sounded once more—it was pink—and the perimeter ring dissolved.

The thief stood beside the Catman for a few more moments. "Will you be all right?"

The Catman nodded slowly, still looking away.

The thief watched him for a moment longer, then vanished. He reappeared at the far side of the Geodex and looked back at the tiny figure of the Catman, standing unmoving. He continued to watch till the police officer walked to the heap of matted and empty blackness, bent and began gathering up the remnants of the panther. The thief watched silently, the weight of the Antarean soul-radiant somehow oppressively heavy in the bag of confounders.

The Catman took a very long time to gather up his dead stalker. The thief could not see it from where he stood, so far away, but he knew the Catman was crying.

The air sparked around him . . . as though he had not quite decided to teleport himself . . . and in fact he had

not been able to make the decision . . . and the air twin-
kled with infinitesimal scintillae . . . holes made in the
fabric of normal space through which the displaced air was
drawn, permitting the thief to teleport . . . the sparkling
points of light actually the deaths of muons as they were
sucked through into that not-space . . . and still he could
not decide.

Then he vanished and reappeared beside the Catman.

"Can I help you?"

The Catman looked away quickly. But the thief saw the
tears that had run down the Catman's black cheeks. "No,
thank you, I'll be all right. I'm almost finished here." He
held a paw.

The thief drew in a deep breath, "Will you be home for
dinner tonight?"

The Catman nodded. "Tell your mother I'll be along in
a little while."

The thief went away from there, in twenty level leaps,
quickly, trying not to see a black hand holding an even
blacker paw.

They sit silently at the dinner table. Neil Leipzig cannot
look at his father. He sits cross-legged on the thin pneu-
matic cushion, the low teak table before him; the
Estouffade de boeuf on his plate vanishes and reappears.
It is wallaby, smothered in wine sauce and "cellar vege-
tables" from sub-level sixteen-North. It continues to
appear and disappear.

"Stop playing with your food," Neil Leipzig's mother
says, sharply.

"Leave me alone; I'm not hungry," he says.

They sit silently. His father addresses his food, and eats
quickly but neatly.

"How was your shiftday?" Neil Leipzig's mother says.

Neither of the men looks up. She repeats the question,
adding, "Lew." His father looks up, nods abstractedly,
does not answer, returns to his plate.

"Why is it impossible to get a civil word out of you in
the evening," she says. There is an emerging tone in her
voice, a tone of whitewater rapids just beyond the bend.
"I ask: why is it impossible for you to speak to your
family?"

Keep eating, don't let her do it to you again, Neil Leipzig thinks. He moves the cubes of soybean curd around in the *sauce madère* until they are all on the right side of the plate. *Keep silent, tough up*, he thinks.

"Lewis!"

His father looks up. "I think I'll go downstairs and take a nap, after dinner." His eyes seem very strange; there is a film over them; something gelatinous; as though he is looking out from behind a thick, semi-opaque membrane; neither Neil nor his mother can read the father's thoughts from those eyes.

She shakes her head and snorts softly, as though she is infinitely weary of dealing with those who persist in their arrogance and stupidity; there was none of that in what the father had said. *Let him alone, can't you?* Neil Leipzig thinks.

"We're out of deeps," the mother says.

"I won't need them," the father says.

"You know you can't sleep without a deep, don't try and tell me you can. We're out, someone will have to order more."

Neil Leipzig stands up. "I'll order them; finish your dinner."

He goes into the main room and punches out the order on the board. He codes it to his mother's personal account. Let *her* pay, he thinks. The confirmation tones sound, and he returns to the table. From the delivery chute comes the sound of the spansules arriving. He stands there staring down at his parents, at the top of his father's head, black and hairless, faintly mottled; at his mother's face, pale and pink, heavily freckled from the treatment machine she persists in using though the phymech advises her it is having a deleterious effect on her skin: she wants a tan for her own reasons but is too fair and redheaded for it to take, and she merely freckles. She has had plasticwork done on her eyes, they slant in a cartoon imitation of the lovely Oriental curve.

He is brown.

"I have to go out for a while."

His father looks up. Their eyes meet.

"No. Nothing like that," he lies. His father looks away.

His mother catches the exchange. "Is there something new between you two?"

Neil turns away. She follows him with her eyes as he starts for the tunnel to his own apartments. "Neil! What *is* all this? Your father acts like a burnout, you won't eat, I've had just about enough of this! Why do you two continue to torment me, haven't I had enough heartache from the both of you? Now you come back here, right here, right now, I want us to have this out." He stops.

He turns around. His expression is a disguise.

"Mother, do us both a favor," he says, quite clearly, "kindly shut your mouth and leave me alone." He goes into the tunnel, is reduced to a beam of light, is fired through the tunnel to his apartments seven miles away across the arcology called London, is retranslated, vanishes.

His mother turns to her husband. Alone now, freed of even the minor restraints imposed on her by the presence of her son, she assumes a familiar emotional configuration. "Lewis."

He wants to go lie down. He wants that very much.

"I want to know!"

He shakes his head gently. He merely wants to be left alone. There is very little of the Catman now; there is almost too much of Lewis Leipzig. "Please, Karin . . . it was a miserable shiftday."

She slips her blouse down off one perfect breast. The fine powder-white lines of the plasticwork radiate out from the meaty nipple, sweep down and around and disappear under the lunar curve. He watches, the film over his eyes growing darker, more opaque. "Don't," he says.

She touches a blue-enameled fingernail to the nipple, indenting it slightly. "There'll be bed tonight, Lewis."

He starts to rise.

"There'll be bed, and sex, and other things if you don't tell me, Lewis."

He slumps back into his round-shouldered dining position. He can hear the whine of generators far back in his memory. And the odor of dead years. And oil slicks across stainless steel. And the rough sensuality of burlap.

"He was out tonight. Robbery on the ninetieth level.

He got away with three tubes of the Antarean soul-radiant."

She covers her breast, having won her battle with nasty weaponry, rotted memories. "And you couldn't stop him."

"No. I couldn't stop him."

"And what else?"

"I lost the panther."

Her expression is a combination of amazement and disgust. "He destroyed it?" Her husband nods; he cannot look at her. "And it'll be charged against your account." He does not nod; she knows the answer.

"That's it for the promotion, and that's it for the permutations. Oh, God, you're such a burnout . . . I can't stand you!"

"I'm going to lie down."

"You just sit there. Now listen to me, damn you, Lewis Leipzig. *Listen!* I will *not* go another year without being rejuvenated. You'll *get* that promotion and you'll get it bringing him in. Or I'll make you wish I'd never filed for you." He looks at her sharply. She knows what he's thinking, knows the reply; but he doesn't say it; he never does.

He gets up and walks toward the dropshaft in the main room. Her voice stops him. "You'll make up your mind, Lewis."

He turns on her. The film is gone from his eyes. "It's our son, Karin. Our son!"

"He's a thief," she says. The edge in her voice is a special viciousness. "A thief in a time when theft is unnecessary. We have everything. Almost everything. You know what he does with what he steals. You know what he's become. That's no son of mine. Yours, if you want that kind of filth around you, but no son of mine. God knows I have little enough to live for, and I'm not going to allow your spinelessness to take *that* from me. I want my permutation. You'll do it, Lewis, or so help me God—"

He turns away again. Hiding his face from her, he says, "I'm only permitted to stalk him during regulation hours, you know that."

"Break the regs."

He won't turn around. "I'm a Catman. I can't do that. I'm bound."

"If you don't, I'll see that someone else does."

"I'm beginning not to care."

"Have it your way."

"Your way."

"My way then. But my way *whichever* way."

He vanishes into the main room and a moment later she hears the dropshaft hiss. She sits at the table staring into the mid-distance, remembering. Her face softens and flows, and lines of weariness superimpose themselves over her one-hundred-and-sixty-five-year-old youthful face. She drops her face into her hand, runs the fingers up through her thick coppery hair, the metal fingernails making tiny clicking noises against the fibers and follicles. She makes a sound deep in her throat. Then she stiffens her back and rises. She stands there for several moments, listening to the past; she shrugs the robe from her slim, pale body and follows her husband's path to the dropshaft.

The dining salon is empty. From the main room comes the hiss of the dropshaft. Menials purr from the walls and clean up the dining area. Below, punishment and coercion reduce philosophies to diamond dust and suet.

Seven miles away, the thief reappears in his cool apartments. The sights and sounds of what he has overheard and seen between his parents, hidden in the main room till his father left his mother, tremble in his mind. He finds himself rubbing the palm of his left hand up the wall, rubbing over and over without control; his hand hurts from the friction but he doesn't stop. He rubs and rubs till his palm is bloody. Then he vanishes, illegally.

Sub-level one:eleven-Central was converted to ocean. Skipboats sliced across from Oakwood on the eastern shore to Caliban on the western cliffs. In the coves and underwater caves sportsmen hunted loknesses, bringing home trophies that covered large walls. Music was bubble-cast across the water. Plankton beaneries bobbed like buoys near the tourist shores. Full Fathom Five had gotten four stars in *The Epicure* and dropshafts carried diners to the bottom to dine in elegance while watching the electro stims put on their regularly scheduled shows among the kelp beds. Neil Leipzig emerged into the pulsing ochre throat of the reception area, and was greeted by the maitre d'.

"Good evening, Max. Would Lady Effim and her party be here yet?"

The maitre d' smiled and his neck-slits opened and closed to reveal a pink moistness. "Not yet, Mr. Leipzig. Would you care to wait at the bar? Or one of the rooms?"

"I'll be at the bar. Would you let them know I'm here when they arrive?"

The thief let the undulant carry him into the bar and he slid into a seat beside the great curved pressure window. The kelp beds were alive with light and motion.

"Sir?"

The thief turned from watching the light-play. A domo hovered at the edge of the starburst-shaped table. "Oh. A chin-chin, please, a little heavier on the Cinzano." The domo hummed a thankyou and swirled away. Neil Leipzig turned back to the phantasmagoria beyond the pressure window. A bubble of music struck the window and burst just beyond the thief's nose. He knew the tune.

"Neil."

The thief saw her reflection, dimly, in the window. He did not turn around for a moment, gathering his feelings. "Joice," he said, finally. "Nice to see you again."

"Then why don't you turn around so you *can*."

He let the seat turn him toward her.

She was still remarkable. He wanted to see dust marks on her loveliness, product of treachery and floating ethics, but he knew she had not really been treacherous, and if there had been an ethical failure, it had been his.

"May I sit?"

"I'm going to be joining a party in a few minutes, but please . . ." He waved her to the seat beside him. She settled into it, crossing her legs. The chiton opened and revealed smooth thigh vanishing up into ivory fabric. "How have you been?"

"I've been excellent, Neil. Breve sends his best."

"That was unnecessary."

"I'm trying to be reasonable, Neil. It's been a long time and I'm uncomfortable with it this way between us."

"Be comfortable. I've got it all straight."

"I'm trying to be friendly."

"Just be reasonable, that'll be enough."

The domo came bobbing through the room and hovered beside the table. It set the chin-chin down. The thief sipped and nodded acceptance. "Lady?" the domo hummed.

"Nothing for me, thanks."

The domo shot straight up and went away just below ceiling height.

"Are you still doing dust?" she asked.

He stiffened and his eyes came to her face with anger as he stopped watching the domo. "Your manners haven't improved any with time."

She started to say I'm sorry. But his anger continued to sheet: "If we run out on *that* topic, we can always discuss Breve's throat!"

"Oh, God, Neil, that's unfair . . . unfair and *lousy!*"

"I understand from one of the twinkle boys that Breve's using some new steroid vexing agent and a stim-sensitive synthetic that lets him vibrate it like mad. Must be terrific for you . . . when he's not with twinkles."

Joice pressed a fingertip against the room-call plate set into the surface of the starburst-shaped table. Near the reception area Max heard the tone on his console, noted it was Neil Leipzig's table, punched up an empty, and made a mental note to let Lady Effim know the thief was in a room, when she and her party arrived. At the starburst-shaped table, the number 22 pulsed in the translucent face of the room-call plate.

"All right, Neil. Enough already. Overkill doesn't become you."

She stood up.

"And mealy-mouth attempts at *bonhomie* don't become you."

He stood up.

"It's simply I see no reason why we have to be on the outs. There are still some good memories."

Side-by-side, they walked across the enormous dining room of the Full Fathom Five, toward the curving wall of glass-fronted private rooms.

"Look, Joice: I don't want to talk about it. You stopped to talk to *me*, remember? I didn't force myself on *you*."

"Just now, or three years ago?"

He couldn't help laughing. "Point for you," he said, opening the door to the private room. The magnifying glass of the room's front wall curved the diners beyond into a mere smear of moving color. From outside, the tableau in the room was cast large for anyone to watch.

"I'm sorry I said that about the dust," Joice said, slipping the soft fabric of the chiton off her shoulders. It floated to the floor like fog.

"I'm not sorry about my comments where Breve is concerned," Neil replied. Naked, he moved his shoulder blades in a loosening movement, realizing the scene with his parents had made him unbelievably tense. He slid into the free-fall cumulus fizz and lay on his back.

"Gardyloo!" she said, and dove into the mist beside him. Her long auburn hair floated wildly around her head.

"What the hell's all this in aid of, Joice?" the thief said. She rolled him under her, sitting astride his thighs, positioning herself above his erect penis.

"Peaceful coexistence," she said, and settled down slowly till he was deep up inside her.

"Has he filed for you?"

"No."

"Does he intend to?"

"I have no idea."

"You've gotten more *laissez-faire* since we were a pair. I can't recall a week when you weren't badgering me to file."

"I loved you."

"And you don't love Breve."

She moved her hips in a circular pattern. He contracted and expanded his penis in a steady pulse. She leaned back and rested her hands on his upper thighs, sliding up and down smoothly.

"I didn't say I don't love Breve. He just hasn't filed and it isn't a problem at the moment."

"Why don't *you* file for *him?*"

"Don't be cruel; you *know* Breve isn't in the Pool."

"So what *is* the problem? Twinkles?"

"Don't be ridiculous."

He freed one hand and, pressing her lower lips, very gently sought out and stroked the mercury heaviness of her clitoris. She shuddered and opened her eyes, then they slid closed once more.

"Then what is?"

"There's nothing wrong between us. He's doing very well, his work is going well, and I'm fulfilled. It's a good merging."

She spasmed, from deep in her stomach muscles, and he felt her contracting around him. When she climaxed it was with a succession of small ignitions. He continued touching her, maintaining a rhythm, and she spiraled upward through a chain of multiple orgasms till she dropped her upper body onto him, reached under to grasp his buttocks, and thrust herself up and down rapidly. He thought of metal surfaces.

She forced air through her clenched teeth and groaned from low in her throat, and he felt her rising for the final ascent. When it came, Neil held his breath and could feel the sudden cessation of her heartbeat. They rolled and turned in the free-fall mist, and Joice spasmed for half a minute.

They lay locked together for a time, and then she raised her head and looked down at him. "Nothing happened."

"For me. You're fine."

"Too much dust, Neil?"

"Too little interest."

"I don't believe that."

"Life is filled with little disappointments."

"You make me feel sad."

"Life is filled with little disappointments."

She pulled off him and reached for a moist and scented serviette in a dispenser on the wall. She dried herself between her legs and swam out of the fizz. Neil Leipzig lay on his back, at a forty-five degree angle to the floor, hanging artfully in mid-air, and watched her. "I don't regret losing you, Joice. I have more to work with, now that your appetites are satisfied at other groaning boards."

"Spare me the metaphors, Neil. Are you aware that in most circles you're considered ridiculous?"

"I seldom travel in those circles. It must get you dizzy."

"Hurting each other won't make the past more liveable."

"I don't live in the past."

"That's right. I forgot. You live in tin cans."

He felt his face getting hot. Too close, she'd come too

close with that one. "Goodbye, Joice. Don't slam the door."

She draped the chiton over her arm, opened the door, and stepped partially into the dining room proper. "Don't get metal splinters in your cock." She smiled a smile of victory and closed the door behind her. Softly.

He watched her striding across the Full Fathom Five to join a group of Twinkles, Dutchgirls, a Duenna . . . and Breve. As she moved, she was comically distorted by the magnifying window. It was like watching her stride through rainbows. She sat down with them and Breve helped her into the chiton. Neil smiled and with a shrug reached for a serviette.

The door opened, and the maitre d' stuck his head in. "Mr. Leipzig, Lady Effim and her party have arrived. The coral room. Would you like your drink sent over?"

"Thank you, Max. No, a fresh one, please. Chin-chin, a little heavier on the Cinzano. And tell Lady Effim I'll be there in a moment."

He lay in the fizz for a few minutes, thinking of metal surfaces, his eyes closed, fists clenched.

The thief had no real, concrete data on what Lady Effim's side-boys did to earn their keep, but he was gut certain it was at least partially sexual in nature; and Neil Leipzig did not dismiss the possibility that another part of their services dealt with various deaths; and that another substantial expenditure of their time in her behalf was legitimately connected with the continent she owned and exploited; and that other time was spent in *il*legitimate pursuits; and darker times spent in places, and doing things, the thief did not wish to dwell on.

The side-boys numbered three this time. Sometimes Lady Effim had six, sometimes eight, sometimes a squad. Never less than three. This time there were three.

One was obviously a twinkle: fishtailed hair parted in the middle, tinted blue-black like the barrel of a weapon, giving off the warm odor of musk and jasmine. Very slim; hands delicate and skin of the hands so pale Neil could see the calligraphy of blue veins clearly outlined; large nostrils that scooped air so the twinkle's chest rose and fell noticeably; skintight weskit suit with metal conchos and leather thongs down both sides; heavy on the jewelry.

"Neil, I'd like you to meet Cuusadou . . ."

The second was some kind of professional student: his like were to be found in the patiently seated waiting lines of the career bureaus, always ready to file for some obscure and pointless occupation—numismatist, dressage instructor, Neurospora geneticist, epitaphologist, worm rancher. His face was long and horsy; his tongue was long and he could bend its tip back on itself; he wore the current fashion, velvet jodhpurs, boots, rhodium manacles with jeweled locks, dark wraparound glasses. He had bad skin and his fingernails were long, but the quicks were bitten and bloody down around the moons.

". . . and Fill . . ."

The third was a killer. He made no movement. His eyes stared straight ahead and Neil perceived the psychotic glaze. He did not look at the third man for more than a second. It was painful.

". . . and Mr. Robert Mossman."

She invited him to join them, and Neil took the empty formfit where the domo had set his chin-chin. He settled into the chair and crossed his legs. "How've you been?"

Lady Effim smiled a long, thin smile of memories and expectations. "Warm. And you?"

"All right, I suppose."

"How is your father?"

"Excellent. He sends his best."

"That was unnecessary."

Neil laughed. "Less than an hour ago I said the same thing to someone. Excuse me; I'm a little cranky tonight."

She waved away his apology with a friendly, imperious gesture. "Has the city changed much?"

"Since when?"

"Last time." That had been six years earlier.

"Some. They turned the entire fourteenth level into crystal cultures. Beautiful. Peculiar. Waste of space. Helluva controversy, lot of people making speeches, the screens were full of it. I went off to the Hebrides."

She laughed. The crepe texture of her facial skin made it an exercise in origami. Neil gave it a moment's thought: having sex with this creature, this power, this force of nature. It was more than wealth that kept three such as these with this woman. Neil began to understand the attraction. The cheekbones, the timbre of her voice, ice.

"Still vanishing, Neil?" She said it with amusement.

"You're playing with me."

"Only a little. I have a great affection for you, darling. You amuse me. You know that. You amuse me."

"How are things in Australia?"

Lady Effim turned to Fill. For the answer.

"Cattle production is up two hundred per cent, trawling acreage is yielding half a million barrels of lettuce a month, tithes are up point three three over last year at this time, and Standard & Poor's Index closed up eight points today."

Neil smiled. "What about all the standard poor bastards who were wiped out when the tsunami hit two weeks ago?"

Everyone stopped smiling. Lady Effim sat straighter and her left hand—which had been dangling a gold-link chain and baited fish-hook in her jeroboam snifter of brandy in an attempt to snag the Antarean piranha before it bellied-up—the hand made a convulsive clenching movement. The killer's eyes came off dead center and snapped onto the thief with an almost audible click: the sound of armaments locked into firing position. Neil held his breath.

"Mr. Mossman," Lady Effim said, slowly, "*no*."

The air began to scintillate around Neil.

"Neil," said Lady Effim.

He stopped. The air settled. Mr. Robert Mossman went back to rigidity.

Lady Effim smiled. It reminded the thief of an open wound. "You've grown suicidal in six years, Neil darling. Something unpleasant is happening to you; you're not the sweet, dashing lad I used to know. Death-wish?"

Neil smiled back, it seemed the thing to do. "Getting reckless in my declining years. I'm going to have to come visit your continent one of these days, m'Lady."

She turned to the twinkle. "Cuusadou, what are we doing for the company peasants who were affected by the disaster?"

The twinkle leaned forward and, with relish, said, "An absolutely splendid advertising campaign, Lady Effim: squawk, solids, car-cards, wandering evangelists, rumors, and in three days a major holo extravaganza. Our people have been on it since almost before the tide went out.

Morale is very high. We've established competition between the cities: The one that mounts the most memorable
mass burial ceremony gets a new sports arena. Morale is
very high." He looked pleased.

"Thank you, darling," she said. She turned back to
Neil. "I am a kind and benevolent ruler."

Neil smiled and spread his hands. "Your pardon."

It went that way for the better part of an hour.

Finally, Lady Effim said to Fill, "Darling, would you
secure the area, please." The professional student fiddled
with the jeweled lock on the right-wrist manacle, and a
sliding panel in the manacle opened to reveal a row of
tiny dials under a fingernail-sized meter readout window.
He turned the dials and a needle in the meter window
moved steadily from one side to the other. When it had
snugged up against the far side, he nodded obsequiously
to Lady Effim.

"Good. We're alone. I gather you've been up to some
nasty tricks, Neil darling. You haven't been teleporting
illegally when you were off-shift, have you?" She wore a
nasty smile that should have been on display in a museum.

"I have something you want," Neil said, ignoring the
chop. She knew he was breaking the regs at this very
moment:

"I have to go out for a while."

His father looks up. Their eyes meet.

"No. Nothing like that," he lies. His father looks away.

*He rubs and rubs till his palm is bloody. Then he
vanishes, illegally.*

"I'm sure you do, Neil *mon cher*. You always do. But
what could *I* possibly have that would interest *you*? If
you want something you go to the cornucopia and you
punch it up and those cunning little atoms are rearranged
cunningly and there you have it. Isn't that the way it's
done?"

"There are things one can't get . . ."

"But those are illegal, darling. *So* illegal. And it seems
foolish to want one of the few things you *can't* have in a
world that permits virtually *every*thing."

"There are still taboos."

"I can't conceive of such a thing, Neil dear."

"Force yourself."

"I'm a woman of very simple tastes."

"The radiant."

It was only the most imperceptible of movements, but Neil Leipzig knew the blood had stopped pumping in Lady Effim's body. Beneath her chalky powder she went white. He saw the thinnest line of the biting edges of her teeth.

"So you did it."

Now the smile was Neil Leipzig's.

"A thief in a time of plenty. So you did it. You clever lad." Her eyes closed and she was thinking of the illegal Antarean drug. Here was a thrill she had never had. Farewell to ennui. She would, of course, have it, at any cost. Even a continent. It was a seller's market.

"What do you want?"

She would have it at any cost. Human lives: these three, his own. His father's.

His mother's.

"What do you want, Neil?"

His thoughts were a million miles away. A lie. They were only arcology levels above and across London.

"*You!* What do you want?"

So he told her.

He would have preferred the other three not be there. The look of revulsion on their faces—even the zombie Mr. Robert Mossman's—made him defensive.

Lady Effim sneered. It did not become her. "You shall have it, Neil. As often as you care to go, God help you." She paused, looked at him in a new way. "Six years ago . . . when I knew you . . . were you . . ."

"No, not then."

"I never would have thought—of all the people I know, and you may be assured, dear boy, I know oddnesses beyond description—of all I know, I would have thought you were the last to . . ."

"I don't want to hear this."

"Of course not, how gauche of me. Of course, you shall have what you need. When I have. What. I. Need."

"I'll take you to it."

She seemed amused. "Take *me* there? Don't be silly, dear boy. I'm a very famous, very powerful, very influential person. I have no truck with stolen merchandise, not even any as exotic and lovely as soul-radiant." She turned to the killer. "Mr. Mossman. You will go with Neil and obtain three tubes from where he has them secreted. No, don't look suspicious, Neil will deliver precisely what he has said he would deliver. He understands we are both dealing in good faith."

The twinkle said, "But he's . . ."

"It is not our place to make value-judgments, darling. Neil is a sweet boy, and what he needs he shall have." To Mr. Robert Mossman: "When you have the three tubes, call me here." To the thief: "When I receive Mr. Mossman's call, Fill will make the arrangements and you'll receive very explicit instructions where to go, and when. Is that satisfactory?"

Neil nodded, his stomach tight, his head beginning to hurt. He did not like their knowing.

"Now," Lady Effim said, "goodbye, Neil."

"I don't think I would care to see you again. Ever. You understand this contains no value-judgment, merely a preference on my part."

She did not offer her hand to be kissed as he and Mr. Robert Mossman rose to leave the table.

The thief materialized on the empty plain far beyond the arcology of London. He was facing the gigantic structure and stared at it for minutes without really seeing it: eyes turned inward. It was near sunset and all light seemed to be gathered to the ivory pyramid that dominated the horizon. "Cradle of the sun," he said softly, and winked out of existence again. Behind him, the city of London rose into the clouds and was lost to sight. The apartments of the Prince of Wales were, at that moment, passing into darkness.

The next materialization was in the midst of a herd of zebra, grazing at tall stands of deep blue grass. They bolted at his appearance, shying sidewise and boiling away from him in a mass of flashing lines of black and white. He smiled, and started walking. The air vibrated with the smell of animal fur and clover. Walking would be a pleasure. And mint.

His first warning that he was not alone came with the sound of a flitterpak overhead. It was a defective: he should not have been able to hear its power-source. He looked up and a woman in torn leathers was tracking his passage across the veldt. She had a norden strapped to her front and he had no doubt the sights were trained on him. He waved to her, and she made no sign of recognition. He kept walking, into the darkness, attempting to ignore her; but his neck itched.

He vanished; to hell with her; he couldn't be bothered.

When he reappeared, he was in the trough of a dry wash that ran for several miles and came to an end, when he had vanished and reappeared again, at the mouth of a cave that angled downward sharply into the ground. He looked back along the channel of the arroyo. He was in the foothills. The mountains bulked purple and distant in the last fading colors of dusk. The horizon was close. The air was very clear, the wind was rising; there were no sounds but those of insects foretelling the future.

He approached the cave mouth and stopped. He sat down on the ground and leaned back on his elbows. He closed his eyes. They would come soon enough, he was certain.

He waited, thinking of nothing but metal surfaces.

In the night, they came for him.

He was half-asleep. Lying up against the incline of the arroyo, his thoughts fading in and out of focus like a radio signal from a transmitter beyond the hills. Oh, bad dreams. Not even subtle, not even artful metaphors. The spider was clearly his mother, the head pink and heavily-freckled, redheaded, and slanting Oriental cartoon eyes. The Mameluke chained between the pillars was bald and old, and the face held an infinite weariness in its expression. The Praetorian with the flame thrower was himself; the searing wash of jellied death appearing and vanishing, being and being gone. He understood. Only a fool would not understand; he was weary, as his father was weary, but he was no fool. He burned the webbing. Again and again. Only to have it spring into existence each time. He came fully awake before the cone-muzzle of the weapon touched his shoulder.

Came awake with the web untouched, covering the

world from horizon to horizon, the spider crawling down the sky toward the weary black man hanging between the pillars.

"You were told I'd be coming," he said. It was only darkness in front of him, but darkness *within* a darkness, and he knew someone stood there, very close to him, the weapon pointed at his head.

He knew it. Only a fool would not have known. Now he was awake, and he was no fool.

The voice that answered from the deeper darkness was neither male nor female, neither young nor old, neither deep nor high. It sounded like a voice coming from a tin cup. Neil knew he had been honorably directed; this was the place, without doubt. He saluted Lady Effim's word of honor with a smile. The voice from the tin cup said, "You're supposed to giving me a word, isn't it?"

"The word you want is *Twinkle*."

"Yeah, that was to being the word. I'm to your being took downstairs now. C'mon."

The thief rose and brushed himself off.

He saw movement from the corner of his eye. But when he turned to look, there was nothing.

He followed the shadow as it moved toward the cave mouth. There was no Moon, and the faraway ice-chips of the stars gave no heat, gave no light. It was merely a shadow he followed: a shadow with its weapon carried at port arms.

They passed into the mouth of the cave, and the dirt passage under their feet began to slope down sharply almost at once. There were two more shadows inside the mouth of the cave, hunkered down, looking like piles of rags, features indistinct, weapon barrels protruding from the shapeless masses like night-blooming flowers of death.

One of them made a metallic sound when it brushed against the wall. It. Neither he nor she. It.

Neil Leipzig followed the shadow down the steep slope, holding on to the rock wall for support as his feet sought purchase. Ahead of him, his guide seemed to be talking to himself very, very softly. It sounded like a mechanical whirring. The guide was not a domo.

"Here you'll stop it," the guide said, when they had descended so deep into the cave passage that the temperature was cool and pleasant. He moved in the darkness, and the thief saw a heat-sensitive plate in the rock wall suddenly come to life with light as the guide touched it. Then a door irised open in the rock wall, and light flooded out, blinding him for a moment. He covered his eyes. The guide gave him a shove through the iris. It was neither polite help nor surly indignity. He merely shoved Neil through to get him inside. It was an old-style elevator, not a dropshaft and not a light-ray tunnel. He had no idea how long it had been here, but probably before the arcology of London.

He looked at his guide in the full light.

He felt, for the first time since . . . he felt for the first time that he wanted to go home, to stop, to go back, to return to himself before . . . to return to the past . . .

The guide was a gnome of spare human parts and rusting machinery. He was barely four feet tall, the legs bowed with the enormous weight of a metal chest like the belly of an old-time wood-burning stove. The head was hairless and the left half was a metal plate devoid of eyes, or nose, or mouth, or skin, or sweat, or pore. It was pocked and flaking metal, riveted through in uneven lines to the bone of the half of the head that was still flesh-covered. His left arm was fastened at the shoulder by a pot-metal socket covered with brazing marks. Depending from the socket were long, curved, presumably hollow levers containing solenoids; another ball socket for elbow, another matched pair of hollow levers, ball socket wrist, solenoid fingers. His right arm was human. It held the cone-muzzled weapon: an archaic but nonetheless effective disruptor. Input sockets—some of them the ancient and corroded models housewives had found in the walls of their homes, into which they had plugged vacuum cleaners and toasters—studded both thighs, inside and out. His penis was banded with expansible mesh copper. He was barefoot; the big toe was gone on the right foot; it had been replaced with a metal stud.

Neil Leipzig felt sick. Was this—?

He stopped the thought. It had never been like this

before, no reason to think it would be like this here. It couldn't be. But he felt sick. And filthy.

He was certain he had seen movement out of the corner of his eye, up there in the arroyo.

The elevator grounded, and the door irised open. He stepped out ahead of the gnome. They were in an underground tunnel, higher and wider than the one above, well lit by eterna lamps set into the tunnel's arched roof. The guide set off at a slow lope, and the thief followed him; illegal, yes . . . but how did they *live* down here, like troglodytes; was this the look of his future . . . he erased the thought . . . and could not stop thinking it.

They rounded a bend and kept going. The tunnel seemed to stretch on indefinitely. Behind him, around the bend, he thought he heard the elevator door close and the cage going back up. But he could not be certain.

They kept on in a straight line for what seemed an eighth of a mile, and when it became clear to Neil that they were going to keep going for many miles in this endless rabbit run, the guide took a sudden right turn into a niche in the right-hand wall the thief had not even suspected was there.

The niche opened into a gigantic cavern. Hewn from solid rock for a purpose long forgotten, decades before, it stretched across for several miles and arched above them in shadows the thief's eyes could not penetrate. Like the pueblo Amerinds of old, whoever lived here had carved dwellings from the rock faces and ledges. From the floor of the cavern below them, all the way up into the shadows, Neil could see men and women moving along the ledges, busy at tasks he could not name. Nor would he have bothered:

All he could see, all he could believe, was the machine that dominated the cavern floor, the computer that rose up and up past the ledge on which they stood, two hundred feet high and a quarter mile in diameter.

"*Mekcoucher*," the half-human gnome said, his voice filled with—

Neil looked down at him. The expression was beatific. Love. Awe, love, desire, respect, allegiance, love. The blasted little face twisted in what was supposed to be a sigh of adoration. Love. Mek-coo-*shay*. The French had invented the word, but the dregs of the Barcelona arcology had conceived the deed. *Mekcoucher*.

The thief touched the gnome's head. The guide looked up without surliness or animosity. His eye was wet. His nose, what there was of his nose, was running. He sobbed, and it came from deep in his stove chest, and he said again, a litany, "*Mekcoucher*. This am all I be here about, dearest shine bright. Fursday, this Fursday, I me I get turn." Neil felt a terrible kinship and pity and recycling of terror. This little thing, here beside him on this ledge, this remnant of what had once been a man, before it had begun dreaming of metal surfaces, of electric currents, of shining thighs, this thing had been no better than Neil Leipzig. Was *this* the future?

Neil could understand the gnome's orison to the machine. It was an installation to inspire homage, to lift up the heart; it was so large and so complex, it inspired deification, idolatry; it was a machine to engender devotion.

It was a sex-partner to consume one such as Neil Leipzig with trembling lust.

They started down the ledge toward the floor of the cavern, the thief with his arm around the gnome's shoulders, both of them moist-eyed and finding it difficult to breathe. At one point, Neil asked the gnome if they could stop, if they could sit down with their backs to the rock wall and just look at the incredible bulk and shapes and shining metal surfaces of the machine in the center of their world.

And they sat, and they watched.

"This is where my place I been stay long time," said the gnome, staring across at the machine. They were now only a hundred feet above the floor of the cavern, and the computer rose up before them, filling their eyes.

Neil asked the gnome his name. "Fursday," he said. "This Fursday, I me I get turn to joy."

A life centralized around his love-partner. No name other than the name that told everyone he would go to Heaven on Thursday. Neil shuddered, but it was a trembling of expectation and desire. And it was there, sitting and remembering the first time, three years earlier . . .

remembering the times since . . . inadequate, searching, fulfilling but not fulfilling the way *this* installation, *this* carnal machine could fulfill . . . he knew it . . . he felt it . . . his bones vibrated like tuning forks, his heart was pudding.

And it was there, sitting beside the gnome, that Mr. Robert Mossman found him.

He came down the ledge behind them, walking lightly, never dislodging a shard of limestone, hardly breathing, the pounder in his right hand. The pounder hit the brain with a laser beam that had the impact of a cannonball dropped from a great height. It could turn the inside of the victim's skull to gruel without marring the outside surface. It made for neat corpses. It was final. It was utterly illegal.

The thief knew there had been noise behind them in the tunnel; there had been movement in the arroyo.

He cursed Lady Effim's word of honor.

He said nothing as the killer came down on them. Mr. Robert Mossman stopped and aimed the weapon at Neil Leipzig's left eye.

"Hey!" Fursday said, seeing the silent killer for the first time. "You aren't being to come down here! I'm me I told to bring him, this one down. Stop!"

Mr. Robert Mossman tracked the pen-point muzzle of the pounder through mere seconds of arc and squeezed the butt of the weapon. Light slashed across the space between them and hit the gnome with the impact of a slammed door. The recoil shuddered the killer; the little metal man was lifted and slung along the ledge. He fell flat onto his back, his human arm hanging over the edge. Neil froze for only a moment, then made a movement toward the gnome's weapon. He knew he would never make it. He could feel the pressure of Mr. Robert Mossman's palm squeezing the pounder. He anticipated the slam of nova heat in his brain, and his eyes filled with light.

But it didn't come. He could not turn around. He knew the killer was savoring the moment. And *in* that moment Neil Leipzig heard the rush of displaced air, the most terrible scream in the world, and the sounds of a struggle.

He turned in time to see the falcon tear away half the

killer's face and, pinions beating a blurred breaststroke against the air, the falcon bore Mr. Robert Mossman over backward.

The killer fell screaming to the rocks below. The falcon skimmed above him, observing, making note of finality, and when it was satisfied that its prey was dead, it dove, ripped loose a piece of meat, and arced back up into the air, banking and turning on a wingtip, and flew to rest on the Catman's shoulder.

The smoldering ember eyes of the two cheetahs stared back at the thief.

The Catman came down the sloping ledge and helped his son to his feet. "Come home now," he said.

Neil Leipzig looked at his father, the lines of tension and sadness and weariness imprinted like circuits across the face. He moved a step closer and then he had his arms around the black man. They stood that way for seconds, and then the Catman's arms came up and circled the thief's back. They stood silently, holding each other.

When they separated, Neil was able to speak. "You didn't stay home, you followed me; all the way from the Five?"

The Catman nodded.

"But how?"

"You to the meeting, then him after you. Come home."

"Dad, it isn't your onshift, you can get yourself in a bad way. Go now, before anyone sees you." The single dead eye of the gnome stared up at the hidden roof of the cavern. Neil thought of metal surfaces. His palms were wet. The air sparkled with scintillance; he stopped it.

"You won't come back with me?"

"I can't. Please, Dad."

"You've seen what this is like. You're my son. I can't let you do it."

"Dad, go *away*. Please! I know what I'm doing."

"Neil."

"*Please*, Dad! I'm begging you. Go away."

"And nothing up there matters more than this?"

"You're not turned away? It doesn't make you sick? Not even here, not even seeing this, not even here will you make a stand? My God, Dad, can't you see you're more destroyed than I'll *ever* be, no matter *what* I do?"

"Make a stand? I'm here, aren't I?"

"Go away!" Then, trying to hurt him because he did not want him hurt, he said, "Your wife is waiting for you."

"Stop it, Neil. She was your mother once."

"The once and never mother to the pervert thief. And you, her consort. Lovely. You want me to come back to that? I won't let my eyes see it again. Not ever."

"How long have you been—"

"How long have I been like this?" He waved an arm at the great machine. "Three years."

"But there was Joice, we thought, your mother and I thought."

"It didn't work. It wasn't enough."

"Neil, *please*, it's not for you. It's—"

"It's what, Dad, it's what? Perverted? Nauseating? Destructive? Pointless? I could apply them all to the way you live with her?"

"Will they come up here after us?" He nodded toward the ledges of cave dwellings and the people moving about them.

"I don't think so, I don't know, but I don't think so. Everything was arranged. I don't know why that one—" and he indicated the body of Mr. Robert Mossman below, "—I don't know why he came after me. But that doesn't matter. Go back. Get out of here. Your promotion, your job, it's almost time for the permutations, God knows that bitch won't give you a moment's peace if she doesn't get rejuvenated. *You're offshift, Dad!* You've never even *bent* a reg before . . . please get the hell out of here and leave me alone."

"You don't understand her."

"I don't *want* to understand her. I've lived with her for twenty-eight years."

"You won't come back with me?"

"No."

"Then let me stay."

The cheetahs closed their eyes and dropped their heads onto their paws. The falcon shrugged and ruffled itself.

"You're out of your mind. Do you know what I'm here for . . . of course you know . . . go *home!*"

So they walked down past the still body of the little

metal and flesh gnome, down the ledge, down to the floor of the great cavern, the thief, the policeman and the animals padding along behind. They paused at the body of Mr. Robert Mossman, and Neil Leipzig, to make certain he knew what he was walking into, took the killer's communication phone from his ring finger, called Lady Effim, and told her what had happened. She said, "I apologize, Neil. My companions are, how can I put it meaningfully, *devoted* to me. Mr. Mossman was very much on his own. I regret his death, but I regret even more that this has caused you to doubt my word. You have my assurance everything was ordered correctly for your arrival. You won't be troubled again. And again, I ask your pardon." He turned her off and he went with his father to the village of the computer.

"For the last time: will you leave now? I don't want you to see this."

"I'll stay. I'll be right over here. Perhaps later . . ."

"No. Even if I go back, I'll only come here again. I know what I need."

"I'll have to keep tracking you."

"That's your job."

The thief held a tiny inhalation tube filled with soft, feathery yellow dust. He had received it from the hand of the cyborg woman who ran the computer's village. It was called The Dust, and spoken of reverently. It was much finer and looked more potent than any Dust Neil Leipzig had ever used. He knew what was going to happen, and could only guess at the intensity of the experience.

The world aboveground was free, totally and utterly free. There were no boundaries, no taboos beyond causing others harm. And even in such a world, *this* was forbidden. The last, the final, the ultimate sexual experience.

"I'll wait."

He didn't answer. He removed his clothes, walked to the towering bulk of the computer and touched it.

The crackle-finish surface of its north flank was smooth and cool to his touch. He felt sensuality pulsing in the machine. They had exposed the leads for him, and he paused for a moment to consider what obligations they must owe Lady Effim for them to give him The Dust, to permit him *Mekcoucher* time with their love-partner. The dwellers in this subterranean hideaway. They were *all* like Fursday. Advanced stages of love commitment to this machine. Part metal, part human, totally the computer's property. Helpless to deny their passion. He grabbed the leads.

The blue lead went into the surgically implanted socket on the inside of his right thigh, the red input lead went into the socket on the inside of his left thigh. The "stim" electrodes found their proper areas through his hair and scalp. He merely placed the medusa cap on his head and they wriggled to their proper clips, sank their fangs, wire snakes. One lead hooked him into the plethysmograph and the Lissajous oscilloscope and the GSR galvanometer. The velcro band containing a million black-dot photocells was ready and he wrapped it around his penis. Then he snorted The Dust, the yellow wonder from Barcelona.

He lay up against the metal body of the machine, arms out cruciform, legs spread, cheek flat to the waiting surface. He could feel the expectancy in the computer, hungry lover.

He thought of the first time he had made love to Joice, the feel of her flesh. It was not enough.

Then he contracted the muscles in his thighs and closed the circuits.

Instantly, the metal of the machine began to flow. He felt himself sinking into the north flank of the computer. His fingers penetrated the metal as easily as if it had been modeling clay. He began to get proprioceptive feedback from muscle activity . . . he could feel the whorls on his fingertips as sucking whirlpools, dark swirling waters that drew his blood and bones through the flesh and out into the machine, spinning the essence of his physical being away from its skin container . . . his chest began to harden, to vibrate with sound like a thunder sheet of aluminum . . . the soles of his feet melted and his arches flattened and his lower legs oozed into puddles of mercury . . . he sank into the machine, was enclosed, its arms around him, welcoming him . . .

The Dust blew in hurricane clouds through his body and

puffed out through the great smooth apertures in his head and back and buttocks. The Dust mingled with lubricant and it was altered, even as he was altered.

He perceived with purest immediacy the sense of his positioning of arms and legs and ferrite cores and LSI circuits and bowels and conductors and limbs and body and plates and fissures and counterweights and glands and wiring in the immediate environment that he was the machine had begun to be him.

Then the auditory and visual feedback began, delayed responses, an instant later than they should have been. He spoke: *Oh, good* and it repeated from another mouth a moment later, *ood.* Echolalia.

He felt his penis engorging with blood and felt the density of light increasing in the capillaries as the plethysmograph measured his arousal in a new language the machine he was the machine interpreted . . . the density of light decreased . . . increased . . . decreased . . . increased . . .

He spiraled upward into the machine—Lissajous pattern oscilloscope sine and cosine waves from the x and y axes actually came together, pulsated in three dimensions and he teased himself the machine he the man with vernier knob stimulation—it came out green and the machine trembled, began to secrete testosterone, estrogen, progesterone . . .

She, the machine, he, the machine, she, the man, he, the machine . . . the man, he becoming she becoming machine . . .

His heart was pudding.

The Lissajous pulsations became hallucinations in the sex organs of the computer . . . galvanic skin response on the galvanometer . . . aching in his spine . . .

Sinking slowly into a sea of oil. Great skyscraper bulk of metalflesh slowly warmly moistly sinking into a sea of blue-black oil. Pumping. Pumping. Wet closing over his head, running in waves over his naked body. Invisible mat of hair covering every plate and surface, a fine golden down, soaking up oil, engorging, coming to climax.

Her breasts were warm, the rivets sensitive to each feather caress of electric stim. Her vagina filled with soft, melting things that went up and up and roughened the oil-slick inner surfaces, sliding to touch and knead the vulva. *So good. Ood.*

His memory, he could see everything in his memory, stored in the banks, every moment of his life from the first dripping emergence from the vats, the running, the extruding, the rolling, the flattening, the cutting, the shaping, the forming, the welding. Every moment of his life: the instant he was first engaged, the circuits closing, the surge of power, the first inputs, the primary runs, every boring clearing procedure, every exercise, every erroneous output.

His mother, his father, great cats and the wet scent of their breath, like coolant on overheated coils, the soft taste of Joice in his mouth, her body moving beneath him, sinking into her, tiniest folding of her labia around his penis, the rising to orgasm, the overloading, the heat, the peace of darkness.

Then he altered his stroke and felt the change to precognitive anticipatory feedback, telling himself how it would feel, fulfilling his own prophecies, the smell of flesh on metal, metal on flesh, the colors of whirling information, increments of semen and fused capacitors.

He was the teleport, additional human faculties, soft sponge pineal gland, polluted adrenalin, strange eyes, this was the best for me the very best I've ever hungry metal lover. They began to converge . . . everything began to converge. He, the machine called Neil Leipzig, was the x axis; he, the machine called love-partner, was the y axis; they began to converge; identical sine waves, out of phase.

His pattern was a growing. The machine's was a throbbing. He passed the machine at a higher level every pulse. The machine grew frantic and drank more power. He tried to catch up, chasing the nymphomaniacal peaks as the machine beckoned him, teased him, taunted him, drew him on, then flashed away. He extended on metal limbs, the machine's soft flesh grew sunburned and dark and leather tough.

Then he peaked out, it, she, peaked out, unable to draw more power from her source. They exchanged modes, as the point of destructive interference denied quantum mechanics and was reached: a millisecond of total sound and utter silence. Orgasm: metal became flesh, human became machine.

The interference pattern was a grating whine that became more and more pure as they came into phase. The machine, in its human throat, began to vibrate in sympathy. She, who had been Neil Leipzig at the start, captured the exponential pattern that had been his, the machine, captured it as it fell away.

They circled, and the image on the Lissajous screen became a circle as she captured the machine and held her in phase again. Prolate and oblate: two dimensional images slowing, softening, dimming, the message of release and surcease .986, 1.0014, .9999986, 1.00000000014

. . .

The first thing he heard was the sound of the two cheetahs attacking something, agony and fury. The first thing he saw was the dying point of green light on the oscilloscope screen. The first thing he felt was the rough metal of his chest against the sweat-soaked north flank of his love-partner.

He was dry. As though he had given the machine a transfusion, as if it had sucked all the juices from him. He understood why Joice and all the others, as free as they had been, had been unable to arouse him in times past, how the first *Mekcoucher* with its promises of *this*, had led him further and further into the inevitability of what he had just experienced.

Now, for the first time in his life, he knew what passion could lead through, what it led to inexorably. And he knew he could never go back. He would stay here, in this terrible place, with these others who shared his lover, and this was all he wanted.

He fell away from the machine and lay on the rock floor of the cavern. His breath had to be drawn in stages. His head reeled. His hand lay on his metal chest.

He wanted to sleep, but the sounds of conflict were louder now, insistent, crowding through the pain and satiation his body felt at one and the same time. He rolled over on his stomach, his chest clanking against the rock floor. *It was the best for you, too,* he thought. *The best you ever had, love-partner. You will never forget me. If I die today, you'll remember always, in every last memory cell.*

At the base of the nearest ledge, the Catman's cheetahs were struggling with one of the love-partner's people. He was down and they were savaging him, but clearly trying to avoid killing him. The thief had seen the technique before. It was called putting, as in *stay put*. The rest of the colony had no part in the melee, and were, in fact, watching with some pleasure—if pleasure could be discerned on faces that were partially metal masks.

A tall, limping, old woman with copper legs came across from the crowd. She hobbled to Neil as the Catman commanded, "Heel!" and the cheetahs left their chewed and semi-conscious prey. The Catman joined the copper-legged old woman.

The falcon looked sleepy. It was an illusion.

"Will you can stay be here with love-partner?" the old woman said. There was a tone of pleading in her voice. "Tewsday," she said, indicating the pile of worked-over flesh and metal the cheetahs had put, "he was for crazy of you with the love-partner. But I'm the saying one for your give machine love never before that fire hot. If you'll be stay this place us can make you what my is being, first lover."

The Catman moved a step closer. "Neil!"

There was raw horror on his face. He had seen his son's body vanish into the machine, had seen the machine turn soft and swallow the thief, had seen the machine sweat and go mad with lust, had seen his son emerge with his parts altered. Neil Leipzig looked at his father, and at the old woman. "I'll stay. Now go and take Tewsday for repair."

The old woman hobbled away, and the crowd went back into their rock-wall dwellings. Neil Leipzig stood facing the Catman.

"You can't. My God, Neil, *look* at you, and this is only the first time. That thing *eats* what it loves. Do you want to end up like—"

He waved a hand at the retreating mob of half-humans.

"This is where I belong. I haven't belonged up there for a long time."

"Neil, please, I'll do anything you want; resign my commission, we can go away to another city . . ."

"Dad," he said, "I have always loved you. More than I've ever been able to tell you. I always wanted you to fight back. That's all I ever wanted."

"You don't understand your mother. She's had bad times, too."

"It's all in aid of nothing. Look at you. You haven't got a dream left in the world. We're killing you a little at a time. It's time I stopped contributing to it and did something final."

"But not this, not down here, son . . ."

But the thief was gone. The air twittered with bright scintillas of fading light.

The first jump brought him back to the world imbedded in the earth a quarter of a mile beneath the arroyo. Had he made such a teleportational error earlier, he would have died. But mating with the machine had altered him. The love-partner had never known a teleport, and in the exchange of modes he had been made less than machine but more than mortal. He expanded his personal space and vanished again. The second jump took him to the surface, and he winked in, out in an instant—seen by no living thing, for even the guards were dead, having been pounded by Mr. Robert Mossman.

The night welcomed him, accepted his mote-outlined shadow, and took no further notice as he vanished again, reappeared, vanished, and in seconds materialized in his mother's bedroom high in London.

He leaned over and grasped her by the wrist, and wrenched her from the doze cocoon where she lay, supple and naked, the powder-white marks of the plasticwork making longitudinal lines on her breasts that glowed faintly in the night light. Her eyes snapped open as he dragged her free.

"Come along, Mom. We have to go now."

Then, clutching her naked body to his naked body, he vanished.

Before merging with the machine, he could not have carried someone with him. But everything was changed now. Vastly changed.

The Catman was high on the ledge leading to the elevator when the thief reappeared with his mother. The cheetahs padded alongside and the falcon was on the wing. The climb was a difficult one for a man that age, even with unnumbered rejuvenations. The Catman was too far away to do anything to stop him.

"Neil!"

"You're free, Dad. You're free now. Don't waste it!"

The Catman was frozen for only a moment. And in that moment Neil Leipzig carried the semiconscious body of his mother to the love-partner. The Catman screamed, a high and desolate scream because he knew what was happening. He began running down the ledge, screaming to his falcon to intercept, screaming to his cheetahs to get there before him, screaming because he could never make it in time.

The thief plugged himself in, his mother pressed flat between his naked metalflesh body and the fleshmetal north flank of his love-partner.

He flexed his thigh muscles, closed the contacts . . .

. . . and offered himself and the suddenly howling woman as the ultimate troilism.

The machine flowed, the oscilloscope formed a design no living creature had ever seen in more than three dimensions, and then, in an instant, it was over. The machine absorbed what it could not refuse, and there was only the single point of green light on the screen, and endless silence once more beneath the earth.

The Catman reached the machine, saw the beads of sweat mixed with blood that dotted the north flank, and heard fading moans of brutality that repeated soundlessly.

The Catman sits alone in a room, remembering.

The child never knew. It was not the mother. The mother always loved, but had no way of showing it. The father had never loved, and had every way of reinforcing it, day after day.

The Catman sits and mourns. Not for the child, gone and without sorrow. For the woman.

For the bond of circumstances that held them together through days and nights of a special kind of love forged in a cauldron of hate.

He will never forgive the child for having destroyed that love out of hate.

He will sit alone now. He has nothing left to live for. He hopes the child burns in a terrible Hell, even as he burns in his own. And after a while, there is always the conversing waterfall.

AFTERWORD

The letter was so casual, I never really paused to consider how incredibly difficult, how close-to-impossible, and how presumptuous I had to be, to even contemplate the assignment. Barry Malzberg wrote and advised me of the nature of *Final Stage*, its by-invitation-only table of contents, and said—in a line—"what we want from you is the ultimate future sex story."

So casually did he write it, and so casually did Ed Ferman talk about it when we had our frequent phone conversations on other topics, that it never really dawned on me, till I sat down to write, what *is* the ultimate sex story? What is it about? In an era of liberal attitudes toward sexual liaisons of *all* kinds, what does one work toward in an effort to ultimize the "sexual experience"?

Clearly, male homosexuality is not where it's at. Gay Lib holds rallies and marches, and only the gauchest *machismo* stud, unconsciously fearing the viability of his own virility (at best) or the preservation of his John Wayne image (at worst), would consider the subject startling. As far back as the mid-Fifties, with the late Charles Beaumont's *Playboy* story, "The Crooked Man," and as recently as this year with David Gerrold's excellent sf novel, *The Man Who Folded Himself*, the subject has been treated in the genre of the imaginative with a variety of views and a range of sympathy. Not to mention Ted Sturgeon's memorable "The World Well Lost."

Lesbianism is hardly daring. Perhaps to anal retentive and bluenosed types in some rural backwash, but certainly not to the vast majority of readers who have seen the subject treated all the way from the sensationalism of the paperback "stiffeners" to articles in *Cosmopolitan* on "lesbian mothers." (Additionally, because of the heavily-weighted sexist attitudes of American fiction in the past, female homosexuality was never really anathema; prurience, apparently, is an AC but not a DC current; the same studs noted above could easily get off with variations of woman-to-woman relationships, where man-to-man liaisons filled them with horror. So, it always was a paper tiger where controversiality was concerned.)

Bisexuality in all its positions and "perversions" has been rather well-explored: an inescapable conclusion when confronted with *Portnoy's Complaint*, *Deep Throat*, the sculptures of Edward Keinholz, the paintings of Richard Lindner and Fritz Wunderlich, the Scandinavian series of "Color Climax" magazines, the sex museum of the Drs. Kronhausen, the Olympia Press novels of Barry Malzberg, the many legitimate theater productions of *The Beard*, and on and on. No, getting laid, whether in terms of Dan Greenburg's *Scoring* or Joyce Elbert's *The Crazy Ladies*, is hardly newsmaking these days. And, say I, hallelujah for our sense of *déjà vu* in the area of bisexual and heterosexual coupling. It means writers will have to work closer to the core of the human condition . . . the audience will no longer accept mere sensationalism or tittilation.

The *ultimate* sexual experience. Mere carnality, whether between man and man, man and woman, woman and woman, adult and child, adult and animal, child and child, animal and animal or variations on the foregoing with merely the substitution of an extraterrestrial (see Philip José Farmer's *The Lovers*; God knows, already over twenty years an established milestone, for evidence that *that* wouldn't be a stunner), isn't the final roadsign. Sado-masochism, sadism and bondage, utter kinkiness . . . that way lies boredom. When *Oui* Magazine does a long

S/M section including a glossary of terminology and a pictorial takeout that lampoons the whole idiom, well, *The Story of "O"* becomes very much beside the point. Besides, to me, as an uptight Jewish lad from Ohio, steeped in the Judeo-Christian Ethic, stitching up a woman's vagina with sailcloth thread, or putting a man's genitalia in a lemon squeezer ain't my idea of never having to say you're sorry.

I deliberated long and freakily, and early on dispatched the easy-out of making it an hallucinogenic mindfuck trip through the use of drugs, known or extrapolated. Subthought A of that line of logic was that such an acid *shtupp* would involve each love-partner feeling the proprioceptive feedback of the other . . . male would get male *plus* female thrills . . . female would get female *plus* male thrills. That was first stage simple, and this was to be the *Final Stage*.

Then I went through futuristic interpretations of incest, satyriasis, nymphomania, auto-eroticism, diabolism, bestiality, onanism, pedicadio (I may not have spelled that correctly; it was once described to me by a fellow named Donald Susan, of Pittsburgh, Pennsylvania, as the act of cutting new fornication-holes in one's love-mate), necrophilia, and new horrors my twisted id created from specially prepared meals of powdered sugar doughnuts, papaya juice, chocolate Malt-O-Meal and warm hair.

None, it seemed to me, came anywhere near what I was looking for. Nor what Malzberg and Ferman (who now assumed, in my mind, a kinship with Burke and Hare) wanted, damn them!

A year earlier, Ed Ferman had sent me a "rough" for a proposed cover on *The Magazine of Fantasy & Science Fiction*. A "rough" is a color sketch of what the artist proposes as the final cover painting. It was by Ron Wolotsky, and it contained a plenitude of elements. I had Scotch taped it to the pivot lamp that hangs over my typewriter. I had begun "Catman" soon after receiving the rough, but had been forced by other committments to set the story aside with only 1,000 words written. All through that year I yearned to return to the story, because it was very much on my mind.

Understand: "Catman" and the story for *Final Stage*

were two very different projects. "Catman" was to have been a character study of a future society thief and a cop from the same world, father and son, who could only operate during their legal shifts. But, inexorably, the two stories grew together in my mind. In stages as follows:

A society where theft is pointless because there is plenty for all.

A thief in such a society.

Why does he steal?

Because he must have something that is so forbidden it is even loathesome to a totally permissive society.

Permissive society.

A sexual proclivity so hideous it remains taboo in a world without taboos.

The ultimate sex experience.

And there I was with two stories that had merged to become one. Perhaps they had been the halves of the that story all along, separated only by a broken link in creativity that needed to be repaired by time.

When the entire story was in my head, I went back to the writing. A year later.

But still I had no specific as to what my "utterly taboo sex experience" would be. Then, one evening, sitting with Lynda watching television, I was making disparaging remarks about the fare on the tube, letting my frequently-dark sense of humor wander. I made some stupid remark about fucking the television set. (It was more than likely a calculatedly offensive sexist remark pertaining to one of the incredibly beautiful ladies who sell products no one really needs.) I didn't even feel the punch Lynda delivered to my head, because in one of those skip-logic switch closings, I leaped across sanity and rationality and knew what my ultimate sex experience would be. The mating of a human with a machine.

Not the way I had used it in my collaboration with A.E. Van Vogt, "The Human Operators," but in a way that would read as logical and scientifically plausible and unsettling as such a—clearly—fantasy concept could be made to seem.

Utilizing the good offices and vast knowledge of three top computer people—two programmers and one authority in the field of CSAI—computer simulation artificial intelligence—I set forth the parameters of the fictional equation, and let them educate me in the areas where I was woefully ignorant.

I've tried this story on a number of people involved with computers, since it was written, and they have all agreed that given the one fantasy input—The Dust—that necessary pseudo-scientific gimmick extrapolated to permit the codification of an impossibility (or is it merely an improbability?)—what I've set down is accurate in terms of what we know today, and what we can postulate for tomorrow.

Having written what will be promoted as the "ultimate story of futuristic sex" I find myself somewhat ambivalent about the possible ramifications of the act. When Sturgeon wrote "The World Well Lost", idle gossip had it that he was gay. I'm sure that will come as a revelation to Ted's wife and children. Robert Bloch, one of the kindest and funniest men God ever set on the Earth, has long had to live with the canard that he is a deranged psychopathic monster merely because he wrote "Yours Truly, Jack the Ripper" and *Psycho*. (Of course, the fact that Bob tells people he has the heart of a small child . ... which he keeps in a jar on the mantle . . . doesn't help those of us who know and love him and would dispell the mist of rumor around him.) Edmond Hamilton, a farmboy at heart, who to this day lives in rustic Ohio farm country, is identified with the *Star Kings* genre of galaxy-spanning, world-smashing epics. God only knows what semi-informed fans think are the realities of Phil Farmer's sex life, or Norman Spinrad's indulgences, or Walter Miller's religious beliefs.

And so, for the record, merely to nip in the bud any ugly conjectures on the part of readers who use their own nasty personal lives as templates for those of the writers' they read, let me say categorically and without shadow of equivocation, I am not now, nor have I ever been, a machine fucker. I have never harbored even the faintest scintilla of lust for my Waring blender or the Pachinko machine in my kitchen. I see nothing sexually attractive in my 1967 Camaro or my Sony tape recorder. Machines do not stir me libidinously.

But I must confess I enjoy the way this Olympia Electric responds to my every touch with a surge of positively paramour-like adoration.

Novels
THE LOVERS, by Philip José Farmer
THE LEFT HAND OF DARKNESS, by Ursula K. LeGuin
THORNS, by Robert Silverberg
ON THE LINE, by Harvey Swados
ULYSSES, by James Joyce

Play
WHO'S AFRAID OF VIRGINIA WOOLF?, by Edward Albee

Short Stories
AFFAIR WITH A GREEN MONKEY, by Theodore Sturgeon
PRETTY MAGGIE MONEYEYES, by Harlan Ellison
THE MASCULINIST REVOLT, by William Tenn
HELEN O'LOY, by Lester del Rey
PASSENGERS, by Robert Silverberg
I HAVE NO MOUTH, AND I MUST SCREAM, by Harlan
    Ellison
THE PROWLER IN THE CITY AT THE EDGE OF THE WORLD,
    by Harlan Ellison
PILGRIMAGE TO EARTH, by Robert Sheckley
THE WORLD WELL LOST, by Theodore Sturgeon
IF ALL MEN WERE BROTHERS WOULD YOU LET ONE
    MARRY YOUR SISTER?, by Theodore Sturgeon

About Harlan Ellison
Harlan Ellison, b. 1934, is a multi-faceted entrepreneur of science fiction, as well as one of its most distinguished writers. He has won numerous Hugo and Nebula awards as editor (DANGEROUS VISIONS), novelist and short story writer (DEATHBIRD STORIES, 1973). Ellison is also active as lecturer, critic, screenwriter (scripted THE OSCAR), and television writer (originator of the new NBC television series, THE STARLOST). He lives in Southern California.

SPACE OPERA

SPACE RATS OF THE CCC

HARRY HARRISON

That's it, matey, pull up a stool, sure use that one. Just dump old Phrnnx onto the floor to sleep it off. You know that Krddls can't stand to drink, much less drink *flnnx*—and that topped off with a smoke of the hellish *krmml* weed. Here, let me pour you a mug of *flnnx*, oops, sorry about your sleeve. When it dries you can scrape it off with a knife. Here's to your health and may your tubeliners never fail you when the *kpnnz* hordes are on your tail.

No, sorry, never heard your name before. Too many good men come and go, and the good ones die early, aye! Me? You never heard of me. Just call me Old Sarge, as good a name as any. Good men I say, and the best of them was—well, we'll call him Gentleman Jax. He had another name, but there's a little girl waiting on a planet I could name, a little girl that's waiting and watching the shimmering trails of the deep-spacers when they come, and waiting for a man. So for her sake we'll call him Gentleman Jax, he would have liked that, and she would like that if only she knew, although she must be getting kind of gray, or bald by now, and arthritic from all that sitting and waiting but, golly, that's another story and by Orion it's not for me to tell. That's it, help yourself, a large one. Sure the green fumes are normal for good *flnnx*, though you better close your eyes when you drink or you'll be blind in a week, ha-ha!, by the sacred name of the Prophet Mrddl!

Yes, I can tell what you're thinking. What's an old space rat like me doing in a dive like this out here at galaxy's end where the rim stars flicker wanly and the tired photons go slow? I'll tell you what I'm doing, getting drunker than a Planizzian *pfrdffl*, that's what. They say that drink has the power to dim memories and by Cygnus I have some memories that need dimming. I see you look-

176

ing at those scars on my hands. Each one is a story, matey, aye, and the scars on my back each a story and the scars on my . . . well, that's a different story. Yes, I'll tell you a story, a true one by Mrddl's holy name, though I might change a name or two, that little girl waiting, you know.

You heard tell of the CCC? I can see by the sudden widening of your eyes and the blanching of your space-tanned skin that you have. Well, yours truly, Old Sarge here, was one of the first of the Space Rats of the CCC, and my buddy then was the man they know as Gentleman Jax. May Great Kramddl curse his name and blacken the memory of the first day when I first set eyes on him . . .

"Graduating class . . . ten-SHUN!"

The sergeant's stentorian voice bellowed forth, cracking like a whiplash across the expectant ears of the mathematically aligned rows of cadets. With the harsh snap of those fateful words a hundred and three incredibly polished bootheels crashed together with a single snap, and the eighty-seven cadets of the graduating class snapped to steel-rigid attention. (It should be explained that some of them were from alien worlds, different numbers of legs, and so on.) Not a breath was drawn, not an eyelid twitched a thousandth of a milliliter as Colonel von Thorax stepped forward, glaring down at them all through the glass monocle in front of his glass eye, close-cropped gray hair stiff as barbed wire, black uniform faultlessly cut and smooth, a *krmml* weed cigarette clutched in the steel fingers of his prosthetic left arm, black gloved fingers of his prosthetic right arm snapping to hatbrim's edge in a perfect salute, motors whining thinly in his prosthetic lungs to power the brobdignagian roar of his harshly bellowed command.

"At ease. And listen to me. You are the hand-picked men—and hand-picked things too, of course—from all the civilized worlds of the galaxy. Six million and forty-three cadets entered the first year of training, and most of them washed out in one way or another. Some could not toe the mark. Some were expelled and shot for buggery. Some believed the lying commie pinko crying liberal claims that continuous war and slaughter are not necessary, and they were expelled and shot as well. One by one the weaklings fell away through the years leaving the hard core of the Corps—*you!* The Corpsmen of the first graduating class of the CCC! Ready to spread the benefits of civilization to the stars. Ready at last to find out what the initials CCC stand for!"

A mighty roar went up from the massed throats, a cheer of hoarse masculine enthusiasm that echoed and boomed from the stadium walls. At a signal from von Thorax a switch was thrown, and a great shield of imperviomite slid into place above, sealing the stadium from prying eyes and ears and snooping spyish rays. The roaring voices roared on enthusiastically—and many an eardrum was burst that day!—yet were stilled in an instant when the Colonel raised his hand.

"You Corpsmen will not be alone when you push the frontiers of civilization out to the barbaric stars. Oh no! You will each have a faithful companion by your side. First man, first row, step forward and meet your faithful companion!"

The Corpsman called out stepped forward a smart pace and clicked his heels sharply, said click being echoed in the clack of a thrown-wide door and, without conscious intent, every eye in that stadium was drawn in the direction of the dark doorway from which emerged . . .

How to describe it? How to describe the whirlwind that batters you, the storm that engulfs you, the spacewarp that enwarps you? It was as indescribable as any natural force!

It was a creature three meters high at the shoulders, four meters high at the ugly, drooling, tooth-clashing head, a whirlwinded, spacewarped storm that rushed forward on four piston-like legs, great-clawed feet tearing grooves in the untearable surface of the impervitium flooring, a monster born of madness and nightmares that reared up before them and bellowed in a soul-destroying screech.

"There!" Colonel von Thorax bellowed in answer, blood-specked spittle mottling his lips. "*There* is your faithful companion, the mutacamel, mutation of the noble beast of Good Old Earth, symbol and pride of the CCC— the *Combat Camel Corps!* Corpsman meet your camel!"

The selected Corpsman stepped forward and raised his arm in greeting to this noble beast which promptly bit the arm off. His shrill screams mingled with the barely stifled gasps of his companions who watched, with more than casual interest, as camel trainers girt with brass-buckled leather harness rushed out and beat the protesting camel with clubs back from whence it had come, while a medic clamped a tourniquet on the wounded man's stump and dragged his limp body away.

"That is your first lesson on combat camels," the Colonel cried huskily. "Never raise your arms to them. Your companion, with a newly grafted arm will, I am certain, ha-ha!, remember this little lesson. Next man, next companion!"

Again the thunder of rushing feet and the high-pitched, gurgling, scream-like roar of the combat camel at full charge. This time the Corpsman kept his arm down, and the camel bit his head off.

"Can't graft on a head I am afraid," the Colonel leered maliciously at them. "A moment of silence for our departed companion who has gone to the big rocket pad in the sky. That's enough. Ten-SHUN! You will now proceed to the camel training area where you will learn to get along with your faithful companions. Never forgetting that each has a complete set of teeth made of imperviumite, as well as razor sharp claw caps of this same substance. Dis-MISSED!"

The student barracks of the CCC was well known for its "no frills" or rather "no coddling" decor and comforts. The beds were impervitium slabs—no spine-sapping mattresses here!—and the sheets of thin burlap. No blankets of course, not with the air kept at a healthy 4 degrees Centigrade. The rest of the comforts matched so that it was a great surprise to the graduates to find unaccustomed comforts awaiting them upon their return from the ceremonies and training. There was a *shade* on each bare-bulbed reading light and a nice soft two-centimeter-thick pillow on every bed. Already they were reaping the benefits of all the years of labor.

Now, among all the students, the top student by far was named M———. There are some secrets that must not be told, names that are important to loved ones and neighbors. Therefore I shall draw the cloak of anonymity over the true identity of the man known as M———. Suffice to call him "Steel," for that was the nickname of someone who knew him best. "Steel," or Steel as we can call him, had at this time a roommate by the name of L———. Later, much later, L——— was to be called by certain people "Gentleman Jax" so for the purpose of this narrative we shall call him "Gentleman Jax" as well, or perhaps just plain "Jax." Jax was second only to Steel in scholastic and sporting attainments, and the two were the best of chums. They had been roommates for the past year and now they were back in their room with their feet up, basking in the unexpected luxury of the new furnishings, sipping decaffeinated coffee, called koffee, and smoking deeply of the school's own brand of denicotinized cigarettes, called Denikcig by the manufacturer but always referred to, humorously, by the CCC students as "gaspers" or "lungbusters."

"Throw me over a gasper, will you Jax," Steel said, from where he lolled on the bed, hands behind his head, dreaming of what was in store for him now that he would be having his own camel soon. "Ouch!" he chuckled as the pack of gaspers caught him in the eye. He drew out one of the slim white forms and tapped it on the wall to ignite it then drew in a lungful of refreshing smoke. "I still can't believe it . . ." he smokeringed.

"Well it's true enough, by Mrddl," Jax smiled. "We're graduates. Now throw back that pack of lungbusters so I can join you in a draw or two."

Steel complied, but did it so enthusiastically that the pack hit the wall and instantly all the cigarettes ignited and the whole thing burst into flame. A glass of water doused the conflagration but, while it was still fizzling fitfully, a light flashed redly on the comscreen.

"High priority message," Steel bit out, slamming down the actuator button. Both youths snapped to rigid attention as the screen filled with the iron visage of Colonel von Thorax.

"M———, L———, to my office on the triple." The words fell like leaden weights from his lips. What could it mean?

"What can it mean?" Jax asked as they hurtled down a dropchute at close to the speed of gravity.

"We'll find out quickly enough," Steel snapped as they drew up at the "old man's" door and activated the announcer button.

Moved by some hidden mechanism the door swung wide

and, not without a certain amount of trepidation, they entered. But what was this? *This!* The Colonel was looking at them and smiling, *smiling*, an expression never before known to cross his stern face at any time.

"Make yourselves comfortable, lads," he indicated, pointing at comfortable chairs that rose out of the floor at the touch of a button. "You'll find gaspers in the arms of these servochairs, as well as Valumian wine or Snaggian beer."

"No koffee?" Jax open-mouthedly expostulated, and they all laughed.

"I don't think you really want it," the Colonel susurrated coyly through his artificial larynx. "Drink up lads, you're Space Rats of the CCC now, and your youth is behind you. Now look at that."

That was a three-dimensional image that sprang into being in the air before them at the touch of a button, an image of a spacer like none ever seen before. She was as slender as a swordfish, fine-winged as a bird, solid as a whale, and as armed to the teeth as an alligator.

"Holy Kolon," Steel sighed in open-mouthed awe. "Now *that* is what I call a hunk o' rocket!"

"Some of us prefer to call it the *Indefectible*," the Colonel said, not unhumorously.

"Is that *her?* We heard something . . ."

"You heard very little for we have had this baby under wraps ever since the earliest stage. She has the largest engines ever built, new improved MacPhersons[1] of the most advanced design, Kelly drive[2] gear that has been improved to where you would not recognize it in a month of Thursdays—as well as double-strength Fitzroy projectors[3] that make the old ones look like a kid's popgun. And I've saved the best for last . . ."

1. The MacPherson engine was first mentioned in the author's story, "Rocket Rangers of the IRT" (*Spicy-Weird Stories*, 1923).
2. Loyal readers first discovered the Kelly drive in the famous book *Hell Hounds of the Coal Sack Cluster* (Slimecreeper Press, Ltd., 1931), also published in the German language as *Teufelhund Nach der Knockwurst Exspres*. Translated into Italian by Re Umberto, unpublished to date.
3. A media breakthrough was made when the Fitzroy projector first appeared in "Female Space Zombies of Venus" in 1936 in *True Story Confessions*.

"*Nothing* can be better than what you have already told us," Steel broke in.

"That's what *you* think!" the Colonel laughed, not unkindly, with a sound like tearing steel. "The best news is that M———, you are going to be Captain of this spacegoing super-dreadnought, while lucky L——— is Chief Engineer."

"Lucky L——— would be a lot happier if he were Captain instead of king of the stokehold," Jax muttered, and the other two laughed at what they thought was a joke.

"Everything is completely automated," the Colonel continued, "so it can be flown by a crew of two. But I must warn you that it has experimental gear aboard so whoever flies her has to volunteer . . ."

"I volunteer!" Steel shouted.

"I have to go to the terlet," Jax said, rising, though he sat again instantly when the ugly blaster leaped from its holster to the Colonel's hand. "Ha-ha, just a joke. I volunteer, sure."

"I knew I could count on you lads. The CCC breeds *men.* Camels too, of course. So here is what you do. At 0304 hours tomorrow you two in the *Indefectible* will crack ether headed out Cygnus way. In the direction of a *certain* planet."

"Let me guess, if I can, that is," Steel said grimly through tight-clenched teeth. "You don't mean to give us a crack at the larshnik-loaded world of Biru-2, do you?"

"I do. This is the larshnik's prime base, the seat of operation of all their drug and gambling traffic, where the white-slavers offload, and the queer green is printed, site of the *flnnx* distilleries and lair of the pirate hordes."

"If you want action that sounds like *it!*" Steel grimaced.

"You are not just whistling through your back teeth," the Colonel agreed. "If I were younger and had a few fewer replaceable parts this is the kind of opportunity I would leap at . . ."

"You can be Chief Engineer," Jax hinted.

"Shut up," the Colonel implied. "Good luck gentlemen for the honor of the CCC rides with you."

"But not the camels?" Steel asked.

"Maybe next time. There are, well, adjustment problems. We have lost four more graduates since we have been sitting here. Maybe we'll even change animals. Make it the CDC."

"With combat *dogs?*" Jax asked.

"Either that or donkeys. Or dugongs. But it is my worry, not yours. All you guys have to do is get out there and crack Biru-2 wide open. I know you can do it."

If the Corpsmen had any doubts they kept them to themselves, for that is the way of the Corps. They did what had to be done, and the next morning, at exactly 0304 hours, the mighty bulk of the *Indefectible* hurled itself into space. The roaring MacPherson engines poured quintillions of ergs of energy into the reactor drive until they were safely out of the gravity field of mother Earth. Jax labored over his engines, shoveling the radioactive *transvestite* into the gaping maw of the hungry furnace, until Steel signalled from the bridge that it was "change-over" time. Then they changed over to the space-eating Kelly drive. Steel jammed home the button that activated the drive, and the great ship leaped starward at seven times the speed of light.[4] Since the drive was fully automatic Jax freshened up in the fresher, while his clothes were automatically washed in the washer, then proceeded to the bridge.

"Really," Steel said, his eyebrows climbing up his forehead. "I didn't know you went in for polkadot jockstraps."

"It was the only thing I had clean. The washer dissolved the rest of my clothes."

"Don't worry about it. It's the larshniks of Biru-2 who have to worry! We hit atmosphere in exactly seventeen minutes, and I have been thinking about what to do when that happens."

"Well I certainly hope *someone* has! I haven't had time to draw a deep breath, much less think."

"Don't worry, old pal, we're in this together. The way I figure it, we have two choices. We can blast right in, guns roaring, or we can slip in by stealth."

"Oh you really *have* been thinking, haven't you?"

4. When the Kelly drive's inventor, Patsy Kelly, was asked how ships could move at seven times the speed of light when the limiting velocity of matter, according to Einstein, was the speed of light, he responded in his droll Goidelic way, with a shrug, "Well—sure and I guess Einstein was wrong."

"I'll ignore that because you're tired. Strong as we are, I think the land-based batteries are stronger. So I suggest we slip in without being noticed."

"Isn't that a little hard when you're flying in a thirty-million-ton spacer?"

"Normally, yes. But do you see this button here marked *invisibility?* While you were loading the fuel they explained this to me. It's a new invention, never used in action before, that will render us invisible and impervious to detection by any of their detection instruments."

"Now that's more like it. Fifteen minutes to go, we should be getting mighty close. Turn on the old invisibility ray . . ."

"Don't!!"

"Done. Now what's your problem?"

"Nothing really. Except the experimental invisibility device is not expected to last more than thirteen minutes before it burns out."

Unhappily, this proved to be the case. One hundred miles above the barren, blasted surface of Biru-2 the good old *Indefectible* popped back into existence.

In the minutest fraction of a millisecond the mighty spacesonar and superadar had locked grimly onto the invading ship while the sublights flickered their secret signals, waiting for a correct response that would reveal the invader as one of theirs.

"I'll send a signal, stall them. These larshniks aren't too bright," Steel laughed. He thumbed on the microphone, switched to the interstellar emergency frequency, then bit out the rasping words in a sordid voice. "Agent X-9 to prime base. Had a firefight with the patrol, shot up my code books, but I got all the SOBs, ha-ha! Am coming home with a load of eight hundred thousand long tons of the hellish *krmml* weed."

The larshnik response was instantaneous. From the gaping, pitted orifices of thousands of giant blaster cannon there vomited forth ravening rays of energy that strained the very fabric of space itself. These coruscating forces blasted into the impregnable screens of the old *Indefectible* which, sadly, was destined not to get much older, and instantly punched their way through and splashed coruscatingly from the very hull of the ship itself. Mere matter could not stand against such forces unlocked in the coruscating bowels of the planet itself so that the impregnable imperialite metal walls instantly vaporized into a thin gas which was, in turn, vaporized into the very electrons and protons (and neutrons too) of which it was made.

Mere flesh and blood could not stand against such forces. But in the few seconds it took the coruscating energies to eat through the force screens, hull, vaporized gas, and protons, the reckless pair of valiant Corpsmen had hurled themselves headlong into their space armor. And just in time! The ruin of the once great ship hit the atmosphere and seconds later slammed into the poison soil of Biru-2. To the casual observer it looked like the end. The once mighty queen of the spaceways would fly no more, for she now consisted of no more than two hundred pounds of smoking junk. Nor was there any sign of life from the tragic wreck to the surface crawlers who erupted from a nearby secret hatch concealed in the rock and crawled through the smoking remains with all their detectors detecting at maximum gain. *Report!* the radio signal wailed. *No sign of life to fifteen decimal places!* snapped back the cursing operator of the crawlers before he signalled them to return to base. Their metal cleats clanked viciously across the barren soil, and then they were gone. All that remained was the cooling metal wreck hissing with despair as the poison rain poured like tears upon it.

Were these two good friends dead? I thought you would never ask. Unbeknownst to the larshnik technicians, just one millisecond before the wreck struck down two massive and almost indestructible suits of space armor had been ejected by coiled steelite springs, sent flying to the very horizon where they landed behind a concealing spine of rock, which, just by *chance* was the spine of rock into which the secret hatch had been built that concealed the crawlway from which the surface crawlers with their detectors emerged for their fruitless search, to which they returned under control of their cursing operator who, stoned again with hellish *krmml* weed, never noticed the quick flick of the detector needles as the crawlers reentered the tunnel, this time bearing on their return journey a cargo they had not exited with as the great door slammed shut behind them.

"We've done it! We're inside their defenses," Steel

rejoiced. "And no thanks to you, pushing that Mrddl-cursed invisibility button."

"Well, how was I to know?" Jax grated. "Anyways, we don't have a ship anymore but we *do* have the element of surprise. They don't know that *we* are here, but we know *they* are here!"

"Good thinking. Hssst!" he hissed. "Stay low, we're coming to something."

The clanking crawlers rattled into the immense chamber cut into the living stone and now filled with deadly war machines of all description. The only human there, if he could be called human, was the larshnik operator whose soiled fingertips sprang to the gun controls the instant he spotted the intruders but he never stood a chance. Precisely aimed rays from two blasters zeroed in on him and in a millisecond he was no more than a charred fragment of smoking flesh in the chair. Corps justice was striking at last to the larshnik lair.

Justice it was, impersonal and final, impartial and murderous, for there were no "innocents" in this lair of evil. Ravening forces of civilized vengeance struck down all that crossed their path as the two chums rode a death-dealing combat gun through the corridors of infamy.

"This is the big one," Steel grimaced as they came to an immense door of gold plated impervialite before which a suicide squad committed suicide under the relentless scourge of fire. There was more feeble resistance, smokily, coruscatingly and noisily exterminated, before this last barrier went down and they rode in triumph into the central control now manned by a single figure at the main panel. Superlarsh himself, secret head of the empire of interstellar crime.

"You have met your destiny," Steel intoned grimly, his weapon fixed unmovingly upon the black robed figure in the opaque space helmet. "Take off that helmet or you die upon the instant."

His only reply was a slobbered growl of inchoate rage, and for a long instant the black-gloved hands trembled over the gun controls. Then, ever so slowly, these same hands raised themselves to clutch at the helmet, to turn it, to lift it slowly off . . .

"By the sacred name of the Prophet Mrddl!" the two

Corpsmen gasped in unison, struck speechless by what they saw.

"Yes, so now you know," grated Superlarsh through angry teeth. "But, ha-ha, I'll bet you never suspected."

"You!!" Steel insufflated, breaking the frozen silence. "You! *You!!* YOU!!!"

"Yes, me, I, Colonel von Thorax, Commandant of the CCC. You never suspected me and, ohh, how I laughed at you all of the time."

"But . . ." Jax stammered. "*Why?*"

"Why? The answer is obvious to any but democratic interstellar swine like you. The only thing the larshniks of the galaxy had to fear was something like the CCC, a powerful force impervious to outside bribery or sedition, noble in the cause of righteousness. You could have caused us trouble. Therefore *we* founded the CCC, and I have long been head of both organizations. Our recruiters bring in the best that the civilized planets can offer, and I see to it that most of them are brutalized, morale destroyed, bodies wasted, and spirits crushed so they are no longer a danger. Of course, a few always make it through the course no matter how disgusting I make it— every generation has its share of super-masochists—but I see that these are taken care of pretty quickly."

"Like being sent on suicide missions?" Steel asked ironly.

"That's a good way."

"Like the one we were sent on—but it *didn't work!* Say your prayers, you filthy larshnik, for you are about to meet your maker!"

"Maker? Prayers? Are you out of your skull? All larshniks are atheists to the end . . ."

And then it was the end, in a coruscating puff of vapor, dead with those vile words upon his lips, no less than he deserved.

"Now what?" Steel asked.

"This," Jax responded, shooting the gun from his hand and imprisoning him instantly with an unbreakable paralysis ray. "No more second best for me—in the engine room with you on the bridge. This is *my* ball game from here on in."

"Are you mad!" Steel fluttered through paralyzed lips.

"Sane for the first time in my life. The superlarsh is dead, long live the new superlarsh. It's mine, the whole galaxy, *mine*."

"And what about me?"

"I should kill you, but that would be too easy. And you did share your chocolate bars with me. You will be blamed for this entire debacle—for the death of Colonel von Thorax *and* for the disaster here at larshnik prime base. Every man's hand will be against you, and you will be an outcast and will flee for your life to the farflung outposts of the galaxy where you will live in terror."

"Remember the chocolate bars!"

"I do. All I ever got were the stale ones. Now . . . GO!"

You want to know my name? Old Sarge is good enough. My story? Too much for your tender ears, boyo. Just top up the glasses, that's the way, and join me in a toast. At least that much for a poor old man who has seen much in his long lifetime. A toast of bad luck, bad cess I say, may Great Kramddl curse forever the man some know as Gentleman Jax. What, hungry? Not me—no—NO! Not a chocolate bar!!!!!

AFTERWORD

How charming they were in those long-lost days of youth: the mile-long spaceships (the construction of any one of which would exhaust a planet's mineral resources), the lantern-jawed and iron-thewed heroes, the lantern-slide flickers of exotic alien cultures. Rich with violence, pressing forward through the tangles of incoherent grammar and limited vocabulary, sexless as the nether parts of a store window dummy, asprinkle with nonsense science—what beady-eyed subteenager could have resisted their appeal? None! The space warps warped, and the alien ichor flowed, and it was a far better world to live in than the one outside. Space opera was irresistible.

I find it very easy to resist now. As an adult, that is. The grandmaster, E.E. Smith, Ph. D., still lives on in his books, still in print, still selling well. I will not denigrate his novels. They are grand stuff for tiny youngsters and a good introduction to science fiction. In time and space, in the history of sf, they were very important, and if they enjoy a half-afterlife now, why then more power to them. The present exercise in crotch-kneeing is not aimed at their memory, but at the modern practitioners of a dead art.

What is wrong with space opera as written today? Put most simply, there is just no excuse for its existence. The originals, more naïve, far more enthusiastic, did it much better. The world has matured, and science fiction has matured and—I hope—put aside childish things. I say hope because, with a feeling of great despair, I continue to read new sf works that concern themselves with space-warps, blasters, strobelights, space armor, all of the dreadful armory of dead cliches. Worse perhaps are the stories that repeat the deadly assumptions behind space opera and hang yet one more grisly plot line upon the dusty skeleton. Bright young things voyage out from Earth in miraculous ships that get anywhere in a flash, to alien planets with oxygen atmospheres where exotically shaped aliens talk colloquial English and think exactly like their American counterparts, where human needs and desires are stupefied, stultified, and denigrated to the lowest possible level. Do you wonder that I am not only appalled but stirred to a red rage?

I find humor the perfect tool for dealing with the situation. If space opera were not laughable we could not laugh at it. And after laughing at this parody perhaps we will also laugh at the so-serious practitioners of this dead art. Why, they might even laugh themselves at the things they are writing and, having once laughed, they might not ever be able to return to their dubious ways.

Novels

FIRST LENSMEN, by E.E. Smith
GREY LENSMEN, by E.E. Smith

CHILDREN OF THE LENS, by E.E. Smith
SKYLARK OF SPACE, by E.E. Smith
SKYLARK OF VALERON, by E.E. Smith
SPACEHOUNDS OF THE IPC, by E.E. Smith
DEATHWORLD, by Harry Harrison

Short Stories
THE ROCKETEERS HAVE SHAGGY EARS, by Keith Bennett

About Harry Harrison

Harry Harrison, b. 1926, is author of BILL, THE GALAC-
TIC HERO, DEATHWORLD I, DEATHWORLD II, DEATH-
WORLD III, THE STAINLESS STEEL RAT, and MAKE ROOM,
MAKE ROOM (which became the successful movie SOYLENT
GREEN), among others, and hundreds of short stories. He
also has edited THE YEAR'S BEST SF series, now into its
seventh volume, THE JOHN W. CAMPBELL MEMORIAL
ANTHOLOGY, AUTHOR'S CHOICE, and NOVA. His first
mystery, MONTEZUMA'S REVENGE, 1972, has sold in ten
countries and six languages. Mr. Harrison lives in San
Diego with his wife, Joan, and two children.

ALTERNATE UNIVERSES

TRIPS

ROBERT SILVERBERG

> *Does this path have a heart? All paths are the same: they lead nowhere. They are paths going through the bush, or into the bush. In my own life I could say I have traversed long, long paths, but I am not anywhere. . . . Does this path have a heart? If it does, the path is good; if it doesn't, it is of no use. Both paths lead nowhere; but one has a heart, the other doesn't. One makes for a joyful journey; as long as you follow it, you are one with it. The other will make you curse your life.*
>
> *—The Teachings of Don Juan*

1.

The second place you come to—the first having proved unsatisfactory, for one reason and another—is a city which could almost be San Francisco. Perhaps it is, sitting out there on the peninsula between the ocean and the bay, white buildings clambering over improbably steep hills. It occupies the place in your psychic space that San Francisco has always occupied, although you don't really know yet what this city calls itself. Perhaps you'll find out before long.

You go forward. What you feel first is the strangeness of the familiar, and then the utter heartless familiarity of the strange. For example the automobiles, and there are plenty of them, are all halftracks: low sleek sexy sedans that have the flashy Detroit styling, the usual chrome, the usual streamlining, the low-raked windows all agleam, but there are only two wheels, both of them in front, with a pair of tread-belts circling endlessly in back. Is this good design for city use? Who knows? Somebody evidently thinks so, here. And then the newspapers: the format is the same, narrow columns, gaudy screaming headlines, miles of black type on coarse grayish-white paper, but the names and the places have been changed. You scan the front page of a newspaper in the window of a curbside vending machine. Big photo of Chairman DeGrasse, serving as host at a reception for the Patagonian Ambassador. An account of the tribal massacres in the highlands of Dzungaria. Details of the solitude epidemic that is devastating Persepolis. When the halftracks stall on the hillsides, which is often, the other drivers ring silvery chimes, politely venting their impatience. Men who look like Navahos chant what sound like sutras in the intersections. The traffic lights are blue and orange. Clothing tends toward the prosaic, grays and dark blues, but the cut and slope of men's jackets has an angular, formal eighteenth-century look, verging on pomposity. You pick up a bright coin that lies in the street: it is vaguely metallic but rubbery, as if you could compress it between your fingers, and its thick edges bear incuse lettering: TO GOD WE OWE OUR SWORDS. On the next block a squat two-story building is ablaze, and agitated clerks do a desperate dance. The fire engine is glossy green and its pump looks like a diabolical cannon embellished with sweeping flanges; it spouts a glistening yellow foam that eats the flames and, oxidizing, runs off down the gutter, a trickle of sluggish blue fluid. Everyone wears eyeglasses here, *everyone*. At a sidewalk cafe, pale waitresses offer mugs of boiling-hot milk into which the silent tight-faced patrons put cinnamon, mustard, and what seems to be Tabasco sauce. You offer your coin and try a sample, imitating what they do, and everyone bursts into laughter. The girl behind the counter pushes a thick stack of paper currency at you by way of change: UNITED FEDERAL COLUMBIAN REPUBLIC, each bill declares. GOOD FOR ONE EXCHANGE. Illegible signatures. Portrait of early leader of the republic, so famous that they give him no label of identification, bewigged, wall-eyed, ecstatic. You sip your milk, blowing gently. A light scum begins to form on its speckled surface. Sirens start to wail. About you, the other milk-drinkers stir uneasily. A parade is coming. Trumpets, drums, far-off chanting. Look! Four naked boys carry an open brocaded litter on which there sits an immense block of ice, a great frosted cube, mysterious, impenetrable. "Patagonia!" the onlookers cry sadly. The word is wrenched from them: "Patagonia!" Next, marching by himself, a mitred bishop advances, all in green, curtseying to the crowd, tossing hearty blessings as though they were flowers. "Forget your sins! Cancel your debts! All is made new! All is good!" You shiver and peer intently into his eyes as he passes you, hoping that he will single you out for an embrace. He is terribly tall but white-haired and fragile, somehow, despite his agility and energy. He reminds you of Norman, your wife's older brother, and perhaps he *is* Norman, the Norman of this place, and you wonder if he can give you news of Elizabeth, the Elizabeth of this place, but you say nothing and he goes by. And then comes a tremendous wooden scaffold on wheels, a true juggernaut, at the summit of which rests a polished statue carved out of gleaming black stone: a human figure, male, plump, arms intricately folded, face complacent. The statue emanates a sense of vast Sumerian calm. The face is that of Chairman DeGrasse. "He'll die in the first blizzard," murmurs a man to your left. Another, turning suddenly, says with great force, "No, it's going to be done the proper way. He'll last until the time of the accidents, just as he's supposed to. I'll bet on that." Instantly they are nose to nose, glaring, and then they are wagering—a tense complicated ritual involving slapping of palms, interchanges of slips of paper, formal voiding of spittle, hysterical appeals to witnesses. The emotional climate here seems a trifle too intense. You decide to move along. Warily you leave the cafe, looking in all directions.

2.

Before you began your travels you were told how essential it was to define your intended role. Were you going to be a tourist, or an explorer, or an infiltrator? Those are the choices that confront anyone arriving at a new place. Each bears its special risks.

To opt for being a tourist is to choose the easiest but most contemptible path; ultimately it's the most dangerous one, too, in a certain sense. You have to accept the built-in epithets that go with the part: they will think of you as a *foolish* tourist, an *ignorant* tourist, a *vulgar* tourist, a *mere* tourist. Do you want to be considered mere? Are you able to accept that? Is that really your preferred self-image—baffled, bewildered, led about by the nose? You'll sign up for packaged tours, you'll carry guidebooks and cameras, you'll go to the cathedral and the museums and the marketplace, and you'll remain always on the outside of things, seeing a great deal, experiencing nothing. What a waste! You will be diminished by the very traveling that you thought would expand you. Tourism hollows and parches you. All places become one: a hotel, a smiling swarthy sunglassed guide, a bus, a plaza, a fountain, a marketplace, a museum, a cathedral. You are transformed into a feeble shriveled thing made out of glued-together travel folders; you are naked but for your visas; the sum of your life's adventures is a box of left-over small change from many indistinguishable lands.

To be an explorer is to make the *macho* choice. You swagger in, bent on conquest, for isn't any discovery a kind of conquest? Your existential position, like that of any mere tourist, lies outside the heart of things, but you are unashamed of that; and while tourists are essentially passive the explorer's role is active; an explorer intends to grasp that heart, take possession, squeeze. In the explorer's role you consciously cloak yourself in the trappings of power: self-assurance, thick bankroll, stack of credit cards. You capitalize on the glamor of being a stranger. Your curiosity is invincible; you ask unabashed questions about the most intimate things, never for an instant relinquishing eye-contact. You open locked doors and flash bright lights into curtained rooms. You are Magellan; you are Malinowski; you are Captain Cook. You will gain much, but—ah, here is the price!—you will always be feared and hated, you will never be permitted to attain the true core. Nor is superficiality the worst peril. Remember that Magellan and Captain Cook left their bones on tropic beaches. Sometimes the natives lose patience with explorers.

The infiltrator, though? His is at once the most difficult role and the most rewarding one. Will it be yours? Consider. You'll have to get right with it when you reach your destination, instantly learn the regulations, find your way around like an old hand, discover the location of shops and freeways and hotels, figure out the units of currency, the rules of social intercourse—all of this knowledge mastered surreptitiously, through observation alone, while moving about silently, camouflaged, *never asking for help*. You must become a part of the world you have entered, and the way to do it is to encourage a general assumption that you already are a part of it, have always been a part of it. Wherever you land, you need to recognize that life has been going on for millions of years, life goes on there steadily, with you or without you; you are the intrusive one, and if you don't want to feel intrusive you'd better learn fast how to fit in. Of course it isn't easy. The infiltrator doesn't have the privilege of buying stability by acting dumb. You won't be able to say, "How much does it cost to ride on the cable-car?" You won't be able to say, "I'm from somewhere else, and this is the kind of money I carry, dollars quarters pennies halves nickels, is any of it legal tender here?" You don't dare identify yourself in any way as an outsider. If you don't get the idioms or the accent right, you can tell them you grew up out of town, but that's as much as you can reveal. The truth is your eternal secret, even when you're in trouble, *especially* when you're in trouble. When your back's to the wall you won't have time to say, "Look, I wasn't born in this universe at all, you see, I came zipping in from some other place, so pardon me, forgive me, excuse me, pity me." No, no, no, you can't do that. They won't believe you, and even if they do, they'll make it all the worse for you once they know. If you want to infiltrate, Cameron, you've got to fake it all the way. Jaunty smile, steely even gaze. And you have to infiltrate. You know that, don't you? You don't really have any choice.

Infiltrating has its dangers too. The rough part comes when they find you out, and they always do find you out. Then they'll react bitterly against your deception, they'll lash out in blind rage. If you're lucky, you'll be gone before they learn your sweaty little secret. Before they discover the discarded phrasebook hidden in the boarding-house room, before they stumble on the torn-off pages of your private journal. They'll find you out. They always do.

But by then you'll be somewhere else, you hope, beyond the reach of their anger and their sorrow, beyond their reach, beyond their reach.

3.

Suppose I show you, for Exhibit A, Cameron reacting to an extraordinary situation. You can test your own resilience by trying to picture yourself in his position. There has been a sensation in Cameron's mind very much like that of the extinction of the cosmos: a thunderclap, everything going black, a blankness, a total absence. Followed by the return of light, flowing inward upon him like high tide on the celestial shore, a surging stream of brightness moving with inexorable certainty. He stands flat-footed, dumbfounded, high on a bare hillside in warm early-hour sunlight. The house—redwood timbers, picture window, driftwood sculptures, paintings, books, records, refrigerator, gallon jugs of red wine, carpets, tiles, avocado plants in wooden tubs, carport, car, driveway—is gone. The neighboring houses are gone. The winding street is gone. The eucalyptus forest that ought to be behind him, rising toward the crest of the hill, is gone. Downslope there is no Oakland, there is no Berkeley, only a scattering of crude squatters' shacks running raggedly along unpaved switchbacks toward the pure blue bay. Across the water there is no Bay Bridge; on the far shore there is no San Francisco. The Golden Gate Bridge does not span the gap between the city and the Marin headland. Cameron is astonished, not that he didn't expect something like this, but that the transformation is so complete, so absolute. If you don't want your world any more, the old man had said, you can just drop it, can't you? Let go of it, let it drop. Can't you? Of course you can. And so Cameron has let go of it. He's in another place entirely, now. Wherever this place is, it isn't home. The sprawling Bay Area cities and towns aren't here, never were. Goodbye, San Leandro, San Mateo, El Cerrito, Walnut Creek. He sees a landscape of gentle bare hills, rolling meadows, the dry brown grass of summer; the scarring hand of man is evident only occasionally. He begins to adapt. This is what he must have wanted, after all, and though he has

"You come all this way on foot?"

"Had a mule. Lost him back in the valley. Lost everything I had with me."

"Umm. Indians cutting up again. You give them a little gin, they go crazy." The other smiles faintly; then the smile fades and he retreats into impassivity, sitting motionless with hands on thighs, face a mask of patience that seems merely to be a thin covering for impatience or worse.

—*Indians?*—

"They gave me a rough time," Cameron says, getting into the fantasy of it.

"Umm."

"Cleaned me out, let me go."

"Umm. Umm."

Cameron feels his sense of a shared identity with this man lessening. There is no way of engaging him. I am you, you are I, and yet you take no notice of the strange fact that I wear your face and body, you seem to show no interest in me at all. Or else you hide your interest amazingly well.

Cameron says, "You know where I can get lodging?"

"Nothing much around here. Not many settlers this side of the bay, I guess."

"I'm strong. I can do most any kind of work. Maybe you could use—"

"Umm. No." Cold dismissal glitters in the frosty eyes. Cameron wonders how often people in the world of his former life saw such a look in his own. A tug on the reins. Your time is up, stranger. The horse swings around and begins picking its way daintily along the path.

Desperately Cameron calls, "One thing more!"

"Umm?"

"Is your name Cameron?"

A flicker of interest. "Might be."

"Christopher Cameron. Kit. Chris. That you?"

"Kit." The other's eyes drill into his own. The mouth compresses until the lips are invisible: not a scowl but a speculative, pensive movement. There is tension in the way the other man grasps his reins. For the first time Cameron feels that he has made contact. "Kit Cameron, yes. Why?"

"Your wife," Cameron says. "Her name Elizabeth?"

The tension increases. The other Cameron is cloaked in explosive silence. Something terrible is building within him. Then, unexpectedly, the tension snaps. The other man spits, scowls, slumps in his saddle. "My woman's dead," he mutters. "Say, who the hell are you? What do you want with me?"

"I'm—I'm—" Cameron falters. He is overwhelmed by fear and pity. A bad start, a lamentable start. He trembles. He had not thought it would be anything like this. With an effort he masters himself. Fiercely he says, "I've got to know. Was her name Elizabeth?" For an answer the horseman whacks his heels savagely against his mount's ribs and gallops away, fleeing as though he has had an encounter with Satan.

5.

Go, the old man said. You know the score. This is how it is: everything's random, nothing's fixed unless we want it to be, and even then the system isn't as stable as we think it is. So go. Go. Go, he said, and, of course, hearing something like that, Cameron went. What else could he do, once he had his freedom, but abandon his native universe and try a different one? Notice that I didn't say a better one, just a different one. Or two or three or five different ones. It was a gamble, certainly. He might lose everything that mattered to him, and gain nothing worth having. But what of it? Every day is full of gambles like that: you stake your life whenever you open a door. You never know what's heading your way, not ever, and still you choose to play the game. How can a man be expected to become all he's capable of becoming if he spends his whole life pacing up and down the same courtyard? Go. Make your voyages. Time forks, again and again and again. New universes split off at each instant of decision. Left turn, right turn, honk your horn, jump the traffic light, hit your gas, hit your brake, every action spawns whole galaxies of possibility. We move through a soup of infinities. If repressing a sneeze generates an alternative continuum, what, then, are the consequences of the truly major acts, the assassinations and inseminations, the conversions, the renunciations? Go. And as you travel, mull these thoughts constantly. Part of the game is discerning the precipitating factors that shaped the worlds you visit. What's the story here? Dirt roads, donkey-carts, hand-sewn clothes. No Industrial Revolution, is that it? The steam-engine man—what was his name, Savery, New-comen, Watt?—smothered in his cradle? No mines, no factories, no assembly lines, no dark Satanic mills. That must be it. The air is so pure here: you can tell by that, it's a simpler era. Very good, Cameron. You see the patterns swiftly. But now try somewhere else. Your own self has rejected you here; besides, this place has no Elizabeth. Close your eyes. Summon the lightning.

6.

The parade has reached a disturbing level of frenzy. Marchers and floats now occupy the side streets as well as the main boulevard, and there is no way to escape from their demonic enthusiasm. Streamers cascade from office windows and gigantic photographs of Chairman DeGrasse have sprouted on every wall, suddenly, like dark infestations of lichen. A boy presses close against Cameron, extends a clenched fist, opens his fingers: on his palm rests a glittering jeweled case, egg-shaped, thumbnail-sized. "Spores from Patagonia," he says. "Let me have ten exchanges and they're yours." Politely Cameron declines. A woman in a blue and orange frock tugs at his arm and says urgently, "All the rumors are true, you know. They've just been confirmed. What are you going to do about that? What are you going to *do*?" Cameron shrugs and smiles and disengages himself. A man with gleaming buttons asks, "Are you enjoying the festival? I've sold everything and I'm going to move to the highway next Godsday." Cameron nods and murmurs congratulations, hoping congratulations áre in order. He turns a corner and confronts, once more, the bishop who looks like Elizabeth's brother, who *is*, he concludes, indeed Elizabeth's brother. "Forget your sins!" he is crying still. "Cancel your debts!" Cameron thrusts his head between two plump girls at the curb and attempts to call to him, but his voice fails, nothing coming forth but a hoarse wordless rasp, and the bishop moves on. Moving on is a good idea, Cameron tells himself. This place exhausts him.

He has come to it too soon, and its manic tonality is more than he wants to handle. He finds a quiet alleyway and presses his cheek against a cool brick wall, and stands there breathing deeply until he is calm enough to depart. All right. Onward.

7.

Empty grasslands spread to the horizon. This could be the Gobi steppe. Cameron sees neither cities nor towns nor even villages, just six or seven squat black tents pitched in a loose circle in the saddle between two low gray-green hummocks, a few hundred yards from where he stands. He looks beyond, across the gently folded land, and spies dark animal figures at the limits of his range of vision: about a dozen horses, close together, muzzle to muzzle, flank to flank, horses with riders. Or perhaps they are a congregation of centaurs. Anything is possible. He decides, though, that they are Indians, a war party of young braves, maybe, camping in these desolate plains. They see him. Quite likely they saw him some while before he noticed them. Casually they break out of their grouping, wheel, ride in his direction.

He awaits them. Why should he flee? Where could he hide? Their pace accelerates from trot to canter, from canter to wild gallop; now they plunge toward him with fluid ferocity and a terrifying eagerness. They wear open leather jackets and rough rawhide leggings; they carry lances, bows, battle-axes, long curved swords; they ride small, agile horses, hardly more than ponies, tireless packets of energy. They surround him, pulling up, the fierce little steeds rearing and whinnying; they peer at him, point, laugh, exchange harsh derisive comments in a mysterious language. Then, solemnly, they begin to ride slowly in a wide circle around him. They are flat-faced, small-nosed, bearded, with broad, prominent cheekbones; the crowns of their heads are shaven but long black hair streams down over their ears and the napes of their necks. Heavy folds in the upper lids give their eyes a slanted look. Their skins are copper-colored but with an underlying golden tinge, as though these are not Indians at all, but—what? Japanese? A samurai corps? No, probably not Japanese. But not Indians either.

They continue to circle him, gradually moving more swiftly. They chatter to one another and occasionally hurl what sound like questions at him. They seem fascinated by him, but also contemptuous. In a sudden demonstration of horsemanship one of them cuts from the circular formation and, goading his horse to an instant gallop, streaks past Cameron, leaning down to jab a finger into his forearm. Then another does it, and another, streaking back and forth across the circle, poking him, plucking at his hair, tweaking him, nearly running him down. They draw their swords and swish them through the air just above his head. They menace him, or pretend to, with their lances. Throughout it all they laugh. He stands perfectly still. This ordeal, he suspects, is a test of his courage. Which he passes, eventually. The lunatic galloping ceases; they rein in, and several of them dismount.

They are little men, chest-high to him but thicker through the chest and shoulders than he is. One unships a leather pouch and offers it to him with an unmistakable gesture: take, drink. Cameron sips cautiously. It is a thick grayish fluid, both sweet and sour. Fermented milk? He gags, winces, forces himself to sip again; they watch him closely. The second taste isn't so bad. He takes a third more willingly and gravely returns the pouch. The warriors laugh, not derisively now but more in applause, and the man who had given him the pouch slaps Cameron's shoulder admiringly. He tosses the pouch back to Cameron. Then he leaps to his saddle, and abruptly they all take off. Mongols, Cameron realizes. The sons of Genghis Khan, riding to the horizon. A worldwide empire? Yes, and this must be the wild west for them, the frontier, where the young men enact their rites of passage. Back in Europe, after seven centuries of Mongol dominance, they have become citified, domesticated, sippers of wine, theatergoers, cultivators of gardens, but here they follow the ways of their all-conquering forefathers. Cameron shrugs. Nothing for him here. He takes a last sip of the milk and drops the pouch into the tall grass. Onward.

8.

No grass grows here. He sees the stumps of buildings, the blackened trunks of dead trees, mounds of broken tile and brick. The smell of death is in the air. All the bridges are down. Fog rolls in off the bay, dense and greasy, and becomes a screen on which images come alive. These ruins are inhabited. Figures move about. They are the living dead. Looking into the thick mist he sees a vision of the shock wave, he recoils as alpha particles shower his skin. He beholds the survivors emerging from their shattered houses, straggling into the smoldering streets, naked, stunned, their bodies charred, their eyes glazed, some of them with their hair on fire. The walking dead. No one speaks. No one asks why this has happened. He is watching a silent movie. The apocalyptic fire has touched the ground here; the land itself is burning. Blue phosphorescent flames rise from the earth. The final judgment, the day of wrath. Now he hears a dread music beginning, a dead-march, all cellos and basses, the dark notes coming at wide intervals: ooom   ooom   ooom   ooom   ooom. And then the tempo picks up, the music becomes a danse macabre, syncopated, lively, the timbre still dark, the rhythms funereal: ooom ooom ooom-de-ooom de-ooom de-ooom de-ooom-de-ooom, jerky, chaotic, wildly gay. The distorted melody of the Ode to Joy lurks somewhere in the ragged strands of sound. The dying victims stretch their fleshless hands toward him. He shakes his head. What service can I do for you? Guilt assails him. He is a tourist in the land of their grief. Their eyes reproach him. He would embrace them, but he fears they will crumble at his touch, and he lets the procession go past him without doing anything to cross the gulf between himself and them. "Elizabeth?" he murmurs. "Norman?" They have no faces, only eyes. "What can I do? I can't do anything for you." Not even tears will come. He looks away. Though I speak with the tongues of men and of angels, and have not charity, I am become as sounding brass, or a tinkling cymbal. And though I have the gift of prophecy, and understand all mysteries, and all knowledge; and though I have all faith, so that I could remove mountains, and have not charity, I am nothing. But this world is beyond the reach of love. He looks away. The sun appears. The fog burns off. The visions fade. He sees only the dead land, the ashes, the ruins,

All right. Here we have no continuing city, but we seek one to come. Onward. Onward.

9.

And now, after this series of brief, disconcerting inter-mediate stops, Cameron has come to a city that is San Francisco beyond doubt, not some other city on San Fran-cisco's site but a true San Francisco, a recognizable San Francisco. He pops into it atop Russian Hill, at the very crest, on a dazzling, brilliant, cloudless day. To his left, below, lies Fisherman's Wharf; ahead of him rises the Coit Tower, yes, and he can see the Ferry Building and the Bay Bridge. Familiar landmarks—but how strange all the rest seems! Where is the eye-stabbing Transamerica pyra-mid? Where is the colossal somber stalk of the Bank of America? The strangeness, he realizes, derives not so much from substitutions as from absences. The big Em-barcadero developments are not there, nor the Chinatown Holiday Inn, nor the miserable tentacles of the elevated freeways, nor, apparently, anything else that was con-structed in the last twenty years. This is the old short-shanked San Francisco of his boyhood, a sparkling minia-ture city, unManhattanized, skylineless. Surely he has returned to the place he knew in the sleepy 1950's, the tranquil Eisenhower years.

He heads downhill, searching for a newspaper box. He finds one at the corner of Hyde and North Point, a bright yellow metal rectangle. San Francisco *Chronicle*, ten cents. Ten cents? Is that the right price for 1954? One Roosevelt dime goes into the slot. The paper, he finds, is dated Tuesday, August 19, 1975. In what Cameron still thinks of, with some irony now, as the real world, the world that has been receding rapidly from him all day in a series of discontinuous jumps, it is also Tuesday, the 19th of August, 1975. So he has not gone backward in time at all; he has come to a San Francisco where time has seem-ingly been standing still. Why? In vertigo he eyes the front page.

A three-column headline declares:

FUEHRER ARRIVES IN WASHINGTON

Under it, to the left, a photograph of three men, smiling broadly, positively beaming at one another. The caption identifies them as President Kennedy, Fuehrer Goering, and Ambassador Togarashi of Japan, meeting in the White House rose garden. Cameron closes his eyes. Using no data other than the headline and the caption, he attempts to concoct a plausible speculation. This is a world, he decides, in which the Axis must have won the war. The United States is a German fiefdom. There are no high-rise buildings in San Francisco because the American economy, shattered by defeat, has not yet in thirty years of peace returned to a level where it can afford to erect them, or perhaps because American venture capital, prodded by the financial ministers of the Third Reich—(Hjalmar Schacht? The name drifts out of the swampy recesses of memory)—now tends to flow toward Europe. But how could it have happened? Cameron remembers the war years clearly, the tremendous surge of patriotism, the vast mobilization, the great national effort. Rosie the Riveter. Lucky Strike Green Goes To War. Let's Remember Pearl Harbor, As We Did The Alamo. He doesn't see any way the Germans might have brought America to her knees. Except one. The bomb, he thinks, the bomb, the Nazis get the bomb in 1940 and Wernher von Braun invents a transatlantic rocket and New York and Washington are nuked one night and that's it, we've been pushed beyond the resources of patriotism, we cave in and surrender within a week. And so—

He studies the photograph. President Kennedy, grinning, standing between Reichsfuehrer Goering and a suave youthful-looking Japanese. Kennedy? Ted? No, this is Jack, the very same Jack who, looking jowly, heavy bags under his eyes, deep creases in his face—he must be almost sixty years old, nearing the end of what is probably his second term of office. Jacqueline waiting none too patiently for him upstairs. Get done with your Japs and Nazis, love, and let's have a few drinkies together before the concert. Yes. John-John and Caroline somewhere on the premises too, the nation's darlings, models for young people everywhere. Yes. And Goering? Indeed, the very same Goering who. Well into his eighties, monstrously fat, chin upon chin, multitudes of chins, vast bemedaled bosom, little mischievous eyes glittering with a long life-time's cheery recollections of gratified lusts. How happy he looks! And how amiable! It was always impossible to hate Goering the way one loathed Goebbels, say, or Himmler or Streicher; Goering had charm, the outrageous charm of a monstre sacre, of a Nero, of a Caligula, and here he is alive in the 1970's, a mountain of immortal flesh, having survived Adolf to become—Cameron as-sumes—Second Fuehrer and to be received in pomp at the White House, no less. Perhaps a state banquet tomorrow night, rollmops, sauerbraten, kassler rippchen, koenigs-berger klopse, washed down with flagons of Bernkasteler Doktor '69, Schloss Johannisberg '71, or does the Fuehrer prefer beer? We have the finest lagers on tap, Löwenbrau, Würzburger Hofbrau—

But wait. Something rings false in Cameron's historical construct. He is unable to find in John F. Kennedy those depths of opportunism that would allow him to serve as puppet President of a Nazi-ruled America, taking orders from some slick-haired hard-eyed gauleiter and hopping obediently when the Fuehrer comes to town. Bomb or no bomb, there would have been a diehard underground resistance movement, decades of guerrilla warfare, bitter hatred of the German oppressor and of all collaborators. No surrender, then. The Axis has won the war, but the United States has retained its autonomy. Cameron revises his speculations. Suppose, he tells himself, Hitler in this universe did not break his pact with Stalin and invade Russia in the summer of 1941, but led his forces across the Channel instead to wipe out Britain. And the Japanese left Pearl Harbor alone, so the United States never was drawn into the war, which was over in fairly short order—say, by September of 1942. The Germans now rule Europe from Cornwall to the Urals, and the Japanese have the whole Pacific west of Hawaii; the United States, lost in dreamy neutrality, is an isolated nation, a giant Portugal, economically stagnant, largely cut off from world trade. There are no skyscrapers in San Francisco because no one sees reason to build anything in this country. Yes? Is this how it is?

He seats himself on the stoop of a house and explores his newspaper. This world has a stock market, albeit a sluggish one: the Dow-Jones Industrials stand at 354.61. Some of the listings are familiar—IBM, AT&T, General Motors—but many are not. Litton, Syntex, and Polaroid all are missing; so is Xerox, but he finds its primordial predecessor, Haloid, in the quotations. There are two baseball leagues, each with eight clubs; the Boston Braves have moved to Milwaukee but otherwise the table of teams could have come straight out of the 1940's. Brooklyn is leading in the National League, Philadelphia in the American. In the news section he finds recognizable names: New York has a Senator Rockefeller, Massachusetts has a Senator Kennedy. (Robert, apparently. He is currently in Italy. Yesterday he toured the majestic Tomb of Mussolini near the Colosseum, today he has an audience with Pope Benedict.) An airline advertisement invites San Franciscans to go to New York via TWA's glorious new Starliners, now only twelve hours with just a brief stop in Chicago. The accompanying sketch indicates that they have about reached the DC-4 level here, or is that a DC-6, with all those propellers? The foreign news is tame and sketchy: not a word about Israel vs. the Arabs, the squabbling republics of Africa, the People's Republic of China, or the war in South America. Cameron assumes that the only surviving Jews are those of New York and Los Angeles, that Africa is one immense German colonial tract with a few patches under Italian rule, that China is governed by the Japanese, not by the heirs of Chairman Mao, and that the South American nations are torpid and unaggressive. Yes? Reading this newspaper is the strangest experience this voyage has given him so far, for the pages *look* right, the tone of the writing *feels* right, there is the insistent texture of unarguable reality about the whole paper, and yet everything is subtly off, everything has undergone a slight shift along the spectrum of events. The newspaper has the quality of a dream, but he has never known a dream to have such overwhelming substantive density.

He folds the paper under his arm and strolls toward the bay. A block from the waterfront he finds a branch of the Bank of America—some things withstand all permutations —and goes inside to change some money. There are risks, but he is curious. The teller unhesitatingly takes his five-dollar bill and hands him four singles and a little stack of coins. The singles are unremarkable, and Lincoln, Jefferson, and Washington occupy their familiar places on the cent, nickel, and quarter; but the dime shows Ben Franklin and the fifty-cent piece bears the features of a heartylooking man, youngish, full-faced, bushy-haired, whom Cameron is unable to identify at all.

On the next corner eastward he comes to a public library. Now he can confirm his guesses. An almanac! Yes, and how odd the list of Presidents looks. Roosevelt, he learns, retired in poor health in 1940, and that, so far as he can discover, is the point of divergence between this world and his. The rest follows predictably enough. Wendell Willkie, defeating John Nance Garner in the 1940 election, maintains a policy of strict neutrality while—yes, it was as he had imagined—the Germans and Japanese quickly conquer most of the world. Willkie dies in office during the 1944 Presidential campaign—aha! That's Willkie on the half dollar!—and is briefly succeeded by Vice President McNary, who does not want the Presidency; a hastily recalled Republican convention nominates Robert Taft. Two terms then for Taft, who beats James Byrnes, and two for Thomas Dewey, and then in 1960 the long Republican era is ended at last by Senator Lyndon Johnson of Texas. Johnson's running mate—it is an amusing reversal, Cameron thinks—is Senator John F. Kennedy of Massachusetts. After the traditional two terms, Johnson steps down and Vice President Kennedy wins the 1968 Presidential election. He has been re-elected in 1972, naturally; in this placid world incumbents always win. There is, of course, no UN here; there has been no Korean War, no movement of colonial liberation, no exploration of space. The almanac tells Cameron that Hitler lived until 1960, Mussolini until 1958. The world seems to have adapted remarkably readily to Axis rule, although a German army of occupation is still stationed in England.

He is tempted to go on and on, comparing histories, learning the transmuted destinies of such figures as Hubert Humphrey, Dwight Eisenhower, Harry Truman, Nikita Khruschchev, Lee Harvey Oswald, Juan Peron. But suddenly a more intimate curiosity flowers in him. In a hallway alcove he consults the telephone book. There is one directory covering both Alameda and Contra Costa counties, and it is a much more slender volume than the directory which in his world covers Oakland alone. There are two dozen Cameron listings, but none at his address, and no Christophers or Elizabeths or any plausible permutations of those names. On a hunch he looks in the San Francisco book. Nothing promising there either; but then he checks Elizabeth under her maiden name, Dudley, and yes, there is an Elizabeth Dudley at the familiar old address on Laguna. The discovery causes him to tremble. He rummages in his pocket, finds his Ben Franklin dime, drops it in the slot. He listens. There's the dial tone. He makes the call.

10.

The apartment, what he can see of it by peering past her shoulder, looks much as he remembers it: well-worn couches and chairs upholstered in burgundy and dark green, stark whitewashed walls, elaborate sculptures—her own—of gray driftwood, huge ferns in hanging containers. To behold these objects in these surroundings wrenches powerfully at his sense of time and place and afflicts him with an almost unbearable nostalgia. The last time he was here, if indeed he has ever been "here" in any sense, was in 1969; but the memories are vivid, and what he sees corresponds so closely to what he recalls that he feels transported to that earlier era. She stands in the doorway, studying him with cool curiosity tinged with unmistakable suspicion. She wears unexpectedly ordinary clothes, a loose-fitting embroidered white blouse and a short, pleated blue skirt, and her golden hair looks dull and carelessly combed, but surely she is the same woman from whom he parted this morning, the same woman with whom he has shared his life these past seven years, a beautiful woman, a tall woman, nearly as tall as he—on some occasions taller, it has seemed—with a serene smile and steady green eyes and smooth, taut skin. "Yes?" she says uncertainly. "Are you the man who phoned?"

"Yes. Chris Cameron." He searches her face for some flicker of recognition. "You don't know me? Not at all?"

"Not at all. Should I know you?"

"Perhaps. Probably not. It's hard to say."

"Have we once met? Is that it?"

"I'm not sure how I'm going to explain my relation-ship to you."

"So you said when you called. Your *relationship* to me? How can strangers have had a relationship?"

"It's complicated. May I come in?"

She laughs nervously, as though caught in some embar-rassing faux pas. "Of course," she says, not without giving him a quick appraisal, making a rapid estimate of risk. The apartment is in fact almost exactly as he knew it, except that there is no stereo phonograph, only a bulky archaic Victrola, and her record collection is surprisingly scanty, and there are rather fewer books than his Eliza-beth would have had. They confront one another stiffly. He is as uneasy over this encounter as she is, and finally it is she who seeks some kind of social lubricant, suggest-ing that they have a little wine. She offers him red or white.

"Red, please," he says.

She goes to a low sideboard and takes out two cheap, clumsy-looking tumblers. Then, effortlessly, she lifts a gallon jug of wine from the floor and begins to unscrew its cap. "You were awfully mysterious on the phone," she says, "and you're still being mysterious now. What brings you here? Do we have mutual friends?"

"I think it wouldn't be untruthful to say that we do. At least in a manner of speaking."

"Your own manner of speaking is remarkably round-about, Mr. Cameron."

"I can't help that right now. And call me Chris, please." As she pours the wine he watches her closely, thinking of that other Elizabeth, *his* Elizabeth, thinking how well he knows her body, the supple play of muscles in her back, the sleek texture of her skin, the firmness of her flesh, and he flashes instantly to their strange, absurdly romantic meeting years ago, that June when he had gone off alone into the Sierra high country for a week of back-packing and, following heaps of stones that he had wrongly taken to be trail-markers, had come to a place well off the path, a private place, a cool dark glacial lake rimmed by brilliant patches of late-lying snow, and had begun to make camp, and had become suddenly aware of someone else's pack thirty yards away, and a pile of discarded clothing on the shore, and then had seen her, swimming just beyond a pine-tipped point, heading toward land, rising like Venus from the water, naked, noticing him, startled by his presence, apprehensive for a moment but then immediately making the best of it, relaxing, smiling, standing unashamed shin-deep in the chilly shallows and inviting him to join her for a swim. These recollections of that first contact and all that ensued excite him terribly, for this person before him is at once the Elizabeth he loves, familiar, joined to him by the bond of shared experience, and also someone new, a complete stranger, from whom he can draw fresh inputs, that jolting gift of novelty which his Elizabeth can never again offer him. He stares at her shoulders and back with fierce, intense hunger; she turns toward him with the glasses of wine in her hands, and, before he can mask that wild gleam of desire, she receives it with full force. The impact is immediate. She recoils. She is not the Elizabeth of the Sierra lake; she seems unable to handle such a level of unexpected erotic voltage. Jerkily she thrusts the wine at him, her hands shaking so that she spills a little on her sleeve. He takes the glass and backs away, a bit dazed by his own frenzied upwelling of emotion. With an effort he calms himself. There is a long moment of awkward silence while they drink. The psychic atmosphere grows less torrid; a certain mood of remote, businesslike courtesy develops between them.

After the second glass of wine she says, "Now. How do you know me and what do you want from me?"

Briefly he closes his eyes. What can he tell her? How can he explain? He has rehearsed no strategies. Already he has managed to alarm her with a single unguarded glance; what effect would a confession of apparent madness have? But he has never used strategies with Elizabeth, has never resorted to any tactics except the tactic of utter candidness. And this is Elizabeth. Slowly he says, "In another existence you and I are married, Elizabeth. We live in the Oakland hills and we're extraordinarily happy together."

"Another existence?"

"In a world apart from this, a world where history took

a different course a generation ago, where the Axis lost the war, where John Kennedy was President in 1963 and was killed by an assassin, where you and I met beside a lake in the Sierra and fell in love. There's an infinity of worlds, Elizabeth, side by side, worlds in which all possible variations of every possible event take place. Worlds in which you and I are married happily, in which you and I have been married and divorced, in which you and I don't exist, in which you exist and I don't, in which we meet and loathe one another, in which—in which—do you see, Elizabeth, there's a world for everything; and I've been traveling from world to world. I've seen nothing but wilderness where San Francisco ought to be, and I've met Mongol horsemen in the East Bay hills, and I've seen this whole area devastated by atomic warfare, and—does this sound insane to you, Elizabeth?"

"Just a little." She smiles. The old Elizabeth, cool, judicious, performing one of her specialties, the conditional acceptance of the unbelievable for the sake of some amusing conversation. "But go on. You've been jumping from world to world. I won't even bother to ask you how. What are you running away from?"

"I've never seen it that way. I'm running *toward*."

"Toward what?"

"An infinity of worlds. An endless range of possible experience."

"That's a lot to swallow. Isn't one world enough for you to explore?"

"Evidently not."

"You had all infinity," she says. "Yet you chose to come to me. Presumably I'm the one point of familiarity for you in this otherwise strange world. Why come here? What's the point of your wanderings, if you seek the familiar? If all you wanted to do was find your way back to your Elizabeth, why did you leave her in the first place? Are you as happy with her as you claim to be?"

"I can be happy with her and still desire her in other guises."

"You sound driven."

"No," he says. "No more driven than Faust. I believe in searching as a way of life. Not searching *for*, just searching. And it's impossible to stop. To stop is to die,

Elizabeth. Look at Faust, going on and on, going to Helen of Troy herself, experiencing everything the world has to offer, and always seeking more. When Faust finally cries out, *This is it, this is what I've been looking for, this is where I choose to stop*, Mephistopheles wins his bet."

"But that was Faust's moment of supreme happiness."

"True. When he attains it, though, he loses his soul to the devil, remember?"

"So you go on, on and on, world after world, seeking you know not what, just seeking, unable to stop. And yet you claim you're not driven."

He shakes his head. "Machines are driven. Animals are driven. I'm an autonomous human being operating out of free will. I don't make this journey because I have to, but because I want to."

"Or because you think you ought to want to."

"I'm motivated by feelings, not by intellectual calculations and preconceptions."

"That sounds very carefully thought out," she tells him. He is stung by her words, and looks away, down into his empty glass. She indicates that he should help himself to the wine. "I'm sorry," she says, her tone softening a little.

He says, "At any rate, I was in the library and there was a telephone directory and I found you. This is where you used to live in my world, too, before we were married." He hesitates. "Do you mind if I ask—"

"What?"

"You're not married?"

"No. I live alone. And like it."

"You always were independent-minded."

"You talk as though you know me so well."

"I've been married to you for seven years."

"No. Not to me. Never to me. You don't know me at all."

He nods. "You're right. I don't really know you, Elizabeth, however much I think I do. But I want to. I feel drawn to you as strongly as I was to the other Elizabeth, that day in the mountains. It's always best right at the beginning, when two strangers reach toward one another, when the spark leaps the gap—" Tenderly he says, "May I spend the night here?"

"No."

Somehow the refusal comes as no surprise. He says, "You once gave me a different answer when I asked you that."

"Not I. Someone else."

"I'm sorry. It's so hard for me to keep you and her distinct in my mind, Elizabeth. But please don't turn me away. I've come so far to be with you."

"You came uninvited. Besides, I'd feel so strange with you—knowing you were thinking of her, comparing me with her, measuring our differences, our points of similarities—"

"What makes you think I would?"

"You would."

"I don't think that's sufficient reason for sending me away."

"I'll give you another," she says. Her eyes sparkle mischievously. "I never let myself get involved with married men."

She is teasing him now. He says, laughing, confident that she is beginning to yield, "That's the damndest far-fetched excuse I've ever heard, Elizabeth!"

"Is it? I feel a great kinship with her. She has all my sympathies. Why should I help you deceive her?"

"Deceive? What an old-fashioned word! Do you think she'd object? She never expected me to be chaste on this trip. She'd be flattered and delighted to know that I went looking for you here. She'd be eager to hear about everything that went on between us. How could she possibly be hurt by knowing that I had been with you, when you and she are—"

"Nevertheless, I'd like you to leave. Please."

"You haven't given me one convincing reason."

"I don't need to."

"I love you. I want to spend the night with you."

"You love someone else who resembles me," she replies. "I keep telling you that. In any case, I don't love you. I don't find you attractive, I'm afraid."

"Oh. She does, but you—don't. I see. How do you find me, then? Ugly? Overbearing? Repellent?"

"I find you disturbing," she says. "A little frightening. Much too intense, much too controlled, perhaps danger-ous. You aren't my type. I'm probably not yours. Remember, I'm not the Elizabeth you met by that mountain lake. Perhaps I'd be happier if I were, but I'm not. I wish you had never come here. Now: please go. Please."

11.

Onward. This place is all gleaming towers and airy bridges, a glistening fantasy of a city. High overhead float glassy bubbles, silent airborne passenger vehicles, containing two or three people apiece who sprawl in postures of elegant relaxation. Bronzed young boys and girls lie naked beside soaring fountains spewing turquoise-and-scarlet foam. Giant orchids burst in tropical voluptuousness from the walls of colossal hotels. Small mechanical birds wheel and dart in the soft air like golden bullets, emitting sweet pinging sounds. From the tips of the tallest buildings comes a darker music, a ground-bass of swelling hundred-cycle notes oscillating around an insistent central rumble. This is a world two centuries ahead of his, at the least. He could never infiltrate here. He could never even be a tourist. The only role available to him is that of visiting savage, Jemmy Button among the Londoners, and what, after all, was Jemmy Button's fate? Not a happy one. Patagonia! Patagonia! Thees ticket eet ees no longer good here, sor. Colored rays dance in the sky, red, green, blue, exploding, showering the city with transcendental images. Cameron smiles. He will not let himself be overwhelmed, though this place is more confusing than the world of the halftrack automobiles. Jauntily he plants himself at the center of a small park between two lanes of flowing noiseless traffic. It is a formal garden lush with toothy orange-fronded ferns and thorny skyrockets of looping cactus. Lovers stroll past him arm in arm, offering one another swigs from glossy sweat-beaded green flasks that look like tubes of polished jade. Delicately they dangle blue grapes before each other's lips, playfully they smile, arch their necks, take the bait with eager pounces; then they laugh, embrace, tumble into the dense moist grass, which stirs and sways and emits gentle thrumming melodies. This place pleases him. He wanders through the garden, thinking of Elizabeth, thinking of springtime, and, coming ultimately to a sinuous brook in which the city's tallest towers are reflected as inverted needles, he kneels to drink. The water is cool, sweet, tart, much like young wine. A moment after it touches his lips a mechanism rises from the spongy earth, five slender brassy columns, three with eye-sensors sprouting on all sides, one marked with a pattern of dark gridwork, one bearing an arrangement of winking colored lights. Out of the gridwork come ominous words in an unfathomable language. This is some kind of police machine, demanding his credentials: that much is clear. "I'm sorry," he says. "I can't understand what you're saying." Other machines are extruding themselves from trees, from the bed of the stream, from the hearts of the sturdiest ferns. "It's all right," he says. "I don't mean any harm. Just give me a chance to learn the language and I promise to become a useful citizen." One of the machines sprays him with a fine azure mist. Another drives a tiny needle into his forearm and extracts a droplet of blood. A crowd is gathering. They point, snicker, wink. The music of the building-tops has become higher in pitch, more sinister in texture; it shakes the balmy air and threatens him in a personal way. "Let me stay," Cameron begs, but the music is shoving him, pushing him with a flat irresistible hand, inexorably squeezing him out of this world. He is too primitive for them. He is too coarse, he carries too many obsolete microbes. Very well. If that's what they want, he'll leave, not out of fear, not because they've succeeded in intimidating him, but out of courtesy alone. In a flamboyant way he bids them farewell, bowing with a flourish worthy of Raleigh, blowing a kiss to the five-columned machine, smiling, even doing a little dance. Farewell. Farewell. The music rises to a wild crescendo. He hears celestial trumpets and distant thunder. Farewell. Onward.

12.

Here some kind of oriental marketplace has sprung up, foul-smelling, cluttered, medieval. Swarthy old men, white-bearded, in thick gray robes, sit patiently behind open burlap sacks of spices and grains. Lepers and cripples roam everywhere, begging importunately. Slender long-legged men wearing only tight loincloths and jingling dangling earrings of bright copper stalk through the crowd on solitary orbits, buying nothing, saying nothing; their skins are dark red, their faces are gaunt, their solemn features are finely modeled. They carry themselves like Inca princes. Perhaps they *are* Inca princes. In the haggle and babble of the market Cameron hears no recognizable tongue spoken. He sees the flash of gold as transactions are completed. The women balance immense burdens on their heads and show brilliant teeth when they smile. They favor patchwork skirts that cover their ankles, but they leave their breasts bare. Several of them glance provocatively at Cameron but he dares not return their quick dazzling probes until he knows what is permissible here. On the far side of the squalid plaza he catches sight of a woman who might well be Elizabeth; her back is to him, but he would know those strong shoulders anywhere, that erect stance, that cascade of unbound golden hair. He starts toward her, sliding with difficulty between the close-packed marketgoers. When he is still halfway across the marketplace from her he notices a man at her side, tall, a man of his own height and build. He wears a loose black robe and a dark scarf covers the lower half of his face. His eyes are grim and sullen and a terrible cicatrice, wide and glaringly crosshatched with stitchmarks, runs along his left cheek up to his hairline. The man whispers something to the woman who might be Elizabeth; she nods and turns, so that Cameron now is able to see her face, and yes, the woman does seem to be Elizabeth, but she bears a matching scar, angry and hideous, up the right side of her face. Cameron gasps. The scar-faced man suddenly points and shouts. Cameron senses motion to one side, and swings around just in time to see a short thickbodied man come rushing toward him wildly waving a scimitar. For an instant Cameron sees the scene as though in a photograph: he has time to make a leisurely examination of his attacker's oily beard, his hooked hairy-nostriled nose, his yellowed teeth, the cheap glassy-looking inlaid stones on the haft of the scimitar. Then the frightful blade descends, while the assassin screams abuse at Cameron in what might be Arabic. It is a sorry welcome. Cameron cannot prolong this investigation. An instant before the scimitar cuts him in two he takes himself elsewhere, with regret.

13.

Onward. To a place where there is no solidity, where the planet itself has vanished, so that he swims through space, falling peacefully, going from nowhere to nowhere. He is surrounded by a brilliant green light that emanates from every point at once, like a message from the fabric of the universe. In great tranquility he drops through this cheerful glow for days on end, or what seems like days on end, drifting, banking, checking his course with small motions of his elbows or knees. It makes no difference where he goes; everything here is like everything else here. The green glow supports and sustains and nourishes him, but it makes him restless. He plays with it. Out of its lambent substance he succeeds in shaping images, faces, abstract patterns; he conjures up Elizabeth for himself, he evokes his own sharp features, he fills the heavens with a legion of marching Chinese in tapered straw hats, he obliterates them with forceful diagonal lines, he causes a river of silver to stream across the firmament and discharge its glittering burden down a mountainside a thousand miles high. He spins. He floats. He glides. He releases all his fantasies. This is total freedom, here in this unworldly place. But it is not enough. He grows weary of emptiness. He grows weary of serenity. He has drained this place of all it has to offer, too soon, too soon. He is not sure whether the failure is in himself or in the place, but he feels he must leave. Therefore: onward.

14.

Terrified peasants run shrieking as he materializes in their midst. This is some sort of farming village along the eastern shore of the bay: neat green fields, a cluster of low wicker huts radiating from a central plaza, naked children toddling and crying, a busy sub-population of goats and geese and chickens. It is midday; Cameron sees the bright gleam of water in the irrigation ditches. These people work hard. They have scattered at his approach, but now they creep back warily, crouching, ready to take off again if he performs any more miracles. This is another of those bucolic worlds in which San Francisco has not happened, but he is unable to identify these settlers, nor can he isolate the chain of events that brought them here. They are not Indians, nor Chinese, nor Peruvians; they have a European look about them, somehow Slavic, but what would Slavs be doing in California? Russian farmers, maybe, colonizing by way of Siberia? There is some plausibility in that—their dark complexions, their heavy facial structure, their squat powerful bodies—but they seem oddly primitive, half-naked, in furry leggings or less, as though they are no subjects of the Tsar but rather Scythians or Cimmerians transplanted from the prehistoric marshes of the Vistula.

"Don't be frightened," he tells them, holding his upraised outspread arms toward them. They do seem less fearful of him now, timidly approaching, staring with big dark eyes. "I won't harm you. I'd just like to visit with you." They murmur. A woman boldly shoves a child forward, a girl of about five, bare, with black greasy ringlets, and Cameron scoops her up, caresses her, tickles her, lightly sets her down. Instantly the whole tribe is around him, no longer afraid; they touch his arm, they kneel, they stroke his shins. A boy brings him a wooden bowl of porridge. An old woman gives him a mug of sweet wine, a kind of mead. A slender girl drapes a stole of auburn fur over his shoulders. They dance, they chant; their fear has turned into love; he is their honored guest. He is more than that: he is a god. They take him to an unoccupied hut, the largest in the village. Piously they bring him offerings of incense and acorns. When it grows dark they build an immense bonfire in the plaza, so that he wonders in vague concern if they will feast on him when they are done honoring him, but they feast on slaughtered cattle instead, and yield to him the choicest pieces, and afterward they stand by his door, singing discordant, energetic hymns. That night three girls of the tribe, no doubt the fairest virgins available, are sent to him, and in the morning he finds his threshold heaped with newly plucked blossoms. Later two tribal artisans, one lame and the other blind, set to work with stone adzes and chisels, hewing an immense and remarkably accurate likeness of him out of a redwood stump that has been mounted at the plaza's center.

So he has been deified. He has a quick Faustian vision of himself living among these diligent people, teaching them advanced methods of agriculture, leading them eventually into technology, into modern hygiene, into all the contemporary advantages without the contemporary abominations. Guiding them toward the light, molding them, creating them. This world, this village, would be a good place for him to stop his transit of the infinities, if stopping were desirable: god, prophet, king of a placid realm, teacher, inculcator of civilization, a purpose to his existence at last. But there *is* no place to stop. He knows that. Transforming happy primitive farmers into sophisticated twentieth-century agriculturalists is ultimately as useless a pastime as training fleas to jump through hoops. It is tempting to live as a god, but even divinity will pall, and it is dangerous to become attached to an unreal satisfaction, dangerous to become attached at all. The journey, not the arrival, matters. Always.

So Cameron does godhood for a little while. He finds it pleasant and fulfilling. He savors the rewards until he senses that the rewards are becoming too important to him. He makes his formal renunciation of his godhead. Then: onward.

15.

And this place he recognizes. His street, his house, his garden, his green car in the carport, Elizabeth's yellow one parked out front. Home again, so soon? He hadn't expected that; but every leap he has made, he knows, must in some way have been a product of deliberate choice, and evidently whatever hidden mechanism within him that has directed these voyages has chosen to bring him home again. All right, touch base. Digest your travels, examine them, allow your experiences to work their alchemy on you: you need to stand still a moment for that. Afterward you can always leave again. He slides his key into the door.

Elizabeth has one of the Mozart quartets on the phonograph. She sits curled up in the livingroom window-seat, leafing through a magazine. It is late afternoon and the San Francisco skyline, clearly visible across the bay through the big window, is haloed by the brilliant retreating sunlight. There are freshly cut flowers in the little crystal bowl on the redwood-burl table; the fragrance of gardenias and jasmine dances past him. Unhurriedly she looks up, brings her eyes into line with his, dazzles him with the warmth of her smile, and says, "Well, hello!"

"Hello. Elizabeth."

She comes to him. "I didn't expect you back this quickly, Chris. I don't know if I expected you to come back at all, as a matter of fact."

"This quickly? How long have I been gone, for you?"

"Tuesday morning to Thursday afternoon. Two and a half days." She eyes his coarse new beard, his ragged, sun-bleached shirt. "It's been longer for you, hasn't it?"

"Weeks and weeks. I'm not sure how long. I was in eight or nine different places, and I stayed in the last one quite some time. They were villagers, farmers, some primitive Slavonic tribe living down by the bay. I was their god, but I got bored with it."

"You always did get bored so easily," she says, and laughs, and takes his hands in hers and pulls him toward her. She brushes her lips lightly against him, a peck, a play-kiss, their usual first greeting, and then they kiss more passionately, bodies pressing close, tongue seeking tongue. He feels a pounding in his chest, the old inextinguishable throb. When they release each other he steps back, a little dizzied, and says, "I missed you, Elizabeth. I didn't know how much I'd miss you until I was somewhere else and aware that I might never find you again."

"Did you seriously worry about that?"

"Very much."

"I never doubted we'd be together again, one way or another. Infinity's such a big place, darling. You'd find your way back to me, or to someone very much like me. And someone very much like you would find his way to me, if you didn't. How many Chris Camerons do you think there are, on the move between worlds right now? A thousand? A trillion trillion?" She turns toward the sideboard and says, without breaking the flow of her words, "Would you like some wine?" and begins to pour from a half-empty jug of red. "Tell me where you've been," she says.

He comes up behind her and rests his hands on her

shoulders, and draws them down the back of her silk blouse to her waist, holding her there, kissing the nape of her neck. He says, "To a world where there was an atomic war here, and to one where there still were Indian raiders out by Livermore, and one that was all fantastic robots and futuristic helicopters, and one where Johnson was President before Kennedy and Kennedy is alive and President now, and one where—oh, I'll give you all the details later. I need a chance to unwind first." He releases her and kisses the tip of her earlobe and takes one of the glasses from her, and they salute each other and drink, draining the wine quickly. "It's so good to be home," he says softly. "Good to have gone where I went, good to be back." She fills his glass again. The familiar domestic ritual: red wine is their special drink, cheap red wine out of gallon jugs. A sacrament, more dear to him than the burnt offerings of his recent subjects. Halfway through the second glass he says, "Come. Let's go inside."

The bed has fresh linens on it, cool, inviting. There are three thick books on the nighttable: she's set up for some heavy reading in his absence. Cut flowers in here, too, fragrance everywhere. Their clothes drop away. She touches his beard and chuckles at the roughness, and he kisses the smooth cool place along the inside of her thigh and draws his cheek lightly across it, sandpapering her lovingly, and then she pulls him to her and their bodies slide together and he enters her. Everything thereafter happens quickly, much too quickly; he has been long absent from her, if not she from him, and now her presence excites him, there is a strangeness about her body, her movements, and it hastens him to his ecstasy. He feels a mild pang of regret, but no more: he'll make it up to her soon enough, they both know that. They drift into a sleepy embrace, neither of them speaking, and eventually uncoil into tender new passion, and this time all is as it should be. Afterward they doze. A spectacular sunset blazes over the city when he opens his eyes. They rise, they take a shower together, much giggling, much playfulness. "Let's go across the bay for a fancy dinner tonight," he suggests. "Trianon, Blue Fox, Ernie's, anywhere. You name it. I feel like celebrating."

"So do I, Chris."

"It's good to be home again."

"It's good to have you here," she tells him. She looks for her purse. "How soon do you think you'll be heading out again? Not that I mean to rush you, but—"

"You know I'm not going to be staying?"

"Of course I know."

"Yes. You would." She had never questioned his going. They both tried to be responsive to each other's needs; they had always regarded one another as equal partners, free to do as they wished. "I can't say how long I'll stay. Probably not long. Coming home this soon was really an accident, you know. I just planned to go on and on and on, world after world, and I never programmed my next jump, at least not consciously. I simply leaped. And the last leap deposited me on my own doorstep, somehow, so I let myself into the house. And there you were to welcome me home."

She presses his hand between hers. Almost sadly she says, "You aren't home, Chris."

"What?"

He hears the sound of the front door opening. Footsteps in the hallway.

"You aren't home," she says.

Confusion seizes him. He thinks of all that has passed between them this evening.

"Elizabeth?" calls a deep voice from the livingroom.

"In here, darling. I have company!"

"Oh? Who?" A man enters the bedroom, halts, grins. He is clean-shaven and dressed in the clothes Cameron had worn on Tuesday; otherwise they could be twins. "Hey, hello!" he says warmly, extending his hand.

Elizabeth says, "He comes from a place that must be very much like this one. He's been here since five o'clock, and we were just going out for dinner. Have you been having an interesting time?"

"Very," the other Cameron says. "I'll tell you all about it later. Go on, don't let me keep you."

"You could join us for dinner," Cameron suggests helplessly.

"That's all right. I've just eaten. Breast of passenger pigeon—they aren't extinct everywhere. I wish I could have brought some home for the freezer. So you two go and enjoy. I'll see you later. Both of you, I hope. Will you be staying with us? We've got notes to compare, you and I."

16.

He rises just before dawn, in a marvelous foggy stillness. The Camerons have been wonderfully hospitable, but he must be moving along. He scrawls a thank-you note and slips it under their bedroom door. *Let's get together again someday. Somewhere. Somehow.* They want him as a houseguest for a week or two, but no, he feels like a bit of an intruder here, and anyway the universe is waiting for him. He has to go. The journey, not the arrival, matters, for what else is there but trips? Departing is unexpectedly painful, but he knows the mood will pass. He closes his eyes. He breaks his moorings. He gives himself up to his sublime restlessness. Onward. Onward. *Goodbye, Elizabeth. Goodbye, Chris. I'll see you both again.* Onward.

AFTERWORD

If science fiction is a literature of infinite possibilities, the subgenre of alternate-timetrack fiction must be one of its most infinite compartments. I find it deliciously liberating. Inventing the future can become a stale business to someone whose profession it has been for almost twenty years, but reinventing the past holds endless and irresistible fascinations for me. In a novel called *The Gate of Worlds*, which no one ever seemed to notice, I explored in careful detail the kind of world that might have developed had the European conquest of the Americas never taken place; in an assortment of short stories I poked at various other alternate-past designs; in my novels *Hawksbill Station*, *Up the Line*, and *The Time Hoppers* I examined some of the paradoxes and complications inherent generally in the philosophically stimulating but physically unlikely concept of time travel.

And now once again a protagonist of mine saddles his horse and rides off in all directions. Instead of methodical exploration of a single alternate track, I've chosen a more dizzying scheme in which the center never holds, and the quest is eternal. No doubt some readers would like to know more about some of the worlds through which Cameron passes. So would I. But the goal here has been to suggest the multitude of experiences, real and possible, that surround and engulf us; and so the scene constantly changes, by way of demonstrating that every moment is a convergence of potential infinities, that every trifling decision sends a billion billion unborn worlds into oblivion.

Novels
THE MAN IN THE HIGH CASTLE, by Philip K. Dick
BRING THE JUBILEE, by Ward Moore
THE WHEELS OF IF, by L. Sprague de Camp
PAVANE, by Keith Roberts
GATE OF WORLDS, by Robert Silverberg
UP THE LINE, by Robert Silverberg

Short Stories
THE PI MAN, by Alfred Bester
FONDLY FAHRENHEIT, by Alfred Bester

About Robert Silverberg

Robert Silverberg, b. 1935, is the author of fiction and nonfiction books totalling over four hundred and fifty, author of two or three thousand magazine pieces, a full-time professional writer since his graduation from Columbia University in 1956. He is best known for his recent science fiction novels (DYING INSIDE, UP THE LINE, THE BOOK OF SKULLS, NIGHTWINGS, THE SECOND TRIP, SON OF MAN, A TIME OF CHANGES) and is a multiple Hugo and Nebula winner. DYING INSIDE received a special 1972 John W. Campbell Memorial Award. Mr. Silverberg presently lives in Oakland with his wife, Barbara.

THE UNCONTROLLED MACHINE

THE WONDERFUL, ALL-PURPOSE TRANSMOGRIFIER

BARRY N. MALZBERG

Haverford sets the controls for PEACE, JOY, AND ACCEPTANCE. Quickly, before his wife can see what he is up to, he brings the helmet firmly over his ears (he always feels that this makes him look somehow like a rabbit) and causes the circuits to mesh. He cannot stand the woman. Really, it is not her fault but he cannot stand her. Less and less has she shown any comprehension of his condition, of the uses and necessity of the wonderful, all-purpose transmogrifier, but even now, as she turns toward him, her mouth opening in rage and knowledge, it is too late, and there is no way that she can stop him. Until the program is played out. Even if she were to rip the helmet from his head she cannot retrieve him now, his rabbity little nose would snuffle into the jungle of the program. He feels all of it sliding from him, the delightful, crosswise, vaulting effect of the program and then, oh boy . . .

PEACE, JOY, AND ACCEPTANCE is his once again in the world of 2114—two hundred and fifty exciting years past the period of the Industrial Revolution. You could look it all up, about the wonderful, all-purpose transmogrifier— which can make all desires real, all possibilities flesh— invented by the Carter Laboratories in 1983; but, because of ruthless government suppression it reached the public only 100 years later. That was after the last and greatest of the Final Wars when the government decided that people were always going to need a way to be transported out of this world and best to give them their way, otherwise they might actually turn on the government itself and what then? The transmogrifier is marketed as a double unit, console and helmet, one basic price, decorations

227

extra. The programs are rented at seventy-five dollars apiece, except for the pornographics, which cost a little more. Installment purchasing brings the machine well within reach of the common man.

PEACE, JOY, AND ACCEPTANCE: Haverford takes himself to be in a small room, not unlike his own furnished unit on the eighteenth level of the Storm Towers. (His helmet is fastened securely against his ears, his hands twitch involuntarily from the effort of the central nervous system to absorb the first impact of the program. There is always a wrench, although it goes away quickly and with experience the shock decreases. The manufacturer and licensor also assure that the possibility of permanent injury or insanity is very low if use is kept within expected limits. One program a day but never more than seven a week.) Haverford, as if in a dream, rises almost absently from the chair, removes the helmet to place it carefully on the illuminated table by its side and strides to the window where he stares down the eighteen stories of the Towers, seeing the twinkling waters, the twisted arches in the distance. The air is unusually clear today, atmosphere almost penetrable, but he decides against a brisk walk. Why risk death? The last time he was outside some years ago he contracted a mild upper respiratory infection. He turns from the window briskly and goes back toward the central area. His wife, from a doorway, confronts him. He had almost forgotten her. He almost had forgotten the woman. But of course the program includes her and in the absence of orders to the contrary she would be in. This is a safety feature.

"What do you think you're doing?" she says. Her name, he recollects, is Ruth. Lively little breasts when he fucks her but who wants to fuck anymore? "What do you think you're doing with your life?" she continues. "Is this right? Is this what we've come to, using helmets and tapes to take us out of the world? Don't you realize that this is exactly what the government wants, what they had in mind for you all the time? They never fought the transmogrifier, that was all a cover story. The real reason was that they couldn't figure out the problem of how to get it into production quickly enough to avoid riots so they had to make all those excuses about danger but that's what they were, simple lies." She does indeed run on but he listens patiently. "The government wants it this way. It wants people like you to spend their lives spinning tapes and making dreams because this way the people that run the world can do anything they want and never be accountable. How did it happen? It's 2114, just 2114, and people like you are living as if it's the end of the world. Face reality! You've got to face reality, face up to who they are and what they're doing to you or it *is* going to be the end of the world. Don't you see that?"

He does not. He never did. But Haverford is in the hold of PEACE, JOY, AND ACCEPTANCE now, feeling a wonderful sense of control. The ethos of the program is a warm and wonderful sense of well-being that underlies even the simplest and most routine of acts. (It is one of the miracles of the process, although the manufacturer, at least to date, has not been able to explain what neural pathways are being massaged in which fashion to yield this result.)

"It's you who don't understand, Ruth," he says kindly. He goes toward her, takes her by the shoulders. In the program she is even attractive to him, although he has not dialed in fucking. Fucking is absolutely out of the question, therefore. "It's not a matter of escaping anything, and actually the government resisted all of this to the bitter end. They only went along with it when they came to understand that otherwise the tensions and pressures of overpopulation—ecological breakdown, culture lag—would destroy everything, even the government *itself*. The world is terrible, you see, and we've got to get out of it: God bless the transmogrifier for giving this to us, and why must you be so stubborn?" He imagines himself with two large front teeth that could penetrate her to enormous distance; his penis bunches against his groin like a carrot. "If *you* tried it," he says, "we could program together, chart out the elements, and things would be so much easier and more pleasant." And then it comes back to him slowly, as it would have occurred quickly in the real: Poor Ruth is incapable of using the transmogrifier. Certain people, for reasons which neither manufacturer nor research can determine, are immune to the effects of the program. These people merely go into catatonic shock or, as in Ruth's case, into a kind of heightened, irritated, paranoid reaction. Neural pathways cannot be spliced or bypassed. There is nothing to be done for the poor woman, then. Locked into the world, she must face it on its difficult terms forever.

"Oh," he says, his penis dwindling in shame to asparagus dimensions, "I'm so terribly sorry, I'm so terribly sorry. I forgot. Forgive me," and turns back toward the chair, still feeling good, thanks be to the program but not so good as he did before. He will sit quietly and muse away the afternoon now, in the lettuce patch of contemplation.

But Ruth is after him, incessant, bitter. She pins him against the wall. "I won't take this anymore," she says, her little face anguished, "I'm not going to stay in this miserable room any longer and watch you dream your life away. I want you to know that I've joined the anti-transmogrifier movement. As a matter of fact, I'm going to go to one of their meetings right now and I'm likely to never come back. In fact I'm quite likely to just leave you—"

"The anti-transmogrifier movement!" Haverford screams. "That's ridiculous. There *is* no anti-transmogrifier movement!" With difficulty he modulates, wondering if he is losing his mind. "The government has authorized an organization for people like yourself so that you can rationalize your failure by thinking it's heightened contact with reality, but nobody takes that seriously. You can't possibly believe that any such movement would mean a thing!" And now the laughter spills, it is really too much, too much for him to take. He could stand her accusations and manage a careful pity for her but the preposterous *earnestness* of her position . . . well, it is really too much for him. Little burbles and hisses of laughter steam, he escapes from her grasp and reels to the chair, feeling almost faint with the laughter. He has not felt this way in years. Truly the transmogrifier is a million laughs; the laughs are the best one could ever have, and he gives himself over to them completely, shaking and shuddering for the duration of the program while his wife moves away cursing. She finds her identifying shield and slams her way from the room, leaving the door moving free in the foul little breezes of the hallway. He does not have the strength to close it. He tries, every now and then, to summon the

will to close that door but every time he is just about to
rise he thinks of his wife at an anti-transmogrifier meeting,
and the laughter starts again. After a long time though, the
program comes to an end as it always, always must, the
ethos begins to darken toward a shallow recrimination and,
try to retard the transfer as he does, matters shift and
slide and Haverford, oh Jesus Christ, he finds himself . . .

. . . Back in the room that he had left, largely un-
changed, except that Ruth's expression is even more
bitter, if this is possible, and the frontal lobes of the brain
are being overtaken with the characteristic throbbing after-
math of a program. Idly, he takes the helmet in his hands,
considers it. He would very much like to program again
today, even though the warnings are quite explicit—more
than once a day if one must but never more than seven
programs a week. Permanent neural damage. He took two
programs yesterday, meaning that he will have to lose one
day already, and if he programs again today he will somehow have to get through two days without release. But the
urge is too strong.

He reaches a hand toward the file.

"Again?" Ruth says.

Haverford nods. "I'm sorry," he says quietly. "I really
can't stand it any more. I've just got to get out." A dim
impulse to tell her about the role she plays in the programs
brushes him casually, like a bird's wing, but he is able to
grapple and hold it down. No point. The inner life is
sacred, just as the manufacturer said.

"I know," she says. She is really a decent woman,
Ruth; it is strange that in the programs she so often takes
an unfortunate role. Of course she must be angry at his
use of the transmogrifier, Haverford thinks, but he is
entitled. She is entitled too, for that matter; he has never
stopped her. Strange, the fantasy when he is in a program
about her being unable to use it; his subconscious must be
working on the problem of her disinclination. "Don't you
think," she is saying, "that you should try to, well, face
up to your problems more than you do? Maybe you
wouldn't need the machine so much that way; the real
world . . ."

"The real world!" Haverford says, and here comes the

laughter again. "There is *no* real world, there's no such thing." And without discussing that dangerous issue further, he slams the new program into the console, plays over the dials to bring them into alignment, and curls down the helmet skillfully over his head. Man, he can hardly wait for . . .

SEXUALITY AND RELEASE . . . to seize him, which it does almost at once, the neural pathways having been unblocked, possibly corroded by excessive use and, almost instantaneously, Haverford takes himself to be leaping from the chair to seize Ruth. Astonished she staggers in his grasp, beats at him, but he is far stronger than she and her clothing falls away like ash. Soon he has pinned her to the floor, mounted her like a crucifix, torn open his trousers so that he can enter her.

Moving in hard, wedging, tearing at her inside, Haverford has a feeling of sexuality and release, just as ordered. Seeing her crumple away underneath him, absorbing that power, only weakly trying to accommodate a force that has transcended her, he feels himself beginning to rush away. Insight drapes him like fire: in the approaching orgasm he feels at last that he understands everything. "Stupid cunt," he says (aggression being for him a large part of the sex experience, he supposes), "stupid cunt, the government fought against this all the way. The government didn't want any part of it. If people are going to be programming seven times a week, right up to the maximum, who the hell is going to do the *shit*? Who's going to do the *work*? Who's left to fight the *smog* and *fog* and *pollution*?" And he would say a good deal more, oh, he is only at the beginning of the point he would like to make, but the fire grips him, little tendrils poke and probe from neck to toe, wrenching him from speech and croaking, trembling, he comes into her instead, pouring what feels like yards of seed into her, his palms scattering and slamming at the rug as if it were flesh. And when he has finally discharged everything within him he falls on top of her heavily, her body just an indentation underneath, and then rolls, rolls from her to his back, lying that way, looking up at the ceiling, his hands reaching instinctively toward the helmet. Yes, it is still there. He has not re-moved it; it remains in place. Once the program has started, the actual presence of the helmet means nothing, but it always seems stronger, subjectively, if it does not come off.

He lies there looking up at the ceiling, and soon a wonderful, warm sense of ease and well-being nibbles, and he closes his eyes. He is not even aware of his wife's breath beside. If she is there, good enough; if she goes that's perfectly all right as well. He is where he wants to be. His eyes close and in small, transitory stages he works his way into sleep, feeling the comforting pressure of the helmet, little fingers grasping his scalp, and then at last, wholly relaxed, he sleeps through the remainder of the program thinking that this time he may never come out but oh, shit, it is always a lie, there is always a return and when he comes out this time Haverford is . . .

. . . Draped over the arm of the chair in unspeakable pain—pain through his belly, disconnection in his skull, an anguish unlike any he has ever had before because he cannot, somehow, define it exactly. The pain is not specific but rather internal and highly diffused, the waxy flexibility of catatonia rooted firmly in his limbs. In pain he looks upward. Ruth, an expression of great concern floating over her face, leans over him.

"You took too much," she says, "you took too many."

He tries to answer but the pain has cancelled speech. He nods dumbly, stricken.

"I *told* you you shouldn't have done it twice," she says. "I warned you, only for your own good. You're twenty-seven years old. You can't take as much of this as you used to. It can be very dangerous."

"Yes," he says. Speech has returned, although he is quacking like a duck. "Of course, you're right." He is able to move his webbed feet a little, he notices. His tail feathers are dry, his beak cuts through the air. Soon he will be able to paddle home.

"You'll have to cut back," she says, not noticing that he has become a duck. "For your own good."

"All right," he says. He flutters to a standing posture,

balances in place preening, then very cautiously swims toward the chair. Not so bad. Not so bad at all. In fact, he is less of a duck than he was an instant ago. Frightening but he is coming out of the grip of it. Brief burnout but functions are returning quickly.

"It's only for your own good, you know," she says, still over him, touching his shoulder, "I want you to be healthy."

"Get away from me," Haverford, no longer a duck, says. "That's quite enough now, just get away from me."

His voice is stronger. Inflection has returned; she reacts. She scuttles away and toward her side of the room. How much like an insect the woman is. Her gestures are that of a cephid, he decides. Of course, rabbits or ducks are in no position to criticize. "All right," she says, "I only wanted to help you. If you don't want to be helped, then I won't bother."

"Good," Haverford says, "that's fine." He feels back to himself now. Yearningly he looks at the helmet which she must have torn off in his distress. It lies crumpled by the chair. He picks it up, smooths it, plays with the wires that trace into the console like little spider fibers.

He would like to put it on and program again. Oh my, oh my, how he would like to program again! But Haverford is no fool, he has seen the signs of real danger in his reaction, and he knows that no matter what happens he must wait a full day before programming. Eat, drink, stroll the Towers . . . but no more for now.

He looks at Ruth, who has returned to her frozen position against the wall. There is some regret in his gaze. In certain aspects, cephid or not, she is an attractive woman. She inflames him as no other figure ever has.

But attractive or not, he must wait for tomorrow until he can insert the program and fuck her again. This is for his own good and he will accept it.

Discipline. Everything was discipline. He thinks of his new-found pride and control, and then something wrenches and claws at him, more profound than anything he has yet felt; he is falling, falling and rising like a man fucking, a man fucking and dying, turning inside and out and then he bursts through the grey, slack waters of the fading program and . . .

THE WONDERFUL, ALL-PURPOSE TRANSMOGRIFIER . . . comes back to herself slowly, like a child picking her way through waters. Holding the helmet in her hands, Ruth looks at the sleeping Haverford across from her, Haverford all ignorant of what she has done (it is always best this way), and then slowly, delicately, puts the program away, sighs, and stands. Back to herself. To be a woman again is a momentary strangeness, having been so recently and in such a complex way a man, but she will manage. She will certainly go on.

Haverford strains in the chair, opens his eyes, comes from sleep like a bather breaking water and looks at her, at the helmet, at the console. "Did you enjoy your program?" he says to her thickly.

Ruth smiles. "You'll never know how much," she says.

"Good," says Haverford. He stands, scratches at his hair. "If you don't mind," he says to her, "I think I'm going to trip for a spot now myself."

"Be me," Ruth says impulsively.

Haverford looks at her slowly, stupidly, then knowledge pierces his face. "Can't," he says. "Sorry. I used that one up last Thursday."

AFTERWORD

Tenn's *The House Dutiful* (the all-purpose servomechanistic house that suspends time and turns its tenants into eternal sleepers) and Kuttner's *The Twonky* (the servomechanism that turns the brains of its masters to jelly, just to be helpful, of course) scared the hell out of me when I was almost too young to be really scared by anything, and I can, twenty years later, quote the plot essentials of both stories with a precision that embarrasses me . . . but this, folks, the Machine That Takes Over, is only the half of it.

The twonky and the house dutiful were extrinsics, agents, devices. They made victims of people who could have solved the problem by getting away from them, burning them up or (best of all) closing the issue of *Astounding Science Fiction* and putting the whole mess away. But we have learned too much in the intervening years about the Enormous Machine. The lessons of modern technology are simple after all:

We are the machines. We are taking over. And we are out of control.

Science fiction is no metaphor anymore, and the twonky, having lit our deadly cigarettes, will not toddle back against the wall. The twonky has gone inside. The house dutiful is burning in the brain.

Novels
BEYOND APOLLO, by Barry N. Malzberg
A FOR ANYTHING, by Damon Knight

Short Stories
THE HOUSE DUTIFUL, by William Tenn
THE TWONKY, by Henry Kuttner and C. L. Moore
THE ENORMOUS RADIO, by John Cheever
NO FIRE BURNS, by Avram Davidson
STREET OF DREAMS, FEET OF CLAY, by Robert Sheckley
AAA ACE SERIES, by Robert Sheckley
THE LITTLE BLACK BAG, by Cyril M. Kornbluth
THE ALTAR AT MIDNIGHT, by Cyril M. Kornbluth

AFTER THE HOLOCAUST

HER SMOKE ROSE UP FOREVER

JAMES TIPTREE, JR.

Deliverance quickens, catapults him into his boots on mountain gravel, his mittened hand on the rusty 1935 International truck. Cold rushes into his young lungs, his eyelashes are knots of ice as he peers down at the lake below the pass. He is in a bare bleak bowl of mountains just showing rusty in the dawn; not one scrap of cover anywhere, not a tree, not a rock.

The lake below shines emptily, its wide rim of ice silvered by the setting moon. It looks small, everything looks small up here. Is that scar on the edge his boat? Yes—it's there, it's all okay! The black path snaking out from the boat to the patch of tulegrass is the waterway he broke last night. Joy rises in him, hammers his heart. This is it. This—is—*it*.

He squints his lashes, can just make out the black threads of the tules. Black knots among them—sleeping ducks. Just you wait! His grin crackles the ice in his nose. The tules will be his cover—that perfect patch out there. About eighty yards, too far to hit from shore. That's where he'll be when the dawn flight comes. Old Tom said he was loco. Loco Petey. Just you wait. Loco Tom.

The pickup's motor clanks, cooling, in the huge silence. No echo here, too dry. No wind. Petey listens intently: a thin wailing in the peaks overhead, a tiny croak from the lake below. Waking up. He scrapes back his frozen canvas cuff over the birthday watch, is oddly, fleetingly puzzled by his own knobby fourteen-year-old wrist. Twenty-five—no, twenty-four minutes to the duck season. Opening day! Excitement ripples down his stomach, jumps his dick against his scratchy longjohns. Gentlemen don't beat the gun. He reaches into the pickup, reverently lifts out the brand-new Fox CE double-barrel twelve-gauge.

The barrels strike cold right through his mitts. He'll

237

have to take one off to shoot, too: It'll be fierce. Petey
wipes his nose with his cuff, pokes three fingers through
his cut mitten and breaks the gun. Ice in the sight. He
checks his impulse to blow it out, dabs clumsily. Shouldn't
have taken it in his sleeping bag. He fumbles two heavy
sixes from his shell pocket, loads the sweet blue bores, is
hardly able to breathe for joy. He is holding a zillion
dumb bags of the *Albuquerque Herald*, a whole summer
of laying adobe for Mr. Noff—all transmuted into this: his
perfect, agonizingly chosen OWN GUN. No more borrow-
ing old Tom's stinky over-and-under with the busted sight.
His own gun with his *initials* on the silver stock-plate.

Exaltation floods him, rises perilously. Holding his gun
Petey takes one more look around at the enormous barren
slopes. Empty, only himself and his boat and the ducks.
The sky has gone cold gas-pink. He is standing on a cusp
of the Great Divide at ten thousand feet, the main pass of
the western flyway. At dawn on opening day . . . What if
Apaches came around now? Mescalero Apaches own these
mountains but he's never seen one out here. His father
says they all have TB or something. In the old days, did
they come here on horses? They'd look tiny; the other
side is ten miles at least.

Petey squints at a fuzzy place on the far shore, decides
it's only sagebrush, but gets the keys and the axe out of
the pickup just in case. Holding the axe away from his gun
he starts down to the lake. His chest is banging, his knees
wobble, he can barely feel his feet skidding down the
rocks. The whole world seems to be brimming up with
tension.

He tells himself to calm down, blinking to get rid of a
funny blackness behind his eyes. He stumbles, catches
himself, has to stop to rub at his eyes. As he does so
everything flashes black-white—the moon jumps out of a
black sky like a locomotive headlight, he is sliding on
darkness with a weird humming all around. Oh, Jeeze—
mustn't get an altitude blackout, not now! And he makes
himself breathe deeply, goes on down with his boots
crunching hard like rhythmic ski turns, the heavy shell
pockets banging his legs, down, going quicker now, down
to the waiting boat.

As he gets closer he sees the open water-path has iced

over a little during the night. Good job he has the axe. Some ducks are swimming slow circles right by the ice. One of them rears up and quack-flaps, showing the big raked head: canvasback!

"Ah, you beauty," Petey says aloud, starting to run now, skidding, his heart pumping love, on fire for that first boom and rush. "I wouldn't shoot a sitting duck." His nose-drip has frozen, he is seeing himself hidden in those tules when the flights come over the pass, thinking of old Tom squatting in the rocks back by camp. Knocking back his brandy with his old gums slobbering, dreaming of dawns on World War I airdromes, dreaming of shooting a goose, dying of TB. Crazy old fool. Just you wait. Petey sees his plywood boat heaped with the great pearly breasts and red-black Roman noses of the canvasbacks bloodied and stiff, the virgin twelve-gauge lying across them, fulfilled.

And suddenly he's beside the boat, still blinking away a curious unreal feeling. Mysterious to see his own footprints here. The midget boat and the four frosted decoys are okay, but there's ice in the pathway, all right. He lays the gun and axe inside and pushes the boat out from the shore. It sticks, bangs, rides up over the new ice.

Jeeze, it's really thick! Last night he'd kicked through it easily and poled free by gouging in the paddle. Now he stamps out a couple of yards, pulling the boat. The ice doesn't give. Darn! He takes a few more cautious steps—and suddenly hears the *whew-whew, whew-whew* of ducks coming in. Coming in—and he's out here in the open! He drops beside the boat, peers into the bright white sky over the pass.

Oh *Jeeze*—there they are! Ninety miles an hour, coming downwind, a big flight! And he hugs his gun to hide the glitter, seeing the hurtling birds set their wings, become bloodcurdling black crescent-shapes, webs dangling, dropping like dive-bombers—but they've seen him, they veer in a great circle out beyond the tules, all quacking now, away and down. He hears the far rip of water and stands up aching toward them. You wait. Just wait till I get this dumb boat out there!

He starts yanking the boat out over the creaking ice in the brightening light, cold biting at his face and neck. The ice snaps, shivers, is still hard. Better push the boat around ahead of him so he can fall in when it goes. He does so, makes another two yards, three—and then the whole sheet tilts and slides under, with him floundering, and grounds on gravel. Water slops over his boot tops, burns inside his three pair of socks.

But it's shallow. He stamps forward, bashing ice, slipping and staggering. A yard, a yard, a yard more—he can't feel his feet, he can't get purchase. Crap darn, this is too slow! He grabs the boat, squats, throws himself in and ahead with all his might. The boat rams forward like an ice-breaker. Again! He'll be out of the ice soon now. Another lunge! And again!

But this time the boat recoils, doesn't ram. Darn *shit*, the crappy ice is so thick! How could it get this thick when it was open water last night?

'Cause the wind stopped, that's why, and it's ten above zero. Old Tom knew, darn him to hell. But there's only about thirty yards left to go to open water, only a few yards between him and the promised land. Get there. Get over it or under it or through it, go!

He grabs the axe, wades out ahead of the boat, and starts hitting ice, trying to make cracks. A piece breaks, he hits harder. But it doesn't want to crack, the axe-head keeps going in, *thunk*. He has to work it out of the black holes. And it's getting deep, he's way over his boots now. So what? *Thunk!* Work it loose. *Thunk!*

But some remaining sanity reminds him he really will freeze out here if he gets his clothes soaked. Shee-it! He stops, stands panting, staring at the ducks, which are now tipping up, feeding peacefully well out of range, chuckling *paducah*, *paducah* at him and his rage.

Twenty more yards, shit darn, *God*-darn. He utters a caw of fury and hunger and at that moment hears a tiny distant crack. Old Tom, firing. Crack!

Petey jumps into the boat, jerking off his canvas coat, peeling off the two sweaters, pants, the grey longjohns. His fingers can barely open the icy knots of his bootlaces but his body is radiant with heat, it sizzles the air, only his balls are trying to climb back inside as he stands up naked. Twenty yards!

He yanks the sodden boots back on and crashes out

into the ice, whacking with the axe-handle, butting whole
sheets aside. He's making it! Ten more feet, twenty! He
rams with the boat, bangs it up and down like a sledge-
hammer. Another yard! Another! His teeth are clattering, his shins are bleeding, and it's cutting his thighs now,
but he feels nothing, only joy, joy!—until suddenly he is
slewing full-length under water with the incredible cold
going up his ass and into his armpits like skewers and
ice cutting his nose.

His hands find the edge and he hauls himself up on the
side of the boat. The bottom has gone completely. His axe
—his axe is gone.

The ice is still there.

A black hand grabs him inside, he can't breathe. He
kicks and flails, dragging himself up into the boat to kneel
bleeding, trying to make his ribs work and his jaws stop
banging. The first sunray slicks him with ice and incredible
goosebumps; he gets a breath and can see ahead, see the
gleaming ducks. So close!

The paddle. He seizes it and stabs at the ice in front of
the boat. It clatters, rebounds, the boat goes backward.
With all his force he flails the ice, but it's too thick, the
paddle stem is cracking. No bottom to brace on. *Crack!*
And the paddle blade skitters away across the ice. He has
nothing left.

He can't make it.

Rage, helpless rage vomits through him, his eyes are
crying hot ice down his face. So close! *So close!* And sick
with fury he sees them come—*whew-whew! whew-whew-
whew-whew!*—a torrent of whistling wings in the bright air,
the ducks are pouring over the pass. Ten thousand noble
canvasbacks hurtling down the sky at him silver and black,
the sky is wings beating above him, but too high, too
high—they know the range, oh yes!

He has never seen so many, he will never see it again—
and he is standing in the boat now, a naked bleeding loco
ice-boy, raging, sweeping the virgin twelve-gauge, firing—
BAM-BAM! both barrels at nothing, at the ice, at the sky,
spilling out the shells, ramming them in with tearing frozen
hands. A drake bullets toward him, nearer—it *has* to be
near enough! BAM! BAM!

But it isn't, it isn't, and the air-riders, the magic bodies of his love beat over him yelling—canvasback, teal, widgeon, pintails, redheads, every duck in the world rising now, he is in a ten-mile swirl of birds, firing, firing, a weeping maniac under the flashing wings, white-black, black-white. And among the flashing he sees not only ducks but geese, cranes, every great bird that ever rode this wind: hawks, eagles, condors, pterodactyls—BAM-BAM! BAM-BAM!! in the crazy air, in the gale of rage and tears exploding in great black pulses—*black! light! black!*—whirling unbearably, rushing him up . . .

. . . And he surfaces suddenly into total calm and dimness, another self with all fury shrunk to a tiny knot below his mind and his eyes feasting in the open throat of a girl's white shirt. He is in a room, a cool cave humming with secret promise. Behind the girl the windows are curtained with sheer white stuff against the glare outside.

"Your mother said you went to Santa Fe." He hears his throat threaten soprano and digs his fists into the pockets of his Levis.

The girl Pilar—Pee-lar, crazy-name-Pilar—bends to pick at her tanned ankle, feathery brown bob swinging across her cheek and throat.

"Um-m." She is totally absorbed in a thin gold chain around her ankle, crouching on a big red leather thing her parents got in where, Morocco—Pilar of the urgently slender waist curving into her white Levis, the shirt so softly holding swelling softness; everything so white against her golden tan, smelling of soap and flowers and girl. So *clean.* She has to be a virgin, his heart knows it; a marvellous slow-motion happiness is brimming up in the room. She likes me. She's so shy, even if she's a year older, nearly seventeen, she's like a baby. The pathos of her vulnerable body swells in him, he balls his fists to hide the bulge by his fly. Oh Jeeze, I mean Jesus, let her not look, Pilar. But she does look up then, brushing her misty hair back, smiling dreamily up at him.

"I was at the La Fonda, I had a dinner date with René."

"Who's René?"

"I told you, Pe-ter." Not looking at him, she uncurls from the hassock, drifts like a child to the window, one hand rubbing her arm. "He's my cousin. He's old, he's twenty-five or thirty. He's a lieutenant now."

"Oh."

"An *older man*." She makes a face, grins secretly, peeking out through the white curtains.

His heart fizzes with relief, with the exultance rising in the room. She's a virgin, all right. From the bright hot world outside comes the sound of a car starting. A horse whickers faintly down at the club stables, answered by the double wheeze of a donkey. They both giggle. Peter flexes his shoulder, opens and grips his hand around an imaginary mallet.

"Does your father know you were out with him?"

"Oh yes." She's cuddling her cheek against her shoulder, pushing the immaculate collar, letting him see the creamy mounds. She wants me, Peter thinks. His guts jump. *She's going to let me do it to her*. And all at once he is calm, richly calm like that first morning at the corral, watching his mare come to him; knowing.

"Pa-*pa* doesn't care, it's nineteen forty-four. René is my cousin."

Her parents are so terribly sophisticated; he knows her father is some kind of secret war scientist: they are all here because of the war, something over at Los Alamos. And her mother talking French, talking about weird places like Dee-jon and Tan-jay. His mother doesn't know French, his father teaches high school, he never would be going around with these sophisticated strangers except they need him for their sandlot polo. And he can play rings around them all, too, Peter thinks, grinning, all those smooth sweating old young men—even with his one mare for four chukkers and her tendons like big hot balloons, even with his spliced mallet he can cut it over their heads! If he could only get an official rating. Three goals, sure. Maybe four, he muses, seeing himself riding through that twerp Drexel with his four remounts, seeing Pilar smile, not looking at him. She's shy. That time he let her ride the mare she was really frightened, incredibly awkward; he could feel her thighs tremble when he boosted her up.

His own thighs tremble, remembering the weak tenderness of her in his hands. *Always before your voice my*

soul is as some smooth and awkward foal— it doesn't
sound so wet now, his mother's nutty line. His foal, his
velvety vulnerable baby mare. Compared to her he's a
gorilla, even if he's technically a virgin too, men are
different. And he understands suddenly that weird Have-
lock Ellis book in her father's den. Gentle. He must be
gentle. Not like—a what?—a baboon playing a violin.
"You shouldn't fool around with older men," he says
and is gratified by the gruffness. "You don't know."
She's watching him now under the fall of her hair,
coming close, still hugging herself with her hand going
slowly up and down her arm, caressing it. A warm soap
smell fills his nose, a sharp muskiness under it. She
doesn't know what she's doing, he thinks choking, she
doesn't know about men. And he grunts something like
"Don't," or "Can it," trying to hold down the leaping
heat between them, but is confused by her voice
whispering.
"It *hurts*, Pe-ter."
"What, your arm?"
"Here, do-pee," and his hand is suddenly taken hold of
by cool small fingers pulling it not to her arm but in
wonder to her side, pressed in the rustling shirt under
which he feels at first nothing and then shockingly too far
in not his own wide ribs but the warm stem of her, and as
his paralyzed hand fumbles, clasps, she half turns around
so that his ignited hand rides onto a searing soft unnatural
swelling—her *breast*—and the room blanks out, whirls up
on a brimming, drumming tide as if all the dead buffalo
were pounding back. And the window blinks once with
lemon light shooting around their two bodies where her
hip is butting into his thigh making it wholly impossible to
continue standing there with his hands gentle on her tits.
"You don't know what you're doing, Pilar. Don't be a
dope, your mother—"
"She's a-way now." And there is a confused interval of
mouths and hands trying to be gentle, trying to hold her
away from his fly, trying to stuff her into himself in total
joy, if he had six hands he couldn't cope with electric all
of her—until suddenly she is pulled back, is asking
inanely, "Pe-ter, don't you have a friend?"
The subtle difference in her voice makes him blink,

answering stupidly, "Sure, Tom Ring," while her small nose wrinkles.

"Dopee Pe-ter, I mean a boy friend. Somebody smooth."

He stands trying to pant dignifiedly, thinking Jeeze, I mean Christ, she knows I don't have any smooth friends; if it's for a picnic maybe Diego Martine? But before he can suggest this she has leaned into the window bay, cuddling the silky curtain around her, peeking at him so that his hands go pawing in the cloth.

"René has a friend."

"Uh."

"He's older too, he's twen-tee," she breathes teasingly. "Lieute*nant* Shar-lo. That's Charles to you, see?" And she turns around full into his arms curtain and all and from the press of silk and giggles comes a small voice saying forever, "And Re-*né* and Shar-*lo* and Pee-*lar* all went to bed together and they played with me, Oh, for hours and hours Pe-ter, it was too marvellous. I will ne-ver do it with just one boy again."

Everything drops then except her face before him horribly heavy and exalted and alien, and just as his heart knows it's dead and an evil so generalized he can hardly recognize it as fury starts tearing emptily at him inside, her hand comes up over her mouth and she is running doubled over past him.

"I'm going to be sick, Peter help me!"

And he stumbles after down the dim cool hall to find her crumpled down, her brown hair flowing into the toilet as she retches, retches, whimpering, convulses unbearably. The white shirt has ridden up to expose her pathetically narrow back, soft knobs of her spine curving down into her pants, her tender buttocks bumping his knees as he stands helplessly strangling a sopping towel instead of her neck, trying to swab at her hidden forehead. His own gullet is retching too, his face feels doughy, and water is running down into his open mouth while one of her hands grips his, shaking him with her spasms there in the dim hospital-like bathroom. The world is groaning, he is seeing not her father's bay rum bottle but the big tiled La Fonda bedroom, the three bodies writhing on the bed, performing unknown horrors. *Playing with her* . . .

His stomach heaves, only what it is, he is coming in his Levis in a dreadful slow unrelieving ooze like a red-hot wire dragging through his crotch, while he stands by her uselessly as he will stand helplessly by in some near future he can't imagine or remember—and the tension keeps building, pounding, the light flickers—a storm is coming or maybe his eyes are going bad, but he can see below him her pure profile resting spent on the edge of the toilet, oblivious to his furious towel; in the flashing dimness sees the incomprehensible letters *S-E-P-T-I-C A-B-O-R-T-I-O-N* snaking shadowy down the spine of his virgin love, while the universe beats black—flash! Black! Drumming with hooves harsher than any storm—hurling him through lightning-claps of blinding darkness to a thrumming stasis in which what exists of him senses—something —but is instantly shot away on unimaginable energies . . .

. . . and achieves condensement, blooms into the green and open sunlight of another world, into a mellow springtime self—in which a quite different girl is jostling his hip.

"Molly," he hears his older voice say vaguely, seeing with joy how the willow fronds trail in the friendly, dirty Potomac. The bars and caduceus on his collar are pricking his neck.

"Yes sir, Doctor sir." She spins around, kneels down in the scruffy grass to open Howard Johnson boxes. "Oh god, the coffee." Handing him up a hot dog, swinging back her fair hair. Her arm is so female with its tender pale armpit, her whole body is edible, even her dress is like lemonade so fresh and clean—no, radiant, he corrects himself. That's the word, radiant. His radiant woman. He shrugs away a tiny darkness, thinking of her hair sliding on his body in the Roger Park hotel bedroom.

"C'mon sit, Pete. It's only a little dirty."

"Nothing's dirty any more." He flops down beside her, one arm finding its natural way around the opulence of her buttocks on the grass. She chuckles down at him, shaking her head.

"You're a hard case, Pete." She takes a big bite of hot dog with such lips that he considers flinging himself upon her then and there, barely remembers the cars tearing by above them. "I swear," she says, chewing, "I don't think you ever screwed anybody you were friends with before."

"Something like that." He puts his hot dog down to loosen his GI tie.

"Thirty days to civvies, you'll be in Baltimore." She licks her fingers happily. "Oh wow, Pete, I'm so glad you got your fellowship. Try the cole slaw, it's all right. Will you remember us poor slaves when you're a big old pathologist?"

"I'll remember." To distract himself he pokes in the boxes, spills cole slaw on a book. "What you reading?"

"Oh, Whately Carrington."

"Whatly what?"

"No, *Whate*-ly. Carrington. A Limey. Psychical research man, they do that veddy seddiously, the Limies."

"Uh?" He beams at the river, blinks to get rid of a flicker back of his eyes. Amphetamine withdrawal, after six months?

"He has this theory, about K-objects. Whatever thing you feel most intense about, part of you lives on—Pete, what's wrong?"

"Nothing."

But the flicker won't quit, it is suddenly worse, through it he can just make out her face turned nurse-wary, coming close, and he tries to hang on through a world flashing black—green—BLACK!—is trapped for unbreathing timelessness in dark nowhere, a phantom landscape of grey tumbled ash under a hard black sky, seeing without eyes a distant tangle of wreckage on the plain so menacing that his unbodied voice screams at the shadow of a metal scrap beside him in the ashes; *2004* the ghostly unmeaning numbers—*STOP IT!*—and he is back by the river under Molly's springtime eyes, his hands gripping into the bones of her body.

"Hey-y-y, honey, the war's over." Sweet sensual pixie-smile now watchful, her nurse's hand inside his shirt. "Korea's ten thousand miles away, you're in good old D.C., Doctor."

"I know. I saw a license plate." He laughs unconvincingly, makes his hands relax. Will the ghosts of Seoul never let him go? And his body guiltily intact, no piece of him in the stained waste cans into which he has—Stop it! Think of Molly. I like Ike. Johns Hopkins research fellowship. Some men simply aren't cut out for surgical practice.

"I'm a gutless wonder, Molly. Research."

"Oh for Christ's sake, Pete," she says with total warmth, nurse-hand satisfied, changing to lover's on his chest. "We've been *over* all that."

And of course they have, he knows it and only mutters, "My Dad wanted me to be an Indian doctor," which they have been over too; and the brimming gladness is back now, buoyantly he seizes the cole slaw, demands entertainment, demonstrating reality-grasp.

"So what about Whately?"

"It's serious-s-s," she protests, snickering, and is mercurially almost serious too. "I mean, I'm an atheist, Pete, I don't believe there's anything afterwards, but this theory . . ." And she rattles on about K-objects and the pool of time, intense energic structures of the mind undying—sweet beddable girl in the springtime who has taught him unclaiming love. His friend. Liberated him.

He stretches luxuriously, relishes a cole slaw belch. Free male beside a willing woman. No problems. *What is it man in woman doth require? The lineaments of gratified desire.* The radiance of her. He has gratified her. Will gratify her again . . .

"It's kind of spooky, though." He flings the box at the river with tremendous effort, it flies twenty feet. "Damn! But think of parts of yourself whirling around forever sticking to whatever you loved!" She settles against the willow, watching the box float away. "I wonder if part of me is going to spend eternity hanging around a dumb cat. I loved that old cat. Henry. He died, though."

The ghost of a twelve-gauge fires soundlessly across his mind, a mare whickers. He sneezes and rolls over onto her lap with his nose in her warm scented thigh. She peers dreamily down at him over her breasts, is almost beautiful.

"Whatever you love, forever. Be careful what you love." She squints wickedly. "Only with you I think it'd be whatever you were maddest at—no, that's a horrible thought. Love *has* to be the most intense."

He doubts it but is willing to be convinced, rooting in

her lap while she pretends to pound on him and then squirms, stretching up her arms, giving herself to the air, to him, to life.

"I want to spend eternity whirling around you." He heaves up to capture her, no longer giving a damn about the cars, and as the sweet familiar body comes pliantly under him he realizes it's true, he's known it for some time. Not friendship at all, or rather, the best of friendships. The real one. "I love you, Molly. We love."

"Ooh, Pete."

"You're coming to Baltimore with me. We'll get married," he tells her warm neck, feeling the flesh under her skirt heavy in his hand, feeling also an odd stillness that makes him draw back to where he can see her face, see her lips whispering.

"I was afraid of that."

"Afraid?" His heart jumps with relief, jumps so hard that the flicker comes back in the air, through which he sees her lying too composed under his urgency. "Don't be afraid, Molly. I *love* you."

But she is saying softly, "Oh, damn, damn, Pete, I'm so sorry, it's a lousy thing women do. I was just so happy, because . . ." She swallows, goes on in an absurd voice. "Because someone very dear to me is coming home. He called me this morning from Honolulu."

This he cannot, will not understand among the flashing pulses, but repeats patiently, "You love me, Molly. I love you. We'll get married in Baltimore," while she fights gently away from him saying, "Oh I do, Pete, I *do*, but it's not the same."

"You'll be happy with me. You love me."

They are both up crouching now in the blinking, pounding sunlight.

"No, Pete, I never *said*. I didn't—" Her hands are out seeking him like knives.

"I *can't* marry you, honey. I'm going to marry a man called Charlie McMahon."

McMahon—Maaa—homm—aa—on-n-n the idiot sound flaps through the universe, his carotids are hammering, the air is drumming with his hurt and rage as he stands foolishly wounded, unable to believe the treachery of everything—which is now strobing in great blows of blackness as his voice shouts "Whore!" shouts "Bitch-bitch-bitch . . ." into a dwindling, flashing chaos . . .

. . . and explodes silently into a nonbeing which is almost familiar, is happening this time more slowly as if a huge energy is tiding to its crest so slowly that some structure of himself endures to form in what is no longer a brain the fear that he is indeed dead and damned to live forever in furious fragments. And against this horror his essence strains to protest *But I did love!* at a horizon of desolation—a plain of endless, lifeless rubble under a cold black sky, in which he or some pattern of energies senses once more that distant presence: wreckage, machines, huge structures incomprehensibly operative, radiating dark force in the nightmare world—the force which now surges . . .

. . . to incorporate him anew within familiar walls, with the words "But I did love" meaninglessly on his lips. He leans back in his familiarly unoiled swivel chair, savoring content. Somewhere within him weak darkness stirs, has power only to send his gaze to the three-di portraits behind the pile of print-outs on his desk.

Molly smiles back at him over the computer sheets, her arm around their eldest daughter. For the first time in years the thought of poor Charlie McMahon crosses his mind, triggers the automatic incantation: Molly-never-would-have-been-happy-with-him. They had a bad time around there, but it worked out. Funny how vividly he recalls that day by the river, in spite of all the good years since. *But I did love*, his mind murmurs uneasily, as his eyes go lovingly to the computer print-outs.

The lovely, elegant results. All confirmed eight ways now, the variance all pinned down. Even better than he'd hoped. The journal paper can go in the mail tomorrow. Of course the pub-lag is nearly three years now; never mind: the AAAS panel comes next week. That's the important thing. Lucky timing, couldn't be neater. The press is bound to play it up . . . Going to be hard not to watch Gilliam's face, Peter muses, his own face ten years younger, sparkling, all lines upturned.

"I do love it, that's what counts," he thinks, a jumble of the years of off-hours drudgery in his mind . . . Coffeeringed clipboards, the new centrifuge, the animal mess, a girl's open lab coat, arguments with Ferris in Analysis, arguments about space about equipment about costs—and arching over it like a laser-grid the luminous order of his hypothesis. His proven—no, mustn't say it—his meticulously *tested* hypothesis. The lucky lifetime break. The beauty one. Never do it again, he hasn't another one like this left in him; no matter! This is it, the peak. Just in time. Don't think of what Nathan said, don't think the word. (Nobel)—That's stupid. (Nobel) Think of the work itself, the explanatory power, the clarity.

His hand has been wandering toward the in-basket under the print-outs where his mail has been growing moss (he'll get a secretary out of this, that's for sure!) but the idea of light turns him to the window. The room feels tense, brimming with a tide of energy. Too much coffee, he thinks, too much joy. I'm not used to it. Too much of a loner. From here in I share. Spread it around, encourage younger men. Herds of assistants now . . .

Across his view of tired Bethesda suburbs around the NIH Annex floats the train of multiple-author papers, his name as senior, a genial myth; sponsoring everybody's maiden publication. A fixture in the mainstream . . . Kids playing down there, he sees, shooting basketball by a garage, will some of them live to have a myeloma cured by the implications of his grubby years up here? If the crystallization can be made easier. Bound to come. But not by me, he thinks, trying to focus on the running figures through a faint stroboscopic blink which seems to arise from the streets below although he knows it must be in his retinae.

Really too much caffeine, he warns himself. Let's not have a hypertensive episode, not *now* for God's sake. Exultation is almost tangible in the room, it's not distracting but integrative; as if he were achieving some higher level of vitality, a norepinephrine-like effect. Maybe I really will live on a higher level, he muses, rubbing the bridge of his nose between two fingers to get rid of a black after-image which seems almost like an Apollo moonscape behind his eyes, a trifle unpleasant.

Too much doom, he tells himself, vigorously polishing his glasses, too much bomb-scare, ecology-scare, fascism-scare, race-war-scare, death-of-everything scare. He jerks his jaw to stop the tinnitis thrumming in his inner ear, glancing at the big 1984 desk calendar with its scrawled joke: *If everything's okay why are we whispering?* Right. Let's get at it and get home. To Molly and Sue and little Pete, their late-born.

He grins thinking of the kid running to him and thrusts his hand under the print-outs to his packet of stale mail—and as his hand touches it an icicle rams into his heart.

For an instant he thinks he really is having a coronary, but it isn't his real heart, it's a horrible cold current of knowledge striking from his fingers to his soul, from that hideous sleazy tan-covered foreign journal which he now pulls slowly out to see the pencilled note clipped to the cover, the personally delivered damned journal which has been lying under there like a time-bomb for how long? Weeks?

Pete, you better look at this. Sorry as hell.

But he doesn't need to look, riffling through the wretchedly printed pages with fingers grown big and cold as clubs; he already knows what he'll find inside there published so neatly, so sweetly, and completely, with the confirmation even stronger and more elegant, the implication he hadn't thought of—and all so modest and terse. So young. Despair takes him as the page opens. *Djakarta University* for Jesus Christ's sake? And some Hindu's bloody paradigm . . .

Sick fury fulminates, bile and ashes raining through his soul as his hands fumble the pages, the grey unreal unreadable pages which are now strobing—Flash! Black! Flash! Black!—swallowing the world, roaring him in or up or out on a phantom whirlwind . . .

. . . . till unsensation crescendoes past all limit, bursts finally into the silence of pure energy, where he—or what is left of him, or momentarily reconstituted of him—integrates to terrified insight, achieves actual deathly awareness of its extinct self immaterially spinning in the dust of an aeons-gone NIH Annex on a destroyed planet. And comprehends with agonized lucidity the real death of everything that lived—excepting only that in himself which he would most desperately wish to be dead.

What happened? He does not know, can never know which of the dooms or some other had finally overtaken them, nor when; only that he is registering eternity, not time, that all that lived here has been gone so long that even time is still. Gone, all gone; centuries or millennia gone, all gone to ashes under pulseless stars in the icy dark, gone forever. Saving him alone and his trivial pain.

He alone . . . But as the mercilessly reifying force floods higher there wakes in him a dim uncomforting sense of presence, a bodiless disquiet in the dust tells him he is companioned, is but a node in a ghostly film of dead life shrouding the cold rock-ball. Unreachable, isolate —he strains for contact and is incorporeally stricken by new dread. *Are they too in pain?* Was pain indeed the fiercest fire in our nerves, alone able to sustain its flame through death? What of love, of joy? . . . There are none here.

He wails voicelessly as conviction invades him, he who had believed in nothing before. All the agonies of earth, uncancelled? Are broken ghosts limping forever from Stalingrad and Salamis, from Gettysburg and Thebes and Dunkirk and Khartoum? Do the butchers' blows still fall at Ravensbruck and Wounded Knee? Are the dead of Carthage and Hiroshima and Cuzco burning yet? Have ghostly women waked again only to resuffer violation, only to watch again their babies slain? Is every nameless victim still feeling the iron bite, is every bomb, every bullet and arrow and stone that ever flew still finding its screaming mark—atrocity without end or comfort, forever?

Molly. The name forms in his cancelled heart. She who was love. He tries to know that she or some fragment of her is warm among her children, but can summon only the image of her crawling forever through wreckage to Charlie McMahon's bloody head.

Let it not be! He would shriek defiance at the wastes, finding himself more real as the strange energy densens; he struggles bodilessly, flails perished nonlimbs to conjure love out of extinction to shield him against hell, calling with all his obliterated soul on the ultimate talisman: the sound of his little son's laugh, the child running to him, clasping his leg in welcome home.

For an instant he thinks he has it—he can see the small

face turn up, the mouth open—but as he tries to grasp the ghost-child fades, frays out, leaving in his destroyed heart only another echo of hurt—*I want Mommy, Mommy, my Mommy*. And he perceives that what he had taken for its head are forms. Presences intrusive, alien as the smooth, bleak regard of sharks met under water.

They move, precess obscurely—they *exist* here on this time-lost plain! And he understands with loathing that it is from *them* or *those*—machines or beings, he cannot tell—that the sustaining energy flows. It is *their* dark potency which has raised him from the patterns of the dust.

Hating them he hungers, would sway after them to suck his death-life, as a billion other remanants are yearning, dead sunflowers thirsting toward their black source—but finds he cannot, can only crave helplessly as they recede.

They move, he perceives, toward those black distant cenotaphs, skeletal and alien, which alone break the dead horizon. What these can be, engines or edifices, is beyond his knowing. He strains sightlessly, sensing now a convergence, an inflowing as of departure like ants into no earthly nest. And at this he understands that the energy upbuoying him is sinking, is starting to ebb. The alien radiance that raised him is going and he is guttering out. *Do you know?* he voicelessly cries after them, *Do you know? Do you move oblivious among our agonies?*

But he receives no answer, will never receive one; and as his tenuous structure fails he has consciousness only to wonder briefly what unimaginable errand brought such beings here to his dead cinder. Emissaries, he wonders, dwindling; explorers, engineers? Or is it possible that they are only sightseers? Idling among our ruins, perhaps even cognizant of the ghosts they raise to wail—turning us on, recreating our dead-show for their entertainment?

Shrivelling, he watches them go in, taking with them his lacerating life, returning him to the void. Will they return? Or—his waning self forms one last desolation—have they returned already on their millennial tours, has this recurred, to recur and recur again? Must he and all dead life be borne back each time helplessly to suffer, to jerk anew on the same knives and die again only until another energy exhumes him for the next performance?

Let us die! But his decaying identity can no longer sustain protest, knows only that it is true, is unbearably all true, has all been done to him before and is all to do again and again and again without mercy forever.

And as he sinks back through the collapsing levels he can keep hold only of despair, touching again the deadly limp brown journal—*Djakarta University?* Flash—and he no longer knows the cause of the terror in his soul as he crumbles through lost springtime—*I don't love you that way, Pete*—and is betrayed to aching joy as his hand closes over the young breast within her white shirt—*Pe-ter, don't you have a friend?*—while his being shreds out, disperses among a myriad draining ghosts of anguish as the alien life deserts them, strands them lower and lower toward the final dark—until with uncomprehending grief he finds himself, or a configuration that was himself, for a last instant real—his boots on gravel in the dawn, his hand on a rusty pickup truck.

A joy he cannot bear rises in his fourteen-year-old heart as he peers down at the magic ducks, sees his boat safe by the path he's cut; not understanding why the wind shrieks pain through the peaks above as he starts leaping down the rocks holding his axe and his first own gun, down to the dark lake under the cold stars, forever.

AFTERWORD

Abominations, that's what they are: afterwords, introductions, all the dribble around the story. Oh, I read them. And often happily, other people's afterwords are often okay. Not mine. The story, that's really all I know. And after I reread any one of my own, the only sincere thing I have to say to the reader who has suffered through it comes out as a kind of obsessed squeal—*Oh gods of the English language, forgive these pages which it is now too late to revise! Reader, can you actually even begin to see*

*what I was trying to bring in through the flak of ill-made
sentences, can you possibly share the vision? How marvellous if you can, but how unlikely . . .*

Now editors don't really want this type of outburst.
They desire author to straighten his underwear and get up
and say something cool, like "The Doomsday theme in
science fiction demonstrates, etc." Well.

All right. The Doomsday theme in science fiction is . . .
a great deal more than a mere theme. Ever since things
got serious, ever since we realized that we really are in
danger of killing ourselves, of bombing or poisoning or
gutting or choking the planet to death, or—perhaps worst
of all—of killing our own humanity by fascist tyranny or
simple overbreeding, science fiction has been the only
place we could talk about it. The mainstream took one
look at it in Orwell's *1984* and promptly caponized itself.
It's too terrible, don't look. Tell me about the agony of
owning too many swimming pools. Tell me Jesus saves.

Science fiction has gone on looking, showing, working
out all the dire roadmaps to Armageddon, the nasty slideways to Entropy and Apocalypse. I loathe you, let me
count the ways. Even the crazy hopeless hopes—remember Bester's last man dragging himself over the radioactive
ruins so that his dead body would fertilize the sterile sea
and start life again? Oh yes, of course we can see occasional traces of adolescent fantasy, bulging out here and
there—is there literary life without libido? But noble,
ingenious, terrifying stories. Which hurt, because the fear
is real.

Now here I learned something else about the Doomsday theme in science fiction. Thinking it would be nice to
end with a bow to the great ones, I went through eight
volumes of science fiction criticism, looking for a list. And
found virtually nothing except a brief European discussion
of anti-utopias and some reviews of specific works.
Writers being notoriously erratic researchers, perhaps I
have missed the definitive Doomsday essay. If not it looks
as if there is an empty place where someone should
assemble and relate the sf warnings of man's end.

A Doomsday study would not only do justice to some
heavy writing; it would, I think, turn up some interesting
things. For example, wouldn't you expect to find a change,

as the menaces became real? How cool the old stories were: Wells's silent landscape under a dying sun, *in the far future*; the exciting *but improbable* disasters of *When Worlds Collide*. Great stories, wild ideas. Thirty years after Huxley wrote *Brave New World* he remarked he had no idea things would move so fast. But somewhere around Hiroshima the tone changes—we suddenly see ourselves *On The Beach* next Wednesday. The stories become immediate: Change our ways or die. And the dooms proliferate. And finally, I think you would find that some of them become so well known that they are only symbolized, become almost interchangeable. Who cares if it's chain reaction or greenhouse effect, imperialism or fecundity? The interest turns to a human mechanism of cause, or possibly, survival. Can you use an imbecile as Mother of the World? And so on. Surely the kindly editors will excuse me now.

But if they insist on a word as to how "Her Smoke Rose Up Forever" attaches itself to the grand procession, well, it does so through that strand of hope. Carrington's work is real, and his speculation on the real nature of time holds out a faint rational hope of a curious sort of immortality. Perhaps, just perhaps, very intense psychic structure might have existence in timeless or "static" time. But Carrington, good man that he was, unhesitatingly assumed that intense psychic structure was *good*, was in fact a sort of Spinozan intellectual love of some aspect of life. A beautiful picture—all the fragments of loving farmers merging around the ideas of earth and seed, bits of philatelists converging forever around a two-penny black, parts of all of us webbed eternally around great poems or symphonies or sunsets. Lovely. But look back in your memory. Moments of pure selfless love, yes—but what about the fearful vitality of the bad past—the shames, furies, disappointments, the lover defected, the prize that got away? As the psychologists put it, *aversive conditioning persists*. One shock undoes a hundred rewards. If by wild chance Carrington's theory is in some degree right, his immortality would be a hell beyond conception . . . until we can change ourselves. Drain the strength of pain from our nerves. Make love and joy as strong as evil. *But how can we?*

Novels
NO BLADE OF GRASS, by John Christopher
RED ALERT, by Peter George
A CANTICLE FOR LEIBOWITZ, by Walter M. Miller, Jr.
TOMORROW & TOMORROW, by Lewis Padgett
EARTH ABIDES, by George R. Stewart

Short Stories
THEY DON'T MAKE LIFE LIKE THEY USED TO, by Alfred
   Bester
NOT WITH A BANG, by Damon Knight
WORLD WITHOUT CHILDREN, by Damon Knight
VINTAGE SEASON, by C.L. Moore
THUNDER AND ROSES, by Theodore Sturgeon
ADAM AND NO EVE, by Alfred Bester
MOTHER TO THE WORLD, by Richard Wilson

About James Tiptree, Jr.

James Tiptree, Jr., an enigma, apparently in his fifties or
sixties, has published brilliant short stories since 1968 in
all of the sf markets. He is probably the most fascinating,
individual talent since the late "Cordwainer Smith" (Paul
Linebarger). Tiptree lives some of the time in McLean,
Virginia.

TIME TRAVEL

A LITTLE SOMETHING
FOR US TEMPUNAUTS

PHILIP K. DICK

Wearily, Addison Doug plodded up the long path of synthetic redwood rounds, step by step, his head down a little, moving as if he were in actual physical pain. The girl watched him, wanting to help him, hurt within her to see how worn and unhappy he was, but at the same time she rejoiced that he was there at all. On and on, toward her, without glancing up, going by feel . . . like he's done this many times, she thought suddenly. Knows the way too well. Why?

"Addi," she called, and ran toward him. "They said on the TV you were dead. All of you were killed!"

He paused, wiping back his dark hair which was no longer long; just before launch they had cropped it. But he had evidently forgotten. "You believe everything you see on TV?" he said, and came on again, haltingly, but smiling now. And reaching up for her.

God, it felt good to hold him, and to have him clutch at her again, with more strength than she had expected. "I was going to find somebody else," she gasped. "To replace you."

"I'll knock your head off if you do," he said. "Anyhow, that isn't possible; nobody could replace me."

"But what about the implosion?" she said. "On re-entry; they said—"

"I forget," Addison said, in the tone he used when he meant, I'm not going to discuss it. The tone had always angered her before, but not now. This time she sensed how awful the memory was. "I'm going to stay at your place a couple days," he said, as together they moved up the path toward the open front door of the tilted A-frame house. "If that's okay. And Benz and Crayne will be joining me, later on; maybe even as soon as tonight. We've got a lot to talk over and figure out."

"Then all three of you survived." She gazed up into his careworn face. "Everything they said on TV . . ." She understood, then. Or believed she did. "It was a cover story. For—political purposes, to fool the Russians. Right? I mean, the Soviet Union'll think the launch was a failure because on re-entry—"

"No," he said. "A chrononaut will be joining us, most likely. To help figure out what happened. General Toad said one of them is already on his way here; they got clearance already. Because of the gravity of the situation."

"Jesus," the girl said, stricken. "Then who's the cover story for?"

"Let's have something to drink," Addison said. "And then I'll outline it all for you."

"Only thing I've got at the moment is California brandy."

Addison Doug said, "I'd drink anything right now, the way I feel." He dropped to the couch, leaned back, and sighed a ragged, distressed sigh, as the girl hurriedly began fixing both of them a drink.

The FM radio in the car yammered, ". . . grieves at the stricken turn of events precipitating out of an unheralded . . ."

"Official nonsense babble," Crayne said, shutting off the radio. He and Benz were having trouble finding the house, having only been there once before. It struck Crayne that this was somewhat informal a way of convening a conference of this importance, meeting at Addison's chick's pad out here in the boondocks of Ojai. On the other hand, they wouldn't be pestered by the curious. And they probably didn't have much time. But that was hard to say; about that no one knew for sure.

The hills on both sides of the road had once been forests, Crayne observed. Now housing tracts and their melted, irregular, plastic roads marred every rise in sight. "I'll bet this was nice once," he said to Benz, who was driving.

"The Los Padres National Forest is near here," Benz said. "I got lost in there when I was eight. For hours I was sure a rattler would get me. Every stick was a snake."

"The rattler's got you now," Crayne said.

"All of us," Benz said.

"You know," Crayne said, "it's a hell of an experience to be dead."

"Speak for yourself."

"But technically—"

"If you listen to the radio and TV." Benz turned toward him, his big gnome face bleak with admonishing sternness. "We're no more dead than anyone else on the planet. The difference for us is that our death date is in the past, whereas everyone else's is set somewhere at an uncertain time in the future. Actually, some people have it pretty damn well set, like people in cancer wards; they're as certain as we are. More so. For example, how long can we stay here before we go back? We have a margin, a latitude that a terminal cancer victim doesn't have."

Crayne said caustically, "The next thing you'll be telling us to cheer us up is that we're in no pain."

"Addi is. I watched him lurch off earlier today. He's got it psychosomatically—made it into a physical complaint. Like God's kneeling on his neck; you know, carrying a much-too-great burden that's unfair, only he won't complain out loud . . . just points now and then at the nail hole in his hand." He grinned.

"Addi has got more to live for than we do."

"Every man has more to live for than any other man. I don't have a cute chick to sleep with, but I'd like to see the semi's rolling along the Riverside Freeway at sunset a few more times. It's not what you have to live for; it's that you want to live to see it, to be there—that's what is so damn sad."

They rode on in silence.

In the quiet living room of the girl's house the three tempunauts sat around smoking, taking it easy; Addison Doug thought to himself that the girl looked unusually foxy and desirable in her stretched-tight white sweater and micro-skirt and he wished, wistfully, that she looked a little less interesting. He could not really afford to get embroiled in such stuff, at this point. He was too tired.

"Does she know," Benz said, indicating the girl, "what this is all about? I mean, can we talk openly? It won't wipe her out?"

"I haven't explained it to her yet," Addison said.

"You goddam well better," Crayne said.

"What is it?" the girl said, stricken, sitting upright with one hand directly between her breasts. As if clutching at a religious artifact that isn't there, Addison thought.

"We got snuffed on re-entry," Benz said. He was, really, the cruelest of the three. Or at least the most blunt. "You see, Miss . . ."

"Hawkins," the girl whispered.

"Glad to meet you, Miss Hawkins." Benz surveyed her in his cold, lazy fashion. "You have a first name?"

"Merry Lou."

"Okay, Merry Lou," Benz said. To the other two men he observed, "Sounds like the name a waitress has stitched on her blouse. Merry Lou's my name and I'll be serving you dinner and breakfast and lunch and dinner and breakfast for the next few days or however long it is before you all give up and go back to your own time; that'll be fifty-three dollars and eight cents, please, not including tip. And I hope y'all never come back, y'hear?" His voice had begun to shake; his cigarette, too. "Sorry, Miss Hawkins," he said, then. "We're all screwed up by the implosion at re-entry time. As soon as we got here in ETA we learned about it. We've known longer than anyone else; we knew as soon as we hit Emergence Time."

"But there's nothing we could do," Crayne said.

"There's nothing anyone can do," Addison said to her, and put his arm around her. It felt like a déjà vu thing but then it hit him. We're in a closed time loop, he thought, we keep going through this again and again, trying to solve the re-entry problem, each time imagining it's the first time, the only time . . . and never succeeding. Which attempt is this? Maybe the millionth; we have sat here a million times, raking the same facts over and over again and getting nowhere. He felt bone-weary, thinking that. And he felt a sort of vast philosophical hate toward all other men, who did not have this enigma to deal with. We all go to one place, he thought, as the Bible says. But . . . for the three of us, we have been there already.

Are lying there now. So it's wrong to ask us to stand around on the surface of Earth afterward and argue and worry about it and try to figure out what malfunctioned. That should be, rightly, for our heirs to do. We've had enough already.

He did not say this aloud, though—for their sake.

"Maybe you bumped into something," the girl said.

Glancing at the others, Benz said sardonically, "Maybe we 'bumped into something.' "

"The TV commentators keep saying that," Merry Lou said, "about the hazard in re-entry of being out of phase spatially and colliding right down to the molecular level with tangent objects, any one of which—" She gestured. "You know. 'No two objects can occupy the same space at the same time.' So everything blew up, for that reason." She glanced around questioningly.

"That is the major risk factor," Crayne acknowledged. "At least theoretically, as Doctor Fein at Planning calculated when they got into the hazard question. But we had a variety of safety locking devices provided that functioned automatically. Re-entry couldn't occur unless these assists had stabilized us spatially so we would not overlap. Of course, all those devices, in sequence, might have failed. One after the other. I was watching my feedback 'metric scopes on launch, and they agreed, every one of them, that we were phased properly at that time. And I heard no warning tones. Saw none, neither." He grimaced. "At least it didn't happen then."

Suddenly Benz said, "Do you realize that our next-of-kin are now rich? All our Federal and commercial life insurance payoff. Our 'next of kin'—God forbid, that's us, I guess. We can apply for tens of thousands of dollars, cash on the line. Walk into our brokers' offices and say, 'I'm dead; lay the heavy bread on me.' "

Addison Doug was thinking, the public memorial services. That they have planned, after the autopsies. That long line of black-draped Cads going down Pennsylvania Avenue, with all the government dignitaries and double-domed scientist types—*and we'll be there*. Not once but twice. Once in the oak hand-rubbed brass-fitted flag-draped caskets, but also . . . maybe riding in open limos, waving at the crowds of mourners.

"The ceremonies," he said aloud.

The others stared at him, angrily, not comprehending. And then, one by one, they understood; he saw it on their faces.

"No," Benz grated. "That's—impossible."

Crayne shook his head emphatically. "They'll order us to be there, and we will be. Obeying orders."

"Will we have to *smile?*" Addison said. "To fucking *smile?*"

"No," General Toad said slowly, his great wattled head shivering about on his broomstick neck, the color of his skin dirty and mottled, as if the mass of decorations on his stiff-board collar had started part of him decaying away. "You are not to smile, but on the contrary are to adopt a properly grief-stricken manner. In keeping with the national mood of sorrow at this time."

"That'll be hard to do," Crayne said.

The Russian chrononaut showed no response; his thin beaked face, narrow within his translating earphones, remained strained with concern.

"The nation," General Toad said, "will become aware of your presence among us once more for this brief interval; cameras of all major TV networks will pan up on you without warning, and at the same time, the various commentators have been instructed to tell their audiences something like the following." He got out a piece of typed material, put on his glasses, cleared his throat and said, " 'We seem to be focusing on three figures riding together. Can't quite make them out. Can you?' " General Toad lowered the paper. "At this point they'll interrogate their colleagues extempore. Finally they'll exclaim, 'Why Roger,' or Walter or Ned, as the case may be, according to the individual network—"

"Or Bill," Crayne said. "In case it's the Bufonidae network, down there in the swamp."

General Toad ignored him. "They will severally exclaim, 'Why Roger, I believe we're seeing the three tempunauts themselves! Does this indeed mean that somehow the difficulty—?' And then the colleague commentator says in his somewhat more somber voice, 'What we're seeing at this time I think, David,' or Henry or Pete or Ralph, whichever it is, 'consists of mankind's first verified glimpse of what the technical people refer to as Emergence Time Activity or ETA. Contrary to what might seem to be the case at first sight, these are *not*—repeat not—our three valiant tempunauts as such, as we would ordinarily experience them, but more likely picked up by our cameras as the three of them are temporarily suspended in their voyage to the future, which we initially had reason to hope would take place in a time continuum roughly a hundred years from now . . . but it would seem that they somehow undershot and are here now, at this moment, which of course is, as we know, our present.' "

Addison Doug closed his eyes and thought, Crayne will ask him if he can be panned up on by the TV cameras holding a balloon and eating cotton candy. I think we're all going nuts from this, all of us. And then he wondered, How many times have we gone through this idiotic exchange?

I can't prove it, he thought wearily. But I know it's true. We've sat here, done this miniscule scrabbling, listened to and said all this crap, many times. He shuddered. Each rinky dink word . . .

"What's the matter?" Benz said acutely.

The Soviet chrononaut spoke up for the first time. "What is the maximum interval of ETA possible to your three-man team? And how large a percent has been exhausted by now?"

After a pause Crayne said, "They briefed us on that before we came in here today. We've consumed approximately one-half of our maximum total ETA interval."

"However," General Toad rumbled, "we have scheduled the Day of National Mourning to fall within the expected period remaining to them of ETA time. This required us to speed up the autopsy and other forensic findings, but in view of public sentiment, it was felt . . ."

The autopsy, Addison Doug thought, and again he shuddered; this time he could not keep his thoughts within himself and he said, "Why don't we adjourn this nonsense meeting and drop down to Pathology and view a few tissue sections enlarged and in color, and maybe we'll brainstorm a couple of vital concepts that'll aid medical science in its quest for explanations? Explanations—that's what we need. Explanations for problems that don't exist yet; we can develop the problems later." He paused. "Who agrees?"

"I'm not looking at my spleen up there on the screen," Benz said. "I'll ride in the parade but I won't participate in my own autopsy."

"You could distribute microscopic purple-stained slices of your own gut to the mourners along the way," Crayne said. "They could provide each of us with a doggy bag; right, General? We can strew tissue sections like confetti. I still think we should smile."

"I have researched all the memoranda about smiling," General Toad said, riffling the pages stacked before him, "and the consensus at policy is that smiling is not in accord with national sentiment. So that issue must be ruled closed. As far as your participating in the autopsical procedures which are now in progress—"

"We're missing out as we sit here," Crayne said to Addison Doug. "I always miss out."

Ignoring him, Addison addressed the Soviet chrononaut. "Officer N. Gauki," he said into his microphone, dangling on his chest, "what in your mind is the greatest terror facing a time traveler? That there will be an implosion due to coincidence on re-entry, such as has occurred in our launch? Or did other traumatic obsessions bother you and your comrade during your own brief but highly successful time flight?"

N. Gauki after a pause answered, "R. Plenya and I exchanged views at several informal times. I believe I can speak for us both when I respond to your question by emphasizing our perpetual fear that we had inadvertently entered a closed time loop and would never break out."

"You'd repeat it forever?" Addison Doug asked.

"Yes, Mr. A. Doug," the chrononaut said, nodding somberly.

A fear that he had never experienced before overcame Addison Doug. He turned helplessly to Benz and muttered, "Shit." They gazed at each other.

"I really don't believe this is what happened," Benz said to him in a low voice, putting his hand on Doug's shoulder; he gripped hard, the grip of friendship. "We just imploded on re-entry, that's all. Take it easy."

"Could we adjourn soon?" Addison Doug said in a hoarse, strangling voice, half-rising from his chair. He felt the room and the people in it rushing in at him, suffocating him. Claustrophobia, he realized. Like when I was in grade school, when they flashed a surprise test on our teaching machines, and I saw I couldn't pass it. "Please," he said simply, standing. They were all looking at him, with different expressions. The Russian's face was especially sympathetic, and deeply lined with care. Addison wished—"I want to go home," he said to them all, and felt stupid.

He was drunk. It was late at night, at a bar on Holly-wood Boulevard; fortunately Merry Lou was with him, and he was having a good time. Everyone was telling him so, anyhow. He clung to Merry Lou and said, "The great unity in life, the supreme unity and meaning, is man and woman. Their absolute unity; right?"

"I know," Merry Lou said. "We studied that in class." Tonight, at his request, Merry Lou was a small blonde girl, wearing purple bellbottoms and high heels and an open midriff blouse. Earlier she had had a lapis lazuli in her navel, but during dinner at Ting Ho's it had popped out and been lost. The owner of the restaurant had promised to keep on searching for it, but Merry Lou had been gloomy ever since. It was, she said, symbolic. But of what she did not say. Or anyhow he could not remember; maybe that was it. She had told him what it meant, and he had forgotten.

An elegant young black at a nearby table, with an Afro and striped vest and overstuffed red tie, had been staring at Addison for some time. He obviously wanted to come over to their table but was afraid to; meanwhile, he kept on staring.

"Did you ever get the sensation," Addison said to Merry Lou, "that you knew exactly what was about to happen? What someone was going to say? Word for word? Down to the slightest detail? As if you had already lived through it once before?"

"Everybody gets into that space," Merry Lou said. She sipped a Bloody Mary.

The black rose and walked toward them. He stood by Addison. "I'm sorry to bother you, sir."

Addison said to Merry Lou, "He's going to say, 'Don't I know you from somewhere? Didn't I see you on TV?' "

"That was precisely what I intended to say," the black said.

Addison said, "You undoubtedly saw my picture on page forty-six of the current issue of *Time,* the section on new medical discoveries. I'm the G.P. from a small town in Iowa catapulted to fame by my invention of a widespread, easily available cure for eternal life. Several of the big pharmaceutical houses are already bidding on my vaccine."

"That might have been where I saw your picture," the black said, but he did not appear convinced. Nor did he appear drunk; he eyed Addison Doug intensely. "May I seat myself with you and the lady?"

"Sure," Addison Doug said. He now saw, in the man's hand, the ID of the U.S. security agency that had ridden herd on the project from the start.

"Mr. Doug," the security agent said as he seated himself beside Addison, "you really shouldn't be here shooting off your mouth like this. If I recognized you some other dude might and freak out. It's all classified until the Day of Mourning. Technically, you're in violation of a Federal Statute by being here; did you realize that? I should haul you in. But this is a difficult situation; we don't want to do something uncool and make a scene. Where are your two colleagues?"

"At my place," Merry Lou said. She had obviously not seen the ID. "Listen," she said sharply to the agent, "why don't you get lost? My husband here has been through a grueling ordeal, and this is his only chance to unwind."

Addison looked at the man. "I knew what you were

going to say before you came over here." Word for word, he thought. I am right, and Benz is wrong and this will keep happening, this replay.

"Maybe," the security agent said, "I can induce you to go back to Miss Hawkins' place voluntarily. Some info arrived—" he tapped the tiny earphone in his right ear— "just a few minutes ago, to all of us, to deliver to you, marked urgent, if we located you. At the launch site ruins . . . they've been combing through the rubble, you know?"

"I know," Addison said.

"They think they have their first clue. Something was brought back by one of you. From ETA, over and above what you took, in violation of all your pre-launch training."

"Let me ask you this," Addison Doug said, "Suppose somebody does see me? Suppose somebody does recognize me? So what?"

"The public believes that even though re-entry failed, the flight into time, the first American time-travel launch, was successful. Three U.S. tempunauts were thrust a hundred years into the future—roughly twice as far as the Soviet launch of last year. That you only went a *week* will be less of a shock if it's believed that you three chose deliberately to remanifest at this continuum because you wished to attend, in fact felt compelled to attend—"

"We wanted to be in the parade," Addison interrupted. "Twice."

"You were drawn to the dramatic and somber spectacle of your own funeral procession, and will be glimpsed there by the alert camera crews of all major networks. Mr. Doug, really, an awful lot of high level planning and expense have gone into this to help correct a dreadful situation; trust us, believe me. It'll be easier on the public, and that's vital, if there's ever to be another U.S. time shot. And that is, after all, what we all want."

Addison Doug stared at him. "We want what?"

Uneasily, the security agent said, "To take further trips into time. As you have done. Unfortunately, you yourself cannot ever do so again, because of the tragic implosion and death of the three of you. But other tempunauts—"

"We want what? Is that what we want?" Addison's voice rose; people at nearby tables were watching, now. Nervously.

"Certainly," the agent said. "And keep your voice down."

"I don't want that," Addison said. "I want to stop. To stop forever. To just lie in the ground, in the dust, with everyone else. To see no more summers—the *same* summer."

"Seen one you've seen them all," Merry Lou said hysterically. "I think he's right, Addi; we should get out of here. You've had too many drinks, and it's late, and this news about the—"

Addison broke in, "What was brought back? How much extra mass?"

The security agent said, "Preliminary analysis shows that machinery weighing about one hundred pounds was lugged back into the time-field of the module and picked up along with you. This much mass—" The agent gestured. "That blew up the pad right on the spot. It couldn't begin to compensate for that much more than had occupied its open area at launch time."

"Wow!" Merry Lou said, eyes wide. "Maybe somebody sold one of you a quadraphonic phono for a dollar ninety-eight including fifteen-inch air-suspension speakers and a lifetime supply of Neil Diamond records." She tried to laugh, but failed; her eyes dimmed over. "Addi," she whispered, "I'm sorry. But it's sort of—weird. I mean, it's absurd; you all were briefed, weren't you, about your return weight? You weren't even to add so much as a piece of paper to what you took. I even saw Doctor Fein demonstrating the reasons on TV. And one of you hoisted a hundred pounds of machinery into the field? You must have been trying to self-destruct, to do that!" Tears slid from her eyes; one tear rolled out onto her nose and hung there. He reached reflexively to wipe it away, as if helping a little girl rather than a grown one.

"I'll fly you to the analysis site," the security agent said, standing up. He and Addison helped Merry Lou to her feet; she trembled as she stood a moment, finishing her Bloody Mary. Addison felt acute sorrow for her, but then, almost at once, it passed. He wondered why. One

can weary even of that, he conjectured. Of caring for
someone. If it goes on too long—on and on. Forever.
And, at last, even after that, into something no one before,
not God Himself, maybe, had ever had to suffer and in
the end, for all His great heart, succumb to.

As they walked through the crowded bar toward the
street, Addison Doug said to the security agent, "Which
one of us—"

"They know which one," the agent said as he held the
door to the street open for Merry Lou. The agent stood,
now, behind Addison, signalling for a gray Federal car to
land at the red parking area. Two other security agents,
in uniform, hurried toward them.

"Was it me?" Addison Doug asked.

"You better believe it," the security agent said.

The funeral procession moved with aching solemnity
down Pennsylvania Avenue, three flag-draped caskets and
dozens of black limousines passing between rows of
heavily coated, shivering mourners. A low haze hung over
the day, gray outlines of buildings faded into the rain-
drenched murk of the Washington March day.

Scrutinizing the lead Cadillac through prismatic binocu-
lars, TV's top news and public events commentator Henry
Cassidy droned on at his vast unseen audience, ". . . sad
recollections of that earlier train among the wheatfields
carrying the coffin of Abraham Lincoln back to burial and
the nation's capital. And what a sad day this is, and what
appropriate weather, with its dour overcast and sprinkles!"
In his monitor he saw the Zoomar lens pan up on the
fourth Cadillac, as it followed those with the caskets of
the dead tempunauts.

His engineer tapped him on the arm.

"We appear to be focussing on three unfamiliar figures
so far not identified, riding together," Henry Cassidy said
into his neck mike, nodding agreement. "So far I'm unable
to quite make them out. Are your location and vision any
better from where you're placed, Everett?" he inquired of
his colleague and pressed the button that notified Everett
Branton to replace him on the air.

"Why Henry," Branton said in a voice of growing
excitement, "I believe we're actually eyewitness to the

three American tempunauts as they remanifest themselves
on their historic journey into the future!"

"Does this signify," Cassidy said, "that somehow they
have managed to solve and overcome the—"

"Afraid not, Henry," Branton said in his slow, regretful
voice. "What we're eyewitnessing to our complete surprise consists of the Western world's first verified glimpse
of what the technical people refer to as Emergence Time
Activity."

"Ah yes, ETA," Cassidy said brightly, reading it off the
official script the Federal authorities had handed him
before air time.

"Right, Henry. Contrary to what *might* seem to be the
case at first sight, these are not—repeat *not*—our three
brave tempunauts as such, as we would ordinarily experience them—"

"I grasp it now, Everett," Cassidy broke in excitedly,
since his authorized script read CASS BREAKS IN EX-
CITEDLY. "Our three tempunauts have momentarily
suspended in their historic voyage to the future, which
we believe will span across to a time-continuum roughly a
century from now . . . It would seem that the overwhelming grief and drama of this unanticipated day of
mourning has caused them to . . ."

"Sorry to interrupt, Henry," Everett Branton said, "but
I think, since the procession has momentarily halted on its
slow march forward, that we might be able to . . ."

"No!" Cassidy said, as a note was handed him in a
swift scribble, reading: *Do not interview 'nauts. Urgent.
Dis. previous inst.* "I don't think we're going to be able
to . . ." he continued, ". . . to speak briefly with
tempunauts Benz, Crayne, and Doug, as you had hoped,
Everett. As we had all briefly hoped to." He wildly
waved the boom-mike back; it had already begun to swing
out expectantly toward the stopped Cadillac. Cassidy
shook his head violently at the mike technician and his
engineer.

Perceiving the boom-mike swinging at them, Addison
Doug stood up in the back of the open Cadillac. Cassidy
groaned. He wants to speak, he realized. Didn't they
reinstruct *him*? Why am I the only one they get across to?
Other boom-mikes representing other networks plus radio

station interviewers on foot now were rushing out to thrust up their microphones into the faces of the three tempunauts, especially Addison Doug's. Doug was already beginning to speak, in response to a question shouted up to him by a reporter. With his boom-mike off, Cassidy couldn't hear the question, nor Doug's answer. With reluctance, he signalled for his own boom-mike to trigger on.

". . . before," Doug was saying loudly.

"In what manner, 'All this has happened before'?" the radio reporter, standing close to the car, was saying.

"I mean," U.S. tempunaut Addison Doug declared, his face red and strained, "that I have stood here in this spot and said again and again, and all of you have viewed this parade and our deaths at re-entry endless times, a closed cycle of trapped time which must be broken."

"Are you seeking," another reporter jabbered up at Addison Doug, "for a solution to the re-entry implosion disaster which can be applied in retrospect so that when you do return to the past you will be able to correct the malfunction and avoid the tragedy which cost—or for you three, will cost—your lives?"

Tempunaut Benz said, "We are doing that, yes."

"Trying to ascertain the cause of the violent implosion and eliminate the cause before we return," tempunaut Crayne added, nodding. "We have learned already that for reasons unknown, a mass of nearly one hundred pounds of miscellaneous Volkswagen motor parts, including cylinders, the head . . ."

This is awful, Cassidy thought. "This is amazing!" he said aloud, into his neck mike. "The already tragically deceased U.S. tempunauts, with a determination that could emerge only from the rigorous training and discipline to which they were subjected—and we wondered why at the time but can clearly see why now—have already analyzed the mechanical slip-up responsible, evidently, for their own deaths, and have begun the laborious process of sifting through and eliminating causes of that slip-up so that they can return to their original launch site and re-enter without mishap."

"One wonders," Branton mumbled onto the air and into his feedback earphone, "what the consequences of this alteration of the near past will be. If in re-entry they do *not* implode and are *not* killed, then they will not—well, it's too complex for me, Henry, these time paradoxes that Doctor Fein at the Time Extrusion Labs in Pasadena has so frequently and eloquently brought to our attention."

Into all the microphones available, of all sorts, tempunaut Addison Doug was saying, more quietly now, "We must not eliminate the cause of re-entry implosion. The only way out of this trap is for us to die. Death is the only solution for this. For the three of us." He was interrupted as the procession of Cadillacs began to move forward.

Shutting off his mike momentarily, Henry Cassidy said to his engineer, "Is he nuts?"

"Only time will tell," his engineer said in a hard-to-hear voice.

"An extraordinary moment in the history of the United States involvement in time travel," Cassidy said, then, into his now live mike. "Only time will tell—if you will pardon the inadvertent pun—whether tempunaut Doug's cryptic remarks, uttered impromptu at this moment of supreme suffering for him, as in a sense to a lesser degree it is for all of us, are the words of a man deranged by grief or an accurate insight into the macabre dilemma that in theoretical terms we knew all along might eventually confront—confront and strike down with its lethal blow—a time-travel launch, either ours or the Russians'."

He segued, then, to a commercial.

"You know," Branton's voice muttered in his ear, not on the air but just to the control room and to him, "if he's right they ought to let the poor bastards die."

"They ought to release them," Cassidy agreed. "My God, the way Doug looked and talked, you'd imagine he'd gone through this for a thousand years and then some! I wouldn't be in his shoes for anything."

"I'll bet you fifty bucks," Branton said, "they have gone through this before. Many times."

"Then we have, too," Cassidy said.

Rain fell now, making all the lined-up mourners shiny. Their faces, their eyes, even their clothes—everything glistened in wet reflections of broken, fractured light, bent and sparkling, as, from gathering gray formless layers above them, the day darkened.

"Are we on the air?" Branton asked.

Who knows? Cassidy thought. He wished the day would end.

The Soviet chrononaut N. Gauki lifted both hands impassionedly and spoke to the Americans across the table from him in a voice of extreme urgency. "It is the opinion of myself and my colleague R. Plenya, who for his pioneering achievements in time travel has been certified a Hero of the Soviet People, and rightly so, that based on our own experience and on theoretical material developed both in your own academic circles and in the Soviet Academy of Sciences of the USSR, we believe that tempunaut A. Doug's fears may be justified. And his deliberate destruction of himself and his team mates at re-entry, by hauling a huge mass of auto parts back with him from ETA, in violation of his orders, should be regarded as the act of a desperate man with no other means of escape. Of course, the decision is up to you. We have only advisory position in this matter."

Addison Doug played with his cigarette lighter on the table and did not look up. His ears hummed, and he wondered what that meant. It had an electronic quality. Maybe we're within the module again, he thought. But he did not perceive it; he felt the reality of the people around him, the table, the blue plastic lighter between his fingers. No smoking in the module during re-entry, he thought. He put the lighter carefully away in his pocket.

"We've developed no concrete evidence whatsoever," General Toad said, "that a closed-time loop has been set up. There's only the subjective feelings of fatigue on the part of Mr. Doug. Just his belief that he's done all this repeatedly. As he says, it is very probably psychological in nature." He rooted pig-like among the papers before him. "I have a report, not disclosed to the media, from four psychiatrists at Yale on his psychological make-up. Although unusually stable, there is a tendency toward cyclothymia on his part, culminating in acute depression. This naturally was taken into account long before the launch, but it was calculated that the joyful qualities of the two others in the team would offset this functionally. Anyhow that depressive tendency in him is exceptionally high, now." He held the paper out, but no one at the table accepted it. "Isn't it true, Doctor Fein," he said, "that an acutely depressed person experiences time in a peculiar way, that is, circular time, time repeating itself, getting nowhere, around and around? The person gets so psychotic that he refuses to let go of the past. Re-runs it in his head constantly."

"But you see," Dr. Fein said, "this subjective sensation of being trapped is perhaps all we would have." This was the research physicist whose basic work had laid the theoretical foundation for the project. "If a closed loop did unfortunately lock into being."

"The general," Addison Doug said, "is using words he doesn't understand."

"I researched the ones I was unfamiliar with," General Toad said. "The technical psychiatric terms . . . I know what they mean."

To Addison Doug, Benz said, "Where'd you get all those VW parts, Addi?"

"I don't have them yet," Addison Doug said.

"Probably picked up the first junk he could lay his hands on," Crayne said. "Whatever was available, just before we started back."

"Will start back," Addison Doug corrected.

"Here are my instructions to the three of you," General Toad said. "You are not in any way to attempt to cause damage or implosion or malfunction during re-entry, either by lugging back extra mass or by any other method that enters your mind. You are to return as scheduled and in replica of the prior simulations. This especially applies to you, Mr. Doug." The phone by his right arm buzzed. He frowned, picked up the receiver. An interval passed, and then he scowled deeply and set the receiver back down, loudly.

"You've been overruled," Dr. Fein said.

"Yes, I have," General Toad said. "And I must say at this time that I am personally glad because my decision was an unpleasant one."

"Then we can arrange for implosion at re-entry," Benz said after a pause.

"The three of you are to make the decision," General Toad said. "Since it involves your lives. It's been entirely left up to you. Whichever way you want it. If you're convinced you're in a closed time loop, and you believe a massive implosion at re-entry will abolish it—" He ceased talking, as tempunaut Doug rose to his feet. "Are you going to make another speech, Doug?" he said.

"I just want to thank everyone involved," Addison Doug said. "For letting us decide." He gazed haggard-faced and wearily around at all the individuals seated at the table. "I really appreciate it."

"You know," Benz said slowly, "blowing us up at re-entry could add nothing to the chances of abolishing a closed loop. In fact that could do it, Doug."

"Not if it kills us all," Crayne said.

"You agree with Addi?" Benz said.

"Dead is dead," Crayne said. "I've been pondering it. What other way is more likely to get us out of this? Than if we're dead? What possible other way?"

"You may be in no loop," Dr. Fein pointed out.

"But we may be," Crayne said.

Doug, still on his feet, said to Crayne and Benz, "Could we include Merry Lou in our decision-making?"

"Why?" Benz said.

"I can't think too clearly any more," Doug said. "Merry Lou can help me; I depend on her."

"Sure," Crayne said. Benz, too, nodded.

General Toad examined his wristwatch stoically and said, "Gentlemen, this concludes our discussion."

Soviet chrononaut Gauki removed his headphones and neck mike and hurried toward the three U.S. tempunauts, his hand extended; he was apparently saying something in Russian, but none of them could understand it. They moved away somberly, clustering close.

"In my opinion you're nuts, Addi," Benz said. "But it would appear that I'm the minority now."

"If he *is* right," Crayne said, "if—one chance in a billion—if we are going back again and again forever, that would justify it."

"Could we go see Merry Lou?" Addison Doug said. "Drive over to her place now?"

"She's waiting outside," Crayne said.

Striding up to stand beside the three tempunauts, General Toad said, "You know, what made the determination go the way it did was the public reaction to how you, Doug, looked and behaved during the funeral procession. The NSC advisors came to the conclusion that the public would, like you, rather be certain it's over for all of you. That it's more of a relief to them to know you're free of your mission than to save the project and obtain a perfect re-entry. I guess you really made a lasting impression on them, Doug. That whining you did." He walked away, then, leaving the three of them standing there alone.

"Forget him," Crayne said to Addison Doug. "Forget everyone like him. We've got to do what we have to."

"Merry Lou will explain it to me," Doug said. She would know what to do, what would be right.

"I'll go get her," Crayne said, "and after that the four of us can drive somewhere, maybe to her place, and decide what to do. Okay?"

"Thank you," Addison Doug said, nodding; he glanced around for her hopefully, wondering where she was. In the next room, perhaps, somewhere close. "I appreciate that," he said.

Benz and Crayne eyed each other. He saw that, but did not know what it meant. He knew only that he needed someone, Merry Lou most of all, to help him understand what the situation was. And what to finalize on to get them out of it.

Merry Lou drove them north from Los Angeles in the superfast lane of the freeway toward Ventura, and after that inland to Ojai. The four of them said very little. Merry Lou drove well, as always; leaning against her, Addison Doug felt himself relax into a temporary sort of peace.

"There's nothing like having a chick drive you," Crayne said, after many miles had passed in silence.

"It's an aristocratic sensation," Benz murmured. "To have a woman do the driving. Like you're nobility being chauffeured."

Merry Lou said, "Until she runs into something. Some big slow object."

Addison Doug said, "When you saw me trudging up to your place . . . up the redwood round path the other day. What did you think? Tell me honestly."

"You looked," the girl said, "as if you'd done it many times. You looked worn and tired and—ready to die. At the end." She hesitated. "I'm sorry, but that's how you looked, Addi. I thought to myself, he knows the way too well."

"Like I'd done it too many times."

"Yes," she said.

"Then you vote for implosion," Addison Doug said.

"Well—"

"Be honest with me," he said.

Merry Lou said, "Look in the back seat. The box on the floor."

With a flashlight from the glove compartment the three men examined the box. Addison Doug, with fear, saw its contents. VW motor parts, rusty and worn. Still oily.

"I got them from behind a foreign car garage near my place," Merry Lou said. "On the way to Pasadena. The first junk I saw that seemed as if it'd be heavy enough. I had heard them say on TV at launch time that anything over fifty pounds up to—"

"It'll do it," Addison Doug said. "It did do it."

"So there's no point in going to your place," Crayne said. "It's decided. We might as well head south toward the module. And initiate the procedure for getting out of ETA. And back to re-entry." His voice was heavy but evenly pitched. "Thanks for your vote, Miss Hawkins."

She said, "You are all so tired."

"I'm not," Benz said. "I'm mad. Mad as hell."

"At me?" Addison Doug said.

"I don't know," Benz said. "It just—Hell." He lapsed into brooding silence then. Hunched over, baffled and inert. Withdrawn as far as possible from the others in the car.

At the next freeway junction she turned the car south. A sense of freedom seemed now to fill her, and Addison Doug felt some of the weight, the fatigue, ebbing already.

On the wrist of each of the three men the emergency alert receiver buzzed its warning tone; they all started.

"What's that mean?" Merry Lou said, slowing the car.

"We're to contact General Toad by phone as soon as possible," Crayne said. He pointed. "There's a Standard Station over there; take the next exit, Miss Hawkins. We can phone in from there."

A few minutes later Merry Lou brought her car to a halt beside the outdoor phone booth. "I hope it's not bad news," she said.

"I'll talk first," Doug said, getting out. Bad news, he thought with labored amusement. Like what? He crunched stiffly across to the phone booth, entered, shut the door behind him, dropped in a dime and dialed the toll-free number.

"Well, do I have news!" General Toad said when the operator had put him on the line. "It's a good thing we got hold of you. Just a minute—I'm going to let Doctor Fein tell you this himself. You're more apt to believe him than me." Several clicks, and then Doctor Fein's reedy, precise, scholarly voice, but intensified by urgency.

"What's the bad news?" Addison Doug said.

"Not bad, necessarily," Dr. Fein said. "I've had computations run since our discussion, and it would appear— by that I mean it is statistically probable but still unverified for a certainty—that you are right, Addison. You are in a closed time loop."

Addison Doug exhaled raggedly. You nowhere autocratic mother, he thought. You probably knew all along.

"However," Dr. Fein said excitedly, stammering a little, "I also calculate—we jointly do, largely through Cal Tech—that the greatest likelihood of maintaining the loop is to implode on re-entry. Do you understand, Addison? If you lug all those rusty VW parts back and implode, then your statistical chances of closing the loop forever is greater than if you simply re-enter and all goes well."

Addison Doug said nothing.

"In fact, Addi—and this is the severe part that I have to stress—implosion at re-entry, especially a massive, calculated one of the sort we seem to see shaping up—do you grasp all this, Addi? Am I getting through to you? For Chrissake, Addi? Virtually *guarantees* the locking in of an absolutely unyielding loop such as you've got in mind.

Such as we've all been worried about from the start." A pause. "Addi? Are you there?"

Addison Doug said, "I want to die."

"That's your exhaustion from the loop. God knows how many repetitions there've been already of the three of you—"

"No," he said and started to hang up.

"Let me speak with Benz and Crayne," Dr. Fein said rapidly. "Please, before you go ahead with re-entry. Especially Benz; I'd like to speak with him in particular. Please, Addison. For their sake; your almost total exhaustion has—"

He hung up. Left the phone booth, step by step.

As he climbed back into the car, he heard their two alert receivers still buzzing. "General Toad said the automatic call for us would keep your two receivers doing that for a while," he said. And shut the car door after him. "Let's take off."

"Doesn't he want to talk to us?" Benz said.

Addison Doug said, "General Toad wanted to inform us that they have a little something for us. We've been voted a special Congressional Citation for valor or some damn thing like that. A special medal they never voted anyone before. To be awarded posthumously."

"Well, hell—that's about the only way it can be awarded," Crayne said.

Merry Lou, as she started up the engine, began to cry.

"It'll be a relief," Crayne said presently, as they returned bumpily to the freeway, "when it's over."

It won't be long now, Addison Doug's mind declared. On their wrists the emergency alert receivers continued to put out their combined buzzing.

"They will nibble you to death," Addison Doug said. "The endless wearing down by various bureaucratic voices."

The others in the car turned to gaze at him inquiringly, with uneasiness mixed with perplexity.

"Yeah," Crayne said. "These automatic alerts are really a nuisance." He sounded tired. As tired as I am, Addison Doug thought. And, realizing this, he felt better. It showed how right he was.

Great drops of water struck the windshield; it had now begun to rain. That pleased him too. It reminded him of that most exalted of all experiences within the shortness of his life: the funeral procession moving slowly down Pennsylvania Avenue, the flag-draped caskets. Closing his eyes he leaned back and felt good at last. And heard, all around him once again, the sorrow-bent people. And, in his head, dreamed of the special Congressional Medal. For weariness, he thought. A medal for being tired.

He saw, in his head, himself in other parades too, and in the deaths of many. But really it was one death and one parade. Slow cars moving along the street in Dallas, and with Dr. King as well . . . He saw himself return again and again, in his closed cycle of life, to the national mourning that he could not and they could not forget. He would be there; they would always be there; it would always be, and every one of them would return together again and again forever. To the place, the moment, they wanted to be. The event which meant the most to all of them.

This was his gift to them, the people, his country. He had bestowed upon the world a wonderful burden. The dreadful and weary miracle of eternal life.

AFTERWORD

The essence of the time-travel story is a confrontation of some sort, best of all by the person with himself. Really, this is the drama of much good fiction anyhow, except that in such a story as this one the moment in which the man meets himself face to face permits an alienation that could not occur in any other variety of writing—alienation and not understanding, as one might expect. Addison Doug-One rides alive on the casket containing the corpse of Addison Doug-Two and knows it, knows he is now two persons—he is split as in a physical schizophrenia. And his mind also is divided rather than united; he gains no insight from this event, neither of himself nor of that other Addison Doug who can no longer reason or solve problems.

This irony is just one of the enormous number of ironies possible in time-travel stories; naïvely, one would think that to travel into the future and return would lead to an increase in knowledge rather than to a loss of it. The three tempunauts go ahead in time, return, and are trapped, perhaps forever, by ironies and within ironies, the greatest one of which, I think, is their own bewilderment at their own actions. It is as if the increase in information brought about by such a technological achievement —information about exactly what is going to happen— decreases true understanding. Perhaps Addison Doug knows too much.

In writing this story I felt a weary sadness of my own and fell into the space (I should say time) that the characters are in, more so than usual. I felt a futility about futility—there is nothing more defeating than a strong awareness of defeat, and as I wrote I realized that what for us remains merely a psychological problem (over-awareness of the likelihood of failing and the lethal feedback from this) would for a time-traveler be instantly converted into an existential, physical horror-chamber.

We, when we're depressed, are fortunately imprisoned within our heads; once time-travel becomes a reality, however, this self-defeating psychological attitude could spell doom on a scale beyond calculation. Here again, science fiction allows a writer to transfer what usually is an internal problem into an external environment; he projects it in the form of a society, a planet, with everyone stuck, so to speak, in what formerly was one unique brain. I don't blame some readers for resenting this, because the brains of some of us are unpleasant places to be in. But on the other hand, what a valuable tool this is for us—to grasp that we do not all really see the universe in the same way, or, in a sense, the same universe at all.

Addison Doug's dismal world suddenly spreads out and becomes the world of many people. But unlike a person reading a story, who can and will finish it and abolish his inclusion in the author's world, the people in this story are stuck fast forever. This is a tyranny not yet possible so readily but, when you consider the power of the coercive propaganda apparatus of the modern-day state (when it's the enemy state we call it "brainwashing") you might wonder if it isn't a question of degree. Our glorious leaders of right now cannot trap us in extensions of their heads merely by lugging some old VW motor parts around, but the alarm of the characters in this story as to what is befalling them might rightly be our own alarm in a lesser way.

Addison Doug expresses the desire "to see no more summers." We should all object; no one should drag us, however subtly or for whatever evidently benign reasons, into that view or that desire. We should individually and collectively yearn to see as many summers as we can, even in the imperfect world we are living in now.

Novels
LEGION OF TIME, by Jack Williamson
LEST DARKNESS FALL, by L. Sprague de Camp
NOW WAIT FOR LAST YEAR, by Philip K. Dick

Short Stories
BY HIS BOOTSTRAPS, by Robert A. Heinlein
TIME LOCKER, by Lewis Padgett
ALAS ALL THINKING, by Harry Bates
AS NEVER WAS, by P. Schuyler Miller
THE RECRUITING STATION, by A. E. van Vogt
THE LITTLE BLACK BAG, by C. M. Kornbluth
THE GHOST, by A. E. van Vogt

About Philip K. Dick

Philip K. Dick, b. 1929, attended the University of California and had a classical music program on Station KSMO, San Mateo. He has been a full-time writer of science fiction for more than twenty years. His best known novels include EYE IN THE SKY, THE MAN IN THE HIGH CASTLE (Hugo award winner), DO ANDROIDS DREAM OF ELECTRIC SHEEP? Mr. Dick lives in Fullerton, California.

Some other books published by Penguin
are described on the following pages.

Wilkie Collins

THE WOMAN IN WHITE
Edited with an introduction and notes
  by Julian Symons

From the moment when the figure in white appears
on a moonlit road in north London, the reader is
caught in the spell of this novel, the greatest mystery thriller in English. The masterful plot revolves
around two almost identical women, and the narrative is composed of accounts by the various participants. Among the many memorable characters,
the most impressive is generally agreed to be Count
Fosco, a villain whose corpulent physique and
eccentric habits add actuality to his melodramatic
role.

Four by Olaf Stapledon

STAR MAKER

A man sits quietly on a hillside. A moment later, he is whirling through time and space on a mind-spinning search for the Star Maker behind the cosmos.

LAST AND FIRST MEN
  and LAST MEN IN LONDON

Here are two science-fiction classics in one volume. *Last and First Men* ranges over five billion years of human evolution, culminating in the extinction of the sun and the dissemination among the stars of the seeds of a new humanity. *Last Men in London* creates a Neptunian, last man's view of the twentieth-century world.

SIRIUS

Thomas Trelone devotes his life to the attempt to produce a superman by hormone injections into various mammals. Sirius is the result of these experiments—the only dog ever born with the brain of a human being. This is a moving story of immense and tragic pathos.

Peter Bowen, Martin Hayden, and Frank Riess

SCREEN TEST
A Quiz Book about the Movies

This volume offers a unique opportunity to test knowledge of films. Sixteen chapters of questions cover every aspect of the cinema—from silent films to science fiction. A sample: Who played the flute, and who conducted the orchestra in *Hot Millions*? What films do these lines come from? Peter Lorre: "We may be rats, crooks, and murderers . . . but we're *Americans*." James Cagney: "I'm from the collection agency . . . I've come to collect my wife." With 188 photographs.